The Wanderer Trilogy

Book Two: Preservation

Dedication:

For my inner child. The girl who held it all together. She cracked so beautifully.

For information, contact:
www.BrittanyHansonWrites.com

ISBN: 978-1-970323-09-2
Printed in the United States of America
First Edition

Content Note:

This book contains scenes that may be distressing to some readers, including violence, grief, and the death of a child.

Chapter 1

Moments before the three battered warriors stepped into Rapture, dusk had already begun its slow crawl across the sky. Scarlet hues bled into the horizon and mingled with the weight of exhaustion that clung to Eva Calloway, a vivid reminder of the battle fought only two days earlier. Echoes of their struggle rang out from the Tiger's Den and rippled all across the region. The Tiger Chief, Jake and Tommy's estranged father, now lay dead. But before The Wanderer and his sons managed to escape, Jake was shot in the arm.

Safety was fleeting, even far beyond those jagged metal walls. McAvoy's bloodthirsty Gang was now seeking revenge. Eva, Jake, and Tommy were forced to travel days without rest. They were injured, exhausted, and starving. After two days of running, their bodies were shutting down. Hope dwindled. They were just empty shells trudging through the Southern wasteland.

Unexpectedly, a sign appeared. A glint of relief. Just enough to push them further into the unknown.

Rapture Welcomes The Wanderer. Four, simple words painted against a well-made wooden sign. Was this a chance at peace and safety? The gates of this walled civilization soon towered over them. They were speechless. Not even The Wanderer had heard of this place. And even if these people welcomed them, death was still waiting beyond the stone.

Only a year earlier, Eva had rescued the McAvoy brothers from a Vault in the northern hills, near the Tiger and

Serpent compounds. They begged her to search for their long-lost father and spent months piecing together clues that ultimately led them to the Tigers. None of them could have predicted that their father was not only the man who sparked a mutiny during the Wanderer's rule over the Serpents, but also the ruthless Chief of the Tigers.

In the end, his sons witnessed the wrath of their father before his demise. "Strike down your *weaker half* and join me or I will cut both of you down." That was the ultimatum that he had given his eldest son. Jake, instead, risked his own life over murdering his brother. He chose to turn against the Chief, only to find himself staring down the edge of his father's weapon.

Lucky for the brothers, Eva had been waiting in the darkness. It was supposed to be a simple plan, executed with precision by The Wanderer. But she never expected the fight to drag on as long as it did. Alarms were sounded. Guards forced their way into the room. Eva quickly plunged her blade into Dan McAvoy's chest, seized Jake and Tommy, and fought her way through the sea of enemies. They made it out alive—barely. But the Gang was right behind them.

Days blurred together as they ran for their lives, until at last they collapsed into the arms of Rapture's Guards, barely able to stand. Well… except Eva.

The Wanderer had grown accustomed to surviving with the bare minimum. Scrounging for scraps of food in the days before she knew how to hunt, Eva was used to the feelings of fatigue and hunger. It had taken a toll on her body, but she was still standing. A couple guards whisked Jake and Tommy down the road and out of sight, but a half-dozen more took their place to greet her. The man at the center wore armor far more intricate than the others. He was muscular yet slender, with sandy-blonde hair and a short, cinnamon-colored beard. But it was not his hair or his stature that caught Eva's attention. It was his eyes. At first, they reminded her of the cold, soulless hue of Chief McAvoy's. But upon further inspection, she realized that there was emotion behind them. *Empathy*. They felt… familiar. In fact, their blue mirrored an autumn midday sky, warm in a way that felt impossible after everything she'd endured. When he cleared his throat, she realized she had been staring.

"I am Captain Gavin," he bowed with a smile. "We've been waiting for you, Wanderer. It's an honor to meet you. Don't worry, you are safe here."

Her gaze drifted right over Gavin's shoulder where a large axe was propped. He, too, noticed the weaponry that Eva carried. The Wanderer's famed short blades slung at her back in an X. The guards surrounding them bore rifles and pistols that glittered with the lingering sun. *We are safe here*, Eva repeated in her mind. *Unlikely... However... given the alternatives, maybe we are safe for now.*

She opened her mouth to speak, but stopped when she heard the all-too-familiar sound of gunfire. Gavin's men raced up ladders to the watchtowers dotted across the city walls and aimed their guns down at the assailants. Voices rose over the whistling wind. The final light of day disappeared. Torches were lit, and the Tigers were waiting for their prey just outside of the walls.

"Give up The Wanderer," one of them demanded. "There is payment that needs to be made."

"You will not win this battle," a guard called back. "We have far more firepower and more men… Return to your compound or you will die."

But the Tigers refused to give up so easily. "Not unless we carry the head of The Wanderer back with us."

"You are not in the position to be making demands," the guard's tone changed drastically. The cocking of guns warned the Tigers that they would fire at any moment. "We've rarely had dealings with the Gangs, but that does not mean we won't start now. Be gone."

Eva pressed her ear against the massive doors. An eerie silence met her from the other side. Since childhood, she had witnessed the devastation the Gangs were capable of. If they decided not to attack now, they would return with more guns and more men. Could Rapture's walls truly keep her, Jake, and Tommy safe? Would the Tigers eventually give up their hunt for The Wanderer? Would she and her family be able to settle down and live the life that Eva had always dreamed of?

"We *will* be back," the Tiger finally responded. "This isn't over."

As the marching of boots trailed off, Eva turned back to Gavin and his guards descending the ladders nearby. He explained that Jake and Tommy had been taken to the Infirmary to be fed, patched up, and given a warm bed to sleep. But unfortunately for The Wanderer, rest would be delayed.

The Captain relayed a request from his superiors.

"I will escort you to meet with our Council," he stated as if reciting a script. "They require your presence. I promise you can rest after they introduce themselves. We have a proposition for your contribution to Rapture… In exchange for your safety, of course."

Somehow, Eva remained standing through the haze of lethargy that continued to decay her body. She had to remain cordial and compliant with Rapture's guards. Otherwise, they would surely sacrifice her to the Tigers. She managed a weak smile and murmured, "There's always a catch, isn't there?"

Captain Gavin left his men to defend the gate and led The Wanderer down the large cobblestone road that cut the town in half. On her left, a large sign read *Market District*. It was one, long, u-shaped pavilion with fifty or more tables crowded under the roof. Even though night had fallen over the town, the market was still bustling with life. Shopkeepers traded with citizens for items like vegetables, fruits, bread, meat, armor, clothing, and trinkets. Between the shops and Market District was Rapture's main farmland and livestock pen. Cows, pigs, chickens, turkeys, and other animals shared a massive area that was fenced off from the rest of the town. Just behind the scent of manure was a massive, freshly-plowed field of crops. It appeared as though the farmers had retired for the evening as the fields were desolate. Further down the main road were hundreds of homes built from clay brick and metal. Each row had completely uniform homes along smaller stone pathways. The larger homes were built closest to the Town Square and furthest away from the main street.

An entire town, she thought. *Self-sufficient? How have I not heard of this place?*

"All of our crops are watered by a stream that flows through the town." Gavin noticed Eva's bewilderment. "You can see the grates around the walls. And there's a forest even further south where we get wood for our fires. Don't worry, we always plant seedlings to replace what we take." He then directed her gaze to the left of the main gate. "We have a lake where we breed fish to eat as well. There is a wonderful garden and meditation area for us to connect with nature. That was Councilwoman Jasmine's idea."

"You're beginning to sound like the Nomads," she said weakly. She desperately wanted to meet the Council and sleep, but also found herself in awe at the grandeur of Rapture.

"That's because they make up a great deal of Rapture's population," Gavin smiled. He scooped his arm underneath Eva's and helped her walk. Although he was slender, he was surprisingly strong. "Long ago, some of our people in the city desired peace. To build a town that could withstand even the greatest enemy. But some couldn't stand living within the confinement of these walls. Rapture allowed them to come and go as they pleased, but most of them never returned. When the North became hostile with Gangs, we closed our gates."

Eva lived with the Nomads for a few years, but never knew that they had once been part of Rapture. Yidi and Masha spoke of their past without a single mention of this city. She pondered Gavin's words as they continued down the main street towards a large building that towered over everything else. It was the most beautiful structure she had ever seen. Monstrous constructs crafted from white brick tripled the height of the walls separating Rapture from the outside world. Circular towers tipped with spires on each corner rose high into the sky as they arrived at the drawbridge surrounded by a stream. This building was a castle.

“Here is where I leave you,” Gavin bowed again. “After speaking with the Council, meet me back here and I will take you to your new home.”

Eva nodded. She rubbed her eyes, trying not to close them for any length of time or she would drop to the ground in a comatose state. Gradually, she made her way to the front doors. As they swung open, The Wanderer was greeted by a massive, crescent moon-shaped table with six people spanning the perimeter. She noticed that the centermost seat was vacant. Without them saying a word, she guessed exactly what their proposition would be.

“Welcome Wanderer,” one of the robed women spoke. Her hand slid from underneath her sleeve and motioned towards the centermost chair. “We have been waiting for you. Please, have a seat. Warm yourself with a drink.”

“I don’t wish to appear ungrateful,” Eva’s boots clicked on the marble floor as she slumped into the vacant chair. “But I am in dire need of rest and food.”

“We promise this will not take long,” a man said and slid over a steaming cup of herbal tea along with a small loaf of bread and some cheese and berries. The Wanderer took a drink of tea and let the warmth spread throughout her body as she looked around. The comfort it brought almost made her pass out. Each of the Council Members wore long, extravagant clothing, but they were vastly different in color and detail. Their hair was neat and clean, just like the rest of the chamber. Eva, on the other hand, was covered in blood, dirt, and sweat. And although she had never minded what other people thought of her before, she felt somewhat uneasy in their presence.

"I think we need to begin with a confession," the first woman spoke again. "Our Scouts have been watching you for some time. In fact, since you first left the Serpents Nest and became The Wanderer, we have been following you…from time to time…"

"What?" Eva said shortly through a mouthful of bread and cheese. Her eyes were starting to become heavy now that her stomach was filling with food. "You've been *watching* me? For that long?"

"Yes. But we simply observed. After tales of your downfall as the Serpent's Mistress reached us. We decided to determine whether you could become a suitable addition to Rapture. Not just an average citizen, you see, but sitting in our most prestigious Council seat, overseeing our army. That is our offer. Do you accept?"

The man to her far right interrupted Eva's response.

"You fight with great skill. Captain Gavin was given charge over the army, but his leadership abilities are… lacking. He simply doesn't have the… experience necessary for his position. If we were forced to fight a larger Gang like the Tigers or Serpents, we would be over powered within days."

"Of course we don't want our people to know that," an older woman chimed in. "But none of us have the tactical ability that you possess. We watched you raise the Serpents to its current size… When you were exiled, we began to plan. Some of us, reluctantly. Ironically, it was your Gang's growth that caused us to worry about Rapture's future."

Eva raised a hand to silence the Council. The woman with glasses stuck her nose to the sky with a *humph*. "I accept." While she craved to return to a position of power and control again, at that moment, she just wanted to sleep. "May I start after I recover?"

"Certainly." They agreed and allowed her to leave.

As promised, Gavin was waiting for her at the bridge. He wrapped an arm around her waist and helped her to the first row of homes on their right. These buildings were significantly larger than the ones she had seen before. He opened the door to the third house and disappeared down the street before Eva could thank him. Jake was waiting for her with his arm wrapped in a sling. Both of them noticed the dark bags under each other's eyes. Not a word was said. They walked over to the bed and instantly fell asleep. Finally, they could settle down for a while.

***

Eva slept for a few days without awakening for much aside from food and water. By the third day, she woke up refreshed enough to explore Rapture while Jake continued to recover. After slipping out of bed, she silently crept into the washroom. On the small wooden end table was a bucket of water and homemade soap. Brown blood and mud dripped down her bare legs and into a drain that led outside. After she finished cleansing herself from days-old combat, she dried off, wiped down her armor, and put it on.

Sunlight and a clear, crisp sky greeted her outside. The scent of early Spring filled her nostrils as she inhaled deeply. Her front lawn was neatly manicured with green buds breaking through the winter frost. Goosebumps rose on her arms as she closed her eyes and let a soft breeze brush across her face, tousling her hair. *This is so serene.*

"Would you like to take a walk, Wanderer?" She opened her eyes and jumped back. Gavin's voice startled her. He was sitting in a chair on the porch next door.

"Please, call me Eva," she said and followed him down the road. "I don't want to be The Wanderer for a while. Maybe not ever again."

He smiled. "Of course… Shall we go to the Gardens? If you are still feeling the stress of battle, this place will wash it away. Even in this weather. But," he looked her up and down. "We have laws in Rapture though… no weapons."

Eva did not realize that she was still carrying all of her daggers and her two shortswords. Her face contorted from confusion to irritation. "Huh?"

"Unless you are on duty," Gavin gestured to a guard on the wall nearby. "We don't allow weapons. Peace is our number one priority in Rapture."

So they lie to their citizens about the dangers out there, she thought.

She looked around and saw that the few citizens nearby did not bear a shred of protection. In fact, a couple of them were looking at her uncomfortably. Nodding and clearing her throat, Eva disappeared back into her home and started disarming. Over the fireplace in the living area were two hooks, a perfect place to display her blades. As she reached down to grab at the holster to place her gun upon the mantle, images of the Tiger Den started to flood her mind. Her heart rose into her throat. *I forgot. My pistol is still there.*

Something dark moved out of the corner of her eye.

After a few hard blinks, Eva was able to shake the dread off of her chest. Gavin whispered from down the hall and she swiftly removed the rest of her smaller knives. Well, all except one. She slid one in her boot between two buckles, refusing to ever be completely unarmed. No. She had spent far too much of her life surviving and would never let herself be vulnerable again. With a few quick steps, she was out the door alongside her new Captain.

Gavin finally spoke as he and Eva passed through the Town Square. Children pressed the final patches of snow into snowmen while their guardians looked on, chatting in the cold air. "So you accepted the offer of becoming our newest Councilmember?"

"I guess," she responded but her eyes remained fixated on the children's faces. They were not worn with fear and exhaustion. No tears stained them. They were laughing and smiling. Blissfully unaware. Not a single one of them had endured torture, hardship, or servitude. Eva wondered whether they had a clue about the unforgiving world outside.

Gavin nudged her and she was pulled from her thoughts.

"It will take some getting used to," she said quickly. "This place. A Council."

Gavin nodded in agreement. "Understandable. You've been alone for many years," he added.

She stopped. Her Captain nearly tripped over her boot as he passed a few paces ahead and turned around.

"It isn't that," she admitted. "Well… it isn't *just* that. Before… When I was the Mistress of the Serpents, I ruled alone. My word was law. There was no compromise. No discussion. No wasting of time."

Gavin frowned. "This isn't a compound, Eva. Rapture has a figurehead from every part of town. Each Council Member represents a portion of the people. It is their *compromise* that keeps this city civil. They all have our best interests at heart, and know their trade and its people well. In fact, the citizens voted for those men and women. You are the first Council Member that was chosen by the Council from outside Rapture's walls."

"Well," Eva started. She wasn't sure whether to take his last comment as an insult or compliment, so she sharply changed the subject. "Your Scouts have apparently been stalking me for years."

"Our town can only handle so many citizens. When we do accept people from the region, we must be sure that they will prioritize Rapture's safety so we continue to thrive. Only those who our Scouts deem worthy are recruited."

She started to raise her voice. "So you have eyes all over the region. To form your *perfect utopia*. While thousands of people suffer at the hands of the Gangs, you sit here with full bellies and smiles on your face? Out there, I was *hunted*. I fended for my life and protected the lives of others for *years*.

And now I'm being told that there were *armed* warriors watching me fight for my life this whole time?"

"Not utopia, but *peace*." They were nearing the garden when Gavin finally stopped. "But sometimes it needs to be forced a little. Nudged into existence. We have to be absolutely *sure* that our choice in recruitment will benefit us to the fullest. Also, I don't believe anyone actually witnessed you fighting. Rapture simply had those in your Nomad Tribe and your Rover Colony report to us. Many of our Scouts are disguised as traders. While I don't always agree with the Council, these are not my rules. I have more respect for you than you could ever imagine."

Eva nodded and stopped with him. Right behind a pine tree were Tommy and Jake. *How did they get here before me?* She had intended to talk to them anyway. Gavin cleared his throat and rushed away, mumbling something about 'tending to his duties'. She watched his figure vanish down the street before turning back to the McAvoy brothers, smiling.

"Well," she laughed sarcastically. "How is this place for safety? They won't even let me carry around weapons unless I'm on duty."

Jake snorted angrily. "You don't have to be an ass about it. *Shit*. We have a permanent home here. Plus, careers, food, and more protection than we need. This place is a dream."

"More protection than *you* need," Eva corrected and jabbed a finger in his direction. "What a perfect place for people who can't fight. I have a bounty on *my* head. The Tigers will come back…"

"Will you relax Eva," Tommy sighed. "They aren't here now. We're safe."

The Wanderer subdued any further comment. She sat down on a nearby stone and ran her fingers through her auburn hair. Scenes of battle bubbled up again. Thoughts of survival, murder, and torture. Unconsciously, her hand slid down to the boot where her lone knife was concealed. *This place just doesn't feel real. It doesn't feel right.* Part of her wanted to run. Escape. The other part begged her to give Rapture a chance. Jake's voice, as usual, pulled her from the darkness.

"Can we talk about what happened with my father—with McAvoy and the Tigers?" he started. "I have so many questions. How did you know where we were?"

"To be honest, I wasn't entirely sure," she said. "I knew that the Tigers had captured you when we infiltrated the compound. You would be enslaved to some extent. But when I found out that your father was the same man that destroyed my life all those years ago… I couldn't let him live. Even if you didn't understand, I *needed* that revenge."

Jake's eyes grew wide. "Wait. Our *father* was the one who staged a mutiny in the Serpents compound when you were their Chief?"

Eva nodded.

"You're sure?"

"I will never forget that man's face."

"Jake said he changed," Tommy chimed in. "From when we were kids."

She shook her head. "That can't be. At least, not since I knew him as Dan Avery. To me, he has always been cruel and vindictive. But I had no clue he was from the Vault and left before… It doesn't matter. Anyway, I posed as a servant, worked the Pits, worked as a Doxie, met Elaine's mother, and killed your father."

"You met Elaine's mother?" Jake gasped. "From the Western Rovers?"

"Yeah. She hid my armor inside the Castle and everything. Risked her life for me. I hope she was able to escape during the chaos. I told her the way out."

"I bet she did," Tommy grinned.

"So you heard about the Chief trying to make me kill Tommy?" Jake refused to call Dan McAvoy his father anymore. After trying to turn Jake against Tommy, and then pulling the trigger on his own son, Jake felt he no longer deserved that title.

"I'm not shocked or surprised to be honest with you. He was like that before."

"Now he's dead. Good riddance. Can I just say that I'm so incredibly sorry we risked your life to find him. We had no idea… I ha-"

"Stop, Jake. You couldn't have known. Honestly, I'm glad I was able to end his miserable existence and live to tell the tale. He caused me so much pain, I was more than happy to return the favor… Is it bad to hope that he suffered?"

Jake and Tommy went silent. They looked at one another, then back at Eva. Was it truly evil of her to wish suffering on another, even after that person caused so much harm? The brothers themselves hoped that he had died slowly, but would never admit it. Eva bit her lip in uncertainty. Neither of them comforted her with their words. Regardless, it was all over. The Wanderer got her revenge. The McAvoy brothers were safe. But most importantly, her Shadow was gone. After no one answered her question, she scoffed and hopped up to take a walk in Rapture's Garden alone.

Once the boys disappeared from view, Eva sat beside a stream, slipped off her boots, and set her sore feet against the cold earth. She leaned into the tree behind her, letting the warm sun and the gentle breeze lull her toward serenity. Then, an unfamiliar voice gently roused her from the quiet.

"I am glad you like my garden," a woman wearing a long lavender dress and animal-hide coat was standing near Eva's feet. Her voice was soft, almost a whisper. "You should experience it in a few weeks, when Spring is fully in bloom. This is the part of the Council that I represent. My name is Jasmine and I am one of the few Nomads who returned to Rapture from the outside. I am a daughter of nature and was chosen by the Goddess, our Mother, to care for this land. The rest of the Council Members do not understand the elements as I do, but it is *essential* to the survival of Rapture… and I think they comprehend that much."

Eva stood up and placed a fist over her heart with a small bow. "Um. Nice to meet you, Jasmine."

"Pleasure, Wanderer." The woman took a step closer. She smiled with the warmth of the sun above them.

"The Wand-er… Eva, please," she corrected. The knife hidden in her boot started to gleam in the sunlight, so she pushed it downward and obscured it with her hand. "So, you are the protector of Nature and I will be the Council Member in charge of war tactics. Two sides of our existence."

"And what is light without darkness?" Jasmine looked at Eva as an equal. Her words bore the same wisdom as Yidi, the Nomad Elder, yet this woman was at least half his age. "Without death, we cannot appreciate life for what it truly is. And what is peace without sacrifice? Fruit is more delicious when you grow the tree yourself. It is the toil that makes it so. That is why Rapture tries to remain peaceful, but will charge into battle if necessary. Everyone has a part to play here. Your friends will be trained to provide for the town as well."

Eva nodded. An unconscious smile spread across her face. "I'll admit, it does feel good to be back in a position of power again."

"The others in the Council wish to introduce themselves to you. Come with me and we will return to The Stronghold."

The young Councilwoman waited while Eva laced her boots, and followed her to the Stronghold, secretly positioning the small blade in her pocket. They strolled down the street as the citizens began their day farming, smithing, tanning, and tending to the domesticated animals. A few shepherds cornered their flock towards the town square to trim the grass. Some of the homes had wooden signs near their respective streets advertising other services like "Tailor" or "Bakery." Everyone seemed blissfully unaware of the daily struggle and death just outside the town. The feeling of peace was bittersweet to Eva. Even though she was now overseeing Rapture's Army, she became nervous that the peace of this town would dull her skills over time.

I will not let that happen. I will train at night if I must.

The Stronghold was more colossal than Eva realized before. She had only been inside the Council Chambers, but this structure was also where Rapture held their festivals, Infirmary, Barracks, and School. The main atrium was the largest room. Enormous, marble columns held the structure from collapse and the flooring was painted with gold and silver filigree. Designs spread like vines up the pillars and exploded into a deep navy-colored ceiling with twinkling silver stars. The Council Table looked like a crescent moon with five Council Members awaiting them. If Rapture's citizens were Nomads, their architecture proved it.

"Welcome Wanderer," the woman on the far left raised her hand to the sky. The black silk robe slid from her sun-worn arm. "I am Maven and I oversee the Workers District. Tanners, Glassmakers, and Smiths are under my protection and the steel and leather they work with is my charge."

Eva took her place at the center of the table. Directly next to Maven was a red-haired man clad in an elegant brown tunic and black trousers. He spoke next as she noted his melodic voice. "And I am Xander. I am he who took charge of the farmers and shepherds here in Rapture. I represent their needs here and help tend our crops during harvest."

Next up was the dark-skinned man closest to Eva's right. He introduced himself as Lee. "I am the Head Healer here. My doctors are vital to the survival of Rapture and its people. Should you ever need a word with me, you can usually find me here. I rarely leave The Stronghold."

It was Eva's turn. These people only knew her as The Wanderer and she wanted to leave that title behind. It was time for a new beginning. Although she would still be using her abilities for battle, there would be others to help protect Rapture. She would not be alone.

"I'm Eva," she stopped. They were looking for a longer introduction. "Well… um… As you know, I *was* The Wanderer. Not any longer. The two brothers that were with me, Jake and Tommy McAvoy came from the Vault in the hills, far to the North of here. Originally, I was tasked with finding their father, but when I discovered that he was the man who betrayed me as the Serpent's Mistress, I killed him. That is why the Tigers were after us."

A long pause permeated the room. She shuffled uncomfortably in her seat. All eyes were on her.

"Invasion of a Gang compound…" the woman to her left spoke. She was wearing something on her face that Eva had not seen in a long time. Glasses. They were round and thick, sitting softly against the bridge of her nose. An emerald robe wrapped around her wrinkled figure and a quill with ink and parchment sat in front of her, meticulously arranged. She scrawled a few notes and placed the quill back in the inkwell. "How quaint."

With a long, drawn-out breath, almost a sigh, the oldest woman in the Council finally introduced herself. "I am Virginia, the Headmistress of the school here. We teach our students not just Old World academics, but also more practical things like growing crops. Unlike your useless skills in bloodshed, *my* school is how they become apprentices after they leave my supervision. Pupils who do not meet my expectations are not allowed to graduate. The younger brother that entered with you should enroll within the week."

Virginia turned her nose up and glared down the bridge of her nose.

Useless skills in bloodshed. Anger prickled through Eva's body and the thoughts of death were still fresh in her mind. Although part of her wanted to separate from the persona as The Wanderer, half of her mind was clinging to the prowess that came with that title. This old woman in round spectacles had already begun to get under her skin.

How about I show you how useless they are? You wouldn't last a second out there.

The last Council Member spoke his name. He was the tallest person Eva had ever seen, towering even while seated. His head and broad shoulders rose far above the throne-like chair. She estimated he must have stood at least seven feet tall. On his face, scars from long-forgotten battles softened by the kindness of his smile.

"It is nice to meet you Eva," he said in a deep, baritone voice. It was so loud that the marble table vibrated slightly with each word. His robe was the same color as the rest of the city, a pale gray. As he explained his position within the Council, Eva understood why his attire was so simple.

"As you can probably tell, there isn't much remaining to oversee within the walls. That is why I took the lead in outside trade, although we scarcely need it. I also disperse our Scouts for recruitment and maintain a good rapport with the Nomads. So, one could say that I have the *most important* job here because I handle the rest of the region."

Unlike the rest of the Council who rolled their eyes or shook their heads, Eva immediately took a liking to this guy. "Oh… and my name is Bruce." He was definitely the happiest one at the table.

"We wanted to introduce ourselves," Jasmine added when Eva caught her eye. "We only meet when one of us calls a Gathering. Otherwise, you are free to roam and perform your duties."

Virginia could not help but to chime in. "But *always* remember Wanderer… your duties are with Rapture and Rapture alone. You no longer have friends outside of these walls."

"It doesn't even seem like I have many *within* the walls," Eva snarled.

The old woman ignored her.

"If I were you." Virginia slowly pushed her glasses up the bridge of her nose. "I would meet with Gavin and your men fairly soon."

Eva had already planned to do so before Virginia's condescending instruction. She had spoken with her Captain and intended to introduce herself to the rest of the army. Respect had to be earned, and her reputation as the Wanderer would lay the foundation for their loyalty. As she rose to leave with the others, Bruce walked over and draped his trunk-like arm around her shoulders. It nearly knocked her off balance.

"Make sure you enroll the young boy in school," he whispered down to her. His ponytail hovered at least two feet above Eva, just past his beard. "And don't bother yourself with Virginia. She is *very* strict about academia, which is why she detests war so strongly. Unlike most of us, she believes that knowledge is the *only* key to peace. She doesn't realize that conflict is a necessity in this world. She has not lived it. Oh…one more thing. The older brother that arrived with you… he can find a master crafter and become an apprentice. Have him choose whatever he likes."

With a hard pat on Eva's back, Bruce stuck his tongue out at Virginia who turned her back and scoffed. He snickered. *Is this man crazy or just abnormally cheerful?* Still, Eva could not help but laugh with the Councilman.

The rest of the Council quickly dispersed to their respective jobs and Eva made her way back home. She told herself that today would be the last day she tarried around Rapture. When the sun came up the following day, she would begin her work. It was just a lot to take in. *There is much to do if I am to train this army properly.*

Jake and Tommy were waiting when Eva returned. The smell of a home cooked meal greeted her at the door. Her mouth watered and stomach yawned in hunger. She saw Tommy in the kitchen, standing over the hearthfire, stirring their evening meal. Jake was staring out the window at the Laborer's District on the other side of town. A cool breeze kept the house at a comfortable temperature despite the fire burning. Eva glanced at the mantle and noticed something was different. Her blades were hung right where she had left them, but a handful of smaller knives were missing.

"What did you trade with?" Eva turned to the young boy.

Silence. He turned his eyes to the pot of soup.

"Tommy? They don't just give out stuff for free here. So don't lie to me."

"Well we didn't have food…" The young boy kept his eyes glued to the cauldron as he stirred. "So I thought that… since you have so many knives… and it wasn't your swords… I could trade a couple of them."

Before Rapture, Eva would have lashed out. Each and every weapon she accumulated was a matter of life or death. But now, she had an army to protect them, so maybe she no longer needed so many weapons. Her response, though, startled both of the McAvoy brothers.

"It's fine. Just… please ask next time before you take my things," and left it at that.

Jake walked to the front door and called back to her. "I heard they gave you a seat on the Council."

"It suits me," she admitted. "Rapture's entire army is at my disposal. My days as a Mistress will pay off, but peacefully."

Jake's arm was still in a sling, but based on the way the wound was bound, Rapture's Healers were the best Eva had ever seen.

"Both of you will have to contribute," she mentioned. "I was told by the Council that Tommy has to enroll in their school before he becomes an apprentice… And Jake, you must choose a profession."

Jake sat at the table as Tommy started to fill up bowls of stew. "Well, I've always wanted to try blacksmithing. Not making weapons. Silverware and trinkets."

"Sounds like a great idea. Whatever you want to do."

There was a long pause. Eva stirred in her seat. Tommy slurped up some of his soup. Jake furrowed his brow.

"Do you like it here, Eva?" he asked.

"I…" She paused and considered the question. "Considering all that's happened to us. Actually… I *do* like it here. I'm just uncomfortable. Not having to fend for myself is weird. And honestly… with my new position, it reminds me of leading the Serpents. Those were the best days of my life. So, I guess I'm just conflicted."

"But these people are *good.*" Tommy tapped his spoon on the wooden table. "Not bad."

"Right Tommy," Eva put a hand on his shoulder. "They took us in, so they have to be good people."

Chapter 2

FIVE YEARS LATER

"We haven't received *any* intel regarding the Gangs." Eva rubbed her tired eyes, spending another long day in a Gathering with the Council. "It's been *months*."

The Council grumbled as Virginia finished another excessive rant that no one really listened to. She had called the previous six Gatherings and the other Council Members were becoming restless. When Eva tried to respond, the old woman interrupted.

"...Then how do we know what their next move will be? Isn't that your job? To gather information about anyone who would harm us? Especially since the Tigers-"

"My *job* is to protect Rapture," Eva said as calmly as she could. Avoiding eye contact, she played with the buckles on the leather armor she had been given years ago. "And I can do that with or without knowing what the Gangs are doing every day. Remember, I led one?"

Bruce was usually on her side during these disputes. They would frequently speak of battle tactics after their meetings. "Eva knows more about the Gangs than we could ever comprehend. These meetings are becoming pointless, Virginia. *I* have my full faith in The Wanderer as does the rest of this Council."

"My daughter and I cannot sleep with this level of uncertainty." Virginia stood up and pointed at Eva violently. "The Gangs have been silent for far too long. How do you think Rapture has been able to sustain this life thus far? We have to know what they are up to, and this is *her* responsibility."

"If you have a problem with how I run *my* army," Eva spat as she slammed her fist against the table. "Then I'm taking it as an assumption that you would like to replace me."

Everyone felt the tension rise in the room. Virginia's gaze narrowed as a flash of anger flickered in The Wanderer's eyes. Uncomfortable silence filled the Council Chambers for a moment, but neither woman would break their stare.

Jasmine attempted to diffuse the hostility. "Please stop fighting. This will get us nowhere."

"I will not dismiss this Gathering until something is done. We need *action* not *reaction*. Nonchalance will not be tolerated by me, and it certainly shouldn't be tolerated by any of *you*."

"*If it will get you to shut up,*" Eva said through gritted teeth, allowing her fingertips to run across the hilt of one of the daggers hidden in her pant leg. She despised having to explain herself. "Councilman Bruce, can you send Scouts north to watch the Tigers and Serpents for a while? And a small brigade west. My spare men are tied up trading with the Rover Warriors, as you asked."

"Aye," boomed the Councilman. He looked around at everyone else who wanted to leave just as bad as he did. "My Scouts are far more stealthy for this job anyway. If the Gangs are planning something, my Scouts will find out."

Lee stood up to leave. "Does this solution please you, Virginia? Can we move on and spend time on more pressing matters?"

"Fine." The woman in emerald stood up, spun on her heels, and disappeared down a hallway.

No one made a sound until Xander and Maven got up to leave. “I guess that means we are adjourned,” Xander said. “Can we please refrain from requesting another Gathering unless it is an *urgent* matter? Spring Harvest is quickly approaching and my farmers need assistance before the festival.”

“You’re speaking to the wrong people,” Eva added. “None of us have called a Gathering in ages. It’s the other one.” She pointed to where Virginia disappeared.

Maven followed Xander through the massive front doors of The Stronghold. Jasmine had disappeared without anyone noticing, as usual. She was a Nomad after all. All that remained was Eva and Bruce, who repeated their requests to one another and parted.

As The Wanderer crossed the drawbridge into the Town Square, she noticed that Gavin was waiting for her near the fountain. He had been a huge influence from the moment she entered Rapture. No matter what happened, he always had her back. When Jake decided to become a Smith’s Apprentice, Gavin was the one who convinced the most skilled blacksmith to take him in.

“So?” he smirked as they strolled to the Training Grounds. “How did it go this time?”

“You don’t want to know,” she shook her head and sighed. “*Trust me*. If this continues, I’ll probably be banished or publicly executed for murdering that woman.”

He playfully elbowed her. “I’m surprised you haven’t already. You know me… I love Rapture’s Council gossip. But seriously, what happened?”

“Virginia is afraid of the silence, once again.” Eva nodded at a few of her men on the road as they passed. It was midday and the guards were changing shifts. “I neglected to tell them that we haven’t sent anyone to check up on the Gangs in over a month. Honestly, it isn’t worth keeping the men away from Rapture. We aren’t really getting additional information that we don't already know. They're quiet. Trade is normal. No attacks on the free peoples."

"True," Gavin nodded as he stroked his beard. "But you know how she is. Paranoid as usual. After her husband died over a decade ago, she worries about every little thing. I feel bad for her daughter. Having to live with that woman…"

The two leaders of Rapture's Army followed the cobblestone path to a cutaway in The Stronghold. Large, gray bricks stacked a wall to their left and a small cliff led to a stream off to their right. A wooden door on a tower further ahead opened up to steps down to the Barracks, where the men rested, awaiting their next shift. The soldiers noticed her right away and gathered around a large crate near the wall.

"Attention men," Gavin's voice rose over the rabble of the townspeople nearby. "Eva has a message from the Stronghold."

The crowd made their way to a large crate to await their Commander's words. Roughly a hundred men and women waited for their orders that day. The apprentices remained in the Training Grounds and continued sparring. Eva climbed onto the large crate and called out to them.

"Virginia called yet another Gathering in regards to the Gangs." The armored men and women sighed loudly. A few booed. "I know. I know. I'm sick of this shit too. But we have, at least, a temporary solution. Councilman Bruce allowed me to utilize some of his Scouts to gather intel from across the region. We will continue to protect Rapture from *inside* these walls. The Scouts are already on the move, so the decision is plain and simple in my mind. Please remember, if you see or hear anything suspicious, report it to myself or Gavin. Questions?"

"Will we need more battalions near the city?" one of her men offered. "Just in case the Tigers try to attack us?"

Eva paused for a moment. She hadn't thought much about the Tigers in some time. It had been years since they threatened to come back for her head. "No. I doubt they will try and attack at this point. They don't have the firepower to get through our walls. Plus, McAvoy was the best Chief they've had, and *he's* dead."

Her men laughed. Gavin smiled.

"And if they do attack," Eva continued. "We will be ready here. Our walls are strong. For now, I will be *personally* training with Gavin for you to observe. I know that this has been requested for a while. All I can say is, I hope you are ready."

She smiled at her subordinate. His eyes lit up and he was grinning from ear to ear. For the last three years, he had been begging for her to train them one-on-one. No one in Rapture had yet witnessed her skill in battle. Instruction had only been given verbally before. Much of their loyalty rested on faith that the stories about The Wanderer were true. But now the moment had come for her to prove why she was their superior.

Eva wasted no time in playfully shoving her Captain to the sparring ring. Apprentices hopped out and she began her instruction. A crowd began to form around them. She laid her blades against a nearby tree stump and dropped down into the ring. Gavin trembled slightly, a mix of anticipation and excitement shivering through him. If the stories were true, the fight would be over quickly.

Suspense pressed hard against The Wanderer. She had trained alone for years, but she hadn't faced a true opponent since Chief McAvoy. Memories of the Tiger's Den clawed their way up, stirring a rising dread. She forced them back down and fixed her focus on Gavin.

"Hand-to-hand combat is relatively simple," she started her instruction as Gavin removed his plated armor. *My Captain's confidence will soon be reduced to nothing.* A devilish smile crawled across her lips. *Let's show them what I can do.*

"Watch closely," she said. Eva had always been competitive, but sometimes overconfidence was her downfall.

"You know I'm not going to let you win." Gavin returned her smile. "I'm not going easy."

"If you do," Eva adjusted her leather jacket and winked. "I'll demote you… But I wouldn't be so confident in winning, Captain. I can see you shaking from here."

The Wanderer, sparring against one of the most skilled soldiers in Rapture. Of course the men would cheer for Gavin. That was expected. He was the underdog. And honestly? That's how Eva liked it. Underestimated.

First, she took two, slow steps towards her opponent and studied a few spots on the ground. The crowd watched as she placed the heel of her boot in front of her. Digging it into the ground, she drew a deep X between her and Gavin in the dirt. He swallowed hard. The crowd quieted and watched intently as she took a handful of steps towards the edge of the ring and slid one leg behind her in a wide stance.

The countdown began. *3…*

2…

1…

Now.

Gavin was the first to attack, just as planned. The Wanderer easily dodged his first blow, aimed at her face. She stayed light on her feet, dodging and parrying as a flurry of jabs and kicks came her way. It didn't take long before her Captain grew increasingly irritated. Not one hit landed on his opponent. Soon, his attempts became sloppy and desperate. Once or twice, as he moved in to throw a punch, he stumbled and nearly collided with one of his men standing at the edge of the ring.

"She isn't even *trying*," one of the men shouted.

"Look at her go," cheered another.

Gavin shot a couple glances around the crowd and taunted his opponent. "Come on Eva, we know you can dodge me. Show me what you've got."

"If you insist," she shrugged.

A blink. Rushing footsteps. Impact.

With one fell swoop, the Captain of Rapture's Army felt his back slam against the hard ground. All the air was sucked out of his lungs. Eva had shifted his weight with her leg and swept him off balance, driving a punch into his chest as she knelt. He landed directly on top of the X. Everything happened so fast, no one really caught exactly how she had done it. They simply stood there, speechless.

Cheers erupted from the crowd. Townspeople who stopped to watch clapped loudly for their new Commander.

A few guards even begged for the chance to test their luck against the Wanderer.

Eva helped up her friend. "How the hells did you do that?" he coughed. "I've never seen anyone move so fast."

"The key is to find weakness in your opponent," she said above the rabble. Her men quieted down for the lesson. "Study them for a moment, if you can. Against most Gang Members, they'll just shoot you dead if you hesitate. However, if you manage to disarm them… take your time. You waste much less energy if you start on the defensive."

Gavin was still catching his breath, but managed to beckon for her. "Again."

"Sorry? What?" Eva turned around and adjusted her belt.

"*Again*," he repeated, beckoning for her. "I think I'll have you this time."

She widened her stance. Again, Gavin came at her with all of his might. *That* was his weakness. He expected her to fall to his brute strength, but she was much too agile. She stepped aside and he barreled right past her into the side of the Sparring Ring. People stumbled over one another as they fell backwards. Voices of anger rose around them. As Eva turned to meet his next attempt at knocking her down, he was already upon her. She was thrown to the ground, but rolled away as he tried to bury his knees into her torso. There was no backing down between these two. *Wow. Not bad.*

Eva ducked to a lower stance as Gavin taunted her. "What's the matter? I thought you were *the best*."

The Wanderer was slightly offended by the remark. A flicker of her old self urged her to strike down anyone who dared question her skill. Her Hooded Demon appeared and vanished in an instant. *Am I imagining things? No. Focus.* Furrowing her brow in concentration, Eva sprinted at her opponent and slid across a patch of dew covered grass on one knee. The other leg was outstretched towards Gavin's leg. She didn't want to injure him terribly, just enough to make him hesitant in challenging her again.

He tried to grab her, missing her arm by a hair.

Eva's boot made contact with his shin and as he staggered backwards in pain, she kicked off with the other foot and wrapped her arm around his neck. Gavin was in a headlock, and she was victorious once again. But this time, they were both winded.

"You should see me with my blades," she whispered in her Captain's ear. Goosebumps tingled over Gavin's arms. Her voice was threatening but playful… and he liked it.

As she released him, the rest of the men dispersed to start training with a new sense of vigor. For the next few weeks, Eva planned to spend her time in the Training Grounds instructing the rest of them. To the dismay of the rest of Rapture's army, Gavin would be her only opponent.

"Well," he cleared his throat and straightened his clothes, still panting. "That was fun. I guess you were still holding back on me?"

"You'll never know," she smirked and wiped the sweat off her neck. "But I look forward to the next time we fight."

Later that day, Eva took a break from her duties to stroll through the Worker's District and visit Jake. In the last five years, he had gradually refined his skill in casting trinkets, silverware, and jewelry. In time, he became the second-best smith in Rapture. Only his Master, who specialized in weapons and armor, was a finer blacksmith. The line outside of their respective shops would wind through the main street each morning. Women awaited eagerly for Jake's newest creations, but he would always save his most beautiful creations for Eva, although she had never been interested in jewelry. *He doesn't understand me*, she thought as she turned down yet another accessory—a broach. *I would much rather have a brand new dagger strapped to my leg than a sparkly necklace.*

Lucky for her, Jake never took it personally.

He didn't even glance up at her when she entered the shop. He was chuckling to himself. "Already heard you made a fool of Gavin. I'm proud of you."

"Sounds like you were doubting me," Eva said as she studied the shelves overflowing with baubles. "You've seen me fight at full capacity."

"Yeah, but not in a long time," he said, tinkering with an intricately delicate necklace. "It's been years. I would have thought you'd slow down a bit. Relax a little. As you *should*."

"My job is to train, Jake," she squeezed between a few older women admiring a pair of earrings and neared him. Tension rose in the store as a few people left silently. "And even if I didn't train, I'd still be more skilled than anyone here. I have more real experience than my entire army combined. But I do train. All day. Every damned day."

"Except when you are called to another Gathering."

"Don't even get me started on that shit… I have it under control for now. Bruce and I finally decided to offer Virginia a resolution to avoid another ridiculous meeting."

"I really don't understand why you toy with the Council Members like that," Jake's tone hushed. "It doesn't look good for us as citizens here."

"What are you trying to say?"

"You had the ability to offer that solution weeks ago. Whatever it was. I know you're smarter than that, but you enjoy making your enemies hate you more every day. You like to give them as many reasons to hate you as possible. You don't like to compromise."

"Oh please." Eva rolled her eyes. Jake was trying to get under her skin, and it was working. She slammed a metal spoon on a stone display and stared at him. The other patrons turned to watch the exchange. "It's only Virginia… Besides, I'm The Wanderer. They aren't going to get rid of me that easily. So stop worrying."

Jake saw that she had bent one of his more valuable items and clenched his fist. He went to yell at her for being insensitive, but noticed the townspeople staring at him. Unlike Eva, he cared about how the people of Rapture viewed him. The Scouts had chosen *her* to join the city, not him or Tommy. He worried that if he did not contribute, they would send him back out into the region. And if Jake left the safety of these walls, he would not survive.

However, Eva understood the prestige of her place on the Council. Everyone in Rapture knew The Wanderer by name. And even if they ever banished her, she would simply slip back into the life she'd always known outside these walls. But deep down, fitting into this society had been difficult for her. Even after five years, she still struggled with the idea of this place.

The Tigers. They're still after me. Suddenly, her chest began to tighten. It was becoming considerably more difficult to breathe. The floor swayed beneath her for a moment. Then, she heard a familiar sound.

The bell attached to the entrance rang with the child's voice. "Mama! Papa!" It was Jake and Eva's daughter, Anya. Racing after her was Tommy McAvoy, his face and tunic smeared with dirt.

Chocolate brown waves bounced as the little girl jumped into her mother's open arms. Because it was midday, the schoolchildren were released for a meal. Tommy must have gone to pick Anya up from the Stronghold when she bolted for her father's shop.

"You shouldn't be running around in here," she scolded. "It's dangerous. There's a lot to break."

"Sorry Mama," Anya frowned. Eva met her daughter's aqua eyes as the girl continued with her explanation. "I saw you walking and I wanted to see you so bad. And I'm not allowed to see you when you're with the army. Uncle Tommy isn't as fast as me. We raced and I won."

Jake chuckled and shook his head. Both he and Tommy had matured significantly since entering the town. They had developed a routine with their own career paths and became more independent with each passing day. While Eva was a vital part of Rapture's Council in addition to the Commander of their army, Jake had been given his own forge after only two years of apprenticeship. Despite being exceptionally talented in metalworking, he refused to make weapons. Just like his partner, he wanted to start over.

"I've spent far too much time surrounded by death," he admitted to Eva one evening. "I can't bring myself to make anything used to end someone's life. If your blades could talk..."

On the other hand, Tommy decided to continue his passion for farming. When they first arrived, he reluctantly attended Virginia's school for three years. After proving to the Council that he had more than enough knowledge to be an Apprentice, and much to Virginia's disdain, they allowed him to start working directly under Xander. From the long hours spent tending crops, his skin had tanned, and he'd shaved off his wavy, dirty-blond locks. He hardly resembled his brother now. Most importantly, Tommy's contribution and Nomad-like connection with nature had doubled the town's harvest since they arrived.

Life within Rapture's walls had changed Eva as well. A few months after she and Jake were granted refuge, she became pregnant. She never imagined herself being a mother, but the moment she brought Anya into the world, she fell in love. It was the first time she could remember crying out of pure joy.

Originally, Jake wanted to marry Eva before they had any children, but she never understood the purpose of marriage. "It's an Old Time thing," she argued. But that didn't stop Jake from asking every year. Anya was now four years old and just a few months ago, Eva finally agreed to be wed.

***

"I know you think it's old fashioned," said Jake. "But I really want to show everyone that I am only ever going to be with you."

"Then only ever be with me," she laughed. "Why do you need a ring and a ceremony to make that official? Is our love for each other not enough?"

"Please Eva." Jake revealed a brand new dagger. "I had the other smith make this for you… instead of a ring."

She slowly unsheathed the blade and studied its details. Every inch of the dagger was meticulously designed. The blade was cast from the most beautiful steel she had ever seen. Gold filigree wound around the hilt and down the middle of the blade. The smith had even etched an *E* on the pommel. It glinted as bright as her swords against the candlelight of their home. This was the most beautiful gift she had ever been given. Actually, it was the *only* gift she had ever been given. Jake knew her better than she realized.

"Alright," she finally agreed, smiling up at him. "You win. I'll marry you."

***

Eva reminisced about the moment she first laid eyes on that dagger. She carried it with her at all times, regardless of whether or not she was working. Gavin noticed it poking out from the top of her boot once or twice, but he said nothing.

He understood that she would never completely trust his people. And it was in her nature to be prepared for an attack at all times. That was one of the reasons the Council had chosen her to lead Rapture's Army. Over the years, Eva grew to accept the town and the safety that its walls provided, but she would never let her guard down entirely.

Anya's tiny hand was patting her mother's thigh. Eva looked down at her child and smiled.

"You are dreaming with your eyes open again Mama," she giggled. "I see you."

"It's time for you to go back to school young lady," Eva said. Her daughter crossed her arms and huffed. "Uncle Tommy has to go back to work just like you."

"And you gotta go back to work too?" Anya's bright eyes sparkled up at her father. "You all do."

Jake nodded. "That's right. I don't get breaks like your mother."

Eva clenched her jaw in a fake smile.

Tommy took the little girl by the hand and walked her back towards The Stronghold. Jake kissed Eva on the cheek as she left. Cool, Spring air greeted her as she stepped outside the hot store. It smelled of rain. Vast, dark clouds above her ignited with a brilliant storm. Eva's eyes drifted to the tops of Rapture's walls. Years had passed since she left the security of the town. She had only ventured into the region once since arriving, traveling to the city to retrieve the journal Jake had given her.

But even that felt like a lifetime ago.

I DON'T EVEN FEEL LIKE MYSELF ANYMORE.

She wrote one evening. **AND I'M NOT SURE WHETHER THAT'S A GOOD OR BAD THING. I MEAN... I WANTED TO PUT BEHIND THAT OLD TITLE. I HAVE**

A CHILD. I'M AT PEACE. I HAVEN'T KILLED ANYONE IN YEARS. PART OF ME IS RELIEVED THAT I CAN FINALLY BEGIN TO FEEL NORMAL... WITH A NORMAL LIFE AND A FAMILY, LIKE THEY DID IN THE OLD TIMES...

I JUST WISH I COULD SAY I'M TRULY HAPPY... BUT THERE'S STILL SOMETHING IN ME THAT CLINGS TO BEING THE WANDERER. AND THAT PART OF ME STARTED REAPPEARING AGAIN... IN THE FORM OF JAKE'S FATHER, DAN MCAVOY. IT ISN'T AS OFTEN AS IT ONCE WAS. JUST FLASHES HERE AND THERE. BUT IT STILL MAKES ME WONDER. WHAT IF I DIDN'T KILL HIM? WHY HAVEN'T THE TIGERS ATTACKED LIKE THEY PROMISED? BUT IT'S NOT LIKE I CAN TELL JAKE OR TOMMY. IF I'M DOUBTING, THEY'LL START DOUBTING TOO. THEY'RE SO HAPPY NOW. I MUST HAVE KILLED HIM. I SWEAR I DID... BUT THEN WHY DOES THIS THING STILL FOLLOW ME?

***

Not long after they arrived in Rapture, Eva finally told Jake about her Shadow for the first time.

Jake peeled away the last of his bandages from the wound his father had left. It was late in the evening, and only he and Eva remained awake. Tommy was passed out on his chair again, feet propped up on a small table. The entire home was silent except for the crackling of the dying fire. Something was on Eva's mind, but wasn't sure how to explain it. Waves of dread washed over her as she opened her mouth to speak. Tonight, the Shadow stood in the corner of the room almost eclipsing the moonlight coming through the window.

"I've been meaning to tell you this for a while," she started slowly, lingering on each word, carefully choosing what to say next. "Like *a long time*. Please don't think I'm crazy."

Jake sensed the severity by the tone in her voice. His heart started racing. "Okay."

"So… um…" She hesitated. Was she certain she wanted to confess to seeing something that wasn't there? No one else could see it, but it appeared so real and was causing her so much distress. Still, the feeling of fear that accompanied it *was* real, and it was suffocating. Eva felt so alone.

With a sharp inhale, she continued. "There's something that I can see… that I wanted to tell you about. I'm sure it's what causes my nightmares. The bad ones. But it's only been following me since I first brought you and Tommy back to the Rover Colony. At least, that's when I started seeing it."

"Huh?" Jake was confused. He was under the impression that Eva was leaving Rapture. Or leaving him. Relief came over him briefly, then uncertainty filled the void.

Eva was becoming frustrated with herself. She wanted to punch the wall, but that would wake Tommy and possibly the neighbors. Instead she slammed her hand against her thigh and an old wound tinged in pain. She winced and started whispering loudly. "You know I'm not good at expressing myself. *Okay*. So I can see some shit… a demon in a black cloak. It follows me *everywhere*. I thought it would leave when we got here. I thought I left it behind when I killed your father. But I was wrong. It's still here. Worst of all, it has your father's face. I don't know why it's here. I don't know what it wants. I don't know why I can see it. But… there."

She had spoken so fast that Jake had to process everything she had said for a moment. The silence was taken as judgment by Eva. Before he could utter a response, she was already jumping down his throat.

"I knew I shouldn't have told you," she threw her arms out and stood up, her throat burning from whispering so forcefully. "I knew you'd think I was crazy. Shit. Maybe I should just stop trusting everyone here. Or anyone at all."

"I never said you were crazy," Jake stood up and put his hands on her shoulders, pulling her into an embrace. "As long as it doesn't affect you, then who cares?"

She pushed away from him. "That's just it. It *does*. It taunts me. Remember when you saw me shaking and struggling to breathe in the Rover Colony? That day I tried to take my own life?"

"Yeah?"

"Well that *thing* appeared and pressured me to kill myself. I didn't even realize that I was actually trying to *do* it. My vision went black and I was being… consumed… by the words it spoke. I lost control."

"Has it happened since the Rover Colony?"

"Yeah. But it hasn't happened in a while. I'm able to push away the negative thoughts… for now. I just don't know what to do."

"Is it here right now?"

Eva slowly pointed to the corner of the room. "And it still has your father's face. The only difference is the red eyes and skeleton hands. No skin, no muscle… just bones."

Jake stared at the space, squinting to see if he noticed anything.

Again, she took it as him mocking her.

"You know what, Jake? I don't know why I tell you anything serious. You just turn it into a joke. Just forget about it."

"Eva… I didn't -"

And like that, Eva had already disappeared into the next room.

The truth was, Jake had no idea how to respond. But ever since that night, he hadn't looked at his partner the same way. Maybe he really did think she was crazy. Eva could feel him pulling away from her. He was clearly afraid.

After everything else that Jake has seen me do, this is what's pushing him away?

***

Because Jake was little help in comforting Eva, she confided in Jasmine. She became tremendously concerned when The Wanderer spoke to her about the Demon. The Nomads held the belief that no sign should be ignored and there was a chance that Eva was not on the path that their "Mother" had set for her. When she recounted the attempts at her own life, Jasmine vowed to watch her every day until the apparition no longer appeared. Five years later, little had changed.

***

"You need to connect directly with nature," the Nomad offered as a final attempt to give Eva some peace. "That will be the only way you can separate from your 'self' as The Wanderer and your 'self' as Eva. Spirits cannot function properly if they are not in balance. Take a walk in my garden each day. I will be sure to keep the citizens away while you relax."

"It's worth a shot," she sighed. At this point, she was willing to try anything.

Eva spent more time than usual in the Gardens that day. She desperately wanted to rid herself of the Shadow before her wedding the next morning. Sitting peacefully in nature was her final attempt at eradicating this dread. And while the meditations had been calming, as soon as she opened her eyes, the specter was waiting. Silent. Observing.

With a deep inhale, Eva removed her boots and loosened her armor. Jasmine escorted the last of the citizens from the area near the lake. In a small cove, Eva sat on a soft patch of grass and studied the space. Waves lapped against the large, rounded stones just a few feet away. Perched in the trees above her head were birds of different colors and sizes, chirping melodically in the shade. A light breeze brushed across flowers around her, sending their intoxicating perfume into the air. They, too, came in all shapes, sizes, and colors. To her left, a small stream fed into the lake from underneath Rapture's wall. She could hear a waterfall through the grates in the sewer tunnel.

I am at peace. Slowly, she closed her eyes and released all of the tension in her body instantaneously.

Jasmine had instructed her to focus on the elements of nature. One at a time. "There are *five* elements that our Great Mother has gifted us to protect—Earth, Water, Air, Fire, and Spirit. Four in our physical body, one connected with every other being. Spirit relies on the other four's existence and balance. Focus on the balance outside… try to bring it into yourself… and it will create stability within your soul."

The scent of blossoming plants permeated Eva's senses. She turned her focus to the Earth element, then Water, Air, and finally, Fire. Because she saw Fire as something dangerous and destructive, it was always the hardest to calm within her. Images of torture bubbled up in her mind and her Shadow would grow. But this time, she fought her rising heartbeat. The painful images started to form, but she forced them out of her mind. *Fire gives life, it doesn't just take it away.*

Eva turned her attention back to Earth. By brushing the grass underneath her, breathing in the scent, listening to the rustling of leaves above her, imagining their movement. She allowed each sense to fill with the element, just as the Councilwoman had instructed. *Earth is the bones in my body, giving me stability.*

Next was Water. The sound of the stream nearby and the rippling of the lake. *The blood that courses through my veins is the water within me. It gives my body life.*

Then Air. A deep inhale and slow exhale. The sound of the wind rustling through the trees. *The air I breathe connects me with the element. It gives me a voice to use as a storm or a whisper of wind.* But as she reached the element of Fire once again, her mind shifted to enslavement. Betrayal. Dan McAvoy. As she tried to focus on calming herself, her Shadow began to whisper.

"Are you sure that you killed me, Wanderer?" it taunted with a low, emotionless voice. "I sense that your confidence is dwindling. Time will tell."

Eva kept her eyes shut tight. A single tear dripped down her cheek and she wiped it away with a clenched fist. Images of torture burned through her entire body, a white-hot pain jolted through her chest. Beads of sweat formed on her forehead and neck. That was when the doubt began to overpower everything. Unconsciously, she stood up and pushed the thoughts away. She repeated the phrase that the Nomads had taught her. *Fire gives life, it doesn't just take it away.*

Fire is the passion within me. It is the warmth of my body and ignites my soul to fight for what I love. Fire gives me purpose. I bathe in it to protect those who would burn.

Suddenly, an unfamiliar calmness spread through her torso. It was warm. First, in her stomach, then outwards through her extremities. She opened her eyes. Where the apparition of Dan McAvoy once stood, there was nothing.

Rabbits sprang through the bushes where she had last spotted it. It seemed to have disappeared without a trace.

Eva waited for a moment to make sure she did not hear the Shadow whisper in her ear. Nothing. Even the dread was gone.

"It-it," she choked. Tears of relief welled in her eyes. "It's gone. The damned thing is *finally* gone."

Jasmine had been tending to the Garden nearby and waltzed over to her. Eva stood up and thanked the Nomad with a hug.

"I didn't think it would actually work," she admitted, grabbing the Councilwoman's hands. "But it did. I don't see *or* feel that 'thing' anymore. *Thank you.*"

"That gladdens me," Jasmine nodded. "I am always happy to be of assistance to The Wanderer and those she deems a friend."

Eva looked around one more time, making sure that the hooded creature was, in fact, gone for good.

"They request your presence in The Stronghold," Jasmine said. "Your wedding ceremony is tomorrow and they had a few more questions about where you would like to host it. Rumor is that the entire town will be there."

The Wanderer took her leave of the Nomad and her magical Garden. For the first time in years, Eva was not accompanied by her haunt. She felt lighter. Calmer. And tomorrow, she would be wed to her companion, Jake McAvoy. Through everything that happened since they met, he remained true to her. He understood her better than anyone else and she loved him more than she thought was possible.

After she fastened her boots and tightened her armor, Eva was on her way. The storm clouds she noticed hours before now loomed directly overhead. Low, rumbling thunder was still north of town, but drops of rain blanketed the dirt-covered cobblestone street. She pulled her hood over her head as the mist transformed to a drizzle. The weather was dreary, but Eva Calloway was in good spirits.

It wasn't until she reached the drawbridge that she could see the Stronghold. Rain accompanied by a thick fog obscured her field of view as she finally arrived at the doors. Against her wishes, the entire town would be present for the exchange of vows.

No one would dare miss the wedding of The Wanderer.

Chapter 3

The city of Rapture had given Jake and Eva the safety and peace they'd always dreamed of. At last, the days of fleeing Gangs, scavenging for scraps, and fighting to stay alive were behind them. Everything they could ever want was available to them.

Finally, after all these years, The Wanderer felt comfortable enough to settle down and marry Jake, even if the reason was only to make him happy.

Why am I not more excited about this? She wondered, massaging the pit in her stomach. *I mean, I love him more than anything.* These vows would be bittersweet. On one hand, it felt like a seal in her new life, but at the same time, the final nail in burying her identity as The Wanderer. Freedom that she once enjoyed, even relished, would be gone. The moment she fully pledged herself to Jake McAvoy, she also fully pledged herself to Rapture.

The ceremony would be held in the Council Grand Chambers, the largest room in the Stronghold, where everyone could attend comfortably. Following the ceremony, it would be transformed into a feast hall. There would be drinking, dancing, and music all throughout the evening.

Eva was deep in thought as she entered the Stronghold. She was not keen on being the center of attention for so long, but it was only for one evening.

I can handle one night for Jake.

A voice she had not heard in years beckoned for her. The recognition made her snap out of her thoughts. "Ahhh, Strong Lioness." It was Yidi, the Elder of the Nomad tribe in the city. Jasmine had requested that he perform the wedding ceremony as a special gift. "It is so wonderful to see you."

Eva greeted him with a fist on her chest and bowed. "Likewise, Yidi. It has been too long. You look well."

Masha, Yidi's wife, had also traveled to Rapture. Eva greeted her with a warm hug. "Indeed. We have been gifted with peace over these past few years. No Gangs have intruded in our territory and we took it as a sign from our Mother."

Something in The Wanderer's stomach churned. *The Gangs aren't even attacking the freepeoples? So strange.* But she quickly ignored the thought for the moment and welcomed her old friends to the town.

"This isn't the first time we have ventured here, my child," said Masha. "Jasmine is our granddaughter."

Eva's eyes widened. "Wait… Jasmine? I didn't know that. We've been friends for *years* now and you haven't told me? Neither of you Elders said anything about this place either. I lived with you in the city for a time and it was not mentioned once."

"It is not important as to what our Great Mother has given to us." Yidi shook his head. "What is more important is how we protect her gifts. It is not our path to illuminate the paths of others. Divine timing is different for all of us. Jasmine's mother and father were taken from us by the Gangs… Slain years ago. That is why we had her travel here."

"When Rapture found out that I had an incredibly strong connection to nature," Jasmine explained. "They granted me a Council seat. Someone had to tend to the Gardens."

"And it has never looked so beautiful dear," Masha beamed. "Your parents' spirits are so proud. More than most of our people, you give to our Mother."

"Anyway," Yidi interrupted. "We would like the ceremony to be in the center, here." He pointed at the crescent-shaped table where the Council held their Gatherings. "Would that be alright with you, Lioness?"

Eva studied the space where she would be standing for a moment. "It really doesn't matter to me. This event is more for him, anyway."

Jake had just stepped out of the rain and into the high-ceilinged room. "This place will be perfect. And Eva, this is for *both* of us."

She turned her eyes to the floor. Her stomach turned into knots as she struggled with the idea of marriage once again. For nearly two decades, she had traveled the region alone. Although the Rovers had looked to her for their protection for a time, Eva was still free to roam the region as she pleased. But the moment she met Jake and Tommy, her life completely changed. She cared for them and loved them like family, but the idea of being eternally bonded to Jake petrified her. He had been asking for so long, Eva considered whether she agreed just to get him to stop. But marriage? It made her feel stuck.

I have to just accept this change for the one I love. He's changed a lot for me... Then she thought about her Shadow disappearing in the Gardens and the smile returned to her face.

"I wanted to tell you tomorrow." Eva glanced around to see if anyone was within earshot. "But I can't wait until then…"

Jake took a step towards her and looked around in confusion. "What?"

"The Demon… It's *gone.* And I don't think it's coming back this time."

"Really? That's wonderful," Jake said as he hugged her tight. "Perfect timing if you ask me. I was starting to worry that you were, you know, losing yourself."

She cleared her throat and nodded.

"Anything else you want to discuss before tomorrow?" Jasmine interjected. "I know you mentioned that you don't care to plan these things, but it is *your* wedding day."

"Jake should be able to make any last-minute decisions," she said shortly. "I never asked for a ceremony…"

Jake's heart sank and he scowled at her.

"Okay." Jasmine sighed. "Just be here by midday tomorrow."

Eva nodded and as she turned to leave, Jake stopped her.

"Why do you always have to act like that?" he asked.

She shrugged. "What are you talking about? I'm being honest. Just like I've always been."

"You're being defensive and it's insulting," he spat. "Do you even *want* to marry me?"

"I already discussed how I feel about the whole 'wedding' thing," she said. "I'm doing it for you. I care about you, but… I just… don't like formalities like this."

Eva tried to push Jake aside, but he took another step in front of her and stopped, blocking the door.

"Are you sure you're okay with this? I don't want to make you do something that you don't want to do…Just tell me the truth. Please."

"Okay," she sighed and bit her lip. "Fine. You really want to know? Too many people in one space makes me nervous. *Really* nervous."

Eva's final comment hung in the air as she left the building. Although Jake understood her discomfort, he had been planning every detail since she had first agreed to marry him. The type of flowers that would be laid across the table and down the aisle. The food to be served. Even Anya would have a part in her parents' wedding. She was thrilled to be the one who poured the four elements over her parents as Yidi spoke his blessing. Afterwards, Masha promised to read the little girls' spirit and bestow appropriate markings. Tommy, Eva, and Jake would all be wearing their Spirit Markings.

And, of course, Tommy was exhilarated to be this close to the Nomads again.

Dinner had been cooked and a steaming plate of meat and vegetables awaited Eva when she finally returned home. She sat down and began to eat with Tommy and Anya when Jake returned. He waltzed in, making it obvious that he was hiding something behind his back.

"Anya," he said and bent down at table level. "I have something for you."

The little girl had already hopped out of her chair and bolted over to see the gift her father was carrying.

"Mama, it's a new dress for me!" Anya exclaimed. She started jumping up and down. "It's *so* pretty."

Jake shrugged at Eva. "I figured you would just wear your armor. I was going to wear mine as well… you know, since the Nomad ceremony is the joining of two warriors. But Anya doesn't have anything to wear."

He revealed the dress. It was sewn from an off-white fabric and ruffled out as a long gown. The tailor had subtly woven shades of purple into several layers of the fabric. Anya had begged her parents for armor because she wanted to be like her mother, but Eva would not allow it so young. She refused to let her daughter follow in The Wanderer's footsteps. Jake, who had been thrown straight into battle after leaving the Vault, was shocked at Eva's firm response. Ever since they met, she had always harped on the importance of fighting for survival, but Rapture, it seemed, had softened that opinion.

Eva examined the small dress. "Wow. It is *very* pretty, my little love." She glanced up at Jake. "And yes, I'm wearing my blades as well. No arguments."

Jake's smile faded but he reluctantly agreed.

"Eat before the food gets cold," Tommy yelled from the other side of the kitchen. "I spent a lot of time cooking this tonight."

And with that, Anya and the McAvoy brothers were eating dinner and chatting about their day. Eva, however, stayed silent. A foreboding feeling arose when the realization of tomorrow's events finally hit her. Up until now, her wedding felt like a dream. Even the Shadow of red-eyed Dan McAvoy seemed more real at the time. And now that it was only one short sleep away, doubt and regret sank its teeth into her chest.

Hours later, Jake was passed out in his chair with Anya in his arms and Tommy had the door to his bedroom shut after cleaning up the evening meal. The house was completely silent. Eva laid in bed alone. She stared at the wooden ceiling, reflecting on her past and questioning her future. Is this life what she truly wanted? Settling down with someone seemed great on the surface, but was it something The Wanderer would do?

The Wanderer is dead, she reasoned. *I am safe. My family is safe. I no longer need to be The Wanderer.*

No matter how hard she tried, she just could not allow herself to let go.

And what happens if Rapture becomes unsafe? How can you protect your family if you let The Wanderer die?

It was a valid point. If Eva continued to be complacent with her new life, her skills known throughout the region would be lost. What if, for some reason, they were forced to leave Rapture? She doubted that would ever happen, but still battled with the assumption of safety here.

Finally, Eva's mind games drained her enough to sleep. There were only a few more hours until the entire town would be squeezed into The Stronghold.

***

The next morning came faster than Eva would have liked, and the lingering feeling of uncertainty did not subside with rest. Still, she refused to ruin her and Jake's special day.

When she considered how much work he put into everything, some of the reluctance faded. He truly wanted the entire town of Rapture to see the strength and beauty of their love.

Maybe I have been a jerk about this whole thing, she thought. *Why do I keep pushing away the only man who is able to love me through all this...shit... that I've been dealing with? Maybe I'll feel better after the ceremony.*

Unfortunately, Eva hadn't been able to spend much time with Jake over the past few months. Gatherings and training had engulfed every free moment that she had. Not to mention, his store was one of the most visited in Rapture. These days, Eva spent more time with Rapture's guards than her own partner. But it was their daughter who suffered most, seeing her parents for only a few hours each evening.

I have to do better. For them.

Both Jake and Eva dressed in solitude while Tommy helped Anya get ready. It had been years since Jake had worn the armor gifted to him by the Rover Warriors, but it stirred a sense of power he had nearly forgotten. He was disgusted by the joy it brought him. Though he would never admit it, he craved to travel with The Wanderer one last time.

"I'm heading for The Stronghold early," he mentioned after finishing breakfast. "I wanted to change some things. To be honest, I'd rather us stand on the Grand Staircase. That way, everyone can see us."

Eva pointed her fork at the door. "Okay. I'm going to take a walk in The Gardens before the ceremony."

"Is every*thing* okay?"

By the way he emphasized 'thing,' Eva knew exactly what he was referring to.

"Yes. I'm *fine*." Eva stood up, grabbed her blades, kissed Anya on the cheek, and walked to the door. "Don't worry about me."

As her blade sheathes wrapped around her shoulders, a chill crept up her spine. She closed her eyes and allowed the emotion to fill to the brim. Familiarity. Images of countless battles flashed in her mind. After all these years, she had forgotten how many victims, both good and bad, fell victim to her wrath. More memories floated to the surface as she replayed various events as the Serpent's Mistress, protecting the Rovers, rescuing Jake and Tommy in the Vault, and infiltrating the Tigers. Just as she was about to reach the scene of Dan McAvoy and her ultimate revenge, Gavin's voice caught her attention.

"Hope you don't mind me asking but," he called from his porch. He was sitting in a rocking chair, enjoying the nice weather. "Why are you armed to the teeth for a celebration?"

"It's tradition," she responded and made her way over to his home. "I just need a walk to clear my head before I head over to The Stronghold."

Gavin's concern came across as more genuine than Jake's for some reason. "Are you doing alright?"

"Yeah," she said. "I'm fine."

"Doesn't sound like it." Gavin stood up and put his cup of tea on the table near the swing. "Let's go together. Down to the Gardens at least."

Eva knew that if she tried to refuse him, he would insist until she gave in. It was better to nod and allow him to accompany her, even if it was in complete silence. Gavin gave her the space she needed to think, only speaking if she invited him to. Something about him seemed different from everyone else. Most of his life had been spent beyond Rapture's walls. Unlike the McAvoy brothers or anyone else in Rapture, he had endured years of running from Gangs, fighting to survive. And that was how he became such a great warrior.

He made her feel… seen.

"... I just don't want to lose who I am," she finally confessed. "I don't know if I'm doing this for me or for Jake."

"Well… sometimes you have to sacrifice a part of yourself to be with someone." Gavin offered. "Compromise in love, not in battle. You will always be The Wanderer. That will *never* change. Follow your heart, as silly as that sounds."

Admittedly, his words were uplifting. By the time Eva had a moment to focus on how she could bring herself to compromise for Jake, they had reached the Gardens. She found a spot near the stream and sat down on a bench nearby. Gavin took a seat beside her and rested his elbows on his thighs, staring at the ground while he waited. He was an extremely patient man.

"You're right," she murmured under her breath. "I guess I just never imagined myself like this… a mother and a wife… and… now that it's a reality… I guess I didn't plan as well as I thought."

"Life shouldn't be a plan." Again, his words were very wise for only being a few years older than Eva. "You should be allowed to enjoy this place without having to worry about what comes next. Neither of us are out *there* anymore." He pointed to the wall. "It's something I have to remind myself every day."

"You know Gavin," Eva glanced over at him and smiled. "I've always wondered how *you* haven't found someone yet."

"Eh," he shrugged. "My work keeps me busy. Not sure if I'd even have enough time to court someone. Plus, I have a *very* specific type."

They both laughed.

Gavin reached up and stroked his reddish beard, cut short and angled along his jawline. But as his hand drifted toward his ear, the color shifted sharply to a sandy blonde. He ran his fingers through his wavy locks and smiled down at the space between his knees. Eva watched him, though he didn't notice.

Midday gave way into Rapture and greeted its people with sunshine. Gavin had given Eva reassurance that she was making the right decision in marrying Jake. They left the serene Gardens for the Stronghold when Jasmine summoned them for the ceremony. Rapture itself was desolate. Only a few guards were stationed in the watchtowers dotting its perimeter. The citizens had already made their way to the castle waiting for The Wanderer and her Captain to arrive.

Jasmine opened the great doors to the Council Chambers. A sea of people dressed in their finest clothes formed a pathway to the staircase. On the landing, Jake waited for her, clad in his armor. Tommy and Anya were on the step below him. Yidi and Masha stood next to Eva's future husband. The Council Members had all lined up the remaining space of the staircase with their families. Virginia was there with her daughter, Mara, whose thin face with flowing golden hair was smiling up at Jake. Her white and golden dress was the most extravagant that Eva had ever laid her eyes on. A tinge of jealousy panged her chest.

Slowly, the people of Rapture noticed the bride had finally arrived. The Stronghold fell quiet. Gavin rushed up the staircase and stood opposite Tommy and Anya. Eva's face became hot. She could feel the eyes of everyone on her. *Just focus on Jake*, she reminded herself.

As she stepped down the makeshift aisle and passed the Council table, her stomach did a backflip.

Just focus on Jake.

Something didn't feel right. Her stomach lurched.

The second Eva reached the landing where Jake and her family were, a shockwave knocked them to their knees.

The explosion was so loud, everyone in The Stronghold went deaf immediately. Eva forced herself to stand against her swimming vision. All she could hear was a loud ringing. Those around her, including Jake and Anya, were stunned. Luckily, she was able to spring into action with Gavin by her side. Rushing over to a secret corridor underneath the staircase, she frantically motioned for the Council Members and their families to escape.

Eva grabbed Jake's shoulders, lifted him to his feet, and screamed at the top of her lungs. "*Get Anya out of here. Now.*"

He couldn't hear, but was able to read her lips. With one swift motion, he scooped up his hysterical child in one arm and grabbed his brother's shirt with the other. The three of them disappeared into the crowd through the side entrance. People of Rapture who hadn't been injured or killed by the explosive were fleeing in all directions. Eva and Gavin were pushing against the mob to try and find the culprit. The epicenter of the bomb was at the very center of the Council's table, exactly where Eva and Jake would have been standing if they hadn't changed locations that morning. Her heart skipped a few beats.

Did someone want her dead? Or possibly, Jake?

Suddenly, a shift in the air caused Eva to regain her hearing. Wailing and groaning filled the room. The sickening yet familiar scent of flesh and blood filled her nostrils. She shouted orders to the guards. "You! Get the healers in here. There are wounded. Everyone else, get the citizens out of here. Go to your homes."

Gavin motioned for his own men, spouting out more commands, "Help the healers. Move the table, it's crushing this man. These children are still alive. Over there. There's someone moving under the rubble."

It took a while before the entire Stronghold was completely evacuated. Only Eva, Gavin, and a few of their men stayed behind. Thirty casualties and fifty more injured. Lee and his Healers carried bodies of the wounded up to the Infirmary on canvas stretchers while Rapture's Guard dragged the corpses that had been blown apart out to the courtyard to be burned in a mass funeral. A handful of guards could not stomach the smell, violently vomiting before rushing out of The Stronghold. One man lifted a pile of extremities. Another carried a few torsos. Blood and remains were everywhere.

Once the chaos had dissipated and dust settled, Eva was able to examine the crime scene.

"What the shit happened?" Gavin was shaking his head. His boots crunched under the broken stone flooring and shards of bones. "This has never happened before. Not since we closed our gates. Who would do something like this?"

Footsteps echoed through the vacated hall. Eva ordered the rest of her men to check up on the citizens to be sure everyone was safe and, if possible, find the culprit. The rest of the Council refused to enter The Stronghold until they were positive that it was secure. The Wanderer continued to scour the site for any shred of evidence.

"I…" Eva still had not fully comprehended what happened when she finally answered Gavin. Both of them were still shaking, covered in a layer of thick, black dust from the dirt below the flooring. "I don't know… Lucky for us, I guess, the building didn't collapse and still looks sturdy. This could have been much, *much* worse."

"Lucky for us, we survived," he added.

Eva shoved a pile of mismatched human remains aside and found a shred of metal that looked out of place. Unlike the pieces around it, this shard was a perfect square made from a thicker metal, almost like it was meant to survive the explosion. It was bent, but otherwise undamaged. When she flipped it over, she dropped it with a clang and began to tremble violently.

Gavin rushed over to her. "What is it?"

Eva couldn't speak. One hand was covering her mouth and the other was shakingly pointing at the sign. He walked over to her, crouched down in the debris, and gasped. Printed against the metal was a clear message.

WANDERER. YOU CAN'T HIDE FROM US FOREVER.

"*It's the Tigers,*" Eva said immediately. Her voice was a loud whisper. "It has to be. I'd bet my life on it."

"Let's not get too ahead of ourselves," Gavin said as she picked up the evidence and examined it. "We don't know that for s-."

She interrupted him. "Who else could have done this? Huh? I have not made a *single* enemy since I got here. There is *no way* this is one of our own citizens. We don't have the tools to make something like this. And even *you* know that the Tigers have been after me all this time. Remember? They promised that they would be back."

Gavin opened his mouth but closed it quickly, then opened it again. "No one has gone in or out of the gates since the Nomad Elders. Our men would have noticed a Gang Member trying to get through our front door."

Without a second to dwell on the Tigers' warning, Eva's Demon reappeared. *Shit, no please no. No. No. No.* She had just gotten rid of the damned thing and it was already back, stronger than ever. She could feel the panic spreading through her body. Just like before, it bore an uncanny resemblance to Dan McAvoy. She just stood there, staring at it in disbelief.

"You okay?" Gavin was startled by the look on her face and squinted at the space where Eva was staring. He saw nothing.

"No," she said as a tear fell down her cheek, voice cracking. "It's back. After everything…"

Gavin's brow rose. "What's back?"

Eva lost it. In a flash, she became hysterical and started screaming at Gavin. "The Shadow! That stupid thing that follows me *everywhere.* That stupid thing that Jake thinks I'm crazy for seeing. All of this is my fault. Everything. Everyone is dead because of me."

"Stop, stop, stop." Gavin grabbed her shoulders as she collapsed to her knees. "Why do you care so much about someone's opinion who knows nothing about the toll that years of battle take on you? You think I'm not broken? I have my ghosts too."

"This is *different*," she cried. "I can't explain it, but it's not a ghost. It's like my mind is… *I don't know*. I… I just can't take it anymore. I can't escape it."

He forced her eyes to meet his. "Listen to me. You are *not* crazy, Eva Calloway. You are the strongest person I know. From everything you've told me and everything I've heard, you've overcome *a lot*. And the Council has known you for years… You are *not* crazy. And you are definitely *not* weak."

"But this thing…"

"We don't have to tell anyone about it. No one heard us, I'm sure. Whatever it is, I think it's a part of you. We all have bad in us… yours just… exists physically… but there is nothing wrong with that in the world we live in… and anyone who thinks differently are the crazy ones. They just can't understand unless they've lived through it. Because of people like you, people like Jake never have to know what it's like."

Eva glanced over at the hooded figure. Her tears did not come from sadness, rather defeat. She was tired of forcing that demon away, only to have it return stronger.

Hopeless and powerless to her curse, Eva attempted to gather herself. Gavin's words calmed her enough to continue. For some reason, this man understood her on a different level than everyone else. His empathy for her past was genuine and unconditional. But Jake wasn't brought up in this world, so how could he be truly empathetic to the mark it left on Eva? Sure, Jake had killed a couple Gang Members before his time in Rapture, but that was either after his hand was forced or by complete accident. Nonetheless, she loved her partner for his innocence because so desperately craved it for herself. It gave her hope.

I don't want people to pity me. I just want my own peace.

Brushing her thumbs across the hammered metal note, Eva rose to her feet and felt the marble crunch underneath her. The Council table was completely destroyed, but she knew that Virginia would still summon a Gathering. It was only a matter of time. This *had* to be the work of the Gangs. There was no other logical explanation. So, how did they get here? The job of Rapture's army was to keep tabs on the Gang's movement, especially since the Tigers had threatened them for sheltering The Wanderer. The Councilmembers would demand an explanation for the dead, even though she had been the intended target. Whatever the case, she had to consult with Bruce before she spoke with the rest of the Council. He may have some insight.

Eva straightened herself and wiped her eyes. "We must find out who is responsible. I don't care how long it takes… Lives were lost today, and this will not go unpunished. I need to speak with Bruce and ask whether his Scouts heard anything from the Tigers before this attack."

Gavin nodded. "I will double our guard and question everyone who comes in and out of Rapture."

She took a deep breath and looked briefly at the message again. Uncertainty began to seep through her skin. Eva had a sickening feeling that this was only the beginning of something much worse. The Hooded Figure was standing near a pillar, snickering under its breath. All of a sudden, it uttered something that made her heart stop.

"You didn't kill him, did you? You couldn't even kill me." it cackled. "Dan McAvoy is still alive. I'm still alive."

"No," she whispered. "I killed you, *and him*. I *swear* I did."

But Eva no longer believed her own words. This attack had only strengthened her doubt. Somehow he survived. She must have missed vital organs when she stabbed McAvoy five years ago. At first, she imagined the severity of the wound would have at least caused him to bleed out, but now…

Now, she wasn't so sure.

***

Eva was finally able to return to her home that evening. She tiptoed into the front room and closed the door behind her with a soft click. For a moment, she lingered in the foyer with her back resting against the door, still caked in dirt. A sigh slipped through her lips. Anya was fast asleep in her bed, curled up with her stuffed toy. Tommy had his bedroom door shut and bolted tight. Only Jake bothered to stay up and wait for Eva. He had already bathed, only clothed in a simple tunic and pants. The look on his face was that of concern, but he could immediately tell that something was off.

As she stepped towards the kitchen, Jake pulled Eva into his arms. "I thought something happened to you. Are you okay? Is everyone else okay? What happened? Anya cried for over an hour asking where you were. I just got her down to sleep."

"I'm fine." She lied. "Completely fine. Nothing's changed. Gavin and I just have to figure all this out before another Gathering is called."

"Bruce stopped by and asked for you," he said and sat down next to the fireplace. Only glowing coals remained in the hearth. "He said he had a feeling you'd want to talk with him before Virginia gets everyone together."

Eva sat beside Jake and wiped the sweat from her forehead. "I do. That's why I'm going back out… I stopped by to check in on my family."

They smiled at each other.

"You know us," he laughed nervously. "We've been through worse."

"I know…" She put her head in her hands and rubbed her tired eyes. "I just thought things would be different here. This place is protected, *by me…* and it just feels like the Rover Colony all over again. Death follows me wherever I go… innocent people die because of me."

"How do you know it was aimed at -" Jake stopped.

Eva had taken the note stamped in the metal plate. She pulled it from a pocket in her jacket and showed Jake. He read it. His eyes widened. He read it again. His shoulders tensed as he read it a third time. The Demon appeared in the doorway, watching them. Just as Jake looked up at her, she was able to look away.

He can't know it's returned.

She stared blankly at the palms of her hands. "I had to tell you… *only* you and Gavin know about this. And I would like to keep it that way… for now. Please."

"Eva…" Jake didn't know how to respond. He just focused on the word *Wanderer* stamped on the metal. There was no mistake. The attack was intended to murder Eva. "You have to tell the Council. This is evidence."

"Not unless I have some evidence of the Gangs' whereabouts," she stood up and backed away from him. "I promised them that I had it under control. If they knew… I would have another situation on my hands. That's why I have to go to Bruce… *tonight*."

"You're withholding information," he argued. "Rapture needs to know."

Eva was taken aback. If she told the Council that her presence was the cause of the attack, they could banish her. Jake, Tommy, and Anya would remain safely in the town while she was forced to fend for herself once again. Except this time, there would be an entire Gang hunting her every move.

"You would have me exiled over this? After all I've sacrificed for you and Tommy? Have my back for once, Jake, because I'm tired of being nothing more than a human shield to you. *Shit*."

"I'm not-"

Before Jake could come up with a retort, she snatched up the metal plate and disappeared towards Bruce's house.

The Councilman lived near the wall, a few blocks down from her home. His wife, who was dwarfed in comparison, answered the door and let The Wanderer inside. Bruce was already waiting for her. He meticulously-kept records of his men's whereabouts lined his dining table in zigzagging stacks.

He motioned for Eva to take a seat. "I've been waiting for you. We have much to discuss."

"Agreed," she said, but neglected to speak of the note that had been left for her in the carnage. "Sorry for coming in so dirty."

"I would expect no less of someone who has worked so hard today." He sat back and crossed his arms, taking a heavy drag from a cigar. "This has not happened in Rapture since our gates were closed a decade ago… This was the exact reason for us shutting off our city to the outside world… and I'm sure you can make that assumption."

Deep down, Eva hoped that the citizens would not attribute this attack to her arrival. That shard of metal proved it. But Gavin was far too loyal to speak of the evidence they discovered. After her argument with Jake, she was not so certain about his intentions.

"...Virginia has already called a Gathering…" Bruce continued. "First thing tomorrow morning. At dawn. In *her* home. Until something is done, or some information is known, she refuses to step foot inside The Stronghold."

Eva feared the worst. "Then we have to figure out what's going on with the Gangs to have an acceptable response to even her most absurd questions. Any luck in getting information from the Scouts?"

Bruce's wife placed a glass of wine at the table for each of them. The Wanderer took a sip of the sweetened alcohol while scanning the papers.

"We have not seen any significant movement," he admitted. "Nothing."

"Virginia won't like that answer," Eva stared blankly at Bruce's notes. "There has to be something from the Gangs. Tigers, specifically."

"None of them have mobilized aside from trade with one another. All of my men have reported the same thing. No

Gang Member has traveled past the city limits into Rapture's territory and most of the travel in the North has been to and from Posts."

"There is no possible way that the attack was from someone here in Rapture."

"I agree… which leads me to the conclusion that it *was* the Gangs."

Eva and Bruce both knew that they would be speaking in circles tomorrow. "But we have no information on them… same as what my men were telling me. Shit…"

"You had your men examine the scene?"

"Gavin and I are taking charge over this. My men are questioning the citizens to see if they know anything. One shred of evidence… that's all we need."

She slid her hand inside her pocket and held the sign for a moment, then released her grasp and placed her hand back on the table. *No. He can't know. I don't trust him enough.*

"Hopefully your men turn up more information than mine," the Councilman sighed. "But, as usual, I'm on your side. I would also suggest having Gavin and your husband present as well. You know, to vouch for you."

"Jake isn't my husband," Eva said shortly. "We didn't make it through the ceremony, remember?"

"Of course," he apologized. "I am sorry. Stay safe."

Eva finished her wine and took her leave of the Councilman and his wife, but chose not to go home right away. Instead, she would visit Gavin, ask him to accompany her to the Gathering tomorrow, and possibly visit the Gardens. Unlike this morning, she was not walking down the desolate street alone. The Shadow of Dan McAvoy glided noiselessly alongside her. It was only when she touched the brass handle on Gavin's front door did it finally vanish into oblivion. She still felt its presence, but could not see it.

"Gavin?" she called from the cracked door. "Can I come in? Are you still awake?"

He rushed into the foyer in a cloth tunic. “Sorry. I haven’t even thought about sleeping yet. I keep thinking about what happened. Are you doing alright?”

“Yes,” she started. “Well, not really, but… I wanted to ask you to come to the Gathering tomorrow morning… at Virginia’s house. I need someone on my side. Otherwise, she’s going to try and destroy my credibility.”

“To be honest,” he closed the door behind her. “I was planning on doing that very thing. I have no clue why that woman has so much hate for you. Ever since you got here, Virginia has done nothing but ridicule your every move and has *not once* acted like that towards another Council Member. It makes my blood boil.”

“I’m much more honest than the others,” she offered, then backtracked when her fingertips grazed the sign in her pocket. “Well… not *honest* but I’m blunt. Always have been. Or maybe she wasn’t part of the vote to bring me here as a citizen. Plus, I don’t give a shit about who likes me and how my words make people feel. If something needs to be said, I say it.”

Gavin laughed. “Yeah, and that’s why the men and I like you so much. But to answer your first question, yes, I will be there tomorrow at dawn.”

“Thank you,” she said and left.

Chapter 4

By the time Eva reached the Gardens district, it was nearly dawn. She was exhausted, but knew that even if she tried, sleep would elude her. If anything, she could get a few moments of serenity before the Council interrogated her relentlessly. And while she wanted to ask Jake to accompany her to the Gathering, the word of a Smith was worth far less than that of a military Captain. She had no doubt that Virginia and the others would dismiss Jake's words given his relationship with Eva. There was also the possibility that he would mention the note left for The Wanderer. Once again, she would have to rely on her friend over her partner.

She must have dozed off before daybreak, but awoke in a familiar place and yet, not where she had fallen asleep. The last thing she remembered before falling asleep was looking at a large willow tree from across the lake. It seemed as though she waltzed over there in a daze. That, or someone had moved her there. After taking a moment to realize where she was, she grabbed her blades and headed to Virginia's home.

The moment she stepped onto the cobblestone path at the center of town, Gavin was waiting for her. He explained that Jake had already left for his shop and dropped off Anya in the Town Square, where classes were temporarily being held until the investigation was completed. Eva took a deep breath and silently followed her Captain to a home on the opposite side of Rapture, near the Gardens. This would be the first time that she had ever visited Virginia's residence.

As they stood at the end of the walkway, Eva took note of her surroundings. Everything inside was just as methodically organized as Virginia and her daughter's persona. Lining the walkway to the door were purple and white hydrangeas in neat rows. The windows were cracked open, but they were all uniform. Two wicker chairs and a matching table were placed neatly on their porch in a diagonal pattern. A line of drying clothes was hung between two metal poles. Even the clothespins were evenly spaced.

The Wanderer straightened up at the threshold. She pressed her ear against the door and tried to listen to the muffled voices on the other side. Gavin stood behind her with his arms crossed. They were obviously the final ones to arrive at the Gathering. Had the Council planned it to be that way? Had Virginia already poisoned the mind of Jasmine, Lee, Maven, and Xander?

The moment the door creaked open, the room fell silent. It was clear they'd been waiting for her, though Gavin's presence at her heels caught them off guard. Eva's gaze locked instantly onto Virginia, who wore a sly smile. Across the room, Mara shot The Wanderer a hateful look as she served food to the other Council members. For reasons Eva had never fully understood, Virginia's daughter harbored the same resentment. Her hair was tied neatly behind her ears, and her small, pointed nose and pale gray eyes lifted toward the doorway as she took in the sight of them.

"Oh I *do* hope you're prepared for this, Wanderer." Virginia's wrinkled smirk had not vanished. She would take pleasure in this interrogation.

Despite protests from others, Mara remained to listen in on the meeting.

"She will be the one taking my place when I pass from this world, afterall," Virginia argued. "Not to mention, this catastrophe affects us *all*, not just the Council."

Gavin placed his hand on Eva's shoulder as she took her seat at the table. Swallowing a lump in her throat, she took a slow, deep breath and prepared for questions to be hurled at her. For a few moments, the other Members were collecting their thoughts without making a sound. Eva could feel her heart pounding in her ears. It was almost overwhelming.

A voice in her mind chimed in. *Why do you still live in Rapture? Every move is questioned here. But they do not understand. They can NEVER understand.*

Virginia jerked The Wanderer from her swirling thoughts.

"If no one else wishes to begin," she said as she gently interlaced her fingers together. "I will… First, I feel like we should thoroughly examine your *capacity* to protect this town."

Eva could feel fear shift to anger when the tone changed in the Councilwoman's voice. Gavin squeezed her shoulder when he noticed her fists clench under the table.

"To be clear," Bruce interjected. "Only *Virginia* seems to think that you lack the ability to do your job."

"Which seems to be a recurring thought," Eva said shortly. "I will answer Councilwoman Virginia's question with a question. How was I supposed to know that there would be an attack?"

Virginia was peering over the top of her glasses. Her daughter stood behind her with her hands loosely resting on the edges of her mother's chair. "You seem to misunderstand your post, Wanderer. *You* are charged with protecting Rapture. That includes the continuous acquisition of information from *every* Gang in this region. It also consists of reassuring Rapture's citizens that they are safe as an extension of your primary duty. I discovered that your men were *interrogating* families this evening prior… Care to explain?"

"First of all," Eva could hear her Demon provoking her to slaughter the old woman. "Whether or not I have pertinent information on the Gangs does not include reading their minds. Inside their walls, my men cannot infiltrate. The expectation for me to uncover their every move is completely impossible and you know it."

"And the domestic interrogations?" Maven was the next to speak. She would not even make eye contact with Eva. "What of those?"

"Since I am *entrusted* with keeping this town safe and apparently reading minds." Eva refused to hold back at this point and Gavin had no intention of stopping her. "With the lack of evidence present at the scene, I cannot rule out one of our own citizens as the culprit to this assault."

Virginia and Mara gasped simultaneously with matched dramatics.

"*Preposterous*!" screeched the old woman. "Absolute *lunacy*. I can't possibly comprehend why you would believe this to be caused by one of our own..."

"Because *some* of you seem to have a *personal* issue with me." Eva slammed her fists on the table, knocking over Xander's glass. "And Bruce's Scouts are unable to turn up any movement from the Gangs in our part of the region. I'm investigating all possibilities."

"How can we be sure that you were the intended target?" Xander asked as he frantically tried to save his wine. "Is there something that you're not telling us?"

"No," Eva said without skipping a beat, although her heart performed a somersault. "But it was our best guess considering the location of the explosive. If Jake had not changed where we were standing yesterday, I would not be sitting here."

Gavin stood behind her with his lips sealed. Their eyes met and he patted her shoulder softly, resolving to speak only if they began personally attacking his superior.

Maven, Xander, Lee, Bruce, and Jasmine seemed to agree with Eva. However, that did not dissuade a specific Councilwoman from continuing her tirade. Both Gavin and Eva were becoming noticeably more irritated by the second.

"None of this is making me feel any better," she spat. "And I believe the lack of comments from the rest of the Council means they agree with me. Whether or not they will admit it is another story. Unlike the fear you may instill in them, *I* am not afraid of you."

"That does *not* mean we agree with you," Bruce slammed his large fist on the wooden table. The rest of the drinks spilled onto the floor. Virginia shot him a hateful look as Mara frantically started cleaning up the mess. "If Eva was the intended target, which I suspect she was, the fear should be in her own heart, Virginia, not yours."

"So then why do we allow her to live here?" Mara chimed in. Her mother nodded in agreement. Her finger was pointed directly at Eva's face. "If her presence alone is enough to put *our own* lives in danger. Send her back out into the region."

"Because." Gavin raised his voice. He wanted to push Eva's chair aside and lunge over the table at the Councilwoman's daughter. "*Everyone* deserves the safety of Rapture. You know nothing of this woman's past and everything she has lived through. People like her are what keeps this town safe. Your maturity is *lacking*."

Virginia stood up so suddenly, it knocked her chair backwards. "Do not speak to my daughter in that way. You are no more than a piece of *meat.* A human shield. *Gang fodder*. Your comments mean *nothing* in this town. *You* mean nothing to this town."

"You disrespect my men, *specifically* Gavin," Eva stood up and met the older Councilwoman's gaze, inches from her face. "Then you disrespect me. Stand. Down. *Now.*"

"Or what?" Virginia taunted. "You'll *kill* me?"

"Worse," she spat. "You'll regret ever crossing me."

"I've never carried a single shred of respect for you," she continued, ignoring Eva's comment. "Honestly, I still cannot comprehend why the Council decided to allow you to join us. You are not a citizen of Rapture… only a senseless, barbaric murderer."

"*ENOUGH!*"

Bruce's shout exploded through the house. Eva and Virginia sat down, glaring at one another. Mara and Gavin relaxed at the corners of the room. "This is *not* how this Council operates. Malicious arguments are not going to help us in finding out what happened yesterday."

"I agree," Maven added. "Proposal that Eva and Virginia both be suspended for the foreseeable future. All in favor?"

"Aye," Lee said.

"Yes," Xander nodded.

Jasmine glanced over at Eva and sheepishly agreed. "Yes."

Now, it was up to Bruce to make the final decision. It had to be unanimous. Only those Council Members who the vote did not effect could have an opinion. He glanced at Virginia whose face was bright red. She was biting her bottom lip so hard, it was nearly piercing the flesh. Then he turned to Eva. Although her face was calm, she was visibly seething from the exchange. He could see the murder in her eyes. The tendency to fall back to her old self was hanging on by a thread.

"This is absolutely ridiculous," Virginia spouted. She could not take the Councilman's silence a moment longer. Her top lip twitched. "You would suspend *me*… after decades of service to Rapture?"

"You come in here and disrespect one of our peers," Lee said. "After an attack on her life… Eva has done nothing but devote time and energy to Rapture since she arrived. For this alone, she deserves your respect."

Virginia and Mara wanted to continue their rant, but Eva had already left without anyone noticing except Gavin. He had abandoned the Gathering with her. Neither of them wanted to be a part of the decision to suspend Eva from the

Council. The Wanderer also did not want to dissuade Bruce from making the choice to side with his equals. With his hesitant vote to suspend her and Virginia, it was a unanimous decision. Eva would spend her days overseeing Rapture's army and nothing more.

"I have no words for what happened in there," said Gavin through gritted teeth. "I am *beside* myself about this. How she treated you…"

Eva laughed angrily. "*Me*? I can handle her attacking me. What about how she treated *you*? *Gang fodder*? That woman and her daughter…" She stopped. "I don't even want to tell you what I am thinking right now."

Gavin punched a nearby sack of hay when they reached the Training Grounds and roared. "You don't have to say a word. I can see it in your eyes… and I *wouldn't* stop you either. Not after that shit."

She sighed loudly and noticed that Jake was waiting for her near the wall of The Stronghold. As she walked over to him, Gavin turned on his heels towards the men as commands cascaded from his mouth. Jake wrapped his arms around Eva who rested her head on his chest. He could sense the defeat in her body.

"Not a good outcome, huh?" He already knew the answer before she spoke.

"Virginia and I were suspended," she mumbled. "She just doesn't stop… I swear, if I met her and her daughter outside these walls, I would have killed her for the way they treated Gavin."

"First of all, you aren't out there anymore. And you can't solve all your problems by killing people," he said half-jokingly, half-serious. She pushed away from his embrace. "Hey, I'm trying to make you feel better."

She raised her voice slightly. "Jake. This isn't a joke. We were almost *killed* yesterday. The whole world is 'kill or be killed,' not just out there. Someone wants *me* dead… and all that *bitch* can focus on is belittling my ability to protect this town. She tried turning the Council against me."

"And you brought Gavin to back you up," he nodded at the Captain who returned the gesture. "Good thinking."

Eva avoided telling Jake the details of The Gathering. She was already too upset to think straight. "It was Bruce's idea."

"Glad I wasn't there," he admitted. "I probably would have lost my composure."

Eva smiled weakly. "Yeah. Gavin and I both did, but so did she… and so did Mara."

"I promise you will figure this out. I believe in you." Jake kissed her on the cheek and traveled back to his shop.

Gavin quickly occupied the vacant space and tried to keep her mind off the negative events. His first offer was to have her spar with him and expel some anger, but Eva knew when to say no.

"I don't want to accidentally kill you," she politely declined. "My anger has no switch. I know that much. If I start down that dangerous path, I could black out and finish the job."

All of the color drained from Gavin's face. At that moment, he realized Eva's true struggle with her own abilities. Sure, she was able to fight better than anyone he had ever seen, but that skill came with a price. When she allowed her emotions to consume her, there was no turning back. She would only stop if her opponent was either on the ground in surrender, or worse, lying motionless in a pool of their own blood.

"I'm sorry," he furrowed his brow. "I think I understand now, Eva. Do you need the rest of the day to relax?"

"No," she brushed by him and hopped up on a crate to get the attention of her army.

"Glad to see you are okay Commander," one of them called from the crowd. News traveled swiftly, once again.

Eva lifted her hand to hush the rumble of voices. "Thank you. As you all know, I am a part of the Council for Rapture. My job in the Gatherings is to make sure *my* men are heard. Apparently, one particular Member is challenging my competence. Because I am tasked with keeping this town safe, I will have to start -"

Suddenly, she heard the indisputable sound of gunshots. In a flash, her men leapt into battle, searching for the source. *Not again.* Gavin grabbed her arm and tore her down from the box. She fell over the raised edges and tumbled to the ground. Spinning around and pulling out a blade from its sheath, she looked at her Captain in disbelief.

"What the *shit* is going on?" she yelled. Without skipping a beat, he pointed to the wall behind where she had been standing. She looked past his head and her eyes widened. Five round holes were blown right through the brick.

Her eyes darted around but nothing suspicious caught her eye. Gavin rushed her to his home and locked the door behind them. They were still breathing heavily as Eva's Demon appeared behind them.

"The men will handle themselves," he reassured. "I will stay here with you. And I didn't want to take you home. If someone is following us, we don't want them to know where you live."

He rushed over to the window and peered into the street.

"But if it's a citizen." She grabbed her chest to try and calm down. The Hooded Figure behind her was breathing down her neck. With each warm exhale, her chest tightened. "They already know."

Gavin blocked the door when Eva attempted to leave. "I will have a guard tell Jake and Anya that you will be home after dark. Then, no one can follow you. For now, I'll keep you safe."

"I can take care of myself, Captain," she puffed out her chest at the last word. "Move aside. That is an *order*."

He refused to budge, but would not meet her gaze either. “I cannot, as your friend, let you go back out there in good conscience. Not yet. If you were shot and killed, I would never forgive myself. So I’m not letting you leave. Not until we find out who did this.”

Eva forced him to look at her. She stared at him for a few moments and then spun on her heels, punched a nearby wall, and disappeared down the hallway. The instant she was out of sight, Gavin let out a long exhale of relief. He was sure he was going to be The Wanderer’s next victim.

***

Days turned into months as Eva became the target of more unexplained attacks. At the end of Summer and throughout Autumn, they became more frequent. Bullets would nearly miss her, pelting the sides of homes and buildings. Each time, from an unknown shooter. She gradually became the only witness for the attacks. Rumors started circulating around the town that Eva was going crazy. Gavin, Jake, Tommy, and Anya were the only ones who would even approach The Wanderer for a time.

But it was the mental toll that began to affect Eva the most. She spent less and less time with her family, afraid they might become unintended victims. Most of her days were spent secluded in the Training Grounds, issuing only the occasional order to her men. At dusk, she made her way to Gavin’s home. He was more than willing to let her stay, if only to keep her family safe. Most nights, they sat together in silence.

Winter soon drifted over Rapture. Red, yellow, and orange hues faded into grays and whites, and with the steady snowfall came an unexpected sense of security. The attacks had abruptly halted with no explanation. In the quiet weeks that followed, The Wanderer was finally able to return to her family in peace.

Virginia had been reinstated into the Council after bribing enough members to secure her return, but Eva still had not received word that she, too, would be welcomed back to her post. Still, the relief of living without fear was enough. With the additional free time she was granted, Eva poured herself into training her men and spending time with Anya.

Eva's Demon showed itself when Eva stepped outside her home. At night, it stood motionless in the yard, red eyes glowing as it stared through her window, pointed teeth fixed in a cruel smile. Sometimes she wondered if McAvoy was real, if the people of Rapture were lying about not seeing him. What if the people of Rapture were lying? The question festered, feeding her paranoia. She tried to push it away, but it always crept back. And yet, every time the figure appeared, Jake and Tommy said nothing. If they didn't see him, then he couldn't be real.

They wouldn't lie to me about seeing it... right?

But one night, the Hooded Shadow invited itself into her home. Jake, Tommy, and Anya had fallen asleep hours before, so Eva was the only one awake. The figure floated over to her bedside from the corner of her room. Before she could react, it was on her. She tensed as skeletal hands wrapped around her throat. She froze—paralyzed. Her mouth opened to scream, but the grip tightened. Darkness swallowed her, dragging her down into a nightmare.

***

Cold. Eva Calloway was standing in a frozen, damp prison cell. Voices came and went with a breeze from an unknown source. The barred, steel door was locked tight. A lone torch lit the passageway. Eva enclosed her hands around the frigid metal and cautiously peered through the bars. Prisoners' arms reached out of adjacent chambers. Groans of starvation, pain, and pleadings of death echoed through the corridor. The sounds alone made the hair on her neck stand straight up. Worst of all, this place felt familiar.

I've been here before... a long time ago. She reached for one of her blades, only to realize she was dressed in nothing but a thin silk gown. It was black, but she could feel a warm liquid sticking to her chest and torso. The familiar smell of blood filled her nostrils. *What is going on?* Peering down at her chest, underneath the gown, she noticed a white linen saturated with blood. It was not her own blood, but someone else's. At that moment, she realized where she was.

The Tiger's prison.

How did I get here? Terror exploded through her body. She had no recollection of traveling outside Rapture's walls. Was she kidnapped and brought here? No. This had to be a dream. *I have to wake up*. Eva walked over to a part of the cell door that had a sharp piece of metal jutting from one of the bars. With one reluctant motion, she wrapped her palm around the pointed shard and squeezed hard. Pain shot up her arm as the steel penetrated her flesh. She bit her lip to muffle her screams and looked at her hand. A fresh wound had been cut into her skin.

Eva began to panic. *Shit. No. This can't be real. Shit. Shit. Shit.* Her ribcage started to constrict around her lungs and she dropped to the stone floor, gasping for breath. Somehow, with a numbing feeling paralyzing her, she managed to drag her shaking body to the wall and rest against it. *I'm dead. How did I get here? Who brought me here? Did someone sell me to the Tigers?* She tried to regain control over her shaking body and frantic mind.

No luck.

All of a sudden, she heard footsteps coming down the corridor.

A tall, slender figure was gliding down the hall. Cradled in its arms was something small and limp. Eva struggled to lift herself to a standing position to meet the enemy's silhouette. The figure stopped at her cell, turned slowly, and stepped into the light of the torch. In that moment, the image hit her like a bolt of lightning. Imaginary shackles held her back from the door and bound her against the far wall. A debilitating pressure shoved The Wanderer to her knees as she was forced to face the one who stood just out of reach, *Dan McAvoy*.

"*No!*" she screamed at the top of her lungs, hysterically trying to reach the smaller figure cradled in his arms. The aqua-eyed child weakly lifted her head and looked at her mother, reaching for her. "Anya, come here sweetie."

"Mama?"

Chief McAvoy ignored his prisoner's screams. He stood tall and rigid, hair perfectly slicked back. His hollow blue eyes stared into the cell. Above his left lung was an oozing wound, exactly where she had stabbed him five years earlier. When he noticed that her gaze locked onto the wound, he spoke.

"You were never meant to have this life. Happiness…" he teased and ran his fingers through Anya's hair. "It doesn't come to those as powerful as you or me. We are, unfortunately, *cursed* to sacrifice normality. To continue to strike down our enemies so that others may live these lives that we so desperately crave. Utopia is only achieved if *we* wipe out anyone and everyone who would stand in our way."

Eva kept her gaze locked on her daughter. "Utopia is not possible," she said through a strained voice. "Not in this life, and not in the Old Times. That was why they dropped the bombs. The world was already *cleansed.* We inherited it and destroyed any chance at utopia."

"Did we? How can you be so sure? Perhaps the wiping out of civilization over two hundred years ago was to lay out the foundation for a better world. A *perfect* world. And what is perfection without failure? We learn from our mistakes… well, some of us…"

"Why are we talking about this? *Let my daughter go*."

"Because, my dear Wanderer… we are not as different as you try so pathetically to convince yourself. We are both murderers… *powerful* killers. It is woven into the very fibers of our being… And it will be the singular thing we are remembered for after we are gone."

"You are *nothing* compared to me McAvoy. I've managed to live a normal life despite my past."

"And yet, I have been able to infiltrate your mind with surprising ease. I'm sure you've noticed your child here, in my arms. *Her grandfather's arms*."

McAvoy's last words chilled Eva to the bone. A searing hatred rose in her throat, scorching every breath. *This is a dream. It has to be a dream.* She tried to wake herself up. Instead, something forced her eyes open. A small knife appeared in the Chief's hands with a green glint of liquid dripping from the blade. *No.* The Wanderer watched helplessly as he made a small cut on Anya's arm and allowed the toxin to drip into the wound.

"Every sin demands payment… and yours are long overdue."

Eva wailed and strained against the tightening shackles. Her daughter's life was diminishing rapidly. She could see the greenish-black liquid spreading through the little girl's veins. "This is a dream. This *has* to be a dream. Wake up, Eva. *WAKE UP.*"

Violent laughter from Dan McAvoy shot through her like a bullet. He let Anya's frail, tiny body drop to the ground with a thud. She was dead. The sickness had overtaken her. Even the whites of the child's eyes were the same hue as the poison. The Wanderer's urge to vomit was almost as strong as the compulsion to kill McAvoy all over again.

"*You're dead*," she screamed as tears cascaded down her face. The flesh on her wrists tore as she pulled against her chains. "*I killed you. I killed you! This isn't real.*" The hole in her hand burned and bled as she managed to squeeze through one shackle. Her hand instantly went straight for McAvoy, but the other was still tethered against the wall.

"Ohhhhh, but it is real," he snickered. "Just as real as your Shadow. Be patient… all will be revealed in time. Perhaps, we will meet again outside the realm of your unconscious thoughts."

***

Without warning, the scene dissolved and Eva jerked awake with a gasp of brisk midnight air. Jake, Anya, and Tommy were huddled in the corner of the room, watching her. Her daughter had a look of pure terror on her face. The entire bed was soaked with sweat. Resting her back against the wall, she tried to regain her breath by pulling her knees toward her chest. When she lifted her hand to push the hair from her eyes, Eva spotted an identical cut on her hand as the one in her dream, still bleeding.

"How…" she whispered, shaking all over. "How did I get this?"

Jake hugged Anya as she began to sob. "I don't know," he said. "But that was the worst nightmare I have *ever* seen you have. *Ever*. And you lied. While you were sleeping, you called out to your Shadow. You swore it was gone. You said *McAvoy…*"

Eva took a shaky breath, "I-I…"

"Are you okay Eva?" Tommy asked. He crept over to the bed and placed a hand on her clammy shoulder. "I came running in when I heard you scream. And Gavin's been pounding on the door for a while now."

Jake scooped Anya up and rushed out of the room to answer the door. If Gavin could hear her screams from next door, other neighbors would have noticed too. "Was I that loud? Tommy? Please tell me I wasn't that loud."

Tommy sighed. "I wish I could. But honestly, the whole block probably heard you…"

"Shit." She looked at the doorway as Gavin burst in, frantically looking around the room, as she put her head in her hands, trying to cover her tears. "I'm so sorry everyone. It was just a dream."

But even she did not believe her own words. The evidence was on her palm.

Gavin and Tommy looked sympathetically at The Wanderer, but Jake frowned and cleared his throat. "Dream or not, Anya is *petrified* of you. She told me she doesn't want you here right now. I think it would be safer… for *all* of us… if you left."

Eva was at a loss for words. She looked up at Jake as her lip began to tremble. He looked away and disappeared into the hallway. Eva's sadness changed to rage. She snatched up her armor and weapons, and punched the doorframe near Gavin's head. He didn't flinch. Instead, he grabbed the pile of clothing and knives and let her pass.

"You can stay with me Eva." He shot a look at Jake, barely catching a glimpse of The Wanderer nodding to him at the front door, trying to hold her composure. "However long you need."

"Thank you," she said softly, voice cracking against the crippling rejection she felt.

Gavin leaned closer to Jake and whispered to him. "You know what? You should give more of a shit about the demons she struggles with. If you were a bit more understanding, your daughter wouldn't be so afraid of her mother."

"She lied to me about the Shadow-thing being gone," he attempted to defend himself. "Witnessing those nightmares… I can't trust that unpredictability around *our* child. She could kill someone."

"When has Eva taken an innocent life since she's been here?" Gavin shoved Jake with his elbow. "You have no sympathy for her pain because you have never had to fight for anything. She's done it all for you. You know what, Jake? You've changed since arriving here…"

Jake swallowed the lump in his throat and watched Eva and Gavin disappear into the yard. He glanced at his brother. Tommy's arms were crossed. Although he would never admit it, Jake agreed with Gavin. He *had* changed. Instead of supporting Eva as he once did, he grew more aggravated with her daily struggles. Obviously, these attacks were weighing heavily on the Wanderer. He was being heartless.

What is wrong with me? I'm being so stupid. I promise I'll change, he vowed. *I love you.*

Chapter 5

Eva spent the next week at Gavin's home. Instead of tending to her duties, she chose to pass her time in the Gardens. Jasmine closed off a section from the other citizens, allowing The Wanderer to relax without interruption. She no longer brandished her weapons or dressed in armor, wearing common clothes instead, hoping to distance herself from the inner darkness that had terrified her daughter. She desperately hoped that by directly connecting with nature as the Nomads do, the nightmares would end.

Jake took every opportunity to tell Eva how much he loved her. When he took a break from his shop around midday, he would visit her in the Gardens. After a few days of profusely apologizing for how he had dismissed her, there was less hostility between them. When Eva finally returned home, Anya seemed like she had completely forgotten about the nightmare.

"Mama," she gasped. "You look so pretty in your dress. Where did your armor go?"

Eva knelt down to her daughter's level and smiled, brushing her wavy hair behind her ear. "I decided to try something new. But when I go back to work tomorrow, I'll wear my armor again."

"Ohhhhhh. Okay." She hugged her mother tight, nodded, and skipped out of the room as if nothing had happened a couple weeks before.

The remainder of that evening was spent at the dinner table, laughing together. Eva seemed to be in high spirits after a short separation from her family. Although the Demon of Dan McAvoy had not left her sight, she was able to ignore it enough to avoid suspicion. When Jake, Tommy, and Anya retired into their respective bedrooms that evening, Eva took the chance to reflect. Just as she stepped to the front window, Gavin caught her eye. She rushed over to the door and opened it before he could knock and wake the others.

"What is it?" Her look of worry vanished when he answered.

"The Council reinstated you," he said. "Bruce wanted me to tell you… because…"

Eva interrupted but tried to keep her voice down. "Let me guess, Virginia called another Gathering."

He nodded, then sighed. "Yes. But no one knows why. We haven't had a major attack since your wedding ceremony. But… the Council Table was repaired and they're returning to the Stronghold."

"I bet it's to try and convince the rest of them to keep me on suspension. Until she gets actual information from the Gangs or they find me dead, she isn't going to let things be. This whole event was a perfect opportunity for her to get what she wants."

Gavin agreed and bid Eva goodnight. She stood on the porch, following his silhouette with her eyes until he disappeared into his home. Nothing stirred. It was only her and the Shadow awake in the whole town. Even the livestock was asleep. Street lanterns flickered against the cobblestone streets. The Wanderer sat on her front steps and watched the waves of grass crest with the breeze. She looked to her right and studied the towering walls of Rapture.

"This place… feels like a prison," she whispered aloud. "These people are afraid of me, just like everyone else. So I have to be careful. I can't be myself."

But you are The Wanderer, she thought. The Shadow nodded in agreement with her private thoughts. *Your legacy is to strike fear into your enemies.*

"But not my friends… or my family."

You cannot change who you are. She was arguing with herself. Well, her two selves. *The more you try to separate from The Wanderer, the stronger that "thing" will become.*

Eva could see the Hooded Demon out of the corner of her vision. It was silent for the moment, but stared at her like it wanted to pounce. Somehow, she felt that it wanted to say something to her, but feared that if she indulged, its darkness would devour her. The night sky that sparkled above her head reminded her of the freedom of the Rover Colony. Liberation beckoned to her.

Go back. Eva longed for life over the wall. *But I was banished. Perhaps the Nomads would take me in. But their lives would be in danger if I left. It's too dangerous out there for me now. The Tigers...*

"Eva?" Jake was standing in the doorway, candlelight illuminated his face. "Is everything okay? Come to bed. It's getting late."

Eva slowly stood up, pausing only to kiss his cheek before walking past him. "I was reinstated in the Council as of tomorrow. Gavin told me that Virginia has already called a Gathering."

"You've got to be *kidding me*," he whispered loudly. "It's such a…"

"Waste of time," she interrupted. "I know. But at least I will be there to stand up for myself again."

"Don't let her have an inch," he said. "Act like you have in the past. The *old* Eva. The Eva I fell in love with."

She winced.

You mean the Eva you're petrified of.

Nodding softly, she trailed Jake down the corridor, lingering at Anya's doorway before retiring for the night. Her daughter was fast asleep, smiling in her dreamland. She would become a monster before letting anything happen to that girl. Even if it meant slaying every last person in Rapture, even Jake, she would do it. Images of her night terror started to bubble up, but she stifled them and managed to fall asleep for a few hours.

***

The Wanderer awoke early in the morning to attend the first Gathering since she had been suspended. Everyone else in her home was still fast asleep when she departed. *I will not be the final Councilmember to enter that chamber.* Long before any of the others had even roused from their sleep, she would be waiting.

"I refuse to let myself be softened by the needs of these people any longer," she said under her breath as she greeted the morning guard with a slight nod. "I thought that just ignoring myself was the answer. But it isn't. I am The Wanderer. That is who I was. That is who I am. And that is who I will be."

Something changed her during the night. Eva felt much more confident than she had the previous day. Maybe it was Jake's nudge to be 'the old her' as a reassurance that she was making the right choice to stand her ground. Deep down, she was The Wanderer. Nothing could change that. Separating herself from the strength that title gave her was not only exhausting, but also useless. Though she refused to become the merciless killer she once was, she would never waver from the woman who fought tooth and nail for what was right.

When the doors of the Stronghold closed behind her, Eva's heart began to race. It was the first time she had entered this building since the attack. Most of the rubble had been cleared away and replaced, but the marble floor was still cracked where the explosive had detonated, right in the center of the crescent moon-shaped table. That, too, had cracked in half, directly in front of her seat. Her mind drifted back to the message that had been left stamped into a shard of metal. *Wanderer. You can't hide from us forever*. The words lingered until her back made contact with her chair.

"Good morning Eva," Bruce's familiarly cheerful voice echoed through the chambers. "You're here rather early."

She looked up at him. "I've had a while to think about my place in the Council and who I am. I think the time off has answered a lot of questions for me. However, that being said… I don't think anyone will be particularly happy about it."

"And why is that?" The Councilman took his place next to her. A look of concern appeared on his face.

"Because," she paused. Bruce had been a close ally for years, but even he may not appreciate the decision that Eva had made. "I will not allow myself to be stepped on anymore. And I am *not* here to compromise with those who have no experience outside of these walls. For starters, I'm the only one in this Council that has single-handedly led an entire community. Everything from Healers, Servants, and Scouts to the Serpents' entire army. I'm also the only one who has been on both sides of this region, friend and foe."

Bruce squirmed in his chair uncomfortably while Eva continued.

"From the moment I entered Rapture, I feel like *nothing* I say is taken with more than a grain of salt. My choices are constantly ignored and questioned, even when it comes to *my* army. And whether or not that's because of me being The Wanderer or any other reason - it doesn't matter. I will not allow it to continue."

Her peer was speechless. He opened his mouth, then closed it, tilted his head, and stroked his beard. She waited for a response, but none came. Bruce simply nodded and waited for the rest of the Council to arrive. There was an agonizing silence between them for about a half hour before Jasmine,

Lee, Maven, Xander, and Virginia were seated and ready to begin the Gathering.

"To be perfectly clear," Maven rolled her eyes. "Virginia, once again, called this meeting. Can we please make this quick? Xander and I have much to do for the Merchants and Farmers and I am sure that the others have duties to address as well."

"I called us here to contest the decision of Eva's reinstatement," Virginia snapped. Everyone else groaned. "I feel like this is a perfect time to get some things off our chests. Perhaps… air some grievances?"

The Wanderer had prepared herself to verbally spar with Virginia since she first entered The Stronghold. "In regards to what, exactly? I haven't been here in *months*."

"Which is precisely why I cannot comprehend your purpose in this Council," she crossed her legs under the table and adjusted her glasses. Her voice was calm but dripped with resentment. "We managed this city without you before… and it seemed to run rather well in your absence. No attacks. Not a single mistake. It was only when you were part of this prestigious group that things seemed to go awry."

"You don't think that's simply a coincidence?" Eva looked around at the rest of the Councilmembers to see whether they would speak up for her. *Fine, if none of you want to help.*

"In the case of anyone else at this table," Virginia started. "Were they in your position, I would say yes… a coincidence. But none of these members are the famed *Wanderer. One who walks in shadow behind footprints of blood*, was it? That's what the Western Rovers call you. No one else at this table has an entire Gang out for their head. Even though your absence in this council has yielded favorable results, many in this city find your continued residence within our walls deeply unsettling. Your… *presence…* has forced this city to reconsider whether its people are truly safe. Which brings me to my point. We should *never* have elected someone of this caliber to our table, let alone, to become a citizen of Rapture."

"So you suggest banishing her for nothing but a title?" Bruce scoffed. "This Gathering is pointless."

"Not just a title," Virginia argued. "The countless massacres that come with that title."

"This is ridiculous," Lee chimed in. "Eva has been an asset to our city since she arrived."

"How? Her life has been nothing but death and torture. Can we be certain that her *daughter* won't become like her?" Virginia threw her arms out to her sides. "We don't know whether this… this *bloodlust...* runs in the family. And we surely cannot say whether there will be more attacks on *our* people. Our job is to keep this town safe. Even at the expense of this… *menace*."

Eva shot out of her seat. "How *dare* you. I ruled over a compound three times the size of this city. It became the most powerful Gang because of *me and me alone*. Your abilities in leadership or war are nothing compared to mine. *Nothing*."

"You see?" Virginia's thin, wrinkled finger pointed at her adversary. "She wants to rule this place at the end of her blade or our army's guns."

"Oh stop dancing around your words, Virginia," Eva clenched her jaw. "If you have something to say, *then say it*."

The old woman raised her eyebrows. She cleared her throat, interlaced her fingers, and smiled bitterly, "You wish for me to be blunt? Fine. I believe *you* orchestrated these attacks to push your barbaric ways into this town. That my people would run scared to the arms of someone who has knowledge of such… *barbarism*."

"This is getting nowhere," Lee yelled over the two. "Virginia. You are being spiteful by calling this Gathering for nothing more than to anger Eva. Your 'theory' has no basis. There is no evidence."

Maven chimed in. "No. She has a point. The state in which Eva entered this town years ago is a cause for concern. Even if the attacks weren't The Wanderer directly. You all remember the Tiger's threat when she arrived. They promised revenge."

"But they haven't attacked," Jasmine interjected. "It has been five years and nothing."

"Then who set off the explosive?" Xander added. "I highly doubt that it was any citizen here. They do not have access to such materials."

"You are all acting like children," Eva said calmly after a long breath. "I would have never allowed this useless argument in my compound. I understand the need for collaboration within Rapture's Council, but that compromise is expected of *sound* minds. *This* is insanity. To accuse me of planning an attack on the very city that took me in when I was desperate? Complete insanity."

She shot a look at Virginia who tried to interrupt, but Eva continued.

"That being said, I knew the purpose of the Gathering today. So, if there is nothing of value to be spoken, I'm returning to my duties."

The room fell silent. All eyes were on her with the exception of the elder Councilwoman. She was staring down at the table mumbling to herself.

Bruce smiled. He had been silent up until now.

"Well, I think that wraps things up today," he said. "Seriously everyone, what has happened to us? Eva's right. We are acting like children. Rapture must be unified, especially at the top level. Otherwise, chaos will begin and we will come undone. Peace here can only be reached by a strong Council that agrees or disagrees *respectfully. Without ridiculous accusations.*"

Eva shoved her chair and walked out of The Stronghold without another word. As usual, Gavin was waiting at the end of the drawbridge and already sensed the rage burning beneath her ribs. He started to ask what happened during their meeting, but Eva beat him to it.

"I am done dealing with this shit. Especially that woman," she started, but corrected herself. "With *all* of them. Maven is starting to change her tone about these attacks. They considered *banishment*. Can you believe that? Aside from Bruce, they know nothing of the world outside these walls. If I didn't have a family here, I would leave."

Bruce's voice made both of them jump and spin around. "But Virginia would like that far too much. Plus, we need you here."

"That's just it." Eva shook her head, chuckling sarcastically. "I don't need *you*."

The comment hit Bruce and Gavin hard. Before they could develop a response, The Wanderer had already disappeared towards the Training Grounds. Gavin turned to the towering Councilman with the scar across his face.

"Was it that bad?" he asked.

Bruce was still staring at the space where Eva had vanished. "Yeah."

As Gavin rounded the wall to the Training Grounds, the sky began to darken. Thunderstorms quickly rolled in from the South, bearing lightning and hail. The guards who were not on duty fled into the Barracks covering their heads and hiding any pieces of metal armor they were wearing. But not Eva. She didn't seem to be fazed by the roaring thunder or explosions of lightning careening down around Rapture. At the corner of the clearing, she sparred with a sack dummy. Her gaze was fixated on the imaginary enemy as she threw strategic punches and kicks. The jolt from a nearby crash of thunder made her spin around and yank a knife from its sheath. Gavin was standing at her heels and barely dodged the blade before his jugular was sliced open.

"It's just me," he said, wide-eyed. If it hadn't been so dark, he would have seen the anger on her face from underneath her hood.

"Leave me alone Captain," she ordered and slowly sheathed the weapon.

"Not in this condition," he yelled over the unrelenting storm. "Come inside."

Eva glanced at the tower of The Stronghold where Virginia had her school. Anya was there. She could see her tiny figure through the window. Inside, teaching the younger children was Mara. Her wispy figure floated around the room, overseeing their work, pointing at them occasionally. Stopping where Anya was sitting and knelt down, her waist-length, sun kissed hair draped over her shoulders. She whispered something in the little girl's ear and stood up, dismissing the students for their midday break.

"Hey," Gavin pulled The Wanderer from her haze. "The storm is getting worse. Let's get inside."

She shook her head. "I'm going home. I promise I'll be fine tomorrow. Send for me if you need anything."

Unenthusiastically, Gavin dismissed her. The Wanderer trudged down the road, passed the town center, toward her home. Water was still pouring off of her leather armor as she stepped inside and shut the door. Her knees were buckling under the dizzying feelings of defeat and fatigue. The presence of her Shadow brought thoughts of bloodlust. Lingering on them for a few moments, she contemplated leaving her family behind and returning to a life of survival. The mere thought of ending Virginia's life was thrilling enough to risk banishment. Or worse.

Anya would be safer without me, she reasoned. *And I could leave this place. Otherwise, I'm scared that staying will be the death of me...* She paused and sighed aloud. *It all sounds so nice... so simple.... but... I can't just LEAVE them. They're my family.*

Her Shadow loomed, nearly draped over her body like a shroud. An eerie blackness pooled on the floor and crept towards Eva's feet. The image of Dan McAvoy's face was still contorted in an evil grin. Her stomach churned. All of a sudden, Jake rushed into the house and his voice was shaking.

"Something happened," he said frantically. Eva's heart dropped. "Anya… she's sick. *Really* sick."

Both of the panicking parents sprinted out of the house and towards The Stronghold. Eva shoved past Jake as they reached the drawbridge. She threw open the doors and skidded across the marble floor in her wet boots, sliding to one knee and making a sharp left turn towards the Infirmary. She bounded up the stairs and down the hall, away from the Council's Chamber. Citizens leapt out of the way as she nearly threw them over the balcony by the time Jake had reached the front door.

"Where is my daughter?" she demanded loudly, gasping for breath as everyone in the Infirmary stopped to look up. A crowd of Healers were huddled around a bed to her right alongside Virginia and Mara. "Where is Anya?"

Jake finally reached Eva, heaving from being so winded. Lee popped his head over the crowd and slowly walked over to them. His eyes were downcast. The look on his face and the recollection of her nightmare told Eva more than she needed to know. Anya was ill. Seriously ill. As Jake went to grab her hand, she tore it from his grasp.

The Head Healer intentionally turned away from Eva's ferocious stare. "I'm so sorry. It was so sudden. None of us have ever seen this sickness before. If only we knew what was wrong… From what Mara told us, one second, she was playing with the other children… the next, she dropped to the ground unconscious. I have stabilized her condition, for now. We are certain that she must have ingested a toxin of some kind. But we have never seen these conditions, so we are working to find a way to reverse the effects. She is… okay… just in a deep sleep."

"How did this happen? She was in class. *School.* We were assured that this would be the safest place for my daughter." Eva demanded to know more. She was screaming in Lee's face. Dan McAvoy's likeness was screaming in her ear. *Torture them. Kill them. Kill them all. They are murdering your daughter and you are just allowing it to happen. Why are you still standing there? Strike. Them. Down.* She could not decipher whether these were her own unique thoughts or from the Shadow. Blinking hard and shaking her head slightly to tone out the voice, she failed in attempts to hear Lee's muffled response.

Jake had already rushed over to his daughter's limp figure. Mara laid a comforting hand on his back. His hands were shaking as they caressed the child's tiny arm and sobbed. Eva could not bear to look at her child in this state. When her eyes met Virginia's, a white hot fury shot through her body like lightning. Restraint caused vomit to bubble up in her throat. *She did something. It has to be her.*

The Councilwoman felt the surge of hostile energy eject from The Wanderer, but approached her anyway. Eva's knuckles whitened and she glanced around the room to see how many people would bear witness to the slaughter of this woman. *No survivors*, a quiet but firm voice said in the back of her mind. Slowly, without anyone noticing, she reached back to one of the smaller daggers attached to her belt. Her Shadow began to shrink.

"You may be the most detestable person I know," Virginia dismissed. Eva's fingertips floated just over the hilt of the blade. "And I dislike you with every fiber of my being…"

Eva gritted her teeth. "Say one more thing. I *dare* you."

"...However… I would never bring your child into our disagreements," she finished, but did not wear an ounce of empathy on her face. "Let alone, intentionally sicken an innocent child. By the look in your eyes, I can tell you are intent on placing the blame on *me*. Rest assured, I would never commit such a heinous act."

"But this happened on *your* watch." Eva was shaking violently. Her hand grasped the blade behind her back. "You are responsible for keeping the children of this city safe, *right*? Seems awfully coincidental, especially after questioning my competence less than an hour ago."

"Can we worry about our child, Eva?" Jake yelled over the quarrel.

Eva looked over Virginia's shoulder and released the hilt of her blade. Both of the women parted ways. Mara stayed with Anya's parents, standing very close to Jake and caressing his back. The Wanderer shuffled her stance the moment she noticed. The willowy woman lifted her hand when Eva cleared her throat.

Aside from the shallow breathing, their little girl lay motionless. A Healer stood at the foot of her bed, documenting her grim condition. Jake was kneeling next to his daughter, holding her cold hand and wiping away tears as they met his neck. Mara watched him with a solemn look, but refused to make eye contact with Eva, who, for some reason, couldn't progress past her rage towards Virginia.

That bitch must've had something to do with this. Eva was sure of it. Her teeth clenched so hard that her jaw began to ache. Her Shadow repeated the woman's name over and over. *Just like my dream. This isn't an illness and it wasn't Dan McAvoy, but a new enemy. Virginia must have orchestrated the explosion to kill me... and now that she failed her first attempt... She's poisoned my daughter.*

Unfortunately, Eva had no proof that Virginia was the culprit. And even if she did, who would believe her? People had already begun to think that The Wanderer had nothing in her heart but murder, control, and madness. The continued attacks would only hurt her credibility. If Virginia's intent was to turn Rapture against Eva, it was working.

Jake left for home and Mara disappeared soon after him. The Healers, one by one, retired for the night, except the designated nightwatch. Eva remained. She vowed to stay by

Anya's side so that no one could harm her further. And as each moment passed in the darkness of the Infirmary, she plotted. Whoever did this would regret it if her little girl did not recover.

***

A week went by and Anya's condition began to improve. There was a time where she could sit up and speak, but was still far too weak to stand. Eva had completely neglected her daily work to stay at Anya's bedside. The only thing her daughter would talk about was how excited she was to see her friends in school again. But her mother's mind was always elsewhere.

"Do you know who did this to you?" she would ask, but Anya never had an answer.

She frowned. "I don't know Mama. My mind is all fuzzy. I can't remember. I'm sorry. I'm really trying to remember."

"That's alright sweetheart," Eva could feel the tears welling up, but she had to stay strong. "I love you. You will be okay."

From time to time, Mara would also visit when Jake was there. After classes concluded for the afternoon, she would escort a few of Anya's friends into the room with gifts to make her feel better. Eva couldn't help but smile at the children's poorly-drawn well wishes.

But in the following days, Anya McAvoy's health suddenly took a turn for the worse. One day, she just could not sit up, no matter how hard she tried. The next day, she could barely speak. Eva was internally hysterical. All she could think about was her nightmare, and each time she dozed off, it would reappear in her mind. The thought of losing her only child was unbearable. Her daughter was the only good thing left in her life. Still, the Healers could not determine the cause of her mysterious illness.

On the fifth day, Eva noticed something she had not seen before. And Jake, Mara, and Virginia were there to witness her breakdown.

When Lee lifted the sleeve on the child's gown one evening, Eva's eyes widened and she staggered backwards, knocking over her chair and a table. It was a dark green spot that crept up the veins towards her neck. Every vein on her arm and chest were greenish-black. She could see it pulsating towards her neck. Lee stepped back in shock. "What is *that*?"

Just like my dream... McAvoy.

"No, no, no," she whispered. She was fixated on her feeble daughter who could not even open her eyes. "It can't be. I *killed* him. There is no way this is happening. Wake up Eva. *Wake up.*"

Her Demon was now obscuring her view of Anya. It hovered over her, the top of its head brushed against the ceiling. Suddenly, Eva could not breathe. The room felt like it was spinning, and flashbacks from her dream were now as plain as day. Reality shifted and merged with her unconscious as she struggled to regain control. Dan McAvoy was right in front of her, holding the lifeless body of her daughter, cackling.

The scene was so real, Eva felt like she could reach out and touch the figure.

"It seems like I have finally found you," he smirked. "Foolish of you to think you could hide from me. But now... I have your daughter's life in my grasp... and next will be your own."

As quickly as it came, the scene dissolved. Eva felt the air rush back into her lungs as she heard the deafening clang of her blades hitting the floor. She stared blankly at the hand that had been clutching it. Unlike the episode at the Rover colony years ago, Jake had not come to her rescue. Instead, he stood between her and Anya, shocked at what he was witnessing. Virginia and the Healers were huddled in the corner. Eva reached up to feel her neck for wounds. Nothing.

The moment her eyes caught the figure shaking in the corner of the room, The Wanderer realized what she had done. Rather than taking an attempt at her own life, this time she brandished her weapon at who she imagined was Chief McAvoy - Mara.

"What the shit just happened?" Jake demanded, his voice breathless with disbelief. "Eva, you tried to attack us. You almost *killed* Mara. Nothing you said made any sense except… except, *Chief McAvoy…*"

"I-I," Eva looked around the room. All eyes were on her. "How long was I like that?"

"Too long," Virginia interjected, but her voice was shaking with fear. "Whatever happened, just now… is intolerable… and must be *punished*."

Mara was doubled over in a bed next to Anya's, crying softly. Her already-pale skin was drained of all color as her terror-stricken gaze remained fixed to The Wanderer. Healers had rushed over to make sure she had not been injured during the event. The sound of thunder crashed overhead. The Wanderer hurriedly sheathed her weapon and rose to her feet, wiping her sweat-covered brow.

Jake spun around and swallowed the lump in his throat. "Please. Eva is sorry. I-*I* am sorry. It won't happen again, Councilwoman. Something must have triggered it."

"My daughter will not fall victim to this… this… *monster*," Virginia spat.

Eva contended. "*Your* daughter? What about *my* daughter?"

Before Virginia or Mara could breathe another word, Eva could not contain her emotion any longer. Tears streamed down her face as she weighed her options. Honesty, in this situation, was her best chance at convincing everyone that she was distraught, nothing more. "You have to understand. I had a dream that this would happen. Anya… she *died*."

"What?" Jake gasped. Genuine concern was on his face as he took another step closer to her. "Who did this? In your dream."

She hesitated and looked at her feet, then to her daughter.

"*Eva*," he repeated, grabbing her shoulders and shaking her furiously. "Damnit. Who. Did. This. In. Your. Dream?"

"Your father," she replied, almost inaudibly.

The Infirmary went silent. Jake recoiled and swayed backwards. Virginia and Mara looked at each other, puzzled.

"Are you *sure*?" Jake asked and whipped his head to the hallway. Tommy was standing in the doorway, just as speechless as his older brother. It was unlike him to trust in Eva's dreams.

"You killed him." Tommy tried to reassure The Wanderer. "I saw you."

"Who is this person?" Mara demanded as Lee helped her to her feet. "Do they mean harm to us? We must know. Withholding information-"

"I *did* kill him," The Wanderer said sternly. Once again, doubt began to seep through the cracks of her brain. Her Shadow cackled. "But that doesn't mean that Anya will… make it through this. It could have been a glimpse of the future and he just appeared in my dream… Either way, he *is* dead. The Chief of the Tigers is dead."

Virginia swiftly rushed Mara out of the room, keeping a close eye on the Wanderer as they left. Jake hugged Eva, who sunk into his embrace. When her mind cleared and she glanced at her vulnerable child, she dropped to her knees and sobbed. She felt so helpless. Tommy walked over and held them both closely. The remainder of Eva's energy was spent hoping that Anya would somehow pull through.

There was nothing else she could do.

***

Anya's condition showed no improvement over the next three weeks. The poison had spread from her neck up to her face, undeterred by Lee and the other Healers' tireless efforts. Jasmine had even sent for Yidi and Masha, who also attempted to stop the poison's spread. They tried every remedy that they could muster, but nothing seemed to work. No one had a clue what they were battling.

One day, the little girl woke up enough to speak. Twinkling stars looked in from the window. When the little girl opened her eyes, she noticed that only her mother was sitting at her bedside. She smiled weakly as their eyes met. Eva could tell that she wanted, so badly, to jump out of bed and hug her mother, but she was too sick.

"Mama?" she smiled. "I'm so tired."

Eva ran her fingers through her daughter's chocolate locks. "It's okay sweetie. We are going to get you all better. And then you can take some time off school."

"Really?" Anya's eyes brightened. "Can I come to work with you one day?"

"Of course." She was fighting back another barrage of tears. Her eyes remained fixed on the dark, spidering poison on her child.

"Where's Papa?"

"He was going to make you some jewelry for when you got better," Eva smiled. "Your father has been working so hard on it lately."

Anya coughed to exhaustion and nearly passed out. The blackening veins in her face pulsated slightly. "Mama. If I don't get better… and I die… what happens after?"

A tear slid down her mother's cheek as she pondered how to answer. Truthfully, Eva had always been negative about the possibility of an afterlife, but did not want her daughter to think that nothing would happen if she were to pass.

She took a deep, shaky breath and forced a smile. "The most beautiful thing happens, Anya. You know how the Nomads always talk about how you are made of five elements?"

“Mhmmm,” she nodded.

“Well, your body returns to the Earth and the Great Mother’s care. She takes your Spirit up in her arms and lets you watch over everyone you love.”

She smiled, thought for a moment, then whispered, “Well then I’m not scared if it’s nice.”

Without a warning, her small body tensed up and she winced in pain. Eva leapt over to her daughter’s side and watched helplessly as her nightmare came alive. Just as she dreamt, Anya’s eyes were consumed with dark green as the poison spread across her face.

Eva couldn’t hold back her hysterics any longer. “Sweetie? It’s okay. Mama’s here. Everything is going to be okay.”

“I love you Mama,” her daughter grabbed her hand. She was blind to everything around her. Panic overwhelmed her voice. “Wait… Mama, I’m scared. I can’t see. I can’t see. Wait…”

“It’s alright sweetheart. I’m here. I’m not going anywhere. I love you so much.”

With one final gasping breath, young Anya McAvoy would never see the age of six. Her tiny body rested softly against the cushion on the bed, a peaceful smile on her face. Eva wept at her side in the Infirmary until dawn. She apologized to her daughter for hours. “I am so sorry. I’m sorry I brought you into this cruel world. I’m sorry that you had to endure all this. Everything is my fault. All of it. It’s because of me.”

Her voice lowered to a whisper, choked with anger and grief. “*I swear on my life that I will find whoever did this to you.*”

Alone, except for her Shadow. Just like every other time before, a laugh echoed in her ear. It repeated the message left for her at the wedding ceremony. She had forgotten about it until that moment.

“Wanderer. You can’t hide from us forever.”

Chapter 6

Jake completely shut down when he went to visit Anya the following morning, only to find that she was gone. He blamed himself for not being there in her final moments. Eva felt hollow. Numb. She refused to let the Healers remove her daughter's body from the Infirmary until Jake and Tommy had a chance to say goodbye. When Tommy entered the room, she had been staring blankly at the corner of the room with red, bloodshot eyes.

"Eva…" he stuttered. "Is-is she?"

She did not reply. Her mind had been suffocated by the nightmare. Images of Dan McAvoy carrying the lifeless body of her child. Anya's eyes wide open, completely black. They were staring right into her mother's soul, tearing it wide open and shredding it into pieces. Clutching her chest in unspeakable emotional pain, alone, in the corner of the room. But no one paid Eva any attention. Not one person came to comfort her.

Not even Jake.

He was waiting for his brother. When Tommy finally made it to the Infirmary, Jake pulled him into a tight embrace, crying loudly into his shoulder. After they had spoken their sorrowful goodbyes to Anya, Lee wrapped her body in white linen and brought her into another room until the following day.

"We can hold a ceremony tomorrow," the Healer explained. Eva was still in her own world but heard Lee anyway. "Her body will be buried in our cemetery."

"No," she slowly stood up, facing away from the small crowd gathered in the room. Although her Demon was becoming progressively louder, she just increased the volume to speak over it. Jake, Lee, Mara, Tommy, and the other Healers simply thought she was shouting.

"No?" Lee repeated, confused.

Eva's face was a ghostly white as she turned to the others. "The Nomads will do a *proper* burial for my daughter. Send word to Yidi and Masha. I promised Anya that she would return to the Earth as the Nomads believe. So, we're going to do this… The *right* way."

Jake went to hug his partner, but she turned away and left The Stronghold. Gavin, who had just entered the Infirmary, rushed out to his Commander's side.

Mara gently grabbed Jake's arm when he tried to follow.

"Leave her," she cooed and caressed his cheek with an empathetic look. "Obviously, something is off. I don't know if anyone can save her now."

Jake touched Mara's hand for a moment, her long slender fingers and warm palm rested gently against the side of his face. Her thin face and light skin almost matched her golden hair. He closed his eyes for a moment, but then tore it away. "No Mara. Eva has struggled with things you would never understand. I can't let her go through this alone. This was *our* child. Someone murdered our child. *Our* sweet little girl."

He burst into tears again.

"I am so sorry about Anya," she replied, staring at the floor in embarrassment. For a moment, she flushed bright red, rubbed her arm, then looked back up at him. "She was such an amazingly happy child. She was always so kind and caring. Like you. I can't even imagine the vile thoughts of the person responsible. Only someone truly deranged could kill a child and let them suffer. Someone who has lost touch with reality…"

Jake agreed. "You're right. Whoever it is better hope that Eva never finds them. Rapture will burn under her wrath if the culprit is a citizen. And I wouldn't stop her."

"No *sane* person could have done this," she repeated, hoping he would understand what she was implying, but he did not catch on. He simply agreed with her again.

With that, he hugged Mara and left to find Jasmine in the Gardens. After he broke the devastating news, he asked her to send for the Nomad Elders. She agreed to leave the safety of Rapture to find them. Jake offered to come with her, but she politely declined.

"I cannot ask your help for this adventure," she stated firmly. "Your spirit is grieving for your daughter, and I would never request that of you or Eva. You have my word. I will find them and return safely."

Jake took his leave of the former Nomad, shut down his shop for the remainder of the week, and returned home to mourn. Eva, on the other hand, had ventured to the far end of the Gardens, where the wall met a small waterfall from outside. It was the space where she had cleared her mind countless times before. A babbling brook surrounded a soft, mossy island. Trees shaded the lapping waves near the lake. That was where Gavin found her, speaking to her Demon.

"...What do you want from me?" she whimpered, voice cracking beneath tears. "I don't understand why you're here. You've taken my daughter… you've taken *everything*."

For the first time, Eva questioned whether the Shadow of Dan McAvoy had ever been imagined at all. *Rapture's citizens could be deceiving me. Jake and Tommy could be lying as well. Everyone could be.*

Gavin stepped closer and looked around to see if anyone was nearby. He put his hands on her shoulders and knelt down. "Are you okay?"

"What do you think?" Eva twisted around and shoved him. He did not budge. "My daughter was *poisoned.* It was the Tigers. I'm *sure* of it. Someone in Rapture is working with them. But nobody believes me. Nobody cares about how I feel. Somehow. Some way. They got in here and they took my Anya..."

"We will find them," Gavin promised.

"*I* will find them," she corrected, wiping the tears from her swollen eyes. "And I'm calling a Gathering."

Gavin sighed. "Virginia already called one after the funeral."

"Of course she did."

Eva clenched her fist at the thought of speaking with that woman or her daughter. Before she could say another word, the Shadow of Dan McAvoy took her attention. Her Captain watched as she glanced over his shoulder and pushed him aside. The Demon's red eyes had changed to McAvoy's icy-blue, lifeless gaze. Even his attire had changed to the same armor from years ago. Most terrifying of all was the gauze wrapped around the exact spot where she had stabbed him before. It was the Chief, in the flesh. Or was it simply her imagination getting better at playing tricks?

"You're not holding together very well, Wanderer," he said softly, grinning from ear to ear. "Are you? I thought it appropriate to attend my dear granddaughter's funeral. I assume you understand... Not that your opinion carries any weight."

Eva furrowed her brow and glanced at Gavin, whose gaze was far past where Dan McAvoy was standing. *Are you seeing this?* She rubbed her eyes to make sure she was not imagining anything. He seemed so real. Was everyone in Rapture playing a game with her sanity? Were they all aware that Chief McAvoy had survived and allowed him to toy with Eva's life?

"If you are wondering whether it was I who poisoned her," he continued. "Understand that you gave me no other choice. You turned my sons against me and tried to kill me. It seemed more than fair that I take something precious of yours. A child for two children seems a bit merciful on my part. Be grateful that I did not take more."

"You *murdered* my daughter," Eva screamed at the image. When she leapt forward and tried to attack him, her entire body went through the mirage. It was her imagination.

"And *you* took my sons," he snarled and refused to disappear. She whirled around to meet his gaze. "Both of them. I may be a figment of your imagination, but I am very *very* real. And I will not be satiated until every last person you love has either betrayed you or fallen by my hand. Only then, will I face you again, Wanderer. You deserve nothing less."

McAvoy's voice transformed to Gavin's. He was shaking her. "Eva!"

"I'm fine," she swayed on her feet for a moment. After a moment of calming herself, she shoved him away, repeating the words. "I'm fine."

Gavin wanted to argue, but looked at her empathetically and released her from his grasp. "Please. Go home. You need rest. I will see you tomorrow for the funeral."

Eva stared at Gavin blankly. She could not comprehend what he said for a few moments. Her mind was torn between the loss of her daughter and the new attributes of her Shadow. Dan McAvoy looked even more lifelike now than ever before. And not a single thing she tried had gotten rid of that *thing*. Finally, after wavering for a moment, she nodded and left her Captain in the Gardens to return home.

The door to her home creaked open and no boisterous child greeted her when she stepped inside. It felt so big and empty now. A suffocating blanket of dread and depression had replaced the positive aura of Anya McAvoy. The last remaining shred of happiness that had pulled Eva from her own darkness was now gone forever. It was only her, Jake, and Tommy now.

***

Neither parent slept the entire night. They spent the twilight hours quietly staring at the ceiling. While Jake spent his evening in the bedroom, Eva sat in the doorway of Anya's room, leaning against the frame, crying softly. Dwelling on the guilt she had for not spending more time with her daughter and the responsibility she felt for her death. *I should have fought back harder. For my baby girl.* But sooner than either of them would have liked, the sun was breaking through the horizon. Today would be the last day to see their child before her spirit would be sent to the Nomad's Great Mother.

"At least… she isn't suffering anymore," Jake offered, grasping for comfort. Eva neglected to tell him about her episode in the Gardens. In fact, she had not uttered a word since returning home the previous evening.

Instead, she lingered heavily on the words she had spoken to Anya about the afterlife. The story of the Nomad's Mother meant nothing to her. Empty words. She did not believe that there was an afterlife or a deity who watches over everyone. So much death and suffering had numbed her into that mindset. But it was Anya's final moments that reaffirmed Eva's belief. The look of terror on her child's face proved that there was nothing after death. And victims from the Old Times who worshiped gods met the same fate when the bombs enveloped the world in destruction. A dark abyss was all Eva believed awaited her when the time finally came.

Still, that nothingness felt kinder than her current existence.

Thousands of Rapture's citizens squeezed tightly into the Town Square. All were clad in dark clothing and disheartened eyes. The death of a child was never a time of rejoicing, but a child's *murder* struck a chord of restlessness across the town. Whether that worry was placed on an unknown culprit or The Wanderer herself was what made Eva anxious. She could feel their eyes on her, judging.

The fountain in the center of the square was nearly obscured by the mass of people in attendance. In fact, the entire Nomad troupe had traveled with their Elders, Yidi and Masha, to pay their respects to The Wanderer's child. That sight brought more tears to Eva's eyes. The reassurance that these people cared for her and her family was touching, but she refused to stand in the middle of the crowd for fear of another attack. Someone still had malicious intent to kill Eva, and she could not put anyone else in danger.

Jake stood near the towering stack of logs in front of the fountain with his brother. Both of them wore their Spirit Markings for the cremation. Masha noticed Eva's arrival and attempted to paint markings on her face. At first, she declined, but when she spotted her daughter's tiny figure atop the timbers, her heart sank. *It is what she would have wanted,* and allowed the woman to trace the symbols of the Lioness across her face. One line from her bottom lip down her chin and neck, one curved line on each cheek with a dot below its center, and a line down the bridge of her nose.

When the old woman removed her wrinkled thumb from Eva's cheek, The Wanderer made her way far from the crowd. Climbing a nearby scaffold, she watched from above. Anya McAvoy would never have her wish of initiation into the Nomad Tribe. It was something she always talked about when Jasmine would join them for meals. Just like Tommy, she was excited to have her Spirit Animal chosen by Yidi or Masha. Eva had promised to do it for her sixth birthday after the attack at her parent's wedding.

Sixth Birthday, Eva rubbed her burning eyes. *She would have been six this Summer*. Just then, Yidi's voice rose over the murmur of the crowd.

"It is with a heavy heart that I return to Rapture," he began solemnly. Masha had her hands in the air, palms facing the sky. "Among my brethren to send this tiny, fragile soul to our Great Mother's loving arms… we bid farewell to a beautiful spirit… so that she may return to our dear Mother and watch over us all."

Paint on Jake's face was already running with a stream of tears, smearing his Spirit Markings as he wiped them away. The Council Members and their families were near the front of where the vigil was taking place. Mara stood with her mother, both dawning elegant black dresses. A crackle of distant thunder and the Spring air became dense with rain clouds. Suddenly, the heavens opened up and drizzle fell over the assembly. Still, no one moved a muscle.

Always remain vigilant. Eva wanted to let her emotions overtake her, but survival instinct enveloped her senses. *Whoever had the gall to attack my family wouldn't take a second thought at attempting to slaughter me while I bury my child.* She paused and glanced over at her Shadow. It spoke.

"If you would have just died by my hand, I would not have to bury my granddaughter."

Eva shuddered. "You aren't real. No one can see you."

"Can't they? Or are they simply ignoring me?"

Eva scanned the crowd. Yidi and Masha had already started their offerings to the Great Mother to keep Anya's soul safe on the journey. No one was looking up at the scaffolding except a few people around the fountain. Jake and Tommy caught her attention, starting at the space behind her, *exactly* where Dan McAvoy stood. *Can they see him? Have they been lying to me all this time?*

"You bring nothing but death and chaos," it taunted.

Shut up, she thought. *Shut up. Shut up. SHUT UP.*

The funeral continued. "... As we can all see, The Great Mother is deeply saddened by this death. A vibrant life, cut short. How someone could torture this child is beyond me or any of my people. We have prayed to the Mother for the swift blade of justice to seek revenge for Anya McAvoy."

A loud crash of thunder scattered through the sky.

I just want to watch the final moments of my daughter, she pleaded.

But the Shadow was relentless. "Do you truly believe that solace will come from this pain? We have to become merciless leaders. That is our fate. Not kind, loving parents and peaceful citizens of a senseless city. *Tyrants. Absolute leaders.* Embrace the darkness before it is too late. Before I *end* you."

Heartbeat gushing in her ears replaced the sound of the storm. Eva watched with an emotionless face as a Nomad walked over to the pyre with a torch. She pulled her hood over her head and felt the grasp of her Demon's nails around her shoulder, digging into her flesh. A single tear fell down her cheek as the fire crackled up to her daughter, flickering at her feet. She could feel the heat from the blaze as a piece of her soul broke off and was carried with the smoke into the heavens. What seemed like a few moments was actually an entire hour that Eva stood there, watching her daughter's body devoured by the flames. It was only when Gavin's hand pressed against the small of her back that she was torn from her haze and realized that she was standing in the rain, alone.

"The Gathering is about to start," he said softly.

Eva wiped what remained of her Lioness markings from her skin and glanced at the Shadow standing at the end of the wooden planks, near a ladder. It was silent for the moment, still indistinguishable from the Dan McAvoy that Eva faced almost six years ago. Numbness crept over her skin, and the fiendish part of her she'd buried deep within her broken soul began to resurface. This time, she chose not to stop it. The same force that once ruled the Serpents stirred. A sharp tingle ran up her spine.

"How are you holding up?" Gavin finally spoke when they reached the drawbridge to The Stronghold. "Do you need me to be there if Virginia tries to start anything?"

She paused. "I think I'm going to handle myself this time. Since I have nothing left to lose."

The tone in Eva's response did not sit well with her Captain. The Wanderer could snap without warning and there was no telling what she would do. Vengeance was clearly on her mind.

Gavin's heart was racing and his palms began to sweat, but he retaliated. "Eva. I'm not going to let you go in there alone. Not with that horrible woman. And definitely not after all that's happened to you. I would never forgive myself if she had you banished from here and I did not speak up."

Despite her wishes, she begrudgingly agreed. If Virginia had persuaded more of the Council to consider her banishment, Gavin's word could hold significant weight. And if she, indeed, was the culprit to poisoning Anya, Eva would need him to restrain her from killing the Councilwoman. Or, possibly, aid her in the slaughter.

The large wooden doors slammed behind them and The Wanderer's gaze immediately locked onto the shallow indent in the floor at the center of the Council Table. Her thoughts of the warning written upon that metal shard flashed in her mind again. Imaginary bodies appeared where the explosive had detonated, allowing her to relive the chaos from a few months prior. *Wanderer. You can't hide from us forever.* Was that only the beginning of the Tiger's tormenting? If so, the protection of Rapture's people was something the Council would likely address during The Gathering.

Bruce's calming, baritone voice greeted them at the end of the table. "Ah Eva… The Council is well aware of the circumstances of the day, so I personally apologize for this *abrupt* Gathering." He shot a nasty look at Virginia. "However, I do agree that we need to address -"

"I understand," Eva said sharply as she took her place at the table, soaking wet. Gavin was right behind her with a reassuring hand on her shoulder. "The protection of Rapture."

She attempted to prepare herself for what Councilwoman Virginia would say.

"We do not want to force you back into your position," Xander explained. "But… if your daughter was in fact *poisoned,* as Lee mentioned, we cannot allow that to happen to another child."

"But they've only been attacking Eva and her family up to this point," Maven added.

"Who knows whether one of us will be the Gang's next target?" Jasmine said quietly. She refused to make eye contact with her friend. "We already have a dozen dead citizens from the explosion here."

She pointed to the cracked marble at the center of the table, in front of Eva's seat.

"*Exactly,*" Virginia exclaimed, gesturing at Jasmine. "We *still* do not have a single shred of information regarding the Gangs… particularly the Tigers. The *very same* Gang that threatened Rapture and The Wanderer's life when she first arrived. As I'm sure you noticed. But this is the point that I have been making for over a year."

Eva took a deep inhale. "And if I can assure you that it won't happen again?"

"Oh, we are *far* beyond that," Virginia scribbled something on her papers and circled it. "First, we must consider why *you* were targeted, as well as discuss your immediate and *permanent* expulsion from this place. And, I do not mean just this Council, but the city itself. We have a compelling case against you, I think. It isn't like you have any family left. So, at this point, you really have no reason to stay, correct?"

The old woman's tone alone was enough to ignite a fire in Eva. It burned so painfully, she half-expected a hole charred into her torso. She turned her head away from the table and glanced over her shoulder where her blades were sheathed. The compulsion to murder Virginia in the midst of the Gathering was almost unbearable. However, the Councilwoman noticed Eva's hostility.

Even her Demon shared the same animosity towards Virginia, sneering at her from the corner of the room.

"Do it Eva," it said in McAvoy's unforgettably cold voice, but appeared more animal-like than before. "Questioning you? Insulting you? Will you let her get away with those words? *End her*."

Before The Wanderer could flinch, Gavin slammed his fist against the back of her chair. "Enough of this shit, Virginia." The sheer force of the punch caused Eva to jump a foot straight out of her seat. "She just buried her daughter. *Today*."

Virginia adjusted the woven belt around her waist and looked at him over the top of her glasses. "I am empathetic to that, Captain. It is a terrible tragedy, no doubt. But we cannot have some outside Gang, which we know *nothing* about, attacking our good people in the name of one citizen. Not to mention, the very same citizen who has taken countless innocent lives in her time. Should we not consider her own… darkened… bloodthirsty past?"

"I'm sitting right here," Eva spat. "How can I rule *you* out as the one responsible for Anya's death? Ever since I stepped foot in this place, you have done nothing but *berate* me and question my every move. Want to talk about coincidence? How fitting that, after the Tigers attack me on my wedding, my daughter falls ill the following year? Under *your* care."

The Councilwoman gasped loudly. "I already told you. I would *never*."

Eva could no longer hold her composure. Gavin took a step back when she suddenly stood up and yelled at the hollow old woman. "You may have fooled the rest of this Council, but not me. I came to this Gathering hoping to compromise with you. Possibly find a common ground. Me and my family have been through nothing but suffering. And after all this, I get no empathy. No sympathy… *Fine*."

"Calm -" Bruce started slowly, but the burning in Eva's chest would not be still.

Virginia scoffed.

Eva pointed violently to the door. "I am having my army, as of this moment, double their shifts *and* number of men. We cannot take any chances of someone sneaking in here, under or over the wall. One guard for every ten feet of wall perimeter. Not just above, but *below* the wall as well. Double guards on the canals and the Gate. We don't want the Gangs sneaking in through the cracks. There. Problem solved."

"That's an awful lot of men in a small space," Virginia added. "Perhaps the Tigers would capitalize on the opportunity of them being in such close quarters."

"Can I do *anything* right in your eyes, Virginia?" Eva snapped. "Anything at all? Or am I just wasting my time trying to appease the high-and-mighty."

"Sounds like *you* know more about the Gangs then you are letting on," Gavin said. His words were ignored by everyone but Eva.

That comment was far too coincidental, she thought. *She was uncomfortably quick with that response.*

"Why did we even allow this mongrel in here?" Virginia argued. "Obviously his gullibility has weakened his decision-making abilities. That's the only reason he is siding with *her*. Because he is a simple-minded fool."

"This is *not* what this city nor this Council stands for," the other members argued.

"We cannot continue this animosity with one another. Rapture is being attacked by an outside source."

"What would you have Eva do, Virginia? We need solutions, not accusations."

"None of us feel safe anymore. What happened to our peaceful city?"

Without further discussion, Eva was already out the door and walking to the Training Grounds with Gavin at her heels. There was no need for a vote. She would make the announcement and personally oversee the evening shift with her Captain. Her head swiveled toward the Town Square and the smoldering coals of Anya's burial. Now, she was *positive* that Virginia had poisoned her. Each Gathering was meant to attack Eva's credibility so the Council will turn on her. *If she can't kill or banish me herself, she'll destroy everything I love and throw me to the Tigers. She will stop at nothing to turn everyone against me. No matter the price. But I won't stop until I get my revenge. I have to be tactful. Careful. Thorough.*

The effort that it took to reason with the other Council Members was useless at this point. None of them cared what happened to her. They only wanted results. As long as someone was still attacking Rapture, they would continue their relentless interrogations.

"Everyone," Gavin's voice boomed. The guards crowded around the scaffolding where Eva had climbed to address them. She raised her hands and the murmur quieted.

Her Shadow was standing amongst the crowd, using its finger to draw an imaginary line across its neck. Eva closed her eyes and pushed thoughts of murder out of her mind for the moment. "As I'm sure you all are aware, we have been attacked by an unknown - possibly outside - source. *My* solution to this problem is to double shifts and guards on the wall. Triple around the gates and canals. We cannot… No, we *will not* allow anything else to happen. Rapture may still be at risk."

The guards agreed without protest. Gavin ushered the younger guards to their positions and the Training Grounds soon became desolate. Her Demon stayed behind when the army dispersed to their respective posts. When it spoke this time, its appearance transformed into Virginia's to recite a single line.

"That's an awful lot of men in a small space," it hissed. "Perhaps the *Tigers would capitalize on the opportunity of them being in such close quarters*."

Eva's heart skipped a beat.

Just as its chambers started to fill with blood, something happened. She was blown off her feet by the shockwave of an explosion.

She was unconscious only for a minute or so, but woke up to find herself face-down, covered in a layer of ash. Reaching up to touch her head, she realized that she could not hear anything except a ringing noise. Blood trickled from the left side of her head, but nothing more. The guards had hardly adjusted to their new posts when it detonated. Bodies were strewn across the Training Grounds, sprayed out from the gaping hole in the wall nearby. As she tried to stand, her head began to swim and she crumpled back to her knees. Everything was spinning as she forced herself into thc chaotic scene.

Her first instinct was to find Gavin.

Fighting the urge to vomit from the wavering ground beneath her, she met the lifeless eyes of a young guard. Both arms had been completely separated from his body and he was missing a leg.

This can't be happening. Not again.

The person she was searching for, she did not see and panicked. *Gavin*, she repeated. *Please don't be dead. Please. Please don't be dead.* Suddenly, she felt pressure around her shoulders and turned her head slowly to find her Captain. He had crawled over and wedged his body between her and the ground to keep them both from falling.

Eva could only read his lips.

"Are you okay?" he screamed.

She nodded. "I think so," she yelled at the top of her lungs. Adrenaline was still coursing through her body, so she did not know whether she was lying. She could not feel anything.

Gavin looked above them with wide eyes. He reacted just fast enough to shove him and Eva away from The Stronghold's wall as it came crumbling down behind them.

Dust exploded up in a plume over their heads as bricks crumbled onto the ground. A section of the outer wall had completely collapsed.

Rapture's Captain and Commander watched the scene as it continued to unfold. Guards were sliced in half, screaming for their mothers and gawking at the space where their limbs should have been. Large pieces of metal from the wall flattened a few unfortunate victims, killing them instantly. Screams of agony and the smell of open wounds caused Eva's stomach to lurch. The swimming in her head had mostly subsided, and she managed to get back to her feet. Amid the chaos, her Shadow stood with its arms outstretched and a smile on his face.

Holding each other up to stabilize their steps, Gavin and Eva tried to spot any structural damage. As the dust began to clear, a gaping hole in Rapture's wall came into view. They coughed through the blackened air and tripped over bodies as they clambered over to it. Both of them scanned the opening to the outside world, searching for any trace of the Tigers. Or any Gang.

But there was nothing.

Something caught their eye on the ground just ahead. They both looked down. It wasn't what they saw through the hole that caused them to jump backwards in fear, but what lay beneath their feet where it once stood.

Painted onto the flat cobblestone road around the outermost ring of Rapture was a message. It was written in fresh blood.

IT WILL NEVER BE ENOUGH, WANDERER. YOU WILL FALL.

"I have to hide this," Eva said in a panic. Her heart was racing so fast, she thought it would burst. "If the Council finds out…"

"Don't you think they'll find out anyway?" Gavin called over the screams and tripped when a dying guard grabbed his leg, screaming for a Healer.

Eva tore him from the writhing man and dragged herself over to a stable wall. "We have to do something. They *cannot* know this is about me. Not until I can think straight. Please, Gavin."

"I'm with you Eva," he said, resting against the side of The Stronghold, attempting to catch his breath. "No matter what. I'm *always* with you."

She wrapped her arms around Gavin and thanked him. It felt like the whole world was against her at this point, but his words were exactly what she needed to hear.

All of a sudden, the ghost of Dan McAvoy appeared right in front of her, wearing the same evil smile as before.

"You. Will. Fall." A voice in her head echoed loudly in her ear. It sounded like he was singing. "I say it again as I have stated before. The Wanderer, soon, will be no more."

Chapter 7

Eva and Gavin were still caked with dirt and dust as they stepped over to further investigate the gaping hole in Rapture's wall. Healers were already on the scene, tending to the wounded and carrying them to the Infirmary. Piles of body parts lined the crumbling wall where the Barracks once stood. Fortunately, under the Wanderer's orders, most of the guards had been stationed along the town's perimeter, far from the explosion.

Hundreds of townspeople had gathered around the carnage, jumping over one another, shoving against the makeshift barricade separating them from the scene. Guards who had not been injured formed a wall between the battleground and the mob of people. Citizens were trying to catch a glimpse of the disaster. There was no way of telling who lost a family member at that time. Many of the victims were unidentifiable.

The Wanderer tried to convince herself she'd made the right call in dispersing her men. "This could have been so much worse. If we'd waited… if I'd waited…"

She trailed off.

"We *all* would have been injured," Gavin filled the silence with his heartfelt words. His lip had been cut and his cheek had already begun to bruise. "Or killed. You made the right choice. There was no way we could have known w-"

"*This is exactly what I am talking about*," a familiar, shrill voice rose over the moans of the wounded. Gavin and

Eva spun on their heels. The Council had just left The Stronghold when Rapture's wall was blown apart. Marching over to the area that had been the Training Grounds, all eyes were on The Wanderer. In the front of the group was the Councilwoman with the long, silver hair. "*I. Have. Had. It.* We receive *zero* intel from the Gangs for *months on end* and they attack again. For once, I'm beginning to agree with The Wanderer. This was *not* an outside source. The answer is right in front of our face."

Virginia kept her gaze fixed on Eva's piercing aqua eyes. Gavin became the partisan who blocked the two women from tearing each other apart. He slowly opened his mouth to speak.

But it was Jasmine who spoke for her friend this time. "Why would Eva try and kill herself?"

Mara had pushed her way through the crowd to stand next to her mother. "But she wasn't killed, was she? Seems awfully coincidental that she's supposedly the intended target but somehow *survives* each attack."

"Exactly," said the eldest Councilwoman. "This isn't staging a suicide. It's about instilling fear into Rapture's people so they will bow to *her* as their savior. She only wants to make it *appear* as though she's the victim. She's probably working with the Tigers right now."

"That's ridiculous," said Lee. "You are making absolutely no sense, Virginia. Why would she work with the Gang that wants her head?"

Virginia looked at her peers, "Because she's obviously a maniac. Don't you see? This is all deception."

"Make one more baseless accusation and we will vote to suspend your duties again, Virginia," Bruce warned. "We have a town to repair and dead to be buried."

For the moment, the rest of the Council appeared to silently side with Eva. The haze of dust cleared and the grotesque scene came into full view. Jasmine strode over to the threshold between Rapture and the outside world. The three of them peered out. Only a few miles stood between them and the crumbling skyline of the city.

Years had passed since Eva had ventured outside Rapture's walls. It was the first time she realized this town was perched on a hill, overlooking the structural remains of Old Time homes and vast forests. But now, any enemy could just walk right in. They had to rebuild. Fast.

"I will begin preparations to give these people a proper burial," the Nomad Councilwoman promised. The wind had knotted her dark hair into her face. She gently brushed it aside. "I want to make sure their souls have not yet left their bodies. We simply don't have enough space or time to bury them in the cemetery. Nor do many of our people choose that ending."

Eva stared blankly at the faint outline of the metropolis. Her mind was still tangled in thought, but Jasmine's words cut through it, leaving Eva confused by what she meant about *making sure their souls had not left their bodies.*

"The Nomads believe that when the soul leaves the body before Last Rights," the young Councilwoman explained. "There's a chance that they sit in a neutral space and they cannot ever return to the Mother."

Smells of death and decay began to permeate the grounds. It was so unbearable that most of the townspeople rushed back to their homes. Virginia, Bruce, Mara, Xander, Lee, Maven, and Jasmine scanned the scene, covering their faces with their clothing. While the odor of death rarely fazed The Wanderer, it was obvious that few in Rapture had witnessed such a sight. Grass all around the Stronghold had been saturated with blood, softening the dirt underneath, staining it red. Countless guards had either vomited, passed out, or broke down sobbing.

"Hey, everything is going to be alright. Okay?" Gavin offered, putting his arm around her. "Please don't let Virginia get to you."

Eva still could not completely grasp what had happened. People were still in shock, and the threatening message at her feet had not yet sunk into her mind. Her Demon was larger than it had ever been before. It loomed over the entirety of Rapture, casting a darkness only she could see.

Luckily, Gavin had already erased the message written in blood before anyone else noticed. Eva's instruction to cover any evidence that directly exposed her as a threat was so the Council would not banish her. Deep down, the thought of exile terrified her. It was just like the Rover colony years ago. She had nowhere to go. Would anyone in the region even remember The Wanderer if she returned? *It's been a long time since I've done anything to deserve that title.*

Still, a small part of her longed for the rush of exhilaration after battle. No sparring match with the guards could ever match the desperation of fighting for her life—or the darker thrill of ending one. For some reason, she found herself craving it more and more.

Jasmine bowed and disappeared around the side of the Stronghold that had not been affected by the explosion. Eva and Gavin continued their investigation when the rest of the Council appeared from around the corner, following them. She swallowed the lump in her throat and wiped the reddish mud from her face. Behind her, the sound of distant gunshots drifted into her ear. She strained to discern how close they were to Rapture, but Virginia, once again, interrupted her train of thought.

"Why do we continue to accept the incomprehensible slaughtering of our people when we already know its source?" she yelled just loud enough for Eva to hear. A number of Rapture's citizens gathered around the shrapnel in the Training Grounds. Councilwoman Virginia jumped on the opportunity to plant the seed of doubt in the people, not just her peers.

"Shit," Eva whispered to Gavin. Suddenly, she grabbed her Captain's left wrist as it slid over the hilt of his weapon. She looked him straight in the eye. He relaxed. "If anyone is going to kill her," she said in a low voice. "It's going to be *me*."

Let's wait and see what this bitch has to say.

"This is *no longer* the issue of the *people*," the Councilwoman shrieked with arms outstretched, attempting to start a coup. She climbed up to a large crate and spoke over the crowd. "But *one person*. The Wanderer who, in our midst, has caused nothing but mayhem since we first allowed her to enter our peaceful town. I will not deny that I supported the decision to have Scouts observe her and grant her entry into Rapture. But I regretted it the instant she arrived. She was trailed by one of the largest Gangs in the North for murdering their Chief. Since that moment, we have lived in fear and uncertainty. We've been attacked. Our friends, neighbors, and family members have sacrificed their lives for *her* safety. Who will be the next to die? Who will be the next human shield for this woman? This… This *monster*."

"Virginia," Bruce went to grab her hand to pull her down off the box, but she tore it away and gasped. "Now is *not* the time for this."

"You see?" she jabbed her finger in the direction of the Councilman. "Some of your *own* appointed Council are on her side. Against *you*. Brainwashed by The Wanderer herself. Look what happens. The Gangs attacked us and more people lay dead… because of *her*."

The people seemed to murmur in agreement with Virginia. Eva's lip quivered. Flashbacks of her banishment at the Rover Colony pierced her mind. The same haunted expressions reflected on their people's faces. She turned to face the crowd, took a deep breath, and climbed onto an unsteady shard of metal from the wall. Her gaze swept over the crowd's hateful stares until it landed on Jake. He was standing next to Mara and both of them averted her gaze. A flicker of emotion rose in her stomach. Jealousy.

"This is crazy," Eva started, but no one was listening. They were insulting her and demanding vengeance for the dead. "I have done nothing but devoted my *life* for the last six years to Rapture and its safety. My child was *murdered*… Not by the Gangs, but by someone in the Council. The culprit? Who else, but someone who despises me? When she was unable to vote me out of this city, she took matters into her own hands."

Virginia continued their verbal battle. "If you are making such an accusation without proof, Wanderer, then enlighten us. *Say* it."

"This Councilwoman and her daughter *poisoned* my daughter and orchestrated these attacks."

"Ha," Mara shouted from the crowd. Her voice squeaked over the noise. "She's delusional. Using any excuse she can come up with to turn you against the Council. How do we know for sure that she isn't working directly with the Gangs themselves? There is more evidence for *that* than Eva's accusation against me *or* my mother."

Virginia chimed in again. "She wants you to be completely oblivious to what is *really* happening. And then, when you least expect it, the Tigers will attack and more of you will die. More of *us*."

Gavin did not skip a beat. His loyalty was unyielding, even against the people he had once vowed to protect. "Virginia will stop at *nothing* until she gets what she wants. If she is willing to villainize Councilwoman Eva, then any one of us could be next. Do you not realize what this woman is capable of? She's trying to turn you against The Wanderer and everything this city stands for. Virginia is not the victim, Eva is. She lost her child, and has nearly lost her life again today."

The tide shifted their attention to the old woman with the perfectly tied bun and glasses. The possibility that Virginia would murder an innocent child was far worse than Eva being the target of a Gang's wrath.

"*Enough*!" Bruce roared over the crowd. His baritone voice rang through the steel walls and into the valley towards the city. Everyone jumped and silenced in a flash. The top of his scar twitched, but he maintained a calm demeanor. "Rapture is *not* fraying like this. *It will not.* Eva, just like everyone else here, deserves the protection of our walls. We have no clear answers as to who poisoned Anya McAvoy, who orchestrated the attacks, or who their true target was. Until any of these allegations are *proven* true, this is the last that I want to hear of this. *Any* of it. Citizens, return to your homes. We will rebuild the wall immediately and Councilwoman Eva will be stationing guards to accommodate this empty space."

The Wanderer could feel the blood drain from her face when she met Bruce's eyes. The anger staring back at her was nothing like she had witnessed since the Tiger Chief. It felt like a boulder had been thrown on her chest. She recalled the warning written in blood. *IT WILL NEVER BE ENOUGH, WANDERER. YOU WILL FALL.* There was no question that the Tigers were behind this, somehow. Whether it was her Shadow's continued warnings and threats, its embodiment of Dan McAvoy, or her knowledge of the Gang itself, it had to be them. But there were still so many questions left unanswered. How did they get *inside* the Stronghold on her wedding? And how did they get to her daughter? Evidence pointed to an informant *inside* Rapture. But who, aside from Gavin, would believe this theory? She had no proof to support it.

Choking on the profound scent hanging around the town center, Jake made his way to Eva. The rest of the Council had already retired to their respective homes and only he, Eva, Gavin, a handful of guards and healers stayed behind. Eerie silence swallowed the grounds.

Jake cried as he hugged Eva. "I'm so glad you're okay. I can't imagine losing you too, after Anya… I don't even want to think about it…"

But she did not return his embrace. Her gaze was fixated on the space where she and Gavin had discovered the note. Now, it was just a swath of red grass and stones. The Hooded Demon returned to a normal size and started making its way up from the hill where Rapture rested. The image of Jake and Tommy's father rose a hand and beckoned for her to step outside the town's walls.

"Is everything okay?" Jake snapped in her face. "*Eva*?"

She turned to him and sharpened her tone. "Yeah, I'm alive if that's what you mean… By the way, thanks for *not* standing up for me just then. Forget it Jake. I don't want to hear your excuses… I just - I - I need to… I need to gather evidence." She brushed him aside. Buried deep within her own mind, she was not completely aware of her surroundings. All of her focus was on the space between the wall and the rest of the world. She could hear a voice, seeming to come from the outside, calling to her.

Jake realized he was standing alone with his arms still outstretched in an embrace. He cleared his throat, dusted off his pants, and walked away in disbelief. For months he had tried to be more sympathetic to Eva's pain. She, too, had lost a child, and was targeted at their wedding ceremony. But lately, her mind seemed to sink deeper into a darkness she could not climb out of. Jake noticed. He always noticed. Though she never admitted her Shadow had returned, he knew better.

I couldn't stand up for her in front of the whole town, he thought as guilt spread through his chest. *I have no idea what's going on. All Eva does is push me away when I ask for information. I just don't know what to believe anymore.*

When her partner was out of sight, The Wanderer returned to her duties. The rabble from the crowd had subsided, leaving space in the air for the sound of gunshots to fill her ears. It was coming from the city. They were distant, but clear as day. Gavin, too, noticed it and stood with Eva at the border of Rapture.

"What do you think that is?" he whispered, craning to listen.

She breathed a sigh of relief. "Oh good, you can hear it too." Eva closed her eyes and tried to discern the direction of the sound. "It sounds like it's coming from the Northeast. But I can't tell whether it's in the city or further than that. The air is clear enough to carry the sound."

"There could still be some evidence of who attacked us there. Should we investigate?"

She considered the question. Truthfully, if she left, there would likely be no returning. Still, a fight for survival felt more appealing than a battle for her reputation. But abandoning Jake and Tommy was out of the question. They were still her family.

Even if they didn't stand up for me... Maybe they're just scared... Maybe...

She could sense the Demon tearing away at her sanity. After all these years, Eva couldn't understand why it appeared in the first place. And no matter how much she fought, she could never rid herself of the dread that accompanied it.

"Eva?" Gavin nudged her from her thoughts. He must have read her mind or the look on her face. "Do you want to leave Rapture? Go back out on your own?"

"Yes," she whispered as she stared into the horizon as a few tears slid down her cheek and to her neck. "More than anything. After everything that's happened… But I can't leave my men… or Jake…"

"You know I would follow you anywhere," he said quickly. For a moment, he waited for a response, staring straight ahead. When he finally gathered the courage to look at her face, he was surprised to find a sheepish smile.

The only one here who doesn't think I'm crazy would gladly follow me into the abyss of my mind. Only to find that he had descended into the same madness that is trying to devour me. No. I must fight this darkness alone. Still...

"What?" Gavin chuckled. "What's so funny?"

"Nothing. Just... Thank you... for your unrelenting loyalty."

Her Captain shook his head and left her to absorb the city skyline alone. She had not laid eyes on it in ages, and still it held the same quiet peace she remembered. Old Time grocery stores, hotels, banks. Names that meant little to her, yet seduced her with whispers of the ancestors who once resided there. Jake and Tommy's ancestors, however, had never known the bombings that nearly wiped out humanity. They stowed away in a Vault to the North, with possibly more elsewhere. There they remained in seclusion, until their descendants were eventually unearthed by the tyrannical Gangs. Not all who came from that Vault were taken by the Serpents. Two would settle in Rapture.

One would become the Tiger Chief.

***

Jake was on his way home when he spotted Mara in the Town Square. She was gliding past the ashes of his daughter's burial mound. She appeared to be waiting for someone. After a few steps, she would stop, her crimson gown would ripple at her ankles, and she would continue circling the pile. He watched her golden hair lift with the breeze, softly caressing her thin face and pointed nose. Suddenly, her gray eyes rose to meet him and she glided over.

"How long have you been standing there, Jacob McAvoy?" The woman began circling the Blacksmith, running her fingertips across his shoulder. "You shouldn't stare at a woman when you already belong to another."

"Belong?" he repeated. "What are you talking about?"

"The Wanderer, of course," she responded.

"I am not her property, Mara."

Her high-pitched voice changed to a sing-song tone. "Could've fooled me. Despite your faithfulness to her, she treats you so poorly. Unrightfully so. She obviously does not…" she corrected herself, "*cannot* love you."

Jake rolled his shoulders. "What do you mean by that?"

"Isn't it obvious? Are you so deeply infatuated that your emotions have blinded you to the truth? You cannot deny that she has distanced herself from… *everyone* here."

"She has a lot on her mind," he said matter-of-factly. "Eva's been attacked *multiple times*. Our daughter was murdered in cold blood. And all your mother can do is try to paint her as the villain of Rapture."

There was a certain sternness in Mara's reply that caused Jake's heart to skip a beat. "The Wanderer's presence is a *danger* to us all, Jake. That's what my mother is trying to convey to everyone. Her job is to keep Rapture and its people safe and her passion for that duty is clearly unmatched. There is no sane reason in keeping *one* citizen safe but threatening the lives of the rest. I don't understand why the Council continues to protect her… why *you* continue to protect her. From what I've heard, Eva is already reverting to what the Scouts have called "her other self"."

"What are you saying?" Jake took a step back, but Mara closed the gap between them, standing to his side.

"They *know* about her Demon," she whispered in his ear softly. Her soft lips caressed his ear lobe. "Eva doesn't love you, Jake. Not any more. She's too far gone. Stop protecting her and save yourself before it's too late."

And just like that, the woman sauntered down the street to her home. Jake was standing in an empty town square, next to the remains of his daughter's burial. The words lingered in the air around him, encircling his head, making it spin. *Stop protecting her and save yourself before it's too late.* Slowly turning his head back to the hole in the wall, he saw

Eva's silhouette, standing at the town's border, staring out into the region.

Maybe Mara's right, he thought. It pained him to think that Eva was losing herself. The knowledge that he had spent more than six years pining for her, only to realize she no longer felt the same, weighed heavily on him. Did he have the courage to ask how she truly felt? Would she even understand the weight of her answer? One thing was undeniable: her Shadow had returned. But how could the Scouts or the Council possibly know? Her mind had been unraveling with each passing day. Every attack over the past year only seemed to widen the gap between Eva and reality.

But Jake still loved her. From the moment they first met to the day she saved them from their merciless father, his love had never faltered. Even when she stood drenched in the blood of her enemies, he still saw her as beautiful. When, in a moment of weakness, she had tried to take her own life, he had still longed to face the future with her at his side. And even on the night she forced him to kill a Gang member, his devotion held fast. How long could love endure when it was carried alone?

Or was that even love at all?

***

Eva and Gavin worked through the day to be sure they hadn't missed a single shred of evidence. Unfortunately, they did not find anything aside from the note written in blood that indicated the Gangs had been responsible, and that had already been erased. They were hoping to have something more concrete that Eva could bring to the Council. Something that would dissuade them from suggesting banishment. But if she showed up empty handed, the result may be exile.

"There has to be *something* here," Gavin sighed. At this point, he resorted to combing through the grass for any sign of a detonation device. Anything. He, too, understood

Eva's predicament with the Council. They were expecting her that evening. In fact, they were most likely awaiting her return already. It was the perfect opportunity for Virginia to persuade even Bruce to banish her.

Only the tone of defeat resonated in her voice as Eva slumped to a nearby rock. "If I tell them that I didn't find anything, they'll know I'm lying."

"Maybe you should tell them about the note," he offered. Flinching when Eva shot a look at him, he straightened up. "It's just a thought."

"No. No." Eva put her head in her hands and wiped the dust off of her face. "You're right. If they catch me in a lie, they're more likely to kick me out of here. Not that it matters anymore. It's only a matter of time before…"

She trailed off. Something caught her attention in the city. It was faint, but she could still make out the glow of a light. It must have been a beacon to reach so far from the border, but it shone right at Rapture, at the hole that had been blown through the wall. Watching it flicker against the clouds, Eva considered whether or not to travel to the source. The gunshots had finally ceased or moved so far away that she could no longer hear it.

I'm not going down without a fight. Her muscles tightened as an unsettling idea settled in.

"What?" Gavin asked frantically. "What is it?"

"I'm ordering a brigade to go North," she said, reaching down to the space where her handgun once sat. The last place she had touched that firearm was in her battle with Dan McAvoy.

"Why send one all the way out there?" Gavin pointed through the hole towards the aging city.

"Let me correct myself. *I'm* taking a brigade North."

Her Captain repeated his question.

"Well," she stood up and spun on her heels to face him. "We need evidence. Nothing we've done so far is working. The Scouts are clearly useless as they haven't turned up anything either. We need to go to the source. If we find out who's behind these attacks *and* information on the Gang's plans for any further destruction, the Council will have to side with me. But most importantly, when I step through those gates, one of two things will happen."

After a pause, Gavin shrugged. "And that is?"

"Something changes in me after I kill someone," she said with casual ease. "Or someone kills me. Either way, I'll know if my skills have dulled over the years. And if I learn anything about the Tigers' motives, I'll have something for Virginia."

"It would be nice to get out there and fight again," he agreed. Gavin had not seen a real battle since he came to Rapture. The thought of it excited him. "I'm coming. I'm in."

Eva nodded and rushed over to The Stronghold. Just as she suspected, the rest of the Council was already waiting. They were deep in discussion when she entered the Chambers, but their voices fell silent the moment they noticed her.

"Yes?" Virginia taunted. "Can't you see the Council was talking?"

Eva snarled. "You mean the Council in which *I* am a part of? Pardon me for being so blunt, but I was under the impression that a Gathering would not be held until *all* Members were present?"

"Your membership at this point is *debatable*," Maven said. "Pending your investigation, I am considering siding with Virginia."

Lee and Xander both chimed in, "As are we. Albeit, reluctantly."

"What is this?" Eva exhaled in disbelief. "You have *secret* meetings, which, I might add, are against the very rules set by The Council. Then you allow Virginia to turn you against me with nothing but hearsay and baseless accusations? I didn't realize you were all so gullible."

"Our decision has nothing to do with you," Lee said calmly, interlacing his fingers together. "We are *all* tasked with keeping this city safe. That means it's people as well. If your presence is risking the lives and safety of Rapture's citizens, the logical choice would be banishment. You cannot deny that."

Honestly, Eva was not surprised by this exchange. Each Tiger attack was more fuel for the fire and Virginia wanted to watch her burn. What they did not count on was The Wanderer's plan.

"Please allow me one more chance," she said. "I'm taking a unit into the region. It appears I cannot trust the Scouts or my men to uncover anything. I am personally overseeing the investigation of the Tigers."

"We will not authorize further risk to anyone's lives who do not wish to sacrifice them," Virginia spat. "You may only take those who wish to go… which, I doubt, will be anyone at this point."

Gavin's voice rang through the Council Chambers. "I'm going with her. It will be better if she and I go alone anyway. My only hope is that this Council changes their tone when we return."

"That will depend on the *manner* in which you return," Virginia dismissed with a cruel grin.

Bruce hung his head in shame.

The Wanderer and her Captain had already slammed the door behind them before anyone could say another word. Traveling down the cobblestone streets, they both stopped at their homes to gather a few pieces of equipment. Eva roused Jake from his nap and quickly told him where she was going.

"I'm not sure how long I will be gone," she said. "But I doubt I'll be able to return if I don't come back with something."

"Do you want me to come with you?" Jake asked, but did not push to accompany her. The offer was only because he worried for her safety, not that he had a desire to go. He was elated when she declined, but slightly hurt when she told him who else would be going.

"Gavin is the only one who agreed to join me at this point," she explained. "But you should stay here with your shop. You haven't fought in ages and I can't have you being a burden to me."

The way she said '*burden*' lingered in Jake's mind as she disappeared down the street. It sounded exactly as it had when they first met. Eva had often referred to him and Tommy as burdens, but had not uttered the word since they entered Rapture. Now, there was no denying it. She was changing. Or rather, returning to who she had once been. The Wanderer. The part of her that had protected them in the region, but was far too unpredictable for these walls. Would another attack make her unravel completely? In Rapture, there was nowhere to hide.

"Is everything alright?" Mara's voice carried softly from the front door, near to where Jake had been sleeping. "My mother just told me about Eva's plan to go into the city. I wanted to check on you."

Her willingness to listen was something that Jake had recently come to appreciate. In fact, there were times that he found himself craving attention of some type. Though Mara seemed to be taking it beyond a simple cordial conversation.

Before he could reply, she was already at his side. "Don't you find it incredibly unusual that she would take Gavin, but not you? Aren't you the least bit hurt by her decision? I mean, you've fought by her side before."

"No," he lied. Part of him *was* jealous of Eva's friendship with Gavin. Lately, they had been spending quite a bit of time together. "To be honest, I never actually fought when we traveled together. It was just Eva saving me and my brother. I have only taken two lives, and one was by accident."

Mara tilted her head. "And the other?"

"Eva…" he started, then changed his tone. Perhaps he had said too much. "It had to be done. They would have tortured and killed Tommy."

"She forced you, didn't she?" She could read Jake like a book. Then again, he *was* terrible at lying. "Let me guess, the man you murdered was helpless. Bound, mercilessly beaten, or something like that?"

The young woman's words dissolved into nothing, and Jake found himself back in the Post, torturing the large Tiger. She had killed the first to make her threat unmistakably clear to the other. Speak, or suffer the same fate. Jake was standing there, shaking, with a knife in his hand. The Wanderer's eyes flashed with exhilaration as she plunged her knife deep into her victim's thigh.

The man's scream echoed in Jake's head as Eva stood aside, forcing his hand to finish the poor soul. Everything in his body held him back, but she pushed him further. He wanted to vomit. The thought of ending someone's life terrified him beyond words. Glancing over to the other body on the floor, Jake felt another shove from behind.

"If you don't do this, he'll go back and tell the others. And then they will *torture and kill* Tommy."

A moment of what he believed to be an understanding of Eva passed. He extinguished the Tiger's life. When his thoughts returned to his home in Rapture years later, with Mara sitting beside him, he realized that his moment of empathy had in fact been one of weakness and coercion.

His long silence was more than enough to answer Mara's question.

"Tell me—Are you certain that Eva loves you?" She brushed her fingers across his hand. "Really, *truly* loves you?"

He thought for a moment. Eva had said she loved him many times, but could not answer whether she really meant it. It was difficult to recognize how she expressed her feelings, so he was not entirely sure how to answer Mara's question. "I...I..."

"She's been distant with you lately," she said with a pout. "Very distant. Jake, you deserve to be loved in the way that you're supposed to love someone. Fully and unconditionally. You need someone who will take care of you. Someone who will never leave your side… especially not for a nameless Captain."

Jake leaned into Mara's hand as it caressed his cheek. He closed his eyes, taking in the warmth of her palm. But, in his mind, there was only Eva. It was always her. She was always there to tear him from unfaithfulness. *Maybe I'm afraid of what she'll do. Maybe this isn't love. Wait.* Regardless of how distant she had been lately, he believed that he still loved her. In fact, he partly blamed himself for Eva's recent detachment, knowing he hadn't been as supportive as he should have been. She was hurting too and he was too concerned about how Rapture viewed him, not how the love of his life was handling her demons.

When he realized his mistake, he sprung out of the chair.

"Y-y-you have to go," he stuttered. "*Now.*"

Mara stood up and scoffed. "You stay with her even though she doesn't return your affection. She doesn't *deserve* you."

Jake jabbed his finger at her. "You know *nothing* about her," he said and pointed to the door.

"Neither do you," she spat. "Otherwise, you wouldn't stay. And when she goes down, she will take you with her…"

And with that, Jake was alone, left to dwell in his thoughts.

Chapter 8

Fresh air filled Eva's lungs as she and Gavin closed the creaking gates of Rapture behind them. A vast graveyard of Old Time homes lay ahead. Crumbling wooden and stone skeletons, clinging to the life that once was. Just beyond, the silhouette of a crumbling city, illuminated by the reds and orange swaths of clouds against the setting sun.

Elation washed over The Wanderer's body as if invisible chains had been broken. But uneasiness settled into Gavin's stomach. He was loyal to his Commander, but a decade had passed since he was forced to survive outside of Rapture's walls. He was unsure how his skill in battle had withstood the test of time.

Unlike her companion, Eva had been practicing. One of her biggest fears was losing the very thing that earned her the title of The Wanderer. The frailty of life intoxicated her. Visualizing a clash between her and the Tigers was both invigorating and petrifying. The clashing of steel against steel. The scent of fear when they realized who stood before them.

Adrenaline coursed through her veins, causing her to shake in anticipation.

"Do you still remember the way through the city?" Gavin asked as they navigated between cracked streets and frames of old vehicles.

She answered in confidence. "With my eyes closed." Memories of Nomad trails through the city rushed in, followed by a sense of freedom. Outside Rapture, Eva's Demon faded from view.

Gavin noticed the change in her demeanor almost instantly. "Why do you stay in Rapture if you are so comfortable and happy out here?"

Silence. Eva buried her chin in her jacket and threw her hood over her head.

"You don't see it, do you?" he said firmly. "No one else does, but *I* do. You belong out here."

"Not when I have an entire *Gang* after me," she said. "I can't fight them alone."

"But you thrive out here," he replied, then stopped. "Unlike most people, you were meant to be out here. And you wouldn't *have* to be alone…"

Eva walked in front of him and blocked his path. "What do you mean by that?"

"You're so much more lively out here," he said. "I can tell just by how you're holding yourself right now."

"No." She crossed her arms. "The other thing."

"Well…With the way Virginia and the rest of the Council treat Rapture's army," he started, but digressed. "Anyway… I've been thinking about it for a while—before you came into Rapture. And I could not think of a better companion than The Wanderer."

Eva paused and silently agreed with Gavin. She was always more at ease beyond the limits of any one town. Even as the protector of the Rovers, she was able to venture through the region whenever she wished. This world was the world she grew up in. Fought for. Ruled. It was where she was most comfortable.

"I can't," she said reluctantly. "Jake…I have to try… for him."

Gavin sighed, nodding as they continued down the street. "Yeah, I know. But there is always the option… if something should change. I just can't let them continue to treat you like shit."

“Well, that’s why we’re out here.” She concealed her smile. “To shut them up.”

The two traveled quietly for a few hours. Only the sound of wildlife and the rhythm of their footsteps surrounded them. Eva would never admit how badly she wanted to get out of Rapture, especially now. It was never in her nature to rule alongside others. Most of the Members disagreed with her tactics and ideas, but none of them had controlled an entire populus by themselves. The Serpents became the greatest Gang in the region because of The Wanderer’s absolute rule.

The Council should be begging me to teach them how to lead rather than fighting me at every turn. Rapture has been around for years, sure, but they’ve never had to deal with a Gang before. Not like the Tigers. Not with their ruthlessness. They know nothing.

Another voice inside her head offered a solution to her frustration and anger.

Then leave.

But she still struggled with how much she still cared for Jake and Tommy. Sure, both of them had become less dependent on her once they settled into their new lives. She hardly saw Tommy anymore because he was so busy leading the Farmers with Xander. And in the days after Anya had passed, Jake and Eva had hardly spoken. Regardless, they were her family, and she loved them.

The sight of collapsing skyscrapers, inhabited by ancient people long ago, greeted them at the edge of the city. The Wanderer had almost forgotten what it felt like to gaze upon these buildings from below. She felt so small, and her problems, insignificant. It was a humbling experience, comforting her like a long-forgotten home. For a moment, she closed her eyes and recalled her time with the Nomads as a young woman, studying the trails built through the city, unknown to others. Much of the rubble was impassable unless you knew the secret ways.

“We aren’t lost are we?” Gavin asked.

Eva opened her eyes and shook her head. "No. I know *exactly* where we're going. Keep up if you can."

She sprinted forward, skidded sharply to the left, and crawled through a building where a part of the wall had broken away. It was barely large enough for either of them to squeeze through, but once they were inside, everything opened up. Eva slid down the gravel pathway and out into the street. The energy radiating from the city was different than she remembered. It felt like an evil presence had settled into the brick, dissolved into the streets, and permeated the air. Had the Gangs overtaken the city? Something did not feel right.

Gavin saw Eva stop suddenly and almost knocked her over. "Did you feel that too? It feels like…"

"The Gangs have been here," she said. "Here or nearby. I can smell blood, faintly. It must have something to do with those gunshots we heard earlier."

"I hope it's not the Nomads." He looked down the street. Nothing stirred.

"I'm sure we will find their carnage sooner or later." Eva lowered her voice. "We're taking a different route to get out of this place. Keep an eye out for any evidence of the Tigers. Or any other Gang."

"Got it." His heart began to race. *I'm not ready for this.*

"Just. Stay. Quiet."

Eva climbed on top of an old dumpster and vaulted up to a fire escape. Rust caked over the steel, creaking under her weight. Gavin wondered whether it would snap if he followed. Fortunately, he didn't have to. A moment after she disappeared, Eva returned with a sturdy wooden ladder so he could safely climb into the building. When he stepped inside, she drew it up and stored it in an adjacent room.

"Man," he breathed. Up until now, he forgot that he was wearing his metal armor, which was more decorative than practical. "You really know your way around this city."

"I did live here for a while," she said and noticed how much sound Gavin was making. "Lose the armor. If we get caught, I *will* gut you before the Gangs do."

That last comment was something the old Eva would have said. It made her chuckle. When Gavin asked why she was laughing, she ignored him. "Just take it off."

"This new you is beginning to creep me out," he joked as he tossed the armor in the same room where the ladder was. "I've never seen this side of you before. But it is nice to see you smiling again."

Eva climbed down an old staircase and motioned for him to follow. The bottom half had been destroyed so they leapt the rest of the way. Out of the building, they were now on another street, stepping through an open window at a nearby store. It took twice as long to wind through the city this way, but it would keep them away from the open streets where the Gangs could discover them.

Hours passed as they wound through endless streets, breathless by the time they reached the eastern border. Just at the horizon, The Wanderer spotted something that made her stomach churn.

Familiar, haphazardly-built shacks protruded from the edge of her view. The Rover Colony lay just about a mile from where they now stood. As usual, their town seemed desolate during the day. Their doors would be locked tight at this time. A flicker of anger ignited in her chest as Eva wondered how they fared since her banishment. For all she knew, they could have been wiped out by a Gang.

Yet the scent of blood lingered. It clung to the air as they neared Gang territory, but neither could tell where it was coming from. One breeze would bring the smell of death from the city. Another would waft in from the forest. Large, dark clouds rolled in from the distant lands to the North, bringing with it, a drizzle of rain. The air grew heavy, extinguishing the smell. As they passed the Rover colony from a distance, Eva turned and watched it disappear into the fog.

"I can hardly see ahead of us now," Gavin said and squinted. "Do you still know where we're going?"

Eva was being much more cautious now that her vision was limited by the haze. Both of her blades were tightly clutched in her hands, ready to strike. "As long as we follow this old highway, we will get to The Blooded Row."

"We're going to The Blooded Row?"

"Possibly, but I want to try another place first. Somewhere *much* closer."

The rest of the day was spent on-edge as the fog refused to clear. They did not quite make it to No Man's Land, but Eva knew that they would reach it the next day. When they found a secluded place behind a cluster of boulders, she decided to stop and rest for a few hours.

Gavin collapsed against the back of one of the rocks while Eva unconsciously caressed her empty gun holster. She was staring in the direction of the Tigers Den, still standing in the rain. Her mind was suffocated with questions. For a while, she was unaware of her surroundings. And as usual, her Captain read her mind with ease.

"Do you think you killed him? Chief McAvoy I mean." he asked.

She jumped at the sound of his voice. "Huh? What?"

He repeated the question.

"I-I-." She paused and glanced at the place where her Demon was now standing. "I don't know anymore. When I fought him, there was so much chaos that I just stabbed him and ran out of there. The whole Gang was after me at that point. But… shit, I *swore* I killed him. He was losing blood so fast, it would have only taken *minutes* for him to bleed out."

"Since the attacks?"

"I don't know… I really want to believe he's dead. I can't think of any possible way he survived. But if he did somehow live through that. That terrifies me. I should have just put a bullet through his brain. I…I just wanted my blades to taste the blood of the man who destroyed my life. I wanted him to suffer. But that may have been my mistake. Overconfidence."

"And you are positive that the Tigers are the ones who are doing this?"

"*Positive.*"

"I believe you."

Those were the words that Eva desperately needed to hear. From someone. Anyone. Lately, so many people had discredited her, doubted her, or ignored her. Memories of the night she ran from The Tiger's Den arose, but the dread did not accompany it. Her Demon was gone for the moment, but McAvoy's voice still whispered in her ears.

You are getting oh so close Wanderer, it said. *If you intend to strike me down, please be sure that you do it correctly this time. My hope is that you finally see the light while encompassed in so much darkness.*

Oh I will, she argued in her head. *You will not control me again.*

The voice laughed. *That's debatable. Even when I'm gone and your blades drip with my blood, I will never truly disappear. Lingering in your waking thoughts and imprinted on your darkest nightmares. I will haunt you for the remainder of your pathetic life. That is... if you can kill the real McAvoy properly.*

Eva waited a while before electing to hunt for their dinner. It had been a while since she had trapped anything, hoping that luck was on her side. Gavin waited at their makeshift camp while she journeyed near the border of the forest that split the region down the middle. Many of the animals would be hopping around at dusk, so she believed there was a good chance of catching something to eat.

Fortunately, a few rabbits sacrificed themselves to her trap as soon as she laid it inside a bush and hid. As she knelt down to pick up the animals, her Shadow brushed against her arm. It was the first time she had actually felt something that was not its claws. The dread seeped in at the point where they touched. And then, it spoke.

"Your doubt is not misplaced," it mocked. Its flat, emotionless voice sounded exactly like the real Dan McAvoy and froze Eva to the core. "I am not dead. Otherwise, why would my Tigers be seeking you out so passionately? Your head will be my most prized possession. Everyone will know that it was *I* who ended The Wanderer."

The Demon's voice echoed in Eva's ear, causing emotions of trauma to start to overtake her, paralyzing her body. She wanted to scream, but no sound exited her lips. Her head began to swim and her vision blurred. Agony tore through her, ripping the breath from her lungs as if her soul were being dragged free. Fire burst across her back, and she writhed, gasping, her body seizing beneath her. The only thing she could do was watch her body from above. Years seemed to pass before the familiar grasp of Gavin's muscular arms wrapped around her torso. A dagger was in her hand, its cold blade pressed against her neck, ready to slice.

It took a few moments for Eva to pull herself fully back into her body, and a few more for the daze to lift. Gavin scanned her body with worry. She opened her mouth and sheathed the blade. Her voice cracked. "I'm so sorry. You weren't supposed to see that."

"Are you okay?" His eyes darted through the darkness of the forest. "Did you see something? What happened?"

He helped Eva to her feet. She grabbed the rabbit carcasses and shook her head. During this particular struggle with her thoughts, she was not trembling as much as she had in the past. She considered whether she was getting used to the nightmares. "For some reason, this happens from time to time. That Shadow-thing touched my arm and then… this happened. All of the pain from my past just… takes over."

Without hesitation, Gavin pulled her into an embrace. "I heard your scream. I thought they had gotten to you," he whispered.

"Hang on. I screamed? I mean, I was trying to, but it was all silent."

"I heard it. You were begging someone to stop hurting you. That's why I thought a Gang attacked."

"No. It was… my mind. It's happened a few times before, and I don't know why. But I can't control it. I black out. Apparently, the only person meant to end me is myself…"

"I would never let that happen."

Eva's lip trembled. "These nightmares are why everyone thinks I'm a monster."

"You are many things, Eva, but a monster is not one of them."

Gavin's short, fire-colored beard held a straight smile that Eva found very attractive. For a half second, she considered leaving Rapture behind and running away with the only person that accepted her for who she truly was, along with her flaws. Jake would force her to change for a sense of normalcy in his own life. He wanted peace at the expense of her sanity. But what *he* wanted no longer suited her. Gavin never questioned her motives and followed her without protest. Quite the opposite. He empathized deeply with her struggle.

"I found dinner," she quickly changed the subject and held up her catch.

They walked back to their makeshift camp for the rest of the evening. Gavin took care of cooking and they ate by a warm fire. Watching the crackling of the flames was calming to Eva, almost hypnotic. Out in the wilderness, she felt at peace. The walls of Rapture suffocated her. She felt like an outcast. A prisoner.

Bright coals soon replaced the flickering blaze and both adventurers laid on opposite sides of the embers, trading stories from their lives before Rapture.

"I know what you were before becoming The Wanderer," Gavin said. "Y'know, the Serpent's Mistress. Most of Rapture knows now, I'm sure."

She felt her face get hot with anger. "Is that why everyone is so terrified of me?"

"Maybe," he responded. "But it doesn't bother me at all. Actually, it makes me respect you. I mean, you created a Gang that could take over all the others around here. Single-handedly. Lucky for the Rovers and Nomads, their current Chief doesn't involve himself with anything outside his walls."

Eva rolled over to her side, facing Gavin. "Respect?"

A word she had not heard or felt since she ruled the Serpents.

"Yeah. I really do. As a *young* woman, you brought a region to its knees. Everyone, at that time, bowed down to you. The first servant to challenge a Chief *and win, unarmed.* Consuming every small town of Rovers except the two that are still here. Developing an unconquerable army. Sure, the Gangs are wicked and cruel, and you were part of that… But accomplishing that feat no matter what side you were on… wow."

"You really think so?"

Gavin sat up. "Eva, *everything* you are, I admire. You are strong and fearless. You stand up for what you believe in and never let anyone take advantage of you… On top of all that, and forgive me if I overstep, but you are indescribably beautiful."

Beautiful. Eva's heart started beating in her ear so fast, it was humming. When her Captain had realized what he said, he cleared his throat and laid back down, facing away from her. Awkward silence fell over the campsite.

"Sorry," he finally said.

"Don't be," she responded. "I… I haven't gotten a compliment in a long time. It makes me feel more like a human than a monster. So, thanks."

"If I have to say this for the rest of our lives, I will. Eva Calloway, you are *not* a monster."

***

The next morning was another rainy day. Eva and Gavin woke up as soon as the torrential downpour began, huddling under one of the boulders for shelter. Once they'd gotten a few more hours of sleep, they were up and closing in on their first destination—the site of many events in Eva's recent past: The Post in No Man's Land.

"How do you know this place?" Gavin was wringing out his tunic when he caught Eva admiring his toned figure.

She cleared her throat as her gaze sharply turned towards the door. "Actually, I found it by accident. When I first rescued Jake and Tommy, we stayed here for the night, but didn't realize it was a Post. A couple Gangs came to trade here… Jake knocked something over downstairs where they were hiding… so I was forced to kill them before they killed us."

Gavin went over to the basement and gripped the door handle when Eva recalled the gruesome scene below their feet. She rushed over and threw the door open, bounding down the stairs ahead of him. Sure enough, skeletal remains were still strewn across the concrete. The glass door leading outside had been broken some time ago and animals had ravaged the bodies. Chew marks covered most of the bones that had found their way to the corners of the room. But they were old. No animal had ventured into this home in some time.

What had not changed was the message written on the wall in browned blood. *Serpents*. Eva felt bone shards crunch beneath her boots as she crossed the floor and brushed her hand over the painted word. Once again, she found herself thinking about leaving Rapture.

"I guess… I feel more *alive* when I'm out here," Eva confessed. "In Rapture… I feel hollow, going through the motions of a fake life. I can't… I don't know how much longer I can keep this up."

Gavin stood beside her. "You don't *have* to stay there."

"But I do," she said. "At least, I feel like I do. For Jake. For me. I deserve the peace that everyone else has there… right? Maybe once the Tigers stop hunting me things will change."

He nodded and patted her back. "Well, if we do find something out here, Virginia no longer has a case against you. And then, maybe, we can all move forward."

For the rest of the day, Eva and Gavin took turns at the front window, watching for any sign of the Gangs. While her Captain was in the foyer, The Wanderer spent her time strolling around the two story building. She could still make out the dark bloodstains on the floor and walls from her battle years ago. Bullet holes riddled the walls on the upper floor. Tiny spider webs filled the voids in the panels. She spent hours studying their miniscule lives. Each time she tore the web apart, the spider rebuilt, its home never quite the same as it had been before.

Maybe I need to be more like these spiders, she thought. *Start over, but a little differently.*

Jake lost a daughter too, another voice in her head argued. *And you can't hold that against him. You are in this together*.

Eva finally came downstairs to Gavin, sitting in the front room, staring into the yard. He rose from his chair and nodded to her. She took his place, sliding both blades from their hilts, laying them to rest against the windowsill. If anyone passed through the street, she would be waiting. Memories of torturing a Tiger for information, her life being threatened, and the fear in someone's eyes as they came to the realization that she was The Wanderer. All of it was oddly comforting. Familiar.

As she settled into the armchair, she felt her Captain standing in the stairwell. Slowly, she turned around and looked at him.

"Something wrong?"

"Sorry," he chuckled and turned around, disappearing into the other room. "I'm just tired. I'm going to lay down for a while"

She resumed her place as the guard for the next few hours, scanning the ancient street for any sign of movement. It was completely desolate, broken only by the occasional raccoon or owl darting through her field of view. A soft breeze rustled the leaves in nearby trees, lulling Eva to a reverie. She sank into her seat and imagined herself no longer as a citizen of Rapture. No Council. No Virginia. No attacks. Just her old self.

The Wanderer.

***

Gavin and Eva spent the next two days in the home, but did not come across a single Gang Member. No one came to trade at all. Both nights, The Wanderer searched the streets and nearby homes for any sign of them. Perhaps they moved their trading posts? Maybe they no longer traded this way. With so little information from the Gangs over the past year, any change was a mystery to her.

When Eva finally grew tired of waiting, she decided to move closer to The Blooded Row. She explained the plan to her Captain. He hesitated, but vowed to follow her wherever she went.

"We aren't going to go *through* The Blooded Row," she explained. "But we need to get closer to the Gangs to see if we can catch any of their members from a distance. I don't want to put our lives in danger. Think of it as me putting our lives 'at risk'."

Gavin raised an eyebrow. "Okay…"

They vacated The Post, covered their tracks, and continued North. Storms had disappeared from the region and a partly cloudy sky broke over them. It was a cool day. Despite the fact that they were heading straight into dangerous territory, their spirits were high. Gavin seized the chance to urge Eva to consider staying out of Rapture again.

"Please." She put up a hand to silence him. "If you keep badgering me, I'm going to change my mind about letting you come with me. At least for now, I'm staying in Rapture. No more talking about it. Just stop."

Gavin apologized. "I'm sorry, Eva. I only want you to be happy."

"Thanks," she sighed. "And things might change. My future could depend on what we find here."

Now, the compounds were just ahead. Their unforgettable steel walls, crowned with rusted barbed wire and shadowed by looming watchtowers, had remained unchanged since Eva last ventured here. Guards paced back and forth, pockets brimming with ammunition and brandishing large firearms. Eva and Gavin crawled behind the shell of an old vehicle, moving closer only when they were sure no one was looking. They came across the ruins of an old building, a place where they could settle in and eavesdrop on the Tigers. If anyone knew of plans to attack Rapture, it would be their high-ranking sentinels.

Lucky for them, the voices from above carried down to them rather clearly. An hour passed and the only thing that the guards spoke about was Doxies, Bondsmen, and the quality of food. It wasn't until the shifts changed around dusk that the discussions became more relevant to Eva's search.

"Too bad nothing's happened yet," a male guard said. "Well, nothing worth talking about."

"Yeah," a woman chimed in. "Keep missing."

Gavin looked at Eva and whispered, "They could be talking about *anything*. The Council will need more concrete -."

"*I know*," she breathed loudly. "That's why I'm trying to listen. Shush."

"... clue what's next," the man said. Eva had missed the first part of the comment. "But he believes it will happen soon. And we'll be ready."

What the shit are they talking about? She mouthed to herself.

Just then, the higher-ranked guards were called away with a "the Chief is asking for you" and their replacements spoke nothing of interest. For a long while, Eva and Gavin sat under a partially collapsed basement, waiting for their superiors to return. But they never did. The only chance that Eva had to obtain any type of evidence may have been cut short by Gavin's remark. He glanced at his Commander. His stomach dropped at the look on her face.

"Eva," he stuttered. "I… I'm…"

"It's fine," she spat. They had waited long enough, and she truly believed that there was no more information to be gathered without actually infiltrating the compound itself. "Not like it matters anyway. Let's just go. I'm done waiting. Dawn is only an hour away and they'll see us for sure. Plus, the longer we're out here, the more likely the Council is going to banish me… since I'm not there to defend myself."

The three day trip was steeped in a hostile silence. Attempts to diffuse the bitterness was shot down by single-word responses by The Wanderer. It wasn't until they had reached the far outskirts of the city on the third day that Gavin could not take her attitude any longer.

"I'm sorry okay?" he said as they left the crumbling city behind them. "I'm not good at this 'sneaking around' shit. I never was. That was why I went to Rapture in the first place. And the *one* time I get to see The Wanderer in action, we come up empty. Not a single battle and no evidence of their plans to attack you."

Eva clenched her fists, but took a deep breath, relaxed, and sighed. "It isn't your fault, Gavin. I doubted the Tiger's tower guards would know much anyway. The only way we would have gotten solid information was to infiltrate the

Gang, and that would just be stupid at this point. This was a last resort plan. I'm desperate."

"Doesn't seem strange to you, though? That we didn't find a single shred of evidence?"

He had a point. It was the very question that had haunted her for the entire return journey. Gangs were loud and messy. Their only enemies were each other, so there was no reason to cover their tracks. It was almost like the silence was intentional.

But how did they know I'd be out here? Once again, all signs pointed to an informant inside Rapture.

"Yeah," she finally responded. "I was thinking the exact same thing… I just don't know what I'm going to tell…"

Suddenly, her thoughts were cut short. She squinted toward the front gates of Rapture. A crowd appeared over the horizon as she closed the distance between them. It seemed as though they were blocking something at the gate. Her stomach began to churn. Would they stop her from entering the town? Had the Council decided on her banishment while she was gone? When she and Gavin finally reached the front entrance, she realized that the reality was *much* worse.

"*There* she is," a familiar, shrill voice said behind Eva as the crowd formed around her. People were spilling out of the gates to catch a glimpse of the display. "Do you recognize these people? *Speak*."

"What are you talking about?" Eva looked over the shoulders of the mob and her jaw dropped. She muttered an expletive under her breath and pushed the people aside. Gavin followed her, hand wrapped around his weapon.

Virginia was ready to strike. "What do you have to say for yourself?" There had to be something placing Eva as the culprit for this horrible scene.

Behind the line of Rapture's guards and citizens were two rows of stakes, one on either side of the gate. Sitting on top of each spear was a disembodied head. But these victims were familiar. Eva recognized them immediately. The smell of blood when she and Gavin were in the city must have come from the Eastern Rover Colony. These were the same men, women, and children she once protected.

Vomit rose into her throat. Dozens of heads were mounted on pikes, blood dripping down like candle wax. Each one had their mouths wide open, signifying the pain of their final moments. But worst of all was what Virginia had in her hand. A piece of parchment waved vigorously in front of Eva's face. Another message.

And this time, someone else had discovered it first.

"This note places the blame of everything *directly* on Eva Calloway." The eldest Councilwoman cleared her throat as the crowd quieted. "It reads: *Dearest Wanderer, I believe that now, I have left you a strong enough trail to find me. And since you have conveniently ensured my previous attempts to contact you went unanswered, I have no choice but to take matters further. This letter should find the hands of the Council before you attempt to cover it up again. Forgive me... for I cannot deny an opportunity to play with parasites like you before ending your miserable existence.*"

Suddenly, Eva was shoved to her knees and her hands were bound tightly behind her back. Bruce stepped out from behind the guards with a morose look. When their eyes met, he turned away, but she continued to shoot daggers in his direction. He started to say something, but the Councilwoman interrupted him.

"Oh I'm not done," Virginia grinned. Mara was standing between her mother and Jake, who watched the scene unfold with a blank stare. His numbness to what was unfolding only fueled Eva's rage. "It goes on and addresses us, the Citizens of Rapture. *If you continue to hide The Wanderer from my grasp, your fates will be similar to that of the Rovers displayed before you. Tigers do not take prisoners who have behaved so recklessly. Mercy is weakness. Nothing more. Consider this your final warning. Defy me again, and no child will be spared.*"

Eva dropped her head and stared at the ground. Her face felt white hot. She wanted to cut down Virginia, adding another stake to the front of Rapture, but there were too many guards on the Council's side now. They were no longer sympathetic to The Wanderer. No one was. Not even her beloved Jake. Only Gavin fought for her freedom. And he, too, was apprehended.

"She deserves protection as much as any of us," he spat as his arms were tied behind him. "We can fight one Gang."

"Not the Tigers," Bruce interjected. "We do not have the firepower to match them. Sure… we could easily protect our land from any of the Western Gangs, but we are unmatched against the East. They are far too large."

"Then put her under house arrest," he pleaded. He struggled against his chains and screamed at the top of his lungs. Eva was shaking her head at him, trying to get him to stop talking, but he ignored her. "*Something*. *Please*. Don't give her to the Tigers. She'll be tortured until she begs for death."

"I never beg," Eva murmured to herself.

Virginia closed her eyes and turned her back. Her perfectly symmetrical smile had not vanished. "It makes no difference to me what happens to her. We simply cannot have her here a second longer. My suspicions were correct since the day she stepped through those gates. It just took until this moment for all of you to see clearly. Just a shame, really. This… *failure*… could have been dealt with much sooner if everyone had listened to me from the beginning. Lives could have been spared. This monster is not one of us. She has *never* been one of us. And now, *all* of our lives are in jeopardy."

Eva's silence began to unnerve the crowd. One by one, their taunts of exile faded, replaced by an uneasy hush. They were beginning to sense it. The Wanderer was nearing her breaking point. Her Demon grew stronger than ever, placing its clawlike hand on her back, coercing her to "destroy them all." Eva could almost sense the heartbeat of every citizen in Rapture, humming ominously. If she was not surrounded by armored guards, she would have gone on a massacre. As she lifted her head to glance up at Jake, he turned away as Mara draped an arm around his shoulders.

Betrayal.

"...She deserves a fair trial." Gavin would not stop arguing. "Anything. Just don't give her to the Tigers. We have rules. This is *not* how Rapture operates."

Bruce held up his massive hand to silence everyone. "I agree… with Captain Gavin. Eva Calloway, you will be placed under house arrest until further notice. The Council needs to deliberate on how to proceed… and to clean up this… mess. Jake and Tommy McAvoy will be housed elsewhere. I believe that we have a few vacant homes that should suffice."

The entire town watched as The Wanderer was forcefully dragged back to her house. Tommy spotted her through the lines of people and, when he tried to intervene, his brother stopped him. Only the Demon followed to comfort Eva.

"Don't worry my dear," it cooed. "After we destroy them, you and I will battle once again."

Chapter 9

With a loud *slam,* Eva's door was locked and barred from the outside. She gradually rose to her feet from all fours and went over to the window. Darkness veiled her rage-filled stare as the guards also placed Gavin under house arrest. They shoved him into the home, kicked him a few times, bolted his door, and left. He called out something to her, but she could not discern what he was saying.

She began pacing up and down the hallway, trying to comprehend everything that had just happened. Without warning, her Shadow appeared from her daughter's old bedroom. It stood in the doorway, shrouded in an eerie silence. Numbness began to overtake Eva's body. A lone thing clung to her mind. One single word. *Revenge.*

"Tommy and Jake *used* you." The Shadow of Dan McAvoy spoke. "They used you as a human shield until you got them to safety… and now…"

"Now they won't even speak against Rapture for my safety," Eva said softly to herself. She turned back and stared at Gavin's home. He was pacing back-and-forth across the window. "Or my life."

She could feel the warmth of her Demon's breath against her neck. "I am the only friend you have left. The only friend you need… but perhaps Gavin's loyalty will prove useful."

"Please," she whispered as a tear fell down her cheek. Her voice cracked with emotion. "I didn't ask for any of this. I just want to be my old self again."

"Oh my dear Wanderer, it is *far* too late for that," Dan McAvoy's voice hummed in her ear. It was melodic, but hollow. "Time to embrace the darkness. If you accept it, I promise that the transformation will be much less painful."

First came sadness. Then anger.

"I will *never*," Eva spun around, nearly knocking over a shelf. Her blade was out in front of her, slicing through the imaginary being.

Her Demon responded with a cackle and floated over to the corner of the room, resting against a nearby wall. "You *will* become me the moment you end me," it warned, then it disappeared.

Eva sheathed her blade and slumped against a nearby table, staring at the space where her Shadow had been. *I killed the real McAvoy. He's already dead.* Any attempt to convince herself that the Tiger Chief had died was now meaningless. When Virginia read the note to Rapture, the truth became undeniable. Only one person would massacre an entire town for spectacle.

"...I have left you a strong enough trail to find me." the voice of her Shadow whispered. It was repeating the words from the note. "...I have no choice but to take matters further."

Eva's heart was racing. The thought of Dan McAvoy's survival made her sick. Denial made it worse. He was alive and he knew exactly where she was hiding. Rather than start a war between Rapture and his Gang, he had chosen to slowly chip away at The Wanderer's sanity. She was much easier to target if there was no one willing to protect her.

Oddly, the part of her that had once ruled the Serpents stirred, faintly impressed by his use of power. *Turning an entire town against me,* it noted. *A bold tactic.*

But there was still one detail that continued to bother her. *There is simply no way he could have done this alone.*

Knowing where Eva was at all times. Planning and carrying out numerous attacks on her and her family without being detected by anyone. There had to be someone within Rapture carrying out his plans. But who?

***

"What a shame." Mara closed the door behind Jake and Tommy. She volunteered her home to be the brothers' temporary residence. Her and Virginia's home had four bedrooms, so they had plenty of space for the McAvoy brothers. Tommy nodded in thanks, dropped the bag with his belongings in his room, and disappeared in the direction of the farms. Jake was far too distraught to continue working. He just went over to a window and stared toward the direction of his home. Mara could sense the tension.

"Jacob, you must understand," she started. "This is *necessary* for our protection. How do you think that Rapture has existed for so long? You are safe. *We* are safe. And whoever's attacking us will stop if Eva is banished or executed. The note-"

Jake clenched his fists as tears welled up in his eyes. "You cannot allow this in good conscience."

"It is not my place to speak for the people," she said.

He grabbed her shoulders and shook her gently. "Then convince your mother. Demand that she change her mind. The rest of the Council will listen to her."

The slender blonde woman crossed her arms and furrowed her brow. "You would follow that woman to oblivion," she snapped. "Asking me to go against my better judgment—and the judgment of the entire town—is complete insanity. Admit it. Eva wants *nothing* to do with you anymore, Jacob. She doesn't love you. She doesn't care about anyone but herself. Otherwise, she would have left a long time ago. If she really loved you, she wouldn't still be here."

Jake closed his eyes tight and faced the wall. He imagined Mara's comment seeping into the brick and began to believe every word. The quietest voice in his head was still fighting for Eva, but it was becoming more and more distant. He struggled with the realization.

Shit. Mara's right. If Eva cared about my safety, she'd understand that staying here only puts us both in danger. Along with everyone else. When I look into her eyes, I don't see the same person I fell for. There's no more warmth behind her eyes. Maybe... she never really loved me, she just believed she did. How could someone surrounded by so much destruction even be capable of loving another person? All she's ever known is death...

Mara noticed his demeanor change and drifted over to him, sliding her hands around his shoulders. He rested his head on hers and closed his eyes. Something seemed comfortable in her embrace. It felt different. Safe. He allowed himself to take in the feeling for a moment before leaving to search for his brother.

As the crowd dispersed in front of Rapture's gates, Tommy returned to the farms, deep in thought. He had been too afraid to speak up for Eva, even though he knew in his heart she wasn't responsible for any of it. She had been relentlessly pursued by the Gangs for most of her life, and her years in Rapture were no exception. But when he was kidnapped by the Tigers, she had risked her own life to save him. Eva was not the monster everyone was trying to make her out to be. He just needed time to make sense of it all.

Luckily, he spotted Jake walking toward his shop.

He rushed over and pulled him aside. "What's going on? I wasn't able to see what happened. Why did they put her on house arrest?"

The older brother paused. "You left so quickly. I looked everywhere for you. Eva's Rovers were murdered by the Tigers. McAvoy left a note. Apparently Eva has been covering up evidence. Can you believe that? She tried to show me something after our wedding ceremony, but I trusted she would have told the Council by now. I hate to say it Tommy, but even if Eva isn't causing the attacks, she's the reason they're happening."

Tommy became angry. Why was his brother so quick to dismiss the woman who saved their lives in the Vault?

"If it was anyone else, Jake, Rapture would not be trying to force banishment so hard," he replied sternly. "It's only because she's The Wanderer."

"Or is it because she caused an entire Gang to target this city?" Jake said. "Her chaotic nature is what made her famous out there, but dangerous in here. We aren't on the move anymore. We can't just *hide* anywhere. The Tigers know *exactly* where we are. And dad… he's still…"

The thought of their father's survival sent chills across their bodies. If he knew where they were hiding, he would stop at nothing to find them. And once they were finally captured, would he torture them? Or would he just end their lives with one fell swoop?

But Tommy's attempt to reassure his brother fell short. "He's dead. Come on Jake. You know he's dead."

"Tommy." Jake sighed. "She didn't kill him. That note… It was him."

Both of them felt their stomachs drop to the ground.

Jake knew his brother supported Eva. But his own thoughts had already begun to shift away from the Wanderer and toward his own survival. His daughter was dead, so Tommy was the only family he had left.

***

Days in solitude passed and Eva's sanity began to decline even further. A negative energy seemed to drape over the home. She felt helpless. Hopeless. The only thing she could do was allow the darkness to fill the desolate rooms. Her Shadow was becoming stronger, and the likeness to Chief

McAvoy was becoming more indistinguishable. She did not sleep more than a few hours at a time. She barely ate. The only solace she found was in the company of her journal.

THEY CANNOT UNDERSTAND HOW MUCH I HAVE SUFFERED. I NEVER CHOSE THIS LIFE. I WAS FORCED INTO IT. I NO LONGER KNOW FOR CERTAIN WHAT IS REAL AND WHAT ISN'T. IS THIS "THING" REALLY JUST A SHADOW? NOW THAT I'M ALONE, HE COULD BE PLAYING TRICKS ON ME. NO ONE WOULD KNOW. EVERYONE IS LYING.

JAKE AND TOMMY SAID NOTHING WHILE I WAS DRAGGED TO MY HOME LIKE AN ANIMAL. PEOPLE OF RAPTURE – A WARNING TO YOU ALL- BE AWARE OF WHO YOU ARE MESSING WITH. MY SANITY WILL SNAP AT ANY MOMENT. IT MAY HAVE ALREADY SNAPPED. I'M EVEN TERRIFIED OF MYSELF SOMETIMES... WHAT I COULD BECOME... WHAT I AM BECOMING... WHAT I HAVE BECOME.

GAVIN MUST BE CRAZY BY NOW. OR MAYBE THIS ENTIRE THING WAS AN ACT AND THEY LET HIM GO THE MOMENT I HID MYSELF. I LOOK OUT BUT I DON'T ALWAYS SEE HIM. MAYBE HE TOOK

MY PLACE? NO, HE WOULDN'T DO THAT. HE ISN'T JAKE. HE HASN'T BETRAYED ME... YET. BUT STILL, WHY WOULD HE BE ANY DIFFERENT FROM ANYONE ELSE? WHY IS HE SO LOYAL TO ME? IS THERE SOMETHING I'M MISSING?

THE HOUSE SEEMS TO BREATHE WITH ME NOW. GROANING WITH EACH INHALE AND WHISPERING WITH THE EXHALE. TO ME, IT'S CALMING. I'M BEGINNING TO ENJOY THE SOUND. I FEEL LESS LONELY. IT'S BECOMING ME. OR AM I BECOMING IT? THE HOUSE OR THE SHADOW? PERHAPS IT WILL KNOW AND MAYBE I SHOULD ASK?

SOMETIMES I TALK TO IT. COMPANY IS COMPANY. HE... IT... THEY... ME? BUT I THINK, MAYBE HE WILL TELL ME SOMETHING I DO NOT KNOW. IF HE DOES, I'LL KNOW IT ISN'T ALL IN MY HEAD. I'LL KNOW HE IS REAL. AND I WILL STRIKE HIM DOWN. SOMEHOW...

The entries became more paranoid and less coherent as sleep deprivation began to set in. Muscles ached and eyes burned. By the fifth day, she closed her eyes and felt herself dive into another inescapable nightmare.

***

The Wanderer found herself standing at the heart of the Tiger's compound, near the bonfires. Jake and Tommy fed wood to the flames, never once looking her way. One by one, others gathered around her. Faces she recognized immediately—Gavin, Wanda, William, Elaine, Yidi, Masha, Anya. Those who had stood by her, fought for her, remained loyal. Each one of them was chained to their place and could not move. Neither could she.

A pedestal appeared beneath her feet and transformed into a stage. It lifted her high above the crowd, so the whole region could watch The Wanderer's final breath. At her back, she could hear the whispers of hundreds of people. Possibly thousands. The moment she turned to face the noise, the color drained from her face.

Victims from her past stood upon the platform. Their faces were gaunt and still bore the fatal wounds that Eva had given them. White rags, saturated in bright red blood. Some had been decapitated, others were disemboweled. There were so many that she could not see them all. After the first few rows of people, it was only the haze of gray silhouettes. But she could hear every single one of them. Their whispers became deafening. And they were all chanting the same thing.

"*Justice for our lives*."

Suddenly, a figure ascended the stairs at the side of the stage, lingering on each one. Her executioner. A cloth hood hid his face, his leather armor the color of midnight, brushed with crimson. She didn't need to see his face to know who would end her life. His voice echoed through the compound, dripping with grandeur.

"Look behind me," Dan McAvoy addressed an unknown audience. "You will see the thousands of lives taken by this woman. One. Single. Person. As the Serpent's Mistress, she unleashed nothing but desolation. Nothing but corpses and a river—nay, an *ocean*—of blood. Today, she will drown in it. The time has come when we finally have our retribution. Behold, the most *lethal* human of our era."

McAvoy wasted no time in unsheathing one of Eva's own blades and placing it at her neck. She could not move, no matter how hard she struggled to break free. She was paralyzed. Now, her throat would be sliced open in front of everyone.

This is the end. This is my execution. My final moments.

As the sharp blade slid across her throat, an intense pain shot down to her legs. Every wound she'd received over a lifetime started to burn. Whippings from her time as a Doxie, bullet wounds from battling Gangs, emotional trauma splitting open her head. The pain was so strong, she made a terrifying noise that sounded completely inhuman. And the moment after the blade was lifted, the scene dissipated.

She woke up.

***

While Eva contained and repressed her Demon once more, Gavin was scheming. He needed to reach the Wanderer's home, where they could plan their escape from Rapture, head north, and search for evidence to clear her name once more. Their last journey had come up empty because of him, and he was determined to make it right. If they managed to escape, maybe Eva wouldn't want to return. Not after everything that had happened. But if she insisted on staying, he would follow her all the same.

Guards had been posted along the street. At dawn and dusk each day, the shift would change, leaving the homes unguarded for about five minutes. That was the only opportunity for Gavin to break out the back door and climb through one of Eva's windows. Because he was not very wide, slipping through an opening would be simple. The difficult part was leaving his home without drawing any attention.

Intuition must have sparked something in Eva's mind because she rushed over to the largest window in her home and carefully pried it open. Across the lawn, she noticed Gavin's silhouette against the candlelight in his home. He waved to her and peeked his head out to see if their street had been vacated. She followed suit. No torchlight bobbing across the cobblestone. Gavin made his move.

As quickly and quietly as he could, he busted open the lock on his back door with a hammer. He braced for the sound. With a loud bang, he threw open the door and peeked outside. The noise echoed towards the Town Square, but nothing stirred. Before Eva could check to see if anyone had heard the commotion, she tripped backwards as Gavin tumbled into her home.

"Shit," he said, placing his hands on his knees to try and catch his breath. "I haven't moved like that in a while. I'm getting out of shape."

Eva laughed under her breath and looked down at him, the weight of it catching her off guard. She had spent her life protecting, sacrificing, enduring. Now, for the first time, she realized someone was willing to risk everything for her—his life, his status—without asking for anything in return.

Suddenly, they heard footsteps coming up the path to her home.

A heavily armed guard rapped hard on the door. Gavin barely managed to slide beneath Eva's bed before they burst inside. One of them slammed her against the wall while the others tore through the home. She stared into the face of the young man who held her back. The scent of fear filled her nostrils as his body quivered against hers.

Fortunately, not a single one of them thought to check under the bed. And just as swiftly as they came, the battalion was down the street and out of sight. Gavin and Eva breathed a sigh of relief and immediately began planning.

"Now that I'm in this as deep as you," he started. "I don't think either of us will get a nice plea bargain with the Council at this point. But we have to hurry. Let's get out of here and try to collect some *actual* evidence."

"No." Eva replied. Gavin's heart dropped. "There is only one piece of evidence that will sway them now. I have to do this alone."

He grabbed her forearm and met her gaze. "You know that I won't let you do that. We're going together. After what the Tiger Chief did to the Rovers -."

"They deserve what they got." When she finished her sentence, her Demon appeared and applauded her cruel comment. "If you didn't know this already, but they also banished me. Look what happened. I warned them."

"I don't care what happened to the Rovers." He started to raise his voice. "I care about *you*. Dammit. Why don't you get that? Obviously, the Tigers have a lot more men than we do in Rapture. And the Council is willing to cast you out to save their own asses. I want to learn from *you* and fight by *your* side. You know that I'm more than capable. Way more capable than the man who claimed he loved you all this time. Then, when you need it most, he says *nothing* when the entire town is calling for your head. I'm sorry, but it seems to me like Jake just risked your life, over and over again, until you brought him and Tommy to safety. Now that they're here, they don't give a shit if you're sent back."

His comments were almost identical to Eva's Shadow. It felt like the entire weight of the house was pushing on her chest. *Maybe Gavin is right.* But she could not convince herself that Jake and Tommy cared so little for her. After everything they had been through in the last six years, the brothers promised to be by her side forever. She had to give them one more chance.

Gavin noticed she was drifting off. "Either way, I'm coming with you. At least to find some sort of evidence. There has to be something out there that points the attacks back to someone inside Rapture. It has to be something undeniable. That's the only way they'll let you go—"

"Stop." She grabbed his hands tightly. "I need you here. You must appeal to the Council. *All of them*. Stall their decision. Something. Anything. I don't care if you have to lie to do it. But when I come back, I need every piece of information that I can get. You need to keep them from carrying out an execution if I return. Gavin, if you are truly loyal to me, please do this. *Please*. I need you."

He let out a long, labored sigh. She pressed her forehead against his and closed her eyes. As much as he wanted to fight by Eva's side, it would have to wait. Her Captain reluctantly agreed. If there was a small chance she would be restored to her original position within the Council, he would act as a spy. If Virginia was planning to banish or execute The Wanderer, they would have to plan.

"Best case scenario," she continued softly. "I find something criminalizing Virginia. Placing her as the culprit for murdering Anya and orchestrating these attacks. If I can get that much… I'll personally oversee her trial. Judge, jury, *and* executioner. Torture would be a merciful punishment for such a crime."

An iciness sparked through Eva's heart. Her bloodlust was becoming blinding. Dan McAvoy was still alive. And if her Demon was foreshadowing another battle between them, so be it. She would gladly strike him down a second time.

Tonight, she thought. *I'm sneaking out. I need to get out of this place.*

She repeated her thoughts aloud. "I'm going into the West. The Warriors know more about their Gangs than Rapture knows of the Tigers or Serpents. They should be able to help me."

"I hope you find whatever you're looking for Eva," Gavin said. "I will be here awaiting your return."

"And I won't return until I'm satisfied."

Gavin did not understand what she meant by the comment, but nodded all the same. He stayed in her home for another hour until the guards disappeared down at the end of the street. Just before he turned to leave through the same window he slipped through before, he hugged Eva tightly, wishing her luck.

"Come back in one piece, okay?" he said and disappeared into the yard.

Eva wasted no time. The moment her Captain was out of sight, she sheathed her blades, threw on the rest of her armor, slid out into the lawn through the same window, and crept through the darkness of the neighborhood. She would escape through the hole in Rapture's perimeter wall, but the trail to the old Training Grounds would be watched by Rapture's army, so she had to focus. She channeled all of her skills in order to survive the three-hundred-foot stretch between her prison and freedom.

From this false utopia, she thought. *What if I don't come back?*

The Wanderer's heart raced with excitement as she wove between homes, ducked beneath windows where citizens ate peacefully, and avoided the night watch. Just beyond the Town Square, she spotted the gaping hole in the outer wall. There was nowhere to hide now. Only an empty field separated her from the exit. Eva's eyes swept the area, her head on a swivel. No guards in sight. She dug the toes of her boots into the earth and burst into a sprint.

Her feet pounded against the stone. *Only a few more feet,* she breathed. Her Shadow floated beside her, matching her pace. *Let luck be on my side.*

Unbeknownst to her, Jake was standing at Mara's window, staring at the hole to the city. A sudden movement caught his eye and he locked onto it, a silhouette at the Town Square. In the moonlight, he could make out a faint figure racing across the cobblestone. It was Eva, and he knew exactly what she was doing.

She doesn't trust this place anymore. Guilt began to twist his insides. *And why should she? I didn't even stick up for her.*

But why would you? Another voice called from inside his head. *She's put your life at risk more times than you can count. You're finally safe. You have a life here. The actions against your father caused the death of Anya. It only makes sense that you and Tommy would be next if she stayed.*

Jake resolved to stay silent about what he had witnessed, but he would no longer allow Eva to pull him into reckless decisions. His mind was made up. She was becoming more dangerous than he had ever known—or perhaps she always had been, and he had simply refused to see it until now. Deep down, he prayed that she would not return. For his safety *and* for hers.

***

Passing through the hole in Rapture's wall and scaling down the cliff, Eva eventually reached the skeletal remains of ancient homes. A wave of relief hit hard enough to bring tears to her eyes. For the first time in years, she didn't have the burden of protecting another's life.

The Wanderer was alone… and it felt good.

Unfortunately, emotions were short-lived. The second she crossed the city's threshold, the energy shifted. It felt like she was being watched. The air was thick with tension and uneasiness. Her stomach began twisting in knots. Before she let the doubt consume her, she caught herself.

Calm down. You can do this.

Eva took a deep breath, closed her eyes, and unsheathed her blades.

Years spent in the "false sense of security" that Rapture provided had undeniably dulled her awareness. As she channeled her old self, the doubt slowly dissolved. Her senses awakened, honing in on the source of the city's negativity. That would be her first target.

Someone is watching me. I can feel it. And it doesn't feel friendly.

It did not take long before she heard the faint noise of crumbling rubble. Whoever was stalking her had tripped. She turned around to try and catch a glimpse of her prey, but only the cloud of dust remained. Suddenly, a crash of metal echoed from a nearby building. *They're getting sloppy.* A sly smile crept across Eva's face. *Gotcha.* It was time to hunt for her prey.

Eva vanished down an alley near the source of the sound. Her movements were silent, but she advanced with agility and speed. Another set of footsteps caused her to whip around, slipping on some gravel. Fortunately, she was able to get her bearings and bolted into a nearby building before being seen.

As she carefully peered around the corner, The Wanderer caught sight of an armor-clad shadow at the next block. They'd heard her, but had no idea where she'd gone. She wasn't close enough to attack. And if it was a Gang member with a gun, she'd be shot before she ever reached them.

No. Confrontation was too risky. She had to stay quiet.

She had to hunt.

If fate was on her side, she could make them talk.

The Wanderer approached the shape from a safe distance. Just like the animals that had trained her in stealth, she waited, studying her prey for a while. Only after she knew who they were would she make her move.

With each step, she matched her opponent's pace so perfectly that the Gang member couldn't tell that she was closing in. Eva soon discovered that this woman was from the Foxes, a Gang she had rarely encountered.

There were only a few details she knew about the Foxes. Every one of their fighters was female, and despite their small size, they were undoubtedly the deadliest Gang in the West. But one fact gave Eva a slight advantage—Foxes always traveled alone. While Gangs like the Tigers prized brute strength, these warriors relied on stealth.

Eva crept around the city until she found a spot where she could kidnap the woman. The place she finally chose to strike was the same motel where she, Jake, and Tommy had spent a winter recovering from their injuries. Back when they had taken care of one another.

So much has changed since then.

Hastening footsteps. A muffled scream. Blade hilt cracking against a skull. The sound of dragging an unconscious body. What was once second-nature to Eva had resurfaced. *Bind with this knot, not that. Search nearby buildings to see if there are more.* This was routine. The Wanderer felt invincible as she sat down and waited for Fox to wake.

Urges to take this pitiful life instantly began to make her sweat. Although her Demon was not visible, its voice whispered in her ear.

"Do it. Finish her. End her miserable existence." Dan McAvoy's voice echoed in the space around her. "Stop resisting or I will take matters into my own hands."

Without warning, Eva felt herself stand up. It was her body, but she was no longer in control. She replaced her blade with a smaller knife. *Closer,* whispered her own disembodied voice. *Closer and more personal. Allow the blood to splatter against your face as you once did. Death becomes you. You are the slaughterer of many. It is what you were born to do. Messenger of Death.*

She began to panic. *What the shit is going on? Stop. STOP.*

A buzzing sound in her ears then all at once, Eva was thrust violently back into her own body. The force was so strong, it knocked her backwards. She rubbed her eyes and looked at the knife in her hand. It was not covered in blood. The woman was still unconscious, but not for much longer.

The Wanderer screamed as her soul slammed back into the shell of her body. Her captive awoke with a start. When the woman realized what had happened, she began to struggle. Eva quickly shook off her shock and stepped forward. Her eyes were locked eyes with the Fox, whose expression flickered with malicious intent.

Eva saw her turn the heel of her boot outward. The glint of a hidden blade caught The Wanderer's attention. Her eyes widened as she scrambled to the boot quick enough to knock it from the Fox's grasp.

"Nice try." Eva pointed the blade toward her captive. "You'd better not try anything like that again. I'm just here for answers. So, if you give me your *complete* cooperation, I may let you live."

The woman spat in her face. "Kill me then. Save us both time. You'll get no information out of me. If you were a true warrior, you would fight me to the death. But all I see is a *coward*."

The Fox's long, brown hair fell over her face as she lunged at Eva. The chair she was tied to lifted off the ground and drug a few feet across the floor. The Wanderer simply took two calm steps back.

"That is not how I play my game. *I* make the rules. Information first, then I may give you an honorable death in which you would have the pleasure of fighting me. Or, if you are incredibly lucky, I will let you leave."

Both of them knew the second option was a lie.

"You are a nobody. I will gut you with ease."

Eva laughed. "A nobody? This *nobody* followed you for hours and now holds your life in their hands. I'll admit, it has been a while since my presence was felt in this region. Five years is a long time… but you should pay closer attention to who you speak to. Especially before you start making promises we both know you can't keep."

The woman matched her cackle. "You speak as though you're a legend or some bullshit. I know *nothing* of the likes of you."

Before the Fox could blink, Eva's blade was pressed against her neck. The woman stiffened and looked down at the weapon, recognizing it immediately. When her chocolate-colored eyes met the aqua gaze of The Wanderer, she gasped.

"You-you-you cannot be her," she stuttered. Beads of sweat formed on her brow, sticking strands of hair to her face. "But t-t-those blades. No. The Wanderer is a *Rover*. She lives with the Rovers."

Eva masked the initial confusion in her mind. "Wrong. It has been and always will be me."

"No. She's been causing chaos in the West for the last few years. All of us have lost numbers. We can't fight the Warriors. They're too strong. They protect The Wanderer and she protects them. Just like she did with the Eastern Rovers before… before the Tigers… How did you get those blades? Did you kill her?"

"Why would you assume that someone who does *not* carry these is The Wanderer?"

"I've never seen her. Only stories. Few who cross her survive. But I've heard of *those* blades. They are legendary. Please. Don't kill me. I-I'm not ready to die."

Eva wasn't listening. "This woman you speak of is nothing but an imposter. Tell me what you know of her… *now*."

The woman broke down. Tears cascaded down her face. As Eva inspected the woman more closely, she realized she was just a kid—barely sixteen or seventeen. She was probably out scavenging the city for supplies. Wrong place at the wrong time. Even the tattoo on her arm looked fairly new—a cursive *F*.

Pity.

Eva grew more concerned about the person using her title to murder members of the Western Gangs. Dan McAvoy and the Tigers would have to wait. She repeated her demand.

"What do you know? I need every detail. *NOW*."

"I already told you," the young woman sobbed. "Her home is with the Western Rovers. She's dark-skinned. Um… also-also… her mother traveled from the East. From the compounds. I only know that because the Tigers sent out Scouts to gather information about escapees a few years ago. Please don't kill me. I told you everything I know. You promised."

Revelation hit Eva like a ton of bricks.

She knew exactly who was impersonating her.

Elaine. You bitch.

Chapter 10

Long after the young Fox's throat was sliced open, The Wanderer's mind fixated on her next victim.

Elaine. Going around and slaughtering the Gangs to try and steal my title? I earned that title. She'll pay for this.

"Play with fire long enough," her Shadow growled. "Eventually, it will burn you."

The Wanderer headed West. Her route eventually took her through the northeastern part of the region, along streets she had seldom traveled. There was a slight chance that McAvoy had Tigers waiting for her in the darkness of the woods, so her instinct was to bypass the forest entirely.

Once she reached the unfamiliar parts of the crumbling metropolis, Eva slowed her pace. The landscape was similar to that of the city's center. Rubble filled the streets and the few buildings that were left standing were far too dangerous to enter. Some pathways had been cut into the rocky hills, possibly by the Gangs or Nomads traveling that direction. It appeared one of the Old Time bombs had fallen in this section of the city as well.

It was grueling work for Eva to traverse these mountains of stone and brick. Where she thought she had a good footing, she would place her boot and instantly sink up to her knees in the loose rock. Underneath the solid material was only fine dust. She cursed and pulled herself to the top of the rubble each time, sweating profusely by the time she made it to a clearing. Exhaustion overtook her limbs and Eva slumped against the corner of a wall and wiped her forehead.

"Shit," she breathed. Her stomach yawned with hunger. "I forgot to pack food."

After about an hour of rest, Eva continued her journey. The initial anger towards Elaine still had not subsided. Rather, plans of exacting revenge arose as she traveled. Eva had admired the Warrior's bluntness when they first met. Now it seemed that same disregard for the Wanderer may have pushed her to take on the name. Perhaps it was envy. Or some delusional sense of retribution and glory. Either way, it must have been her mother, Wanda, who told Elaine everything that happened in the Tiger's Den. That was the only way she could have known Eva had deserted the region.

"But why?" That was the real question. "What possessed her to do this? And to what end?"

McAvoy must know that Elaine's not the real Wanderer. Otherwise, he would be attacking the Warriors, not Rapture. That's proof Virginia's working with him.

"Why are you still trying to deny my survival?" The skeletal hand of her Shadow clawed across her back as it slid from one shoulder to the other. She winced as the clawmarks burned beneath her armor. "There is no other rational explanation for these events. You know this to be true, yet you still continue to deny the facts. It will be the death of you. Just embrace it. Embrace me."

The Wanderer pushed the thoughts of battle out of her mind and focused on getting to the Warrior colony, finding Elaine, and exacting her revenge. Only a half-day journey now stood between her and the Western Rovers, but she no longer had to zigzag through the city. She could make it in a few hours if she hurried.

And she didn't waste a second. Soon, at the edge of the horizon, the faint outline of shacks emerged in rigid rows. She neared the bustling settlement and spotted their leader,

William, immediately. The flash of fear in his eyes when they went to shake hands caught her off guard.

"Wanderer, I believed you to be dead," he admitted, bowing his head. "But what folly it is that I would believe such a thing. 'Tis not in my nature to trust word of mouth and rumors for the untimely demise of someone so great."

"Cut the shit," Eva was tired of playing around. William's games made her suspect that he was hiding something. "Tell me where Elaine is."

He flinched. "She left yesterday. Truly. But why do you wish to speak to her? Is there nothing I or my people can aid you with?"

"Quit playing around. You know why I'm here." Eva did not want to intimidate William with her blades because a small group of his Warriors now surrounded them. But that did not deter her from using a threatening tone.

"She simply desired to carry on your name," he confessed. "At least, that is what she told us. But we know nothing of her actions. I swear it on my honor. I took her at her word, for she has never given me reason to believe she was deceiving us. Now that I see you here, I begin to question her true intentions. Perhaps trusting her was foolish of me."

"In the city, I came across a Fox. She told me that *The Wanderer* was murdering Gang Members all across the West."

William shook his head. "This is not good at all. Absolutely not. We cannot have this happen. They will join forces and wipe us off the map. We can hold back a single Gang, but war against them all… It would be inconceivable."

"What Gangs are left here?" she demanded.

"The previous time you stepped into our midst, as you are well aware, the Wolves were attacked by the Rats. Both of their compounds were decimated. And rather than battling into oblivion, they are now bound by a peace treaty and operate two smaller settlements. Aside from that, there have been no changes. We took the stillness to mean that they were operating peacefully."

"There is *never* peace between the Gangs. Because of Elaine's actions, they'll probably strike soon. That peace treaty may have been to unify at first, but with a common enemy… your town is under threat. Which one is her home?"

The Warrior's leader pointed to the closest shack to their Meal Hall. "I cannot bestow justice with the heaviness in my heart. Will you help us? Please?"

Eva paused and decided to deflect the question. "I have unfinished business that I need to attend to."

"I understand," William nodded softly. "All of us are at fault for this one. We cannot expect you to fight our own battles for us. But Elaine's actions cannot continue."

"And I intend to end them," Eva started walking towards Elaine's home. "*Permanently*."

William knew what The Wanderer intended and still did not try to stop her. He, too, understood the grave mistake that Elaine had made. She was putting her family and friends at risk of invasion, torture, or a slow, painful death. Because their leader did not raise a hand against Eva, the rest of the Warriors allowed her to enter Elaine's home and wait for her return. A cook even handed her a plate of food as she passed.

No one would come running when they heard the screams that night.

***

Weighing every possible outcome of her encounter with Elaine, Eva resolved to get as much information from her as possible. The Rover would have much more intel on the Gangs than many of her other allies. And that could be useful in gathering evidence to bring to Rapture. But there would undoubtedly be a scuffle. Elaine was a trained Warrior, and every movement had to be precise if Eva was going to subdue her without killing her.

That's what she would want. Eva stared out the window from a shadowy corner of the room. *She will beg for death. Getting out any information will be difficult, but I'm always up for a challenge.*

She was starting to sound like her old self again. Not the Eva Calloway that guarded the Rover colony, but the young woman that overthrew the Serpent's Chief unarmed, only to grow into a merciless tyrant in an attempt to unify the Gangs under one leader. Although she would never admit it to Jake, Tommy, or possibly even Gavin, she longed to return to the Serpents. With an ever-growing army at her disposal and the ability to conquer those around her, she would be almost invincible.

Almost.

Eva studied the Warriors from Elaine's window while she waited. They were much more spirited than the Eastern Rovers she once protected. Children played in the streets, practicing fighting techniques with sticks and makeshift wooden swords. A few of their parents watched and critiqued them while others tended to their gardens and sparred with the other Warriors. Eventually, everyone made their way to the Food Hall for the evening meal. Eva stole a few pieces of fruit from Elaine's cupboard and finished up the plate of food she was given. As dusk settled over the town, the imposter returned from her journey.

Elaine sensed another presence the moment she entered her home. The Wanderer watched from the shadows as the Warrior unsheathed one of her daggers and crept around, lifting furniture and looking behind her doors. But Eva was ready.

"Hello *Wanderer*," she said melodically. Elaine dropped her weapon as she spun and tripped. She scrabbled to her knees, reaching for the blade. Her fingers brushed the hilt, but she struck it too hard. The knife skidded across the floor to Eva, who pinned it beneath her boot and dragged it out of reach. "Thought I was dead, *huh*? Now that you know I'm alive, I'm sure you can guess why I'm here."

The Warrior started backing up when Eva brandished her blade. Her hands raised in her defense. "Calm down. You have to understand. I only wanted to carry on your name–"

"Wrong," she interrupted. "You wanted to carry on the *fear* that my name brings. Even William understands that your recklessness is putting The Warriors in danger. They aren't even going to stop me for what I'm about to do to you. But first… I need some information."

"If my life will still be ended whether or not I give you the information, why should I cooperate?"

"Because I haven't made up my mind yet. Perhaps the evidence you've gathered from the Gangs will change the outcome of my decision."

"I don't believe you. The Wanderer never shows mercy."

"Are you willing to risk your life against that belief?"

A pause. A sigh. Then the imposter dropped her head in submission.

The Wanderer used the tip of her blade and pointed to a nearby chair. Elaine sat down, awaiting the first question. Voices from outside the home had all but disappeared. Eva lied about sparing the Warrior's life, but it was necessary to gain any shred of useful evidence. She drew shut the curtains and lit a candle, placing it on the table between them. After clearing her throat, she began the interrogation.

"So before I begin, I suppose I owe you an explanation as to where I have been the past few years." *Not that it matters anyway, since you will be dead in a few hours.*

Elaine nodded slowly, keeping her gaze fixated on Eva's blade.

"After infiltrating the Tigers' compound and attempting to kill their Chief to save Jake and Tommy, we were forced out of the region. We ended up in a town I'd never seen before. Rapture. They took us in and gave me a position on their Council. I had a child…"

She trailed off and became enveloped by grief. *Anya. My little girl. The only light in this horribly dark world.* She recalled her daughter's final moments and the words "I'm scared," echoed in her mind. Elaine noticed.

"So you are human after all." The dark-skinned Warrior leaned in, her face illuminated by candlelight. Any trace of fear had vanished from her eyes.

Eva's hand clenched tighter around the hilt of her blade until her knuckles turned white. "I said *had.* She was murdered. I was attacked… and I believe it was the Tigers. But when I found out that *you* had been going around impersonating me… I figured we should have a little *chat* to see what you know."

Silence crept through the shack. Eva could faintly make out the hum of voices down the street. Crickets chirped just outside the door, and the chitter of birds had grown softer than it had been an hour earlier. As twilight deepened, the forest echoed with the haunting cries of wolves and coyotes.

The true Wanderer grew restless. She slammed her blade against the doorframe, the clang cutting through the quiet. "Let's begin, shall we? Assuming that you were able to get *some* information out of the Gang Members that you tortured during your rampage, perhaps you've heard something about the Tiger's Chief. I need to know what you know. *Everything*."

Eva could tell by the way that Elaine looked at her that she had an answer. When she spoke, the interrogator saw straight through her lie. "That shit doesn't matter to me. I don't know shit about the Tigers *or* their Chief."

"Strike one, Elaine. I have a sixth sense about people, you know. And you are a very poor liar. It makes you look just as guilty as them. *Speak*, or I will remove a hand. Or possibly… a foot. You would be useless… What would William think?"

Veins in Elaine's neck pulsated violently and she swallowed hard. The last comment seemed to have hit the hardest because she squirmed in the chair. Eva rose to her feet and took a step around the table, towards her. The Rover Warrior straightened up. During their first meeting, long ago, the woman had seemed strong and brave. That fearlessness vanished at the tip of the Wanderer's blade.

The only person in the region who was not afraid to face me was Dan McAvoy…

"Please don't kill me," the dark-skinned Warrior begged. "If I tell you what I know, just don't kill me. Would I have known that you were still alive…"

Eva finished her sentence and then raised her voice. "...You wouldn't be *pretending*, right? Fulfilling a fantasy that you knew you could never live up to? It was for your own sick pleasure, nothing more. So tell me what I want to know or present your throat so I can rip it out." The Wanderer's voice cracked with anger.

Elaine was just stalling for time, hoping someone would rescue her. She threw her hands up in surrender. "Okay, okay… I'll tell you. Just - don't - do - anything - stupid."

Suddenly, The Warrior sprung out of her chair, knocking it over, and hurled a knife at Eva. There was a clang of metal on metal as The Wanderer barely dodged the weapon. It skidded across the floor and clanged against the wall. Just as Eva looked up, Elaine knocked the blade out of her hand and they wrestled to the ground, but Eva was far more practiced in hand-to-hand combat.

Ten seconds later, the Warrior lay pinned beneath her. Eva's blade was back in her hand, pressed against the woman's neck.

"*Enough is enough*," she warned through gritted teeth. "I'm not playing anymore. You are going to tell me what I need to know or you will *wish* you were dead. No one is coming to save you. Understand? William knows what I'm doing here and actually asked me to help him by ending your life. Actions have consequences. You are a danger to these people. They care *nothing* for you anymore."

She let out a shaky laugh as a tear slid down her cheek. "Me? What about you? You deserted the Rovers you once protected. They were massacred by the Tigers. You want to know about their Chief? I *saw* him… dressed in black and clad with a crimson cape."

"You saw him?" Eva repeated, eyes widening. "Describe him. What did he look like… *tell me*."

"Why does it matter what he looked like? He wiped your people off the face of the earth. They didn't stand a chance. Bullets and blood everywhere. The screams of children echoed through the forest while you sat in the safety of your haven. The *old* Wanderer abandoned her people. Not me…"

Eva had already resolved to kill Elaine, but her words only hardened the decision. Still, she needed to know what the Tigers' Chief looked like. She had to be certain it was Dan McAvoy. Maybe Elaine remembered who had been with him—anyone out of the ordinary. If her worst fear was confirmed, perhaps she wouldn't seem so crazy after all.

The silver weapon started to cut into the Warrior's jaw, right below her ear. Drops of thick burgundy slid down the edge of the metal and dripped onto the wooden floor. Seeing the blood sparked a sudden urge in Eva to finish the job. Her Demon whispered in her ear, encouraging her thoughts. "Do it. Kill her now."

"*Tell me what I want to know*," Eva screamed. Elaine's face drained of color at the way her opponent looked at her. It was like a hungry predator, ready to feast.

"Okay. I'm sorry… Um… The Chief… um… looked older, but not too old. Um, black hair with streaks of white, combed behind his head… and… um his eyes."

Elaine paused. Too long for Eva.

"What about his eyes? Icy? Emotionless? Dead?"

"Y-y-yeah… *all* of those things."

"Who was with him? An older woman? Gay hair, thin. Didn't look like she belonged there?"

"There were a few women with him, so I don't know. They all had their backs turned, slaughtering the town.... Wait."

Eva felt hot. *Evidence. She knows something.* "Spit it out."

"One woman. I didn't see her face. She was tall, slender. Held herself a bit higher than the others. S-seemed very...um... clean. That's why I thought it was unusual."

"*More.* I need more."

"I couldn't tell if she was older or not. But-but... she said something to The Chief about Rapture. I couldn't make out anymore. She just seemed like she wasn't from here. Please, Eva. That's all I saw. I'm sorry. I-I'll change. *Please.*"

A surge of dizzying rage exploded through The Wanderer's body, merging with a sense of utter and complete failure. Dan McAvoy still lived. Her blow was not fatal. Every death in Rapture, including Anya's, was his doing. Questions she struggled with over the past year were now answered. But one truth stood out above all else. Virginia *was* working with the Tigers. She needed to know more. Unfortunately, that meant traveling back to Rapture for further investigation. Now the concern was whether they would allow her back into the city at all, even as a prisoner.

I have to break into her house and look for her tie to the Tigers. Armor. A weapon. One letter. That's all I need and I'm free.

As her gaze dropped to Elaine, Eva felt the Demon at her back—its fingers burrowing into her skull, its shadow sinking into her muscles. She was losing control again.

The tip of her blade traced a line from Elaine's neck to her chest. One last glance into the Warrior's eyes, wide and frozen with fear. Then the darkness took hold, forcing the blade downward—straight through her heart.

A single, ear-piercing scream.

Blood pooled across the floor, spreading until it nearly reached the corner of the room. Elaine thrashed, hands slick as she tried to stop the bleeding. But it was no use. Eva stood over her, watching as the Rover knelt and took her final, gasping breaths.

A sickening sense of satisfaction washed over The Wanderer as her Shadow slipped away near the doorway. In its place stood another familiar face.

Wanda.

"My daughter!" she gasped and rushed over to the limp figure at Eva's feet. She was hysterical. "My baby! Why would you do this? She has done *nothing* to deserve this."

The Wanderer's response was calm and cold. "William knew my intentions. Your daughter was impersonating me. Killing Gang Members and tarnishing my name. Putting *you* and the rest of this town in danger. It is a crime worth more than the swift death that I gave her. Only because I had a shred of respect for her did I choose not to lengthen her suffering."

"You are a *monster*. Do you hear me? *Monster*. And to think… I believed the good in you once. How foolish I was. I should have never saved you in the compound. I should have died there. Before my daughter. Before unleashing this… *demon* in you."

"Nothing but justice was served here, Wanda. Even her own people did not stop me. Whatever you think of me does not matter. Your daughter was delving into dangerous territory and using my name to do so. Since I've been gone, The Tigers have attacked my home and murdered my daughter."

"*You think you're better than them? You're no different from the ones who whipped and starved me in that compound!*"

"The difference is that my daughter did nothing to deserve her death."

Eva blinked. An elbow caught her in the stomach, the air was immediately sucked out of her lungs. She doubled back in pain and saw Wanda unsheath a few knives from Elaine's corpse and spring towards her. She was quick and nimble despite her age. The Wanderer was narrowly able to withstand the flurry of strikes.

"I was a *slave* for over half my life," the old woman screamed as she shoved Eva into a wall. Tears streamed down her dirt caked face. "I thought my daughter had been taken. And then you… *you* told me she was still alive. I escaped the Tiger's Den and ran for my life. Days passed and I *finally, finally* made it here. But my baby girl, my Elaine, did not know my face. I had to convince her that I was her mother. It took *weeks* for me to hold my daughter in my arms again. And with one swoop, you stole her away from me. You are no better than McAvoy. *You are exactly the same.*"

A cut on Eva's shoulder was nothing compared to her opponent's intent to drive a blade through her eye. Luckily, the weapon had lodged in a wooden beam inches from her face.

Wanda was down one weapon.

Eva took advantage of the momentary daze, slamming her arm into her opponent and smashing her against the wall. She nearly tripped over Elaine's body as she stepped back, blade raised to parry the next strike. The reverberation spidered painfully up her arm, but she held her grip. Another slash nicked her skin.

The Wanderer continued to deflect the Warrior's blows. "Don't make me kill you, Wanda."

But her pleas were ignored.

"Your death will bring this whole region peace," Wanda bawled through labored breaths, jabbing wildly at Eva. "There is no peace in this region because of *you*. Any time there is an agreement or peace, *you* come in with your 'justice' and screw it up. I'm starting to think that the Chief's preachings of utopia were true."

"There is no such thing as utopia."

"Correct. As long as The Wanderer draws breath, there never will be."

Eva noticed the misstep that Wanda took when she attempted to strike and took advantage of the woman's shifted balance. With one strike of the leg, the Doxie was on the floor and The Wanderer kicked the knives from her reach. Her blade was still dripping with Elaine's blood when it touched the old woman's flesh.

An audience had gathered in the doorway and through the windows to watch the Wanderer cut down her second victim. A hush blanketed the house and surrounding yard. Only a shuddered breath met Eva's lips as William stepped through the threshold and into the home. His gaze was fixated on the mother and daughter, now slumped over one another in an eternal embrace. She watched his demeanor change, but could not read the shift in emotion until he spoke.

The leader shook his head. "This is a shame," he sighed. "Only one life was given to you with our backs turned. And yet, you take more. Wanda's soul was brimming with suffering and her only relief and freedom was within these walls. And on this day, she rests in an unexpected and unjustifiable peace."

Eva did not realize how much blood covered her during the scuffle, from her victims as well as her own wounds. She imagined that the Warriors now saw her as a demon or bloodthirsty killer. As she opened her mouth to speak, explaining that she was attacked first, William raised his hand in protest.

"...Understand Wanderer," he said sternly. "Whether this life was taken in self-defense or otherwise, it is unjustified. However, it is not my intent to request your life be taken by my people. That would be wholly unwise. However, knowing your title and those who know you as *one who walks in shadow behind footprints of blood*... we cannot continue to allow this senseless life taking in our midst."

"Just spit it out," she said. Once again, she was forced to take a life, and her accusers refused to hear her story. *I no longer care what the weak think of me. They will not last long enough to see me return to the prowess that I deserve.*

William was understandably taken aback by The Wanderer's tone. He cleared his throat and continued. "You are, forthwith exiled from this town. No longer will you receive hospitality in any form within the borders of my kin. Begone. So we may now bury our dead."

"Doesn't matter anyway," she snapped and shoved her short sword back into its hilt. "I got the information that I came for. Justice has been served. But I will tell you what I told the other Rovers. As a warning to you all."

The crowd's energy shifted to fear. Any threat from The Wanderer would surely play out in time. Only their leader seemed to remain strong amidst Eva's words.

"Hope that I do not return. If the Gangs do not take you, I will. Everyone who has wronged me has met their end sooner or later."

She shoved William in the shoulder as she passed and left the Western Rover Colony without turning back. In the pit of her stomach, something told her that she would return here. But in what manner, she did not yet know.

Darkness had fallen over the noiseless town as she crossed its borders. She left a trail of crimson boot prints behind her that disappeared into the grassy edge of the forest. Thoughts of Dan McAvoy assaulted her mind. Although she already had an idea that he had lived during their battle, her suspicions were now confirmed.

At least my journey back to Rapture is a couple of days, she thought. *I have time to process all of this. When I return, I tell Gavin. Then I get into Virginia's house—unseen.*

Chapter 11

"I told you they won't find her." Mara sipped her tea during breakfast. Jake stared into his plate blankly. "Not that they're looking too terribly hard anyway."

"I wonder if she'll come back," he said. For the first couple days, only he and Gavin knew Eva had escaped. Now the entire town knew.

"She would be idiotic to do so," she commented fervently. "Besides, who cares? All that matters is that *you* are safe, my dear."

He nodded and half-smiled as the graceful woman stood up and slid her arms around his shoulders in a tight embrace. As she rested her chin near his neck, he closed his eyes and buried his face in her golden locks. He inhaled deeply. The intoxicating scent of berries and vanilla filled his senses. Beneath it, there was something more. Something he felt. It may have been her soft, milky skin against his work-hardened palms but an extreme calm spread throughout his core and filled him to the brim.

A knock on the door startled both of them. Mara stood up and made her way to the front of the home, peering through the peephole to see who it was. Tommy's muffled voice was barely audible through the metal and wood structure. The younger brother pushed through Mara to get to Jake.

"There's a line outside your shop," he said irritably. "One of the citizens walked all the way to the farms to come get me. Why they didn't just come here, I don't know. Get your ass out here and go to work…"

Jake was already out the door by then, arguing with his brother about being late. Mara watched from the porch until they reached the Workers District before leaving for The Stronghold in time for classes to begin.

The brothers took their leave of one another. Watering crops was Tommy's duty for the day in preparation for the Autumn Harvest and Jake had to stock his shelves with more jewelry and silverware. It had been difficult for him to work consistently after the death of his daughter. The dress that Anya had worn to her parents' wedding was hung at the back of the store, still blackened with soot from the explosion. Displayed right beside it was the blade that he had made for Eva.

***

Once the Council discovered The Wanderer had escaped, Jake was allowed to return home to gather a few things. Guards combed every inch of the house for a clue to where she had gone, carelessly tossing things all over. Tables and chairs were slid in the corner of the room and animal-hide rugs had been overturned in an attempt to find out how Eva escaped. But it was Jake, in fact, who discovered the open window.

"She must've escaped through here," he told the replacement Captain of the Guard. They studied the small space and spotted a small patch of leather that had torn off while squeezing through the tight space. "Her gear got caught."

"Virginia is requesting a detailed report of the home," one guard commented. "In the event that she returns, The Council asked us to build a case against her."

Just under Eva's pillow, near the nightstand, lay a small black book. Guesses of what could be written within the pages scattered through Jake's mind. Incriminating evidence or a possible link to Eva being responsible for the attacks? Crazy ramblings of an already distressed mind? Whatever it was, Virginia would turn it against her. He knew that much. And although he no longer cared for Eva's recklessness, Jake couldn't bring himself to let the Council see her private thoughts, however dark they may be.

With his back against the edge of the bed, he moved smoothly from the foot up towards the pillows and snatched up the book before anyone noticed. Once they left the home, he would return it back to the exact same place. He shuddered to think what Eva would do if she couldn't find her journal. Or what she would do if she learned he had taken it.

Jake tarried at home, pretending to look for specific items that he knew he would never find. The moment that the last set of footsteps disappeared, he wedged Eva's book underneath her pillow. His fingertips tarried on the leatherbound cover. A voice in his head coaxed him to read it, but he was far too afraid of what he would find written inside.

If she doesn't come back, I'll destroy it.

***

Frederick, the other blacksmith, had visited Jake's shop regularly to help him cast more inventory. Everyone could discern the work between the two. Jake excelled at crafting small, intricate items, while his counterpart handled larger, more demanding builds. When it came to jewelry, silverware, and other baubles, Jake McAvoy was unmatched.

But the young man thanked the blacksmith nonetheless. Speaking with the people of Rapture made the days pass quickly, and he only dwelled on Eva's whereabouts now and then. With each evening spent in Mara and Virginia's home, the woman who had once risked her life for him faded further from his thoughts.

It was the golden-haired woman who made sure Jake was taken care of now. A warm meal waited for him the moment he walked through the door each night.

"She isn't coming back," Mara said sternly one night. Virginia and Tommy had already gone to bed and only she and Jake were awake in the parlor. "And even if she does, would you even take her back at this point? Look at what she has done. Look at how much more peaceful we have been these past few days."

He thought for a moment, but the answer no longer pained him. "No. You're right. Eva has been selfish by putting our lives in danger… It's just…"

She let out a long sigh. "Just what Jake? Every time I ask you about this, you always hesitate. Are you afraid of loving someone else? Are you afraid of her? She doesn't love you anymore. She *barely* spoke to you before she left. You need someone who can be there for you. Someone who truly loves you for who you are and would never try to change you."

"I-um…"

But Mara was already pulling him to his feet. Her long, slender fingers moved up his chest and caressed his cheek gently. Before he could stop himself, Jake's lips met hers. Heat flooded his face, but he didn't pull away, letting his lips linger against hers. Their heartbeats pounded, echoing loudly in his ears. She pulled him closer by the arms, and his hand slid to her waist. *Wow. This feels... different.*

Wait.

The moment shattered as the sense of being watched settled in. They pulled away. Everyone in the house was asleep. But when they turned toward the front door, they gasped. A figure stood there, watching from the threshold. Both of them knew exactly who it was. The smell of blood gave it away.

"Eva!" Mara and Jake said simultaneously.

Too late. She had caught them both.

"Jake, I—"

And then there was a pause. Seconds turned to minutes. It was the longest pause that Jake had ever witnessed in Eva's presence. Normally, she was able to act on her instincts, but seeing him standing there kissing Mara had frozen her to the core. The obvious hesitation petrified them all.

Worlds crashed down around Eva's mind as she wavered in the doorway, caked in the dried blood of Elaine and Wanda. Blind rage reddened her field of view and tunneled to Jake and Mara. Their figures illuminated only by the sparse candles throughout the room and the crackling fireplace. Fear plastered on both their faces.

The Wanderer stepped through the doorway. Jake jumped backwards and put his hands up. Slowly and meticulously, she unsheathed her weapon and pointed it toward him.

"I don't know if I can muster the words for this, Jacob McAvoy," she whispered and wiped her eyes with her sleeve. She tried swallowing the lump in her throat, but it was no use. The tears came anyway. "It could have been anyone… *anyone* else and I would have let you go. Out of all the women in Rapture, the one family that hates me more than anything… you… you…"

Jake had no explanation to give. In truth, there wasn't one. Even if he could manage a response, Eva wouldn't listen. She would see through any lie… and that would only infuriate her more. He felt his arms go cold when Mara opened her mouth. As he reached forward to try and stop her from stepping in between them, she shoved him away.

"Who did you kill this time?" she sneered with an upturned nose. "Another innocent child?"

Mara's laughter was cut short when The Wanderer placed the tip of her sword against her chest.

"One more step *bitch*," she warned. Her gritted teeth upturned to an evil snarl. "One more word. I dare you."

The young woman's voice squeaked and cracked. "Y-y-ou wouldn't dare. You're outnumbered. The guards would come and dispose of you… *you disgusting excuse for a human being*. If that is what you really are. They will find you here."

"As long as my blade gets a taste of you and your mother's blood," Eva put her head down, but kept her glare locked onto Mara. "Then I am satiated."

"Eva don't." The weapon was now pointed back at Jake. He kept his hands raised in submission, but continued. "Please. You don't have to do this."

She cocked her head to the side. "Don't I? Huh? Why don't I deserve revenge for all the shit you put me through? And now *this*? You betrayed me. I came back to this place for *you*. I stayed here for *you*. Even after everyone begged for my head, I stayed here for *you*—"

Jake tried to interrupt, but The Wanderer continued.

"*Who* risked their life for you before this place? Mara? Ha! She wouldn't lift a finger to defend you now. She's practically rattling her bones standing in my presence. Tell me, Jake… did you *really* want to spend your life with me? Or did you just lie your way to safety at the expense of my sanity? Using me as a human shield to be safe from the shit out there, right? I don't know why I thought I could care for someone like you. Your whole existence is a complete… and utter… failure."

Raising an arm over her head, Eva attempted to cut down Mara and Jake with one sweep, but something caught her forearm mere inches away from them. She glanced over her shoulder and saw Gavin. He was shaking his head. Rumbling footsteps neared the house.

"If you do this," Gavin whispered in her ear. "Then you'll be executed. I can't allow you to throw your life away like this. We will get through this. I have a plan. I promise."

Eva was taken away in shackles and her blades were placed in her Captain's care. The Council's decision for the present moment was to put The Wanderer in a cell. Rapture's

Prison was seldom used, but there would soon be a single inhabitant. Metal bars slamming shut and the cold, wet ground felt all too familiar. She sat in the corner of the cell and faced the wall. Alone.

Moments later, Jake stepped into the jail without a word. His footsteps echoed down the hall toward Rapture's prisoner. Something was concealed in his jacket—something the guards didn't notice.

He stopped in front of her cell, hesitating, just long enough for Eva to wonder if she had imagined him entirely. His hand lingered inside his jacket before he reluctantly drew out the package. A soft thump echoed through the corridor, followed by a quiet sigh. Then, the sound of his retreat faded up the stairs.

When Eva was sure he was gone, she turned toward the bars.

Her journal.

Her Demon reappeared.

"Why do you trouble yourself with the emotions of others?" it asked, as if Dan McAvoy himself stood in the prison with her. He cast no shadow in the torchlight.

She slowly stood up and walked over to the leatherbound book. "I shouldn't," she said as she noticed the pencil nearby. There was no telling how long she would be a prisoner here, and no window to measure the days passing, writing could be the only thing that kept her from losing herself completely.

"And yet… you continue to hesitate in striking down the weak? Those who have deceived you? *Betrayed* you?"

Her voice was small, almost a whimper. "I just wanted to help people. I wanted to care for someone so they could care for me. So *someone* would care for me."

"And now?"

Eva broke down. Her lip trembled and tears streamed down her dirty face. "I feel so… empty. So used."

"Don't pity yourself. Pity is for the *weak*."

She stopped and looked up at the Shadow. A sense of clarity came over her, falling softly on her shoulders. It felt oddly comforting. Her face hardened as did her tone.

"Yes. You're right. I am *not* weak. I don't need someone to care for me. They don't deserve my tears… And I won't give them anything else."

***

No one visited The Wanderer during the first two days of her imprisonment. Only by the light of the torches was she able to write. Her Shadow kept her company, striking a conversation here and there. She slept only when exhausted, collapsing deep into horrifying nightmares. When the guards brought her meals, they slid the tray through the bars and rushed away in unease. Eva felt like a caged animal, waiting to strike.

Gavin wanted nothing more than to check on Eva, but was forced to fight the Council for her life instead. Virginia and the others no longer wished to hear a rebuttal after learning that The Wanderer had directly threatened Jake and Mara. The question of invoking an ancient law of public execution split the Council down the middle. Maven, Virginia, and Xander called for her hanging in the Town Square, while Bruce, Jasmine, and Lee pushed for banishment instead.

"We haven't executed anyone in *decades*," Gavin pleaded. "I know the history. I understand what those people did to deserve that kind of punishment. But Eva was *targeted.* Ever since she set foot in this city, we have done nothing to protect her. And still, after every attack, she's tried to protect this city. And now you want her head over a threat? Her entire world is crumbling down around her. She's lost everything. All she was doing was protecting herself—because we didn't. Rapture… *we* failed her."

"Putting aside the fact that she attacked two of our citizens," Maven snapped, "her existence puts our lives in danger because of the Tiger's threats. If we banish her, who is to say they won't continue to attack us? If we deliver her head, then we prove she is no longer a threat to this region."

She fixed Gavin with a hard stare. "Your feelings for her have clouded your judgment, Captain."

Gavin flushed, but the heat in his chest did not fade. It settled, sharp and steady.

"No," he said, voice tight. "What's clouding this Council is *fear*. I *respect* her. And I believe she deserves better than this. We should speak to her. She may have returned with proof of who is actually responsible for all of this."

Virginia lifted her hand to abruptly silence the room. Her tone was sickeningly smug now that the rest of the Council was finally on her side. "What she found is irrelevant. Proof changes nothing. When violence follows you, it isn't coincidence, it's *consequence*."

Bruce shot a hateful glance at his peer. "Unlike the rest of us, Eva's name is known throughout the region. Her title attracts all sorts, good and bad. We should have considered the risk of having someone of that caliber within our walls… especially given the circumstances of her arrival. I'll admit partial responsibility for that decision. It was only a matter of time before her actions would catch up with her. We were just standing between her and her fate."

"She only killed the Chief because they captured Jake and Tommy sir," Gavin argued. "I—"

"But The Chief *still* lives," Virginia barked. "The truth is plain to see. Our barrier to the outside world has been destroyed. Countless citizens lie dead. How much more carnage will she bring before it is too late? I will not stand for another moment of this."

Lee interlaced his fingers and leaned forward. "But would we put Rapture in further danger if we impose this capital punishment? What then? If their Chief is seeking revenge and we take it from him, we could push him to destroy us all. You've all seen the devastation this maniac can unleash.

If we simply banish The Wanderer, we are guiltless to her fate."

Xander stood up in impatience. "There is danger in associating Rapture with The Wanderer. If we simply *banish* her, we may still be a target for the Tigers. Unless Eva's head is on a silver platter for their Chief, we will never be sure."

"I will not allow an execution for someone who has done nothing wrong," Jasmine sniffed. Her fists were clenched. "Simply because an enemy wishes to do her harm, I believe that banishment would absolve us of any wrongdoing. The Chief wants *her, not us*."

***

IT HAS BEEN ONLY TWO DAYS I THINK. THREE? FOUR? I'VE ALREADY FORGOTTEN WHAT THE SUN LOOKS LIKE. WHAT DOES THE RAIN FEEL LIKE? TRAPPED. CAGED. IT'S SO QUIET. ONLY THAT THING SPEAKS TO ME NOW. HE JUST TALKS AND TALKS AND TALKS. QUESTIONS. SO MANY QUESTIONS... BUT THEN HE PREACHES ABOUT UTOPIA. WHAT IS UTOPIA? IS IT THE STRONG LEADING THE WEAK? SUBSERVIENCE? ACHIEVABLE? IS IT POSSIBLE? POSSIBILITIES... WHEN I GET OUT OF HERE, I WILL TRY. TRY TO ACHIEVE A WORLD WORTH LIVING IN... EXISTING IN... FOR EVERYONE... MAKE MY OWN PEACE,

BECAUSE I CAN'T FIND IT HERE. THERE IS NO PEACE FOR ME IN THIS PLACE. I WAS MISTAKEN. USED. ABUSED. BETRAYED... AGAIN.

BUT FIRST, I NEED TO FINISH MY JOB. MY ENEMIES WILL FALL. DAN MCAVOY, THE REAL DAN MCAVOY. WILL. DIE.

Eva slammed her journal shut. Some days she would just write words, random words or phrases that popped up in her mind. On others, she would plan exactly how she would run Rapture, just as she did with the Serpents. Solitude was something that she had relished before, but being confined in a cell was driving her mad. All she could do was wait.

"You could kill them all," the Hooded Demon finally offered. Its face had changed to Eva's for the time being. "You have the skill. Become what you once were, but greater. Allow the anger and darkness to consume… and nothing will stop you. No one will best you in battle. Not even McAvoy."

The Wanderer considered the request, and each time her thoughts returned to her daughter. The memory left her seething with anger and hollow with grief. Anya would not have wanted her mother to become a monster. Eva's true anger had terrified her once before. She wondered if fear was the last thing Anya thought of her mother.

FEAR. A FUNNY WORD. ON ONE HAND, A GREAT TOOL WHEN DEALING WITH THOSE WHO ARE WEAK. BUT NOT MY DAUGHTER. MAKES ME SICK JUST THINKING ABOUT THAT NIGHT. IF I BECOME THE DARKNESS, THEN I WILL NOT BE

WHAT ANYA WOULD HAVE WANTED. I WISH I COULD HAVE GIVEN MY LIFE FOR HERS. I WISH ANYA WAS STILL HERE. BUT I WONDER... CAN I TASTE REVENGE WITHOUT DARKNESS?

VIRGINIA WILL BE THE FIRST TO DIE.

As the days passed, Eva continued the internal struggle of whether to succumb to her Demon or not. Deep down, she knew it spoke the truth. Was she capable of taking down the entire town of Rapture? It would be far too risky. Once she snapped the neck of the guard who brought her food and took his keys, the militia down the hall would be next, and then the army and the Council. No. She could not put her life against hundreds of Rapture's citizens.

***

"Eva?" Gavin's gentle voice echoed through the stone corridor. Finally, the Council had come to a tentative decision and he raced to tell her. As he neared the cell where his friend had been imprisoned, he came face-to-face with what seclusion had done to her. Lost in conversation with the Hooded Shadow, she failed to notice Gavin's presence. He called out again.

She gasped and rushed over to the door. "Gavin?" *Is he real?* Her fingers slid around the frigid metal bars and slowly wrapped around his. She sighed in relief that she hadn't been imagining again. "Please. Get me out of here. Shit. I need to get out of here."

He agreed and immediately noticed her bloodshot eyes. "Oh, Eva. I am so sorry they did this to you. I have some good… and some bad news."

"What?" she said frantically. "What happened?"

Gavin sighed. “The Council voted to execute you, but delayed the hanging to build the gallows again. Bruce convinced everyone but Virginia to let you ‘see the sun’ before they… you know. House arrest again. I was able to trick them into believing I was on their side. I said some nasty things about you that weren’t true. But I was able to convince them to let me be your personal guard. Don’t worry, if anything else happens, I’ll be by your side. And I’m certainly not going to let them kill you.”

She smiled for the first time in days. It was a weary smile, but a smile nonetheless. “Thank you Gavin… I just don’t know if I deserve your kindness. You’ve been the only one who has stuck with me through all of this. And you risked your own neck for mine.”

“How could you say that? You deserve nothing but kindness,” he said softly. “You don’t deserve any of this shit people have put you through.” He trailed off, then cleared his throat and quickly changed his tone. “But we need to come up with a plan to get out of Rapture before they finish the gallows or the Tigers attack again. We’re getting out of here, once and for all.”

“We?” she repeated, then tiredly rested her head against the bars. He leaned forward, pressing his forehead to hers.

“I swear on my life that I will *never* betray you Eva Calloway,” he whispered. “I am so sorry I didn’t come sooner. I was so focused on keeping you safe… and *Virginia*… Anyway, I know that all this may seem like empty words to you right now. Especially after everything you’ve been through. All of the empty promises in your life. But in time, I will prove my devotion.”

Eva recalled the scene she’d witnessed in Virginia’s home—Jake and Mara holding each other, unafraid, uncaring of anything beyond themselves. Anger bubbled up in her stomach again as she took a step back from her cell. Her mind shifted to Dan McAvoy and their battle in the Den. Now that she knew he had survived, an overwhelming urge to finish what she started washed over her.

"Let's go," she said sternly but quietly. "We have some planning to do."

The Wanderer's Captain unlocked the door and handed the keys to another guard. Eva stepped out of the prison cell with her journal tucked in her jacket, turned back to find her Shadow shaking its head in disappointment. Gavin and his prisoner made their way up the stairs and into the blinding sunlight. Once the swimming in her head subsided, a gruesome scene appeared throughout the Town Square.

Gavin was trying to make sense of it all. "It was broad daylight. Thi-This-This wasn't here when I went down to get you. It was a matter of minutes and… and this…"

A small child was the first to discover the sight, pointing in confusion at the three words scrawled across the square. Written in blood—a name, and a warning. Just above the word was a single victim, completely eviscerated.

Last chance, Wanderer.

Not again, Eva repeated in her head over and over. *Not again. Not again.* The sound of a familiar voice startled her from behind. She spun around so quickly that she nearly tripped over her own feet.

"She was in prison," Bruce said over Virginia's loud accusations. "There was no possible way that this was her."

"I am aware that wasn't her, *imbecile*," the old woman said sharply. Her long, emerald dress rippled violently as she raced towards them. Eva turned to her. "No one has listened to a word I've said from the *beginning*. The Tigers will not stop until she is dead. Hurry the gallows. We cannot afford a single wasted second."

Before anyone could say another word, Eva was whisked away to her home before more citizens could see her standing near the message. Gavin locked the door behind him and turned to her. His face had gone ghostly pale, and even his cinnamon beard looked stripped of color. Eva, herself, felt sick. A mixture of rage, confusion, despair, helplessness, and fear fought for control over her body. She reached a hand up to the empty space where her blades would be sheathed.

Her Captain never missed a beat. "I know where they are. I'll steal them for you," and was out of the house in a blink.

Silence shrouded the home. Echoes of voices slowly rose from outside, but The Wanderer could not discern whether or not they were a figment of her imagination. Some of them sounded like Rapture's citizens, but others felt like the whispers of her victims from a nightmare. The moment her mind transfixed on Dan McAvoy, her Shadow appeared again. This time, she approached it. This time, she was not quite as afraid. His face. His icy, lifeless eyes. Even his presence felt real.

"Losing your grip Wanderer?" it taunted, inches from her face. She was shaking and glanced outside. A crowd had formed around the scene in the Town Square. Eva shut her eyes hard and put her head in her hands. The room was spinning so quickly that she had to use a door frame for stability. The closer she got to the figure, the harder it was to breathe. *Come on Eva, get yourself together*.

"Tisk tisk," it taunted. "You've lost your touch… When you face me, it will be far too easy for me to end you. Pity. I was hoping for a fair fight."

The Wanderer's fist met nothing but air as she punched at the specter. Her entire arm shot right through Dan McAvoy's torso. She straightened her stance and stared into the blazing red eyes of her Demon. "When we meet again, I will *gladly* return the suffering you've caused me."

Gavin's return jerked her back to reality.

"I found them," he breathed. "They were in the evidence chest. Had to sneak around some guards to get them."

Eva snatched the blades out of his hands, thanked him, and sheathed them behind her. "Just in case," she said, glancing outside again. "Although I'm stuck here, they could still come for me. We can't leave right away, though. Not yet."

"You need to find out who is doing all of this." Gavin was staring at the same spot where Eva's eyes were fixed. "Enough people have died. It has to be someone in Rapture. We don't want the Tiger Chief and someone in the city to be after you."

"Virginia," Eva interrupted his thoughts. "Who else? There *has* to be something I can find to put an end to all this. I know McAvoy's alive... I just have to prove that he's working with *her*. Once we get out of here, I have a feeling that the answer will come to us."

"I'm staying with you," he said. "We can figure this out together."

She nodded, her auburn hair bounced off her shoulders. The Demon had disappeared for the moment, but its remark lingered. *You've lost your touch.* It branded itself into The Wanderer's being. Rapture had taken everything from her. Her life. Her name. Her daughter. Her sanity.

"Not anymore," she said under her breath. "I cannot allow this place to be the end of me. I'm stronger than this. Pain is a part of who I am. I will have my revenge."

Gavin heard every word. He did not comment, rather, just placed his hand on her shoulder reassuringly. It was warm and welcoming. The feeling spread across Eva's cold, numb body. Another spark of her old self ignited within the pit of her spirit. Then they heard a knock at the door.

It was Jake.

But she shook her head at Gavin who walked over to the door and bolted it. She spoke through the door. "I have no words for you, Jacob McAvoy. Go away. Live your fake, peaceful life with a woman who would have me hanged. Your words mean nothing. I now know who is truly loyal... and it is not you."

Near the Town Square, the citizens began to wail in horror at the massacre around the fountain.

Chapter 12

Jake nearly tripped over the porch step as he backed away from his home. Eva had finally given up on him. And even knowing he deserved it, he still felt the need to make things right. *I have to do something. She doesn't deserve this.* Wiping his burning eyes, Jake raced over to the fields to find his brother working with Xander, as usual. To get away from the traumatic events that were taking place in Rapture, Tommy kept to himself. It was the only way he could cope. When Jake pulled him aside and explained what had happened, the teen's face hardened.

"Don't you realize what you've done, Jake?" he shook his head, staring at his shovel. "I can't believe you would fall for Mara, of all people. I've noticed you two when you think I'm not looking, but I was hoping you would say something to Eva. But you didn't. She has every right to be angry. Now they're going to *kill* her."

"...I know," Jake reluctantly admitted. "I know. You're right. I should have told her earlier. I was scared. But Mara was right all along. About everything. But… I mean… Eva tried to kill both of *us* when she found out."

Tommy just stared at his brother for a long while, waiting for him to think clearly. All that had happened to The Wanderer over the last year building up to the moment where she found her supposed-to-be-husband kissing another woman. Not just any woman, one of the two people in Rapture that despised her more than everyone else combined.

Jake did not seem to feel his words deserved further introspection, so Tommy made himself very clear.

"You *betrayed* her, Jake," he said angrily, just quiet enough for the other farmers not to hear their argument. "Her trust. Her love. Her sacrifice. *Everything*. When she needed you to speak against her for the Council, you stood by and watched her suffer. Kissing Mara was the final straw."

"Me?" Jake gestured aggressively at himself, drawing attention from those nearby. "What about you? I never heard *you* say anything either."

"I have my own guilt to deal with, but we both know I'm not at fault for this one, *brother*."

Jake clenched his fists so tightly that his knuckles whitened.

"I just don't understand why anyone would do this to Eva." Tommy changed the subject as he took notice of people nearby beginning to stare. "Someone in this town has to be helping The Tigers. We have to do something. I'm not going to sit here and let her die."

Jake sighed and relaxed his stance. "We don't have any more information than Eva did. But I agree with you. We have maybe a week to stop this execution."

The dirty-blonde haired boy frowned. "The Nomads know everything," he offered. "We should start there. But… um… are you okay going back out there?"

"No. But we have to try. This is the last chance we have. Are you?"

"Eva taught us how to survive. I think we can handle making it into the city. After that, I don't know. Hopefully, we don't have to go that far. And if dad is really still alive…"

"His Tigers will be after us."

"Yeah. But. I'm in."

They hurried back to Mara's home and explained their plan. Her eyes narrowed when she realized their intention was to *help* The Wanderer. Despite her opinion on the matter, she decided to accompany them.

Jake crossed his arms and huffed. "You don't *have* to come with us. I'm just not going to let Eva be executed without a fair trial."

"It isn't that," she said shortly. "No matter what I say, you refuse to see what's right in front of your face, love. At some point, you'll realize the monster she truly is. And when we return, justice may already be served."

"And what if she's completely innocent?" Tommy asked, visibly offended.

"I reserve my judgment based on current facts," she snapped. The golden-haired woman began speaking like her mother. "However… in the case that new evidence becomes contradictory to my beliefs, I will adjust my opinions accordingly."

Jake slammed his fist down onto the wooden table, flinging a metal plate against the wall with a clang. He was already dressed in the armor that Rapture had gifted him years before. Mara glared at him out of the corner of her eye as she disappeared down the hallway. A few minutes later, she returned to the brothers clad in a surprising amount of armor and brandishing her own weaponry.

"Wait…" the elder brother stopped while she pulled her hair into a tight bun. Her light steel armor gleamed against the sun rays peeking through the windows. At her hip was sheathed a longsword that Jake swore was too heavy for her thin figure. But there she was, carrying it with ease. "When did you get *that*?"

"I have always adored the art of war," she responded in her sing-song voice. "I even trained with the men here long ago. Oh, don't act so shocked. There's more to me than you will ever know."

The brothers exchanged a glance as she pushed past them, then followed her out the door. Tommy remained in his tunic and trousers, wielding only a few knives, a sack of food, and a canteen of water. Years before, when Eva had taken him and his brother to the city for survival training, he treasured the skill of preparation. And although he wasn't too keen on taking a life, he was willing to do whatever needed to be done. He just hoped that his brother would do the same.

Mara led the brothers to Rapture's front gate. They traveled down the cobblestone street that separated the city and passed citizens scrubbing the town square clean of blood. Jake turned towards the direction of his old home. He may have been imagining it, but he swore he saw a shadow float across the window. Was it Eva?

"All I want to do is clear her name," he mouthed to himself, grasping the hilt of his blade. In the back of his mind, he could not escape the danger she brought to this town. *If she was gone, I could live in peace. She gets her freedom, and so do I.*

Towering above them, almost pressing against the sky, they stood at the foundation of the exit. Trickling water from the drains around the Gardens was the lone sound around them until a guard on the wall spoke out.

"State your business."

Mara stepped ahead of Tommy and Jake with a voice of confidence. "We wish to leave Rapture to enter the city. We will only be gone for a few days. Do not inform my mother."

"As you wish, Miss Mara."

And just like that, the gates opened and closed behind them. Paralyzing unease spread across Jake's body. His hands dropped down to his hips and became cold. Gradually, it grew more difficult to breathe. Mara's hand at his back made his heart skip a few beats. The horizon seemed so far, yet so close. Broken, dilapidated homes speckled the landscape and beyond them, the unforgettable skyline of the ancient city. All of Eva's stories about the Old Times ran through Jake and Tommy's mind. In some way, their fear became comforting. Familiar.

"The Nomads, you say, should know where to find information?" Mara mentioned as they made their way down the dirt path. "Are you certain they won't just tell you what you want to hear?"

Jake considered the question, but his brother answered for him. "Because they've been the only group to fully take us in. They believe in truth as the highest form of respect to their Mother. Eva saved them before and they owe it to her to be honest."

"She only saved them because her presence brought the hostility in the first place," she argued. "It always has, ever since she was the Serpents' Mistress."

"But—." Jake realized he had no response to Mara's words. She was right. Ever since the night The Wanderer rescued him and his brother from the Vault, danger had followed them. Whether it was for the fame of killing her or because she truly was dangerous no longer mattered. Being with Eva meant fighting for your life.

"But what?" Mara smiled back at him. Not a sly smile, but she knew that he did not have a rebuttal. Even Tommy could not defend the criticism. "Silence? Because you *know* I'm right. So again, why are we here? What is the point?"

"*Because I have to know*." Jake exploded. Confusion and anger that was bottled up for the last year had finally burst. "*For me, for my daughter. I have to know what is going on. I don't care about Eva. I want a life for myself.*"

Everyone stopped. Tommy slowly turned to his brother, wide-eyed. Mara raised an eyebrow. Jake's voice echoed through the streets and bounced back to them. A few seconds passed before he shoved between them and continued down the path. Forming in his throat was a lump he could not swallow.

I just admitted that I don't care about Eva, was all he repeated in his head as they continued their journey to the city. *I'm not even out here risking my life for her*.

Mara kept to herself for a while. She only wanted Jake to see what type of a person that Eva was, not upset him. As they journeyed through the ancient streets between Rapture and the metropolis ahead, she scanned the horizon. The Gangs seldom traveled this far from the city, but since her town had been attacked numerous times in the last year, the Tigers could be waiting anywhere.

Just as they crested one of the last hills before the city, a familiar sight came into view. The three travelers stopped for a moment to study it. Its painted blue letters were now cracked and sun-worn, flecking off and being carried by the wind like autumn leaves. A few boards, rotted and water warped on the ground. Nearly six years ago, this sign was a glimmer of hope.

But now, it echoed a lie.

Shattered storefronts replaced decaying homes and Rapture's walls disappeared completely from view. Jake and Tommy had forgotten how claustrophobic the city felt. Buildings appeared nearly on top of one another. Danger could be lurking around any corner, with no time to run. Neither of them could fight properly. Mara claimed to have trained with Rapture's Guard, but they were skeptical. They had doubted Eva once, too.

But Mara, Councilwoman Virginia's daughter, was not the Wanderer.

Gravel and bits of brick crunched beneath their boots. Jake was now leading the way, deeper into the city's center, but had no idea where he was going. The Nomads were constantly on the move, and he could only hope they'd stumble upon them by chance.

He could sense the excitement in his brother as they rounded each block. Tommy had always adored the Nomads and their way of life. Jasmine, Yidi, and Masha were always incredibly welcoming, no matter the circumstances. And Tommy always resonated with that.

"So we aren't even out here to clear Eva's name." Mara could no longer contain her bitterness. "And you no longer feel safe in Rapture with her living there. So, *why* are we out here, Jake?"

"Pretty sure I've already answered that question," he responded shortly. "To make sure I know that it isn't Eva causing all of this death."

"Because of her past?"

Jake hesitated. "Yeah… because of her past."

Tommy scowled at his brother.

"So what if the answer you find isn't what you are hoping for? Will you *finally* believe me then? That she's at fault for each and every death in Rapture? Even Anya?"

Both brothers felt their stomachs drop. Jake's palms began to sweat and Tommy felt his legs freeze. She stood between them and the next street, arms crossed, awaiting a response. Silence. Her foot began to tap against the pavement in impatience. They both looked at each other, back at Mara, then nodded in agreement. Their response was good enough for her. She adjusted her hair, spun around, and continued down the street.

As they reached the center of the city, the familiar scene of disintegrated buildings came into view. Jake and Tommy stumbled over the rubble more than they cared to admit, while their guide seemed to navigate it with ease. Around the next corner was a sign that brought back a flood of nearly-forgotten memories. *MOTEL*. It was the same place that Eva, Jake, and Tommy had spent an entire winter after the Rover Colony had exiled their protector. Bittersweet as it was, the brothers found themselves being beckoned by that building, but the scent of death deterred them from entering. They couldn't have known Eva had been there only a few days earlier with a young Fox as her prey. Memories engulfed them so powerfully that neither brother noticed that Mara had vanished.

"Why does everyone want to banish someone who works so hard to keep them safe?" Tommy questioned, although his gaze remained glued to the scarce remnants of a bonfire that Jake had lit over five years ago. Little had changed since then, aside from the building becoming more overgrown with foliage.

"The Rovers banished her for bringing danger to them," Jake sighed. "And now she's done the same to Rapture. She is cursed."

"She's cursed because she fights to protect the weak."

"Yeah… I know. Look, Tommy… I don't want her to be executed, but she also can't stay in Rapture. Mara was right, she-"

Jake paused and looked around. Their companion was nowhere to be found. He started panicking. The entire block was devoid of life. Had she been captured? Not possible. The Gang would have captured the brothers as well. When he thought about it, he half-heard her mention something about 'coming right back'. Perhaps she found the Nomads. But not long after Jake and Tommy began traveling north again, the Nomads found them, and Mara was not among the crowd.

The sound of footsteps ceased all at once, and the tribe fell silent. Painted faces gleamed in the dwindling daylight and the crackling firelight of their torches. Each Nomad bore distinct markings, tied to the animal spirit that resonated with their soul. Just behind the first row stood the Tribe's Elders, Yidi and Masha. Their sun-worn smiles greeted the boys, but Jake barely noticed.

Where did Mara run off to? he wondered. Tommy jabbed an elbow at him. Yidi was addressing him and repeated his question.

"Eva is not with you?"

Jake shook his head and shot a look at his brother, who could have answered the question. "No. She's been attacked by the… erm… Tigers again. Well, not *her* exactly. Um… the town… Rapture."

"Why are you two out here alone?" Masha stepped forward as her warriors moved away.

"So much has happened since Anya's funeral," Tommy said, shoving his brother aside. His voice rose, fractured with emotion. "Eva's been attacked. She thinks Anya was *murdered.* I'm scared we might be next. We don't know what to do. But now that the Tigers know that the Council and others…" he shot a side glance at Jake, "are against her, they're targeting the rest of Rapture. The Council just voted to have Eva *hanged.* There isn't enough time. We need help. We need information. Please. Something to keep Rapture from hanging her."

"Young one," the old woman put her hands on Tommy's shoulders and stared into his glittering eyes. "I can see you are hurting terribly. My spirit pains for Eva *and* for you. Nonetheless… We have only heard whispers of the Tigers, nothing more. In fact, we have not been attacked by any Gang in some time. Quite unusual, but we are vigilant all the same."

Jake rolled his shoulders. *So this was a waste of time too.* His thoughts drifted back to Mara and he scanned the block around him and over the tops of the Nomad's heads. Yidi said something but he ignored the mumbling. When Tommy dug his elbow into Jake's rib cage, he doubled back in pain.

"Ow. What?" he yelled and threw his arms out to his side. "Where the shit is Mara? We need to find her. The Tigers could have kidnapped her."

"Eat with us Coyote Spirit," Yidi put his hands up to calm him. "The Tigers are not in this city or we would know. She must have been exploring elsewhere and I am confident that she will return to you."

Tommy shrugged and stared at his brother, motioning for them to follow the Nomads to their camp for food. "We should go with them."

“They just said they don’t have any information about the Gangs. Apparently no one does.” Jake huffed.

“Who cares right now?” his brother scolded. “You are so worried about finding information instead of letting it come to us. We always find the answers to our problems by complete accident. Let’s try something different for once. Come on.”

Masha overheard the brothers' argument and Tommy’s words of wisdom. She whispered something about ‘having the spirit of a true Nomad, a true warrior’ and scurried back to her place ahead of the group. Jake wanted to argue, but perhaps his brother was right, maybe they would find information about the Gangs at the camp. Maybe Mara would find them too.

He just hoped she was okay.

***

It would be another two days before Mara met up with the brothers again. She left the city behind, confidence in her footsteps, following the Old Time highway north. Buildings gave way to forest and rusted vehicles, animals skittering through both. To her right stood the Rover Colony once protected by the Wanderer. It was silent now, heavy with the scent of death. But Mara barely noticed. Her attention was fixed on the human-shaped figure ahead.

As cautiously as she could, Mara drew her sword and slowly approached the silhouette, slinking behind the corroded shell of a car. As she peeked over the hood, her head slammed into the mirror with a sharp crack. Her heart stopped when the figure turned and spoke to her.

“If that’s you,” it called out in a deep voice. “I’m here to escort you. Chief McAvoy figured you’d need some company. Especially with that clunky weapon.”

Slowly, Mara rose to her feet and returned her sword to its sheath. “Ian, right?”

"Yes." He walked over to her, gun in hand. "Know that I have been waiting for you for days. The Chief assured me that you would be here earlier."

"My last letter did not have a date," she responded shortly as she studied the man, attempting to match his tone. "Remember that my job requires tact and subtlety. I knew that those moronic brothers would leave Rapture looking for clues eventually. Not that they would ever guess who is behind all this."

"Have you been compromised?"

"No. I doubt even The Wanderer knows it's me, let alone have the evidence to *prove* it. Presently, she believes the informant to be my mother."

"And what of your mother?"

A wicked grin crawled across her face. "Her hatred for The Wanderer has blinded her to any possibility that her *sweet, innocent* daughter has been helping you. Trust me, she's just as oblivious as the rest of them."

Ian nodded. Moonlight washed over him, catching in his coarse black hair and the deep brown of his skin. A small, reddish scar glinted from his cheek to his ear. He would never admit it, but a bullet grazed his face when Eva, Jake, and Tommy escaped the Tiger Den. Chaos and disorganization nearly cost him his life, and he would never allow that to happen again. In fact, it was his idea to enlist the help of someone inside Rapture to bring chaos into The Wanderer's life.

"We need to get her out of hiding," Mara mentioned as they headed towards No Man's Land. They were still about a day from the compound, but the golden-haired girl was happy that she had someone to accompany her, especially someone so high ranking within the Gang.

The Tiger's Second-in-Command remained stone-faced. No emotion. Just like his superior. "Agreed. The Chief asked me to mention something. A message for you to relay. Should Rapture's Council vote to execute his target, he instructed my men to *burn your city to the ground.* Understand that he requires the privilege of her slaying for himself. So I would caution you… make that happen or the punishment will be your head *and* your city."

Mara swallowed hard. She nodded. He continued.

"So, what was the promised price for your aiding us? It must be steep for risking your life on both sides."

"Freedom from that place," she said. "Along with a reasonable rank within the Gang without having to fight for it."

"Genuinely," he glanced at her. "Do not take my tone as thankless. You do us a great service. Much of what has occurred in your town could not have been done without your help."

Mara paused. Something had been eating at her for a while. A request. "Do you think I could ask for more?"

"I doubt the Chief will give you more at this point. He has revenge on his mind, always. But I could be wrong. What more could you want?"

"That he would grant a pardon to one of his sons."

Ian stopped in front of a home and looked at the woman. He cocked his head to the side and furrowed his brow, staring at her with an uncomfortable intensity. Owls from the nearby roofs cried their evening song. A distant wolf sent an eerie howl through the forest. Before The Tiger's Second-In-Command could respond, movement from the Post caught their attention.

Rather than running, the two travelers entered the home with their weapons ready. Ian did not know of any trades that day and felt compelled to investigate. He crept towards a window and squinted through the dirt-caked glass. To his surprise, he found his own kin gathered in the foyer with members of the Wolves. Ian burst through the front door and fired a shot through the skull of one of his Tigers. His aim was impeccable.

"What are you doing?" Mara shrieked. "That was one of *your* people."

"This was not authorized," he said calmly over the screams of horror and surprise. "Get on the ground. Face me."

Mara stood in the doorway as Ian slowly entered the room, his gun fixed on the survivors. After a quick glance over her shoulder to ensure no one else would witness the execution, she leaned against the doorframe and watched.

"Where did you obtain the approval for this trade? Who allowed this?" The Tiger's voice brimmed with anger, but his expression gave nothing away. Clearly, he had done this before. Two from his Gang still survived, along with three from the Wolves. They were all knelt around a chest overflowing with weaponry.

Five Gang Members at the mercy of one.

Neither Wolf nor Tiger moved a muscle towards the crate of loaded weapons.

"We did not know this was an illegal trade," one of the Wolves spoke. "We were led to believe that your Chief was giving this shipment on good graces."

"*Good* graces?" Ian repeated and pointed the barrel of his handgun at her. "Do you really think I would believe that? You think the Tiger Chief cares about your dwindling, shitty Gang? If *you* believe that, then you're a fool."

The other Tigers remained silent.

"We heard that the Tigers and Serpents were unifying," the woman continued. Her voice shook as she raised her hands in defense. "Our Chief believed it to be unifying with the West too."

"Now why would you think a Gang the size of the Tigers would be trying to appease someone we could obliterate in a day?"

No one responded to the question. The Wolves looked at each other and started pleading for their lives. Mara's eyes widened as, one by one, Ian took them out. Three gunshots and the Wolves lay motionless on the floor. From the lingering tension in the air, Ian still had unfinished business with his own members.

The last Wolf body thumped to the floor and Ian continued his interrogation. "How long has this been going on? Who is involved?"

Both Gang members remained silent. They looked at one another, then down to their dead comrade. Mara did not believe they would answer the question, so she stepped in. She wanted to prove her worth.

"Ian," she shifted her weight and crossed her arms. "Allow me to crack them open."

The Tiger Commander stood aside as the slender woman approached the two remaining Gang Members. She took a few strides in front of the pair, circling them like a vulture. Humming an ominous tune, she attempted to prod at their minds.

"You know *The Wanderer* is being held in Rapture's prison because of me," she said softly. "Until now, I am the only one who has been able to take her down. How, you ask? Because I *excel* at manipulation."

The Tiger to Ian's right opened his mouth to speak, but she ignored him.

"But words never stung enough for me, so I decided to delve into the art of torture. *That* is what excites me. Pleas to end their miserable lives. The warmth of fresh blood on my fingertips. Sounds beyond anything you could fathom from a human being. Nothing compares."

She was shocked at her own words, but continued nonetheless.

"You brand your servants, yes? I am sure you have heard their cries, smelled the pain. Maybe I could return the favor that you have granted so many."

"Enough playing and do your worst," the young Tiger spat. "I call bullshit."

Mara's embarrassment twisted her stomach. *He saw right through me. It's so different out here.*

In a flash, the warm barrel of Ian's gun was pressed against a young boy's temple. The question was posed again. "Who. Else. Is. Responsible?"

The Tiger squealed. "Just us, sir. No one else was involved. We-we-we just needed some extra trade goods. Please! It won't happen again."

"No," Ian paused, then pulled the trigger again, killing the boy. A second explosion rang out, and the last Tiger fell into a growing pool of his own blood. "No it won't."

"Wait," Mara said as Ian pushed past her and continued towards The Blooded Row. "You're just going to leave this stuff here? Won't that raise suspicion? Why not make it look like a trade gone sour?"

"I will have some of my men return for the goods. The Tigers do not need to stage an accident. We have no need to cover our tracks. Our mark on this region will be known."

Nothing was said for the next day as the two traveled further and further towards the Den. Mara had a nauseating excitement watching Ian extinguish the lives of his traitors. This was the life she wanted to live, not a monotonous existence in Rapture.

But as she thought more about her future, she couldn't get Jake out of her mind. In the beginning, she hadn't been attached to him; when she first struck an agreement with the Tigers, she had cared little for his fate. Now, she found herself considering something far more dangerous—bartering for his life.

Perhaps Chief McAvoy would recognize her unwavering obedience to his orders. And if not, she would find another way. Leverage was never hard to come by.

***

Towering metal gates opened to Mara and her escort. The scent of rotten food permeated the yard as the fires were started for the day. Soot-caked servants stood in queues to be served their meal before work. A cool breeze stopped halfway through the crowd, cut by the heat of the bonfires. Right behind the large barrels of molten metal lay a heap of bodies, slowly mummifying with the dry heat. Mara wanted to vomit, but any scent of decay did not reach them. It may have been the smoke from the fires that masked it, but the sight alone was gruesome enough to make her heave.

The Rapture-woman followed closely behind Ian, weaving through the sea of Doxies and Bondsmen toward the Castle. As they passed the Pits, a few Guards nodded in acknowledgment. Gaunt, ghost-white faces turned to watch the willowy woman, though their eyes never met hers. Finally, the Tiger whisked her from the yard and up the sturdy steps leading into the building.

"He is expecting you," Ian said before turning on his heels and leaving Mara in the stairwell, alone.

Cold sweat slicked her palms. This would be her first time meeting the ruthless Dan McAvoy face to face. She knew the stories and they terrified her. But what sickened her most was having to plead a case to spare Jake. Although it was The Wanderer that he wanted most, she knew that Jake and Tommy had betrayed him as well, and that was not taken that lightly. *Revenge is on his mind, always.*

"Well, well, well," Chief McAvoy's frigid voice carried across the crimson carpet of his chamber. Back turned to Mara as she entered the room, he stared out at the yard from the window, hands clasped behind his back, watching his servants toil away. As he turned to face her, she was taken aback.

"My apologies sir, I didn't -" she hesitated. "I didn't expect you to be so striking. But, then again…" She neglected to mention how he reminded her of Jake.

"I could say the same about your beauty, Mara," he smirked, but his eyes remained pale and emotionless. "I would welcome you as one of my personal Doxies if you'd like. But that does not appear to be your intent. You wish to be a warrior for me."

"Yes," she replied quickly. "And I come with news."

His smile vanished. "News that I have already received. You are not quick enough, I'm afraid. What I want from you is The Wanderer."

"The Council has called for her execution."

"Yes… and I am running out of time to coax her to battle me. Your pathetic excuse for a Council is driven by the weakest emotion known to humankind… *fear*. Pitiful. Typical. Understand, Mara I do not wish to undermine your efforts, but you are not the only one who serves me in Rapture."

Mara took a step closer to McAvoy's desk and asked him to repeat his last comment. He obliged. "How do I not know about this?"

"Your job does not require you to know." He placed his hands on the desk and looked into her eyes. "I am far too experienced to plan for a single spy. I needed someone… if you should fail."

Fail. That word made Mara's stomach twist in painful knots. Her mind raced through everyone in Rapture, considering who might be working for the Tiger Chief. Whoever it was, they hid their secrets far better than she did.

"What would you have me do sir?" she finally said. "I am at your service."

"Excellent." He moved his right hand over to a sealed piece of parchment. Slowly and meticulously, he slid it over to her. "I've decided to resort to a more… direct approach. This task must be done with the utmost haste. I need you to hand-deliver a message to The Wanderer herself."

Chapter 13

"I can feel the heaviness of your Spirit." Yidi said amid the evening festivities. "The first night was rather quiet, but the Nomads decided to feast on the second. "Does our Lioness wish to be free of the bonds of Rapture? Lions were never meant for a cage."

Jake and Tommy had been given their Spirit Markings and sat down for the feast. And although the elder brother's mind stayed fixed on Mara, he did not feel as though she was in danger. Eva, on the other hand, could be executed at any minute if the Council grew impatient enough. Images of The Wanderer hanging in the Town Square reached his mind, but Mara's voice extinguished it with accusations of her danger.

She put you, your family, and the rest of us in danger by her mere existence. It rang. *She deserves nothing but death.*

Then it was his own father's voice that replaced hers. *You should have joined me when you had the chance. I will not forgive such pestilence. The only sufficient punishment is death.*

Jake's internal struggle drowned out any opportunity to enjoy the Nomad's company that night. Children danced around him, laughing and playing, but he took little notice. He began to realize how much that this world had changed him. For the first time, he yearned for the safety of the Vault. Friends and acquaintances with long-forgotten names and faces. Meals that left him sickeningly full and laughing until his sides hurt. Skipping school without a care in the world.

Endless passages winding through the hills and sealed off from this horrible wasteland. All of it felt impossibly far away, like a borrowed memory.

Suddenly, he recalled his mother's face, as clear as day. Her chocolate-colored eyes nearly matched her thick, long hair. She was smiling. It felt so real, Jake could almost reach out and touch her face, but deep down, he knew that it was just his imagination.

I miss you most of all, mom, he shut his eyes tightly to hold back tears.

Yes. She misses being out here," he said. "But she stays for us. Now that the Council wants her executed, we're just trying to stop that from happening—even if it means she comes back out here again."

He paused and cleared his throat. "I think I finally understand. Rapture was never safe for her. Not really. The second something went wrong, everyone turned on Eva."

"Tigers are merciless," the old man closed his eyes and nodded. "But pain from those close to us cuts so much deeper. Death follows that woman wherever she steps. We just have to hope she continues to step down the right path… or that could spell tragedy for all of us."

The younger brother massaged the pit in his stomach. Even the Nomads understood how dangerous Eva was. Although she spent years risking her life for the McAvoy brothers and the Eastern Rovers, the Gangs would always follow the trail of blood right back to her. When she was alone, The Wanderer was harder to trace. But it was Yidi's last sentence that gave him chills.

Jake had finally snapped out of his reverie. "Regardless of whether Eva directly or indirectly caused these attacks, her presence is a danger to our home… *and* herself. I don't want her to be killed anymore than you do, Tommy. You act like I don't care about her anymore."

"Do you?" Tommy lifted an eyebrow. "Do you care about her, or is this just about you? Because it feels like you're just trying to get Eva out of Rapture so you don't have to admit *you* didn't stand up for her. And now she's going to *die* because of it."

His brother shoved his empty plate off to the side, hitting a young woman to his right. Standing up, his voice rose over the group. "You know what? Even Eva would say that survival is all about yourself first. Stop making *me* the bad guy. She's brought nothing but death to our family."

Tommy shot up to his feet and stared up at his brother. "And *we* would both be dead if it weren't for her."

"Sure. Years ago. But she's changed."

"*So have you.*"

The entire tribe was staring at the McAvoy brothers at this point. A few of them were brandishing weapons in case a fight broke out. Tommy's final words cut right through his older brother's soul, causing him to take a step back. By the time Jake came up with a response, his brother was already heading in the direction of Rapture. Anger filled his core.

"Where do you think you're going? You've never killed anyone. You'll be a target for the Gangs…"

Tommy disappeared behind a building, saying nothing.

Jake looked at Yidi, who pointed towards the darkness of the street. "Coyote. A warning. Do not make enemies with your own family. He is all you have left. Your words are not without truth, but they are also borne from emotion. Please, do not allow them to kill Eva. I feel as if she still has a part to play in the unfolding of this world."

Questions engulfed Jake like an ominous cloud as he wound through the ancient city, praying to run into either Mara or Tommy. When the sound of the Nomads silenced, the landscape instantly became eerie. Danger lurked around every corner, and Jake knew that he would hesitate if he came across a Gang Member. *Just let me get back safe.* His heartbeat was loud in his ears and his palms began to sweat. After an hour of searching, Tommy finally revealed himself.

"You are so loud when you walk around here."

Jake jumped and stumbled against the side of a building.

He rushed over and shushed Tommy. "What if the Gangs hear you?"

"Then I hide, which you suck at. Do you know how long I've been following you? The whole time. And you didn't even notice. You never learned *anything* Eva taught us. You never *listen*."

"What is wrong with you?"

"*Me*?" Tommy shouted. "You're the one who doesn't give a shit if she dies. After all she's done for us."

"You aren't even thinking about *all* she's done. Eva is the reason that people in Rapture are dead. *She's* the reason that the Rovers are dead, and *she's* the reason that Anya died."

Jake did not recall the impact of Tommy's fist against his face, only the pain that followed. By the time his head cleared enough that he could see straight, his brother had, once again, disappeared back into the city. Laying his hands in his head, he felt the warmth of his throbbing cheek.

Oddly enough, he wasn't angry with his brother. If anything, the strength of the punch impressed him.

"That was *dad*, not Eva," Tommy had said before he left his brother alone in the street. "And don't bother looking for me. I'm done."

Slowly, Jake wavered to a standing position, pulling himself up with the aid of a nearby brick wall. He was alone. Again. But seconds later, Mara was rushing through the streets and nearly ran over him. The look on her face when she noticed who was in front of her was fear, then relief, then fear again.

She looked around frantically. "Where's Tommy? Are you okay, Jake? What happened to you? Were you attacked?"

Jake only answered the last question. "Yeah. By Tommy. He's fine and is probably back with the Nomads already. Leave him. By the way, where were you all this time? I was worried."

"I'm sorry I left you. I had to follow my gut."

Mara stuffed something in her pocket that looked like a note. Jake squinted in the darkness to try and make out where it was from, but she concealed it too swiftly to discern who had given it to her. When he inquired about it, she gave a short but satisfying answer.

"It's evidence."

Jake nodded and followed her through the remaining part of the city towards their home. Soon, a familiar view appeared as they climbed through the last set of buildings to the hill that overlooked the remains of what was once a vibrant town. Sunlight crept in from the east, washing the land before them in a soft orange glow. In the distance, Jake faintly spotted a small silhouette heading the same way as he and Mara. It was Tommy. It had to be. Tapping his companion on the shoulder, he pointed to an old home where the shadow had just slunk behind.

"There's Tommy," he said. "See? He'll be fine."

"What about you?" she asked as they carefully made their way down the cliff. "Are you finally on my side about Eva?"

Jake paused and bit his lip, hopping down to the pavement. As he rubbed the dirt off of his face, he realized his Nomad markings were still there. He wiped it away and tried to formulate an answer. Part of him wanted to scream the truth at the top of his lungs, but only a nod and a short remark escaped his lips.

"Yes," he muttered. "I'm on your side. But that doesn't mean I want her dead."

After at least an hour of silence, Jake watched his brother's figure disappear towards Rapture. *I guess he didn't return to the Nomads.* He looked down at Mara and immediately noticed the sealed parchment hanging out of her pocket. Something was wrong, though he couldn't put his finger on what. Rather than dwell on it, he gathered the courage to ask.

"Where did that come from?" He gestured at the letter. "Where did you get that? And why did you leave us in the city?"

Mara twirled a lock of hair around her finger. She attempted to mask her nervousness. "Why so many questions?"

"Oh please," Jake huffed. "You don't think it's a *little* unusual that you tell us that you know how to get information, but you won't let us join you. Then, you come back with a sealed note that you won't let me read."

"It isn't for your eyes," she replied sternly. "It's for the Council. Proof that Eva is innocent. I *helped* you and this is the thanks I get?"

He stopped, opened his mouth, then closed it again. *Why do I feel so guilty about this?* Mara noticed the uncertainty on Jake's face and pounced on the opportunity.

"Don't you realize how much Eva has gotten to you? She's making you question *everything*, even those who care about you. That is how *she* lives, suspicious about everyone and everything. Why do you think she has so many enemies? Her *honor*? Ha. She's messed with your mind so badly that you can't even think for yourself anymore. Instead, you think like her—and that's exactly what she wants."

The armored woman's tone was so terse that Jake backed into a foundation, nearly falling into an old basement. Clenching an old stone to hold himself upright, he winced and looked past Mara's shoulders. Secretly, he hoped that a Gang Member would attack them to avoid this confrontation, but she would not budge. Each time he would step to the side, she would follow his lead, blocking his path. He would avert his gaze, but she quickly became frustrated, unsheathed her sword and pointed it at his neck, lifting his chin.

"Quit denying the truth, Jacob McAvoy," she snapped. "I may be saving her from Rapture's execution laws, but out here… there is nothing to protect her. She will get what she deserves."

"If she dies, who will protect those out here?"

"Someone will take her place."

Jake stopped. *No one could take her place* is what he wanted to say, but he believed that Mara was right. *Maybe that's a good thing.* True, she had saved him and Tommy more times than he could count. But would they have needed saving at all if she had not been with them? Mara had always warned that Eva's presence invited danger. And she wasn't wrong. From the Rovers to Rapture itself, death and destruction followed The Wanderer wherever she went.

"You're right okay?" Jake threw his arms out as his voice echoed through the street. "Is that what you wanted me to say? I don't want Eva in my life anymore. I want *you, Mara.*"

The willowy woman drew a breath to speak, but Jake's lips found hers first. The rush of emotion hit so hard they both buckled, knees weakening as the moment swallowed them whole. Their world narrowed to a single, breathless moment. When they finally pulled apart, Jake spoke more gently.

"I don't love her, Mara. But I won't sleep at night if we let the Council execute her. I won't stoop to her level of murder as the only solution. Please, just ask them to banish her. *Beg* them to banish her. Do that much for me."

"And what if she joins a Gang, brings her men back here, and wipes Rapture off the face of the earth?" Mara whispered, still reeling from the kiss.

"She would never do that," he pleaded. "Please. We can be together as soon as this weight is off my shoulders."

She stood up and sighed. Slowly and reluctantly, she nodded in agreement. "I will do what I can," she promised.

Jake smiled weakly.

"Don't worry. This letter will help," she lied.

The two remained silent for the remainder of the trip. When the colossal walls of the town rose above them, Mara announced her presence to the guards and the gate groaned open. Once their eyes adjusted to the sunlight's reflection off the pale cobblestone, Jake half-expected to witness another gruesome scene left by the Tigers. But it was just a normal day in Rapture. He turned towards the farms and noticed Tommy working diligently alongside Xander, as if nothing happened. *So he did come back.* Faintly painted on his face was the markings of an Owl given to him by the Nomads. That much, Jake could see.

Mara started towards her home and Jake began to follow until she held her hand up in protest. "I have work to do. If The Council sees me with you for too long, my mother will not accept her banishment. She'll assume that you've gotten to my head."

"Where am I supposed to go?" Jake asked.

"Come to the house tonight," she said. "Go back to work for now."

He realized that he had not opened his shop in a few days. "Okay." And with that, he rushed over towards the Worker's District to his shop, thinking little of The Wanderer's fate. He trusted that Mara would do the right thing.

***

The informant understood her duty. Chief McAvoy gave her a note to deliver directly to Eva, but how? Gavin was in the home and the rest of the guard would become suspicious if they discovered anything. Could it really be as simple as placing it on the porch, knocking on the door, and hiding around the corner to ensure it found its way into Eva's hands? Planning the attacks on Rapture were much more simple. More lucrative. This menial task was difficult, but Mara had to do it if she wanted a place within the Tiger's ranks. If she ended The Wanderer, Dan McAvoy would surely appoint her to Ian's position of second-in-command. The idea thrilled her.

As she passed the note through her fingers, tracing over the crimson seal. *I wonder what it says.* But she was afraid of what the Gang would do to her if they knew she opened it. They could be watching. She had been loyal without question, and she could not falter now. Unfortunately, she could only imagine what was written on the parchment.

"Tonight," she whispered to herself, "will be the beginning of the end."

***

"Tonight?" Eva whispered as guards passed the door. Gavin and she had been plotting their escape for the last few days.

They both knew the gallows were nearing completion. At Virginia's insistence, the woodworkers worked day and night. The sound of hammers carried through the town at all hours. From her home, Eva could only watch.

"I don't think we have much more time than that," Gavin said with a pained look on his face.

"No," she replied. "Tomorrow morning. The guards change shifts at dawn. When they do, we leave."

Her Commander stroked his beard and nodded. "Okay. I just hope the Council doesn't have you hanging by then."

"I won't go down without a fight," she said, stroking the hilt of her blades. "Trust me. I would sooner massacre the entirety of Rapture before letting them get to me. Or you. You're all I've got now. Although… it is a bit sad…"

"Sad?"

"They have no idea what they're messing with. I have not been myself since I set foot in this place. But after some clarity on who I can trust, The Wanderer is back. I'm not hiding who I am anymore. And something tells me that vengeance is in the future."

A chill spread through Gavin's arms, giving him goosebumps, as a smile crawled across his face. Eva looked at him and smiled as he took her into his arms and squeezed her tightly.

"I would be honored to fight by your side."

She smiled and brushed her fingers along his cheek. "I wouldn't have it any other way. You're the only one who has stood by me through all this. Unwavering. Loyal. But why? I feel like I knew you from a lifetime ago…"

Thumping on the door startled the both of them. By the time Gavin made his way over to the front entrance and threw the door wide open, whoever had been on the porch was gone. At his feet, a sealed note. He bent down and picked it up, looking down the street in both directions. The only life in the street was a guard, marching towards the house. Quickly, he shut the door and stepped back into the kitchen. Eva watched and her eyes widened when she locked onto what Gavin was holding.

"*Tigers*," she gasped. "I'd recognize their seal anywhere."

Gavin held the letter at arms length and slowly opened the note, wincing as the wax popped off the parchment. Nothing happened. Eva instructed him to place the letter on the table as she unsheathed a dagger. The moment that it touched the wood, carefully opened the letter with the tip of her blade. When she saw that it was only parchment, she stepped closer to read it. The handwriting was meticulously perfect, each line had its purpose. Her heart was beating so fast that she could barely hear herself think.

WANDERER,

FORGIVE MY INTRUSION INTO YOUR PERFECT, UNEVENTFUL LIFE. BUT YOU MUST UNDERSTAND, I DID NOT WANT THIS FOR MY SONS. YOU SEE, IT WAS I WHO ORCHESTRATED THE RAID ON THE VAULT WHETHER THE SERPENTS KNOW THIS OR NOT. AND THE DETAILS DO NOT MATTER. WHAT MATTERS IS THAT THIS INVASION WAS A TEST FOR JACOB AND THOMAS. THE REMAINING

VAULT DWELLERS WERE SIMPLY COLLATERAL. BUT WHO WOULD HAVE FOUND MY SONS IF NOT THE INFAMOUS WANDERER? NOTHING IN LIFE IS DRIVEN BY COMPLETE COINCIDENCE. THERE ARE COUNTLESS THREADS OF FATE WOVEN BETWEEN US ALL. NEVERTHELESS, I MISCALCULATED YOUR KINDNESS. I BELIEVED YOU TO BE A RUTHLESS TYRANT. PERHAPS I HAVE BEEN LIVING IN A FANTASY WORLD. A WORLD WHERE SOMEONE, ONCE SO DEADLY, BECAME SO SOFT.

A SUBSTANTIAL AMOUNT OF TIME HAS PASSED SINCE WE LAST MET. THERE IS MUCH TO DISCUSS. THESE ATTACKS WERE FAR TOO MERCIFUL, I CONFESS. THEIR PURPOSE WAS TO FORCE YOU OUT OF HIDING OR LOSE YOUR MIND, WHICHEVER CAME FIRST. ANOTHER MISCALCULATION ON MY PART. I WAS HOPING TO HAVE A RESOLUTION BY NOW. UNDERSTAND, RAPTURE DESERVES EVERY CASUALTY FOR KEEPING YOU FROM ME, BUT I AM RUNNING OUT OF OPTIONS TO END YOU. SO THIS IS MY DIRECT ATTEMPT AT REMOVING YOU FROM HIDING. I SHALL ENTICE YOU TO MEET ME IN BATTLE ONCE MORE. YOU HAVE LOST <u>EVERYTHING</u>, SO HOW COULD I POSSIBLY ENTICE YOU? ASIDE FROM THE REVENGE THAT I KNOW YOU HAVE COURSING THROUGH YOUR VEINS. WE ARE NOT SO DIFFERENT, YOU AND I. VENGEANCE—THE VERY SAME FIENDISH CRAVING THAT WE SHARE.

NEVERTHELESS, I HAVE ANOTHER PAWN TO MOVE BEFORE A CHECKMATE IS CALLED. PERCHANCE I CAME INTO POSSESSION OF SOMETHING, RATHER SOMEONE, THAT YOU THOUGHT YOU HAD LOST LONG AGO.

DOES THE NAME KELLYN SOUND FAMILIAR?

Eva's hands began to shake. *What? How?* She could scarcely believe what she was reading. So many questions flew through her head that it was making it spin. Her Shadow appeared, cackling in the corner of the room. Gavin stood patiently in front of her. There was more to read.

Yes, Your first love, if his words are true. Unfortunately for him, he let that slip. When you deserted your Gang years ago, he should have been slaughtered… but I spared him for the sole purpose of using him against you should the opportunity present itself. I *always* prepare, *always* plan. That is how I remain five steps ahead of you and the rest of that pathetic city.

And if that isn't enough, perhaps it's time I shared the secret that's been consuming your every thought. Tell me—who do you think is behind the carnage that stains your peaceful little town? Which of Rapture's loyal citizens has served as my hand in every act of destruction?

I am a man of my word. Do you trust me? I suppose you will have to find out.

But I digress. The purpose of this message is to pull you out of hiding to die an honorable death. Otherwise, the alternative is hanging as I am told. You would agree that execution is a coward's death, yes? Perhaps Kellyn's life means little to you now. But if I know you, and I do, The Wanderer would never pass up an opportunity for revenge. Once you see how I have redecorated the battlefield, my hope is that your anger is fresh. Let your tears guide the way, if you are even capable of having any human emotion at this point.

WHEN I FACE YOU FOR THE FINAL TIME, I WISH FOR IT TO BE A BATTLE RECOUNTED THROUGH THE AGES. MY NAME WILL BE CRIED THROUGHOUT THE REGION AS THE ONE WHO STRUCK DOWN THE WANDERER. PERMANENTLY.

Fury was already boiling over by the time Eva slammed the letter onto the table. She could feel her face heating up and shot a look at Gavin who placed his hand on her shoulder. He slid the note closer, scanned through it, and a perplexed look appeared on his face. Eva was staring blankly at the floor, deep in thought.

"What does he mean by, '*once you see how I have 'redecorated' the battlefield*'?"

She shrugged. "I was wondering the same thing. But where is this battlefield?"

"There must be a clue somewhere on here." Gavin started to reach for the note to flip it over and knocked over his glass of water, soaking the entire paper. For a split second, Eva's anger was directed at Gavin's carelessness, but then, something appeared on the paper before them. Was this a stroke of sheer dumb luck? *Let your tears guide the way*… A general map of the region gradually appeared across the back of the note with a large X over a very familiar place—The Eastern Rover Colony. *Of course that's where it is.* The Wanderer looked up at her Commander.

She jumped out of her seat urgently. "We have to go. *Right now*. We can't wait until nightfall. If we make it to the gate…"

"They will try to kill us," Gavin whispered loudly.

She pointed at him. "Or they will let us go. Less that the Council has to worry about. We have to take that chance." Eva began to mumble to herself. "No… no… not the gate… the hole near the Training Grounds. That would be quicker and we wouldn't have to wait until they opened it… yes."

"Are you crazy?" Gavin said. "We would be exposed…"

"What are you so afraid of?" she smirked. "I've done this once already."

"I-uh…" he paused and cleared his throat, stiffening his stance. "Shit. You're right. Let's go."

Eva nodded. A knot formed in her stomach as her mind drifted back to the Rover Colony. What had Dan McAvoy done to the survivors? Enslaved them? Some of the Rovers had been used as a warning to Rapture before, but had he indeed massacred the entire town? Her final words to those she once protected made her uneasy. *"You… All of you… had better hope that you can survive without me. Your days are numbered and your thankless attitudes are what led you to this fate… Banishing me will do nothing to appease them."*

"You sealed their fate," a familiar voice whispered in her ear softly. It was her Demon who had stolen the voice of her adversary, Chief McAvoy, once again. "You left. I killed them. Too bad."

"Yeah," she whispered under her breath so Gavin could not hear her. "Too bad for them."

She slowly picked up the soaked letter, turned it over, and stared at a name that she had not seen for years. It had been all but erased in her memory. A spark of hope that Kellyn was still alive ignited faintly, that was, until she looked over at Gavin. Her feelings were stronger for a man who had fought by her side when no one else would.

Revenge was branded onto her heart with a white-hot flame. *That's what I'm facing McAvoy for. Not Kellyn.*

Gavin patted her shoulder and nodded towards the door.

"I'm ready."

Chapter 14

Gunshots, screams, and heavy breathing echoed through Rapture at dusk. Their fugitives had escaped house arrest and made a break for the hole in the wall near the Stronghold's Training Grounds. And it was none other than Mara and Virginia who had spotted them racing across the Town Square. Jake rushed out of his shop, working late, and caught a glimpse of the chaos before Eva disappeared around the side of the Stronghold with a half-dozen guards after her. But he didn't realize that Gavin was with her until Mara said something.

"At least *someone* has her back then," he half-smiled. The weight of regret settled in the pit of his stomach, laced with a sickening flicker of joy.

I won't see her ever again... but now I can finally start over... the way I want to... with Mara.

Just as Eva reached Rapture's border, she turned back. Not towards where Tommy and Jake were staying, but towards the Town Square. The very place where Anya's funeral had taken place. Memories flooded her mind as she pushed through the last few steps and out of the cracked wall. A hail of bullets pelted around her from the guards, but none of them met their mark.

Her Hooded Shadow floated at her heels.

Cool air filled The Wanderer's lungs. *I'm never going back. I'm not a prisoner anymore.* The sacrifices she made for her broken family would wither, but a new chapter in her story was about to begin. An immense weight seemed to lift off her shoulders as they reached the dilapidated homes between Rapture and the city. Gavin turned back to his new companion and wrapped an arm around her.

"How do you feel?" he smiled and laughed nervously. "Shit… I'm terrified. Haven't been out here in years, Eva… *years*. Well, except our last little adventure."

Eva could feel Gavin trembling, but she wasn't sure whether it was from excitement, uneasiness, or a combination of the two. They both knew that there was no turning back now. Rapture was now as hostile as the Gangs. A few more steps down the road and she cut in front of him, looked up into his blue eyes and felt a warmth spread across her body. He smiled back at her and shrugged.

"What? Is it something I said?"

"Just trust in your skill," she said. "We will be fine."

Just as she turned her back to Gavin, her smile faded. The note was still in her pocket and its words were still hanging around her like a noose. A name continuously repeated in her ear, *Kellyn*. She jumped when the next question to escape her Commander's lips was about this mysterious name and the owner of it.

"So um," he started. "Who is this guy? Kellyn. And why is he with the Tigers?"

Eva dropped her head and stared at the ground as they walked. "I can only answer the first question because I don't know the answer to the second. When I was a young Doxie in the Serpent's compound, Kellyn was a Bondsman about my age. His parents were killed and we were shoved in a small tent with a ton of older Bondsmen. They… tried to… um… have their way with me. Kellyn. H-he fought them off and protected me while I slept. He was kind and caring, and always made sure I had food to eat and a safe place to sleep. That was long before I gathered the courage to face the Chief. We were never *lovers*, just children…"

"Wow," said Gavin. "You really cared for him."

"I did. Once." She pulled her hood over her head, concealing her face. A deep breath, a shaky sigh, and a pause filled the air between them.

"The Bondsmen bribed the guards. I guess they got sick of him trying to protect me. And one day… he was just gone. I never saw him again."

Her voice lowered. "That was the same night I challenged the Chief. The night I became Mistress."

Gavin slowed his pace as she continued.

"We were supposed to do it later. Together. But after what happened… I wanted revenge. It was the first time I remember losing myself. Feeding the rage that burned inside me. I cut down the Chief and slaughtered every last one who had wronged us."

"Shit Eva… I'm so sorry."

"Don't be. Now I know the guards sold him to the Tigers all those years ago. And somehow, McAvoy found out about our connection. If he's still alive…"

She trailed off as they entered the city. Only their footsteps echoed through the desolate streets. A barrier of unease formed between her and Gavin until Eva finally exploded.

"I don't need your sympathy okay?" she whispered quickly. "And I don't have feelings for him anymore. I just want to make sure he's okay. I owe him that much. He kept me alive all those years. I was weak. I couldn't return the favor. I-"

Gavin interrupted. "Eva, stop. I don't pity you. You're The Wanderer for shit's sake. I would never think of you as weak…"

She cleared her throat and nodded softly. "I'm sorry. I haven't felt right lately. Like I have to prove to myself that I'm The Wanderer again. Maybe I have to be out here for a while until things start feeling normal again."

"Well we have all the time in the world now."

Suddenly, she spun on her heels and stared down a motionless street. Was it a sound that caught her attention? Perhaps, she saw something. It happened so fast, she couldn't discern what had caused her to turn around in the first place. Gavin followed closely behind as she crept down the road, scanning each building and alleyway as they passed.

No wait, she thought. *It must have been a sound. I heard something.* Crumbling rubble behind Eva startled her again. Shoving Gavin out of the way, she slipped around the corner of a nearby building. As her eyes adjusted to the darkness of the narrow passageway, she caught a glimpse of something dart around the corner. It could have been anything.

"What did you see?" her companion whispered.

The Wanderer stared straight ahead and did not move a muscle. "I-I'm not sure. I thought I heard something following us."

"Can you tell if it's a Gang Member?"

"No. That's why we need to take another path."

The nearly empty streets soon gave way to loosely packed rubble, unstable footing, and jagged beams of structural steel jutting from the ruins. Even The Wanderer, who had traversed this path dozens of times, found it difficult to keep her footing on the dust-blanketed boulders. On the other hand, Gavin's meticulous watch and slow pace kept him from impaling himself on a rusty piece of metal here and there. The decision to change direction delayed their progress to the Rover Colony, but Eva no longer had the harrowing feeling that someone was following her.

But her Shadow still lingered nearby. If she filled her mind with other thoughts, its cackling and threats faded to a dull roar. Still, with every breath she took, it seemed to steal something from her. Energy? Her soul? Her life? The thought terrified her. She wondered if this feeling would turn her into something far more terrifying.

Gavin noticed her deep in thought, but his comment was rather unusual.

"I'm not sure if I'm looking at Eva Calloway or The Wanderer right now," he began. "Whichever you decide to be… I'm just deciding which one I like better."

"Huh?" Eva stopped on a landing and looked at him. "Sorry, I.. didn't catch that."

"Nevermind. Are you alright?"

"Fine… Let's keep moving."

Yanking her deeper into the abyss of her mind, the likeness of Dan McAvoy began to speak again.

"I grow tired of this game," he hissed. "Now… if you do not end your miserable existence, I must. Both of us cannot be allowed to live. One. Will. Die."

And it will be you. Just wait.

Midday greeted the two adventurers as they reached the center of the city. After stopping at an ancient storefront, Eva and Gavin decided to rest for a while. Luckily, they had stuffed enough food in their pockets for a couple meals. If they rationed out what they brought, it should last them the entire journey.

"Do you think he'll show up?" Gavin asked as he peered out into the street. "McAvoy, I mean."

"Not sure," she admitted. "This may be another one of his games, but I am in no position to deny a chance at payback."

"And if it's a trap?"

"Then you turn around and run as fast as you can. Don't look back. Don't be a hero."

Gavin hesitated and rubbed his tired eyes. "Okay."

Eva tore a chunk from a loaf of bread and ate in silence. She started to think about Anya again. Her innocence. Her kindness. She pictured her daughter laughing and telling long, pointless stories of dragons and princesses. She smiled. Questions of 'what if' started appearing and transforming the scene. *What would she have been like growing up? A writer? A warrior? Would she have found love? Would she be free from the chaos of this world and live in peace?* But those thoughts would remain unanswered. Unfulfilled. Pain tightened in Eva's chest, tears burning as she remembered her daughter would never have the chance to reach her dreams.

"Ready to go?" Gavin stood up and dusted off a few lingering crumbs from his armor. "We should reach the Rover Colony tomorrow, I think."

To her left, Eva noticed a familiar structure. It was the large, marble building where she spent an evening watching Jake and Tommy perform survival tasks when they had first met. From the top of it, she could see the city and the vast landscape beyond. A desire to climb those stairs gnawed at her legs—possibly to relive the past or even to shed the burden of the present.

Happily giving into the urge, she ascended the stone steps into the marble foyer, ignoring protests by her companion. A wolf leapt out from behind a counter carrying the carcass of a rabbit in its mouth. When it caught the scent of the travelers, it took a few steps closer with bearing teeth. As swiftly and silently as she could, Eva unsheathed one of her blades and brandished it at the animal. Gavin let out a deafening roar to scare it away, echoing through the building. It worked. For the moment, they were alone in the dust-covered entrance. The familiar sight ignited something in Eva's body, no, her soul. She inhaled deeply and rushed up the stairs, leaving Gavin behind.

"I'll be right back," she called from the stairwell.

Her commander did not respond. He simply found a pillar and leaned against it, staring out into the street. Only tumbling leaves and mice moved about. He yawned but remained vigilant.

If a Gang were to ambush them, she would notice from above and Gavin, from below.

The sound of her boots against the steps stopped as she reached the top floor. Gusts of wind rippled through her jacket, lifting her hood off her head. To her left, the roof had crumbled since she had last been there. A tinge of fear spread through her stomach and she wondered if it was safe enough to continue. By the time she considered the risk, her feet were already dangling off the edge of the roof, taking in the view.

Off in the distance was billowing smoke. It was coming from the direction of the Gangs, but it was also the same area as the Rover Colony. She was unable to pinpoint the exact location as both the town and the compound were just at the horizon and the smoke obscured them both. That sight alone told her more than enough, though. Follow that signal. Death. She knew it was death.

"I saw a signal North of here," she said to Gavin as she raced down to the entrance. "I saw smoke, so it must be fairly recent."

He followed at her heels down the next alleyway.

"This has Dan McAvoy's name written all over it. Whether he decided to overthrow the Serpents or burn the Rover Colony to the ground… people died… that much is clear to me."

"We still have a day ahead of-"

"I know, Gavin. I don't expect to find any survivors. If there was anyone left, they would be in the compounds slaving away by now. I highly doubt that though. McAvoy isn't known to keep survivors."

"Then why didn't he just finish off Rapture? Why didn't he have his contact burn the city to ashes?"

Eva jumped in front of him and shoved him in the shoulder. Her face was red with anger. "Come on, Gavin. Don't you get it? He's been *toying* with me this whole time… with Rapture. To him, it's about fear. Everything he's done is part of his little *game*. He destroyed my credibility so I would lose everything. He wanted me… alone. Because I'm his enemy. His goal was to drive me insane until I finally lashed out."

Her Shadow said nothing as she looked over her shoulder, then back to Gavin.

"Last time we met, I escaped. He almost lost his life. It made him look weak, and he had to *balance the scales* again. But I won't allow that to happen. I will give him the slow, painful death he deserves. This time, there will be no mistakes."

***

"Our lives are still at risk." Virginia's spectacles glinted in the candlelight of the Council Chambers. Xander, Maven, Jasmine, Lee, and Bruce agreed to yet another Gathering. This time, the tone had changed to fear and uncertainty. Little did they realize, Tommy McAvoy was in their midst, hiding just off the main hall and eavesdropping on the voices echoing through the corridor.

"But she's gone," Bruce interjected. "She and Gavin *just* deserted us before you called this nonsensical Gathering. If they attempt to return, they will be met with lethal force. This is a blessing in disguise. The last time we agreed to a public hanging—"

"Was decades ago," Maven added. "And it was well-deserved and necessary for the safety of Rapture. As is this."

"She's *gone*," he repeated. "We should rebuild our walls and live our lives again."

Virginia scoffed. "Why do you have such an unyielding loyalty to her?"

The burly Councilman shot daggers in her direction. "It isn't loyalty, Councilwoman." His hands curled into fists. "It's pragmatism. Rapture has softened my lust for blood, but *you* have never had to fight for your life. You will never understand. Eva is different. Her thirst for battle will never be satiated. Unlike the Gangs, though, she fights for good. But it is better for all of us that she remains out there."

Xander shook his head. "Does she truly fight for good, though?"

Virginia answered for Bruce. "*Good* for her own selfish agenda."

"Why do we care so much if she stays in her part of the region?" Jasmine's voice rose over the rabble. "We only felt the effects of her presence while she resided here."

"She's *The Wanderer,*" Virginia raised her voice as if the Nomad had said something offensive. A few of the Council Members rolled their eyes at the old woman's theatrics. "She's already brought upon us so much harm… so much death. For all we know, she could come back with an army and kill us all!"

Bruce stood up. "Shut up Virginia." His booming voice rattled the table and caused everyone to jump. A vein in his neck pulsated as he narrowed his gaze at the woman. "What you are suggesting is pure madness. Idiocracy at its best. You are completely out of your mind and out of line. Sending out men to kidnap her and return her here for execution is out of the question. Not to mention, dangerous for our people who have already suffered enough."

Silence greeted him when he looked to his kin for some sort of reassurance. All of them averted his gaze. He exhaled sharply and continued.

"I can't believe this Council…" he said, shocked. "You would have us waste the lives of *more* men to track down and kill the most lethal warrior in the region? And what of Captain Gavin? We murder him as well?"

Virginia pushed her glasses up the bridge of her nose. "Precisely. He has chosen his side. Unfortunately for him, it was the wrong choice."

Bruce glanced at each one of Rapture's Council Members. They all stared at the table in front of their seats. All except Virginia. "So is this your decision—Xander, Lee, Maven, *Jasmine*? Is this your *actual* decision?"

Together, they slowly nodded. Even Jasmine, the former Nomad, unenthusiastically agreed with the masses. The moment the silence began to set in uncomfortably, Bruce sat down and put his head in his hands, laughing in disbelief. "None who seek her out will survive this. It's a suicide mission."

Tommy slunk away after the nearly-unanimous vote. As soon as the rain outside splashed against his face, he sprinted towards Jake's shop, bursting open the door and panting heavily. It scared his brother so badly that he nearly dropped a piece of white-hot iron onto his foot.

"What?" Jake asked frantically. "What happened?"

"Eva," Tommy said in between gasps. "We… can't… let her die."

"Tommy. What are you talking about?"

"The Council. Virginia voted. Everyone is scared."

Jake grabbed his brother's shoulders and shook him. He was speaking nonsense. "Calm down. Tell me exactly what happened."

While the elder brother ushered the rest of his patrons out of the shop, explaining that he was closing early, Tommy sat down in a nearby chair to catch his breath. Both of their minds were racing. After locking the door and closing the shades in the shop, Jake pulled a chair over to his brother, sitting nearly knee-to-knee, waiting for him to speak.

Tommy looked around, and leaned in. His voice was barely audible. "Virginia has gone completely crazy. They're sending the guard to kidnap her and bring her back to be executed. I thought Eva running away would keep her safe. But Virginia called another Gathering. I heard her talking to Mara about it yesterday. Apparently they have turned every single Council Member against Eva—"

"No." Jake shook his head. "Mara would never do that. She has been trying to *help* The Wanderer's case."

"What are you talking about Jake? She's been fighting to hang her this whole time. You don't even use Eva's name anymore. What's happened to you?" Tommy's face contorted into a look of disgust.

His brother paused for a moment, then spoke. "Underneath all of that *heroic* attitude is a selfish woman. She's done nothing but put our lives in jeopardy. I don't know how many times I have to tell you that."

Tommy laughed sarcastically. "You have no idea what you're saying anymore. Eva fighting against the Gangs is what put us in danger. She wasn't the one who chose to infiltrate a Gang compound, *twice*. *We* persuaded her to do that. She risked her life out of kindness. She was *trying* to be better than she was before. But you want to talk about selfishness? There is *no one* more selfish than you, brother. You used her, abused her, and cast her aside. Now you have completely lost it and fell for Mara's stupid tricks. And all this time, I thought you were smarter than that."

Jake could not come up with a single rebuttal. Tommy continued nonetheless.

"—And now, I feel like I'm the only one who gives a shit about her anymore. Obviously, she doesn't trust us. But we need to help her. Somehow. We need to warn her before the scouts find her and, if we have to, fight."

Jake stood up, making his brother feel small. "*No*. I'm not fighting again. I'm tired of all this shit. You hear me? I'm *done.*"

"How do you think *she* feels?" Tommy jumped to his feet and punched his brother in the stomach, hard. "You owe her. *We both owe her.*"

But Jake refused to back down. Doubled over, his voice cracked under the turmoil he felt in his gut. "I'm not going. Wherever she's going is a trap and I can't see anyone else die. I'm *not* watching anyone else die."

Tommy roared in anger, shoved his brother out of the way, and slammed the door closed behind him. Jake stood there for a moment, considering his decision, and returned to work with a boulder of guilt on his shoulders. Air from the bellows sent an eerie glow out the shop's windows as he opened the door and ushered in a few of the townspeople. In the distance, he could see his brother leaving Virginia's house, carrying a bag of supplies and clad in the armor and weapons that he had been given long before their time in Rapture.

As Tommy McAvoy exited the front gates of the city, he scanned the horizon. Hazy clouds dropped low in the valley between him and Nomad territory. If he was persistent, he could reach the far side of the city, hopefully running into Eva and Gavin along the way.

I hope she'll listen to me, he thought and started walking quickly down the hill and away from Rapture. Over his shoulder, he had a few small blades strapped to a leather carrier and a larger blade against his belt. Each time a small animal skittered past him, he would unsheathe the weapon so fast that he nearly detached his leg from the rest of his body. Right around the time nightfall blanketed the region, Tommy felt completely alone.

At first, the uneasiness loomed over him like a raincloud, and a heavy one at that. Pressing downwards on his chest, the emotion made it difficult to breathe. *Remember your training*, he repeated under his breath, barely a whisper. Even though he had not taken a single life since being thrown into this new world, Tommy had a knack for stealth. Over the years, he'd mastered his craft, much like The Wanderer had mastered the art of combat. Only Eva, he believed, could ever match him. Tommy's apprehension melted into confidence.

The ancient homes seemed to beckon to him. The same pull Eva had spoken of long ago. A quiet curiosity stirred within him, drawn to the lost stories of the Old Times. Though his current mission could not wait, he silently vowed to return someday.

Maybe it was the weather lulling him into a hypnotic drift, urging his thoughts toward these remnants of the Old Times. Or maybe it was simply the feeling of living beyond the safety of Rapture's walls again.

For the briefest moment, he wondered if choosing to live within the town had ever truly been the right decision.

Distant drumbeats echoed through the city as Tommy stepped into the first few blocks of the metropolis. At first he thought it was his imagination, but there was no doubt it was the Nomads and their jubilant dancing, expressing thankfulness to their Great Mother. His heart ached to join them, but he couldn't abandon Eva and Gavin to the mercy of Rapture's guards. All he had to do was find The Wanderer, deliver his warning, and then he could finally go wherever he wished.

Maybe I will go back to the Nomads, he thought. *They have always treated me like family... better than Jake.* He scoffed. *He probably wouldn't even notice I'm gone...*

Tommy's chest tightened with sorrow for his brother. Mara had poisoned his mind of reason. There was a time when Jake would have run to help Eva without hesitation. Now, he could only see her as a monster.

Throughout the next day, the lonely teenager scavenged for a small meal as he continued zigzagging through the streets. Fatigue set in, but he remained persistent. If Eva could go without sleep for a couple days, so could he. Climbing through buildings, sliding down piles of rubble, Tommy nearly sliced open his torso on shards of rusted metal a number of times. Dusk came and went swiftly, as did the twilight hours. Still, the boy continued. Scraped and bruised, he finally made it through the center and remainder of the city. The welcoming horizon appeared before him as an early morning haze parted.

To his left lay the forest where he, his brother, and The Wanderer had bound themselves with rope and ventured blindly through the night toward the Warriors in the West. To his right, a plume of smoke and the crooked shacks of the Eastern Rovers stood as a memory of what Eva once defended. Between them ran the old highway, littered with the husks of Old Time vehicles and the ghosts of the stories they once held. It was there that Tommy spotted two silhouettes.

Was it part of a Gang? Perhaps it was a couple Rovers. A mere glint of light against something one of them was carrying told Tommy exactly who they were. Silver blades. It was the unmistakable blades of the famed Wanderer. He was close.

At first, he wanted to call out to them, hoping that his voice would carry far enough. But that might alert any Gang Members that were skulking around the city behind him. Waves of exhaustion crashed over his body and paralyzed him for a moment as he pondered what to do. One spark coursed through his body, lifting him from the ground and carrying him forward. There wasn't much time before Rapture sent their assassins out to kill Eva. He had to move quickly.

Tommy started down the steep hill towards the highway, carelessly allowing his feet to drop wherever they pleased. He was able to make it past the first few steps before he twisted his ankle over a pile of rubble, dropped to his knees, tumbling down the remainder of the decline. With each attempt to gain his footing, his fatigue weakened his limbs enough to where he could do nothing but wait until he stopped. Luckily, he landed on his back in a patch of soft grass. And despite his wounds, he was able to stand with little difficulty.

Adrenaline shot through his body like lightning the moment he realized how much noise he had made. He quickly scampered over to a large boulder and hid for a moment, listening carefully to the echoes in the city. Looking over his shoulder towards the direction of Eva and Gavin, Tommy saw that they had not noticed him. The gap between them was growing, so he sprung back to his feet and raced down the remainder of the hill. Soon, his feet began to hit asphalt. Just as he neared them, they made a hard right, straight for the Rover colony. But when he turned his head in their direction, something felt different about this town. He had not noticed the smell of charred remains at first. But when he did, it was unsettling.

***

Hours passed before either Eva or Gavin spoke again. Eva only watched the thin veil of clouds attempt to shroud the ever-sinking sun. The rustling of trees swept past them and upwards towards a V-shaped skein of geese. Normally, The Wanderer would have stopped and taken in the scenery, but her mind was just as distant as the stars that began to twinkle behind the lavender and peach sky.

Kellyn, she repeated in her mind. *Unless he is, in fact, alive... there is no way McAvoy would know who he was. Perhaps... no... he would not make a trade... he spares no one. Still... to possibly find out who is responsible for everything in Rapture? Now that is an answer I need to find out...*

"You really think I would come to my senses?" her Shadow mocked. It was breathing right over her shoulder, following her quickening stride. As it spoke, it reached its skeletal hand and grabbed her shoulder, digging its claws into her flesh. Suddenly, trickles of blood began to appear where the bones had pierced her skin. Eva's heart skipped a beat as she leapt backwards through the specter, grabbing at the searing pain on her upper arm.

Gavin was in front of her, so he did not notice for a moment. It was just long enough for Eva to come to her senses and realize that the pain and the blood was simply a figment of her imagination. When her companion inquired about what had just happened, she brushed it off.

He nodded and they continued down the path towards the Old Time Highway. Although The Wanderer kept her head down and her face concealed by her hood, she could feel Gavin's eyes still on her.

"What?" she asked without lifting her chin.

"Nothing," he started. "Well... actually... I was just wondering what you'll do after you kill McAvoy?"

Eva stopped as they reached the Rover Colony. She felt a presence behind her, but it was what waited ahead that drew her in. When Gavin started to repeat his question, she threw her hand up in the air to silence him. As she reached back to grab the hilt of her blades, the scent of decay assaulted her senses. They neared the closest shacks and her jaw clenched.

"I knew it."

Chapter 15

The scent of charred remains drifting through the colony made Gavin heave. The Wanderer motioned for him to stay back as she moved in to investigate. Taking a few careful steps forward, she could tell from the smell alone that the bodies had been dead for some time, but their bodies were burned within the last day. The realization struck her all at once.

Those gunshots I heard before, she thought. *The smoke.* She slammed her back against the side of a shack, the cold metal sent a shiver across her body. *If it was the Tigers, they could still be here. They could be hiding in the shacks. This is either a trap or a display.*

"Is everything okay?" Gavin whispered loudly.

Tommy remained out of sight, hiding behind a large oak tree.

Eva turned back to her Commander and shook her head, put a finger up to her lips, and continued creeping towards the center of the colony. Dusk was approaching, and the lines to the Feast Hall would have already started around this time. Nothing stirred within the homes. No chirping birds or chatter of small animals reached this cemetery. Even the wind had fallen still. The only sound was the faint crackle of smoldering remains.

Death had poisoned the earth here.

"I don't even have to admit my hand in this," her Demon spoke as The Wanderer stepped over a few bodies. "You already know that I was responsible. However, if I remember correctly, this place was cursed long before I set its people ablaze. *You* cursed this place. It was your words that damned them."

"Words are just that," she whispered back as she tried to take in the scene. Every time she attempted to focus on the massacre, the Shadow's claw would sink further into her shoulder, distracting her. She winced.

"The moment you left them, the clock started ticking," it continued. Eva shut her eyes hard and tilted her head towards the sky as another piercing pain splintered through her body. "My dear Wanderer, it was only a matter of time before I started making examples out of these parasites. Their very existence is meaningless. They only lasted this long because of you. Most importantly, they kept you from realizing your true potential. I did what I had to."

Suddenly, all at once, the Shadow disappeared and The Wanderer was able to see with enough clarity to overwhelm her senses. The sight. The smell. The taste. Even a tactile change in the space around her. She felt everything. Rover's faces, cemented with fear. Some had escaped the flames, but not their end. Their eyes stared into the world, open to everything, yet seeing nothing. Men, women, and children lay twisted in odd poses. Bullet holes and slash marks riddling their lifeless bodies. Others were so badly charred that they were unrecognizable. The rain had bloated their remains into grotesque, swollen shapes. Green and brown mold had already begun to spread across them, and some bodies had been torn apart by scavenging animals. Overhead, vultures circled.

Without a doubt, this was the work of the Tigers—merciless and chaotic. And although this sight would have brought Eva to tears before, the Rover's banishment hardened her heart. Only rage and a thirst for repayment filled the void.

"Eva?" It was not Gavin's hand, but Tommy's that touched her back. "I came after you. I have something to tell you."

She spun around on her heels and pointed a blade towards him. "How did you get out here? Why did you follow us? *Speak.*"

Rather than throwing his hands up in surrender, he drew one of his daggers and pointed it back at her. The Wanderer drew a sharp breath. She took a step back, then hardened her stance.

He continued. "The Council voted to have you *assassinated...* you and Gavin. They're going to try and take you back to Rapture to hang. I had to tell you…"

Gavin watched as they stood there for a moment, absorbing the words that were spoken. Eva sheathed her blade. As she started to back up, she tripped over a bloated corpse, causing the bullet holes to ooze horrid-smelling liquid. Gagging violently, she hurried to her feet and looked at the two men. Perched on her back again was the red-eyed Shadow, whispering into her ear. A chill ran up her spine.

"Losing your touch, Wanderer?" it taunted. "Lucky for you, I know how to stop all of this delirium. *It is time*. You must embrace me. Embrace the darkness inside you. Before all of this, you were truly a sight to behold. Stories of The Wanderer were whispered all throughout the region at one time. Now, you are nothing but a shell that cannot even stand on her own two feet. Continue down this path, and no one will recognize you. Embrace me… or you will never be strong enough to face what waits for you."

Gavin could tell that Eva was no longer listening. He tried to get her attention, but he knew that something internal had taken hold and was not going to let go without a fight. She was staring blankly at the ground. Tommy caught the Commander's eye and they just watched as The Wanderer battled with her demons.

"...What harm is there in becoming what you were meant to be? You would have everything." The Shadow shifted through a series of mangled faces before finally settling into Eva's own likeness, and her own voice. "You would be the greatest warrior in the region again. All would fear you. All would bow… No… *tremble* at your greatness. But if you continue to fight your fate. *You. Will. Fall.*"

Yes... You're... right. I need this strength to battle both McAvoy and Rapture. I give in.

The world beneath her feet suddenly shifted. A resurgence of darkness ripped through her with such ferocity, it knocked her off her feet. Eva felt a dark, piercing haze pressing into her, merging with her physical form. Two entities battled for the space under her skin for eons and seconds simultaneously. Indistinct memories flashed before her eyes. And just as quickly as the feeling came, everything dissipated and she was left on all fours, gasping for air.

As she looked up at Gavin and Tommy, opening her mouth to speak, she saw a group of silhouettes behind them. She looked over their shoulders and scrambled to her feet. Shoving past her Commander, Eva tore her blades out, awaiting who she believed to be Rapture's guard.

It wasn't.

Expect the unexpected, she mouthed to herself. Her Shadow sank deep into her chest, and a fierce confidence rose in its place. As the ringing in her ears faded, footsteps echoed through the haze. The Tigers surrounded her—leather-clad with their insignia stitched boldly across their arms and backs. One near the center dragged a shape across the ground. A body. One by one, the Gang stepped into view. But to her surprise, Dan McAvoy, though promised, was nowhere among them.

"Our Chief sends his regards," one of them bowed mockingly. "Unfortunately, he will not be able to join us tonight."

Gavin and Tommy caught an unusual twinkle in The Wanderer's eye. Swiftly, she flicked her hood over her head. Her voice was playful yet tinged with fury. Inside, a fire ignited in her chest with an intensity she had all but forgotten. Her spirit—an unknown predator—was ready to pounce. She felt herself become the anger, self-doubt, and inner conflict that had manifested as her Demon. The power she felt as she grasped her blades was indescribable.

I am The Wanderer.

"That's too bad," she mocked, concealing her face. "Pity. Guess I'll just have to send a message with *one* of you."

An incredibly large, burly Tiger pushed past one of his members. "I wouldn't be making threats ma'lady. We got yer friend here. W'as his name?"

"Kellyn," a few of the Gang Members chimed in. "Got him right here."

Even in the ten or so years that Eva had last seen him, Kellyn looked worse than she remembered. His hair was matted and long, a few strands were hanging over his scar-ridden face. Underneath his eyes were dark bags that scarcely differentiated from the dirt and bruises that blackened his skin in patches. And then, there was his frame. The entirety of his body was so thin, he looked as though he would shatter if the Tiger moved him too rough. On his arms, Eva could see fresh whip marks.

"E-E-Eva?" His voice was raspy and dry. "It-it can't be… I thought you were-. Y-you *you* are the Wanderer?"

Her heart softened a bit, but she masked it. "No, Kellyn. Clearly, I'm not dead. But I believed you had been killed long ago."

His cough was labored, nearly rendering him unconscious. "I wish I was, believe me. They won't let me die… yet."

A few of the Tigers snickered. The one holding the rope that bound Kellyn's arms and neck kicked him to the ground, giving him a mouthful of grass. There was no way that he could push himself back to his knees, so the Tiger yanked him backwards. The prisoner did not even try to cushion the fall. He was far too weak and could only shut his eyes and prepare for the impact. Eva started to take a step forward, noticed that the Gang was watching her closely, and considered whether her life was worth that of an old friend. She lifted her head and confronted the man who appeared to be their superior.

"I ask again… Where is your Chief? Is he too much of a coward to face me?"

A Tigress dismissed her. "Bold comment coming from someone who couldn't even finish the job the first time, *Wanderer*. Your namesake is far too grandiose. When it comes down to it, your execution is… *lacking*. And that is a direct message from the top, from Mr. McAvoy himself."

"Why claim to face me?" Eva ignored her. "And when the time comes, hide in his castle and let filth do the bidding."

All of the Gang Members laughed in unison. "*You* are outnumbered."

"We will see." A sly smile crept across her mouth. "But I've been underestimated countless times before."

"Sounds awf'lly confiden'," the large Tiger growled.

"Here are my terms. Release your prisoner, as promised in the letter from your superior. And if this goes smoothly, I will let you all live."

A moment of silence spread over the Gang as they looked at one another in confusion. Two counted their numbers and wondered how The Wanderer could make such a demand. Gavin slowly turned his head to Eva, Tommy following suit. Their eyes were wide with fear. Tommy convinced himself that if she was not afraid, he should not be either. Perhaps the Tigers would let Kellyn go without question. However, Eva knew there would be a battle. But she was ready. *Outnumbered but not outmatched.* Lucky for her, the Tigers must not have anticipated a firefight as none of them bore a gun.

A particularly observant Gang Member noticed her studying them. "We were instructed to kill you slowly, so I'd wipe that smirk off your face. Cuz this ain't gonna be pretty."

Kellyn's matted hair and face were now caked with dirt and blood as he spoke. "Eva, we both know I'm not supposed to survive this exchange."

"Don't say that," Eva glanced down at him. "You will be free in a moment. *Now*, Tiger, release him or face m-."

"Goodbye Eva," Kellyn interrupted. "It was nice to see you… one last time."

Before Eva could shout, the burly Gang Member had already unsheathed his machete, grabbed a handful of Kellyn's hair, and hacked at his neck. The blade was so large and so sharp, it decapitated him in a single swipe. Blood cascaded from the wound like a waterfall as Eva watched, shock and anger bubbling up from her stomach, but her demeanor remained stoic. Beside her, Gavin and Tommy let out noises of disgust and horror.

"Surprised this don't make you angry, Wanderer," the massive Tiger taunted.

He tossed the severed head and it rolled right to Eva's feet. She looked down at the look of defeat forever plastered on the face of her old friend. Part of her wanted to cry, but the moment she finally accepted her Demon's words, no emotion allowed itself past her chest. Just the same as she was long ago, Eva allowed it to pass through her without a trace, never to be spoken of again.

"With anger," she explained. Gavin and Tommy watched her closely. "Comes the possibility of making fatal errors. You, however, have made one yourselves."

The Tigers started to laugh, but The Wanderer continued.

"Laugh if you must, but I promise it will be one of the last sounds you ever make. The final will be you choking on your own blood."

Gavin and Tommy pulled out their weapons to fight alongside the Wanderer, but she had other plans for the McAvoy boy. "You have no place here. Go back to the safety of Rapture's walls. *Do not come back.*"

"But Eva-," he started.

"Go, Tommy," she glanced back at the sandy-haired boy. "You are not fit for the world out here. And thank you for warning me about Rapture. I will anticipate their arrival. That is, after I deal with this lot."

By the look in her eyes, Tommy knew that The Wanderer was serious. The longer he stood there, among the tense air of battle, the more he worried about her reaction if he did not leave. Something unseen was rising in the space between them, and it petrified him.

Tommy's feet had already carried him far beyond the Rover Colony before the rejection began to set in. Still, he did not turn back.

He would not dare face The Wanderer again.

***

Gavin kept his back near a Rover shack so the Tigers would not completely surround him. Eva, however, stood in the middle, reckless but ready. No one moved a muscle. Both sides awaited the first strike and The Wanderer grew impatient.

"If you've come to kill me," she called out to them. "Then do it. Quit stalling."

"You first," one of the Gang called out. "We're waiting."

The air became increasingly intense, but The Wanderer refused to budge. A calming patience floated around her. She knew that if she attacked first, she could not assess a weak point and would give away the perfect position to strike from any angle. If she were to be backed into a corner like her Commander, her fate would be similar to that of her friend, Kellyn. She sheathed a single blade and reached down to her back pocket and discovered the hilt of a small dagger. As she slowly removed it, she studied each one of her enemies.

Leave one alive, she decided. *That way, they can carry a message.*

Another voice echoed from the darkest part of her mind. *But that does not mean you can't maim the chosen survivor. If they can make it back to the compound, that would be enough.*

Gavin was visibly sweating from the anticipation as his gaze darted between The Wanderer and the Tigers. Palms sweating, he tightened his grip on his blade and a loud, shaky breath escaped his lips. The Gang noticed and turned their attention to him.

"Wanderer," the largest Tiger boomed over the jesting. "Your friend here won't be able to assist you if he can't keep his legs from falling out from under him."

But Eva refused to turn her back on her enemies. That was their pitiful attempt at distracting her, and it failed miserably. At that point, she'd had enough. She hurled the dagger at the Tiger who had murdered Kellyn. Straight through the eye, the blade lodged itself into the man's skull, dropping him to the ground in a motionless heap. An audible gasp spread through the group. With that single blow, she had accomplished two goals—staying firm in her location as well as asserting her dominance over these unskilled warriors.

Gavin tried to step forward, but The Wanderer stopped him. "Just watch," she said softly. "Watch and learn."

In the blink of an eye, she had calculated where each Tiger stood, their weaponry, and stance. A warmth spread from her spine to her arms as she readied her blades, awaiting the first strike. But even that did not take long. The first assailant was already upon her. Cut down with ease, she simply stepped to the side and swiped downward, dislodging his arm from his shoulder. The piercing scream that exploded from the Gang Member's lips excited something inside Eva. She wanted more.

Scrambling until his back was against one of the shacks, the first Tiger grabbed the stump where his arm had been. Blood spurted from the artery onto the ground nearby. His skin began to lose color. Gavin watched in utter horror as Eva's first victim slowly weakened and stopped moving, slumped in between two pieces of scrap metal. As the life drained from the Tigers' eyes, a numbness spread through the Commander's mind and he began to feel an irresistible urge to stand alongside The Wanderer. By the time his gaze shifted back to the battle, another Tiger was upon her.

Eva parried the first strike. A loud clang from her sword echoed through the colony. Her opponent attacked again, nearly knocking Eva off balance while trying to block. The woman, twice her brawn, carried a heavy hammer. Each time it came crashing down, the ground would gain another small crater. Beads of sweat began to form on Eva's brow, dripping down her cheeks.

And this is only the second opponent. Just as the thought crossed through her mind, she turned around to find another Tiger attempting to stab her in the back. Before Eva could spin around and roll away, his arm was slicing down at her. His first and final blow was barely dodged as Gavin's weapon chopped the Gang Member almost completely in half.

He had saved Eva's life.

She nodded in thanks as the woman behind her began attacking again. Two against seven now. Eva shoved Gavin out of the way so that he would not receive a fatal blow from the Tigress. He nearly tripped over Kellyn's disembodied head as he came tumbling down into a pile of charred remains. Another Gang Member was now on top of him. He lifted his weapon's long hilt to block the next blow. Both opponents were disarmed in the struggle. The Tiger pounced and wrapped his hands around Gavin's neck.

Lucky for her companion, The Wanderer noticed immediately after striking down the burly Tigress. She quickly kicked an axe over to his reach, dodging another Gang Member lunging towards her.

"How many more?" Gavin growled as he embedded the blade of his axe into the Tiger's stomach, lifting him into the air and over his head with a thud.

Eva counted quickly. "Five. Wait." She tripped another Tiger, stabbing him in the back, killing him instantly. "Four."

It was almost like The Wanderer knew her opponents' next move. She had always been confident in her skills, but this time, it felt different. It *was* different. She felt unbeatable. Immortal, even. Tigers fell in heaps, adding to the body count of the lifeless Eastern Rover Colony.

Soon, Gavin and Eva were covered in mud, blood, and sweat. One Tiger, chosen by The Wanderer as the most terrified and weak, stood in their midst. He was shaking so violently that his knees were knocking together. Gavin stepped forward to attack, but The Wanderer stopped him.

"Drop your weapon," she demanded of the young kid. "*Now.*"

The Tiger obeyed.

Eva stepped closer and snatched up a handful of his shirt in her fist. She jerked him towards her. "I have a task for you, so listen. I'm *sparing* you to send a message to your Chief. I. Will. Be. Waiting. Tell him that I want him here. No more games. No more bullshit."

"W-w-what?" The Tiger stuttered. His eyes were darting from The Wanderer to his own fallen comrades. "You-you murdered them all…Y-you did this. H-How?"

It was obvious that the young kid was still in shock. Eva could feel his heart beating in his chest. His pupils were dilated and he couldn't seem to get enough air to amply fill his lungs. For a second, she considered whether she had chosen the right Tiger to send a message to Dan McAvoy, but her gut told her that she had. She lifted her gaze to Gavin. Weapon still in hand, he glanced at her and shook his head.

"He isn't going to say anything," he attempted to argue. "Why don't we just kill him and get it over with. Shit.

We could send the message ourselves when you fight like *that*."

Eva laughed. Her Commander became slightly offended. "Seriously Gavin? You and I against thousands of armed Gang Members? Please tell me you're joking."

"Yeah," he admitted. "You're right." Then, he slammed his weapon against a wall, sending an ear-shattering clash through the bodies of everyone nearby. His eyes were on the Tiger. "You'd better listen. You just witnessed what we're capable of. Consider your fate today… because torture is *much worse*."

She turned back to the boy and leaned forward, whispering in his ear. "He has *no idea* what I can do to people. I've done far worse than what I did to your friends here. Now, if you aren't going to listen, you are useless to me and all we have now is time. Would you like to see what I am capable of?"

All of a sudden, Eva's head began to swim. A voice. The voice of Dan McAvoy. It started to take over, a sharp pain shot up the back of her neck, and she let go of the Gang Member's clothing. Just as quickly as it came, the wave of confusion was gone, but only a single comment resonated in the space between her ears.

"Don't worry dear Wanderer," it said. "I'm coming for you."

Goosebumps spread through Eva's body as she returned to the present. Before either Gavin or the Tiger had a moment to absorb what had happened, she grabbed the boy's arm and yanked him to her face.

This time, she screamed her demands. The tone in which she spoke frightened her a little. "I don't have time to play anymore games, child. You will do this or I *will kill you*."

"Anything," he repeated. "Anything. Anything. Please. Don't kill me. Please don't kill me. Please -"

Eva was now nose-to-nose with the Gang Member. She could feel the terror between them. "Shut up."

There was silence.

"You will *run* back to your compound and go directly to Chief McAvoy. I don't care what your superiors say. Directly to him. Tell him I want him. *I WANT MCAVOY.*"

The Gang Member started running in the direction of The Blooded Row, nearly tripping over himself as he turned back to The Wanderer. However, Eva had one more message to his leader.

"Tell him I will be waiting. I'll be ready."

As soon as the messenger disappeared from view, The Wanderer slumped to the ground and massaged her temples. Breathing heavily and somewhat worn, Gavin slumped near the bodies. Weapons dropped to the ground. They put their head in their hands and rested for a moment.

"You alright?" he asked.

She lied. "Yeah. Fine. You?"

"As good as I can be," he responded. "After all that."

The more she tried to recall what had happened, the more her head began to hurt. Something had happened. Something she could not explain nor recreate. It felt like the real McAvoy was in her head for a split second.

Was it the real him? Impossible. But the sensation felt so different from her Shadow.

"You need to stay away from me until I end him," Eva finally said. Her aqua eyes shimmered with tears, but she knew exactly how dangerous she could be. Since she had entered Rapture, unexplained feelings had overwhelmed her thoughts and she was afraid of accidentally hurting Gavin. She became convinced that the only way she could rid herself of her Demon and regain full control over her body was to kill Dan McAvoy himself.

This has to work, she reasoned. *If not, I don't know what else to do.*

"I'm not leaving—" Gavin started.

She put her hand up in protest. "I didn't say to leave. I can't make you do that. Up until now, your loyalty has been unwavering, despite everything. You even fought with me and saved my life. And shit, you battled *well.* Just… don't come near me until this is all over."

"Do you think it will be over soon?"

"I hope so, Gavin. I hope so."

With that, Eva stood up, sheathed her bloody blades, and dragged her feet over to a familiar shack. Once, years ago, it had been her home. As she stepped through the doorway, she looked around at what remained. Dust had collected in thick layers over her tables, shelves, and bed. Even the Rovers had not touched it. Her fingers drew lines across her end table as she passed it. *Perhaps they thought this place was cursed.* Holes in the sheet metal cast a few, deep rays of foggy sunlight into her home.

For the first time in what felt like an eternity, she felt whole again.

Chapter 16

Tommy listened to the echoes of battle coming from the Rover Colony. The wind carried screams through the valley, but he kept his back to it. Only the look in Eva's eyes occupied him as he walked quickly towards the city, hands in his pockets. Something in the way she looked—or the way she spoke—told him he had to go back to Rapture. *Maybe I'm not fit for out here. She's probably right. I've never killed anyone... even if I can sneak around like her.*

He reached the outskirts of the city while pondering his next move.

Should I return to Rapture? Would I really be able to convince the Council to stop the assassins? Or would I even make it in time?

What if I return to the Nomads... trust that Eva does the right thing? That she kills Dad and somehow puts this region back together?

I could always turn around and return to the colony. Fight at her side.

Jake...

At the very least, he had to warn his brother. To make him understand that Eva wasn't to blame for everything that had happened. They owed her that much. For all the times that The Wanderer risked her life for them, it was their turn to repay that debt. And Tommy knew Eva well enough to predict her next move. She'd spare one Tiger and force him to carry a message back to the Chief. It was only a matter of days before McAvoy would appear. This time, there would only be one winner.

"Child of the Owl Spirit," Masha's voice called from around a corner. The boy thought it was his imagination at first, but saw the Elder Nomad a moment later. "I thought it was your presence I felt." Alongside Masha was a small troupe of her kin. They were all brandishing large weapons, mostly spears. He thought it odd that they were so close to the city's edge.

They greeted each other with a warm embrace. "Where are Yidi and the other Nomads?" Tommy asked.

"With the rest of the clan…" She paused. "We have been forced to venture further out from our home, further from the center, to find supplies. Lucky for us, our Great Mother has blessed us with food to hunt nearby. She has even graced us with safety as of late. But…"

Masha looked over Tommy's shoulder and lowered her voice. "Yidi believes this peace will meet a swift end. He's had crippling visions of war. *A great War*. The region bending a knee to a singular form."

"Do you think he's going crazy?" he asked.

She sighed. "For our own sake," she looked into his eyes. "I hope so."

"And if not. Does he know who this person is? In his dreams?"

"No. He cannot control these visions. Time and place are also unknown. This could happen tomorrow or years from now. Or, it may not even happen at all. If it is a glimpse into our fates, it can always be rewoven."

The boy's mind immediately materialized a battle between Eva and his father. If the Nomad's premonition was correct, his father would send the Tigers to wipe out the rest of the region after he finished The Wanderer. Rovers, Nomads, and other free peoples would burn. Walls of compounds would crumble and the Gangs would be given a single choice. *Join or perish.*

Tommy's decision was made. Rapture had to know.

"Will you not stay with us young Owl?" Masha offered.

"I will someday," he said. "I swear. But I have to warn others."

"Then take some food with you young one."

Tommy thanked Masha and stuffed his mouth full of bread and a handful of seeds and nuts. He quickly bid her and the others farewell and continued on his way.

Overhead, clouds darkened and obscured the winding paths ahead. Thunder rolled through the nearly-desolate metropolis and resonated between the rows of crumbling buildings. However, not a single drop of rain came from the heavens. Tommy's feet crunched over fallen leaves and scattered rubble as he wandered deeper into the ruins of the Old Times. For hours, he followed what he believed was the right path, only to realize he kept circling back to the same broken stretch of land he had crossed before. Panic surged through him as he hurried off in a new direction.

Trust your instincts. The Wanderer's voice whispered in his mind. *You think too much*.

But no matter how hard he tried, Tommy couldn't quiet his mind enough to let instinct take over. Exhaustion weighed heavily on him. Though he felt the relentless pull to keep moving, he knew he would never make it back to Rapture without stopping to rest.

After calculating that it would take at least two or three days for Eva's messenger to reach his compound, deliver the message to their Chief, and return to the Rover colony, Tommy finally allowed himself to stop. He found a place to lie down, cold pavement biting through his clothes. The second his head touched the ground, his eyes fell shut, and he plunged into a dream.

***

“Stand up and face me,” said an unfamiliar voice.

Tommy felt his legs begin to buckle, but managed to stay on his feet. As his eyes adjusted to the torch-lit room, he did not recognize it. The space stretched so wide he couldn’t make out the walls. Shadows deepened the vastness, leaving only a crimson carpet, a set of stairs, and a looming throne visible before him. A figure rested upon the throne, motionless and imposing. Behind it stood two silhouettes, one on either side. To the left was the familiar outline of a human, and to the right, a figure that shifted in a way that defied nature itself.

“There are those who would not deem it wise to stand before me.” Again, Tommy could not place the voice with anyone he knew. It sounded muffled and distorted, as if the person did not want to reveal their identity in his dream.

But this didn’t seem like a dream at all. It felt real.

Suddenly, something drew his attention to the foot of the stairs. He questioned whether it had been there before, but could not convince himself either way. Facing its back to Tommy was a limp, graying corpse. Dark blood pooled on the floor around it. *Who is this?* He couldn’t tell. And no matter how hard he tried to move, his legs would not budge. With his head on a swivel, he searched for a way out.

Wake up, he repeated inside his head. Nothing.

Tommy could hear his own voice, but he could not control what he was saying. “You have massacred so many of us. I am here to avenge the dead.”

“*Are you*?” A laugh of pure-evil boomed from the hooded figure. “How quaint. They send a *child* to face me. So, *you* are their hero? Their champion? Please… You insult me.”

A blade appeared in Tommy’s hand as he raised it above his head. Paralyzing fear spread through his body while he stood frozen, watching his opponent rise to their feet. He inhaled sharply as it advanced towards her at an alarming speed. With his weapon out in front of him, he slashed down at the enemy, missing by mere inches.

The figure drove its shoulder into Tommy's stomach, sending him stumbling backward and knocking the weapon from his grasp. It skidded across the stone floor, stopping just out of his reach. The two warriors struggled, but Tommy soon felt cold hands tighten around his neck, crushing his airway. He fought against the weight of his enemy's arms, trying to pry them loose, clawing at the shadowed limbs to no avail.

His extremities grew numb. Warmth spread through his body. Darkness overtook his senses. Life slipped away.

He closed his eyes.

***

The scene dissolved as Tommy McAvoy was rattled back into consciousness. Drenched in a cold sweat, he rubbed his eyes and tried to catch his breath. Remnants from the dream faded excruciatingly slowly. He stood up, wavering on his feet for a moment, and stepped outside into the brisk midday air.

What was that? Who was that? Was that really me?

But he couldn't linger on questions. He had an important message to deliver.

Trust your instincts, Eva's voice repeated. Finally, Tommy was able to clear his thoughts and take a route he had never ventured before.

Before he knew it, the city was behind him, and Rapture loomed on the horizon. Tommy had only two days to convince the Council to halt the assassination of Eva and Gavin, persuade them to offer help, and force Jake back to the Rover Colony.

A few hours remained until he reached the gates, and all he could do was hope they let him in.

Winding through the timeless streets, he recalled the moment he, Jake, and Eva first set foot inside the walled city. They were wounded, tired, and scared. With the Tigers at their heels, Rapture offered comfort and safety. Six years had passed since then, and the world they once believed in had unraveled into something far different from the truth. People were slaughtered. Anya had been murdered. Jake had fallen under Mara's influence, consumed by his own fear. Worst of all, Eva was losing touch with reality.

Suddenly, an unsettling feeling spread throughout Tommy's body. Something… or *someone* was watching him. Carefully, he unsheathed his weapon and began checking the houses on either side of the street as he moved forward. The complete absence of life made his skin crawl. He quickened his pace and kept his head on a swivel, eyes darting to the source of every subtle movement. Soon, his footsteps became maddening. He feared they masked any other noise that might warn him of danger, so he shifted onto the grass, careful to avoid fallen branches and dead leaves. Even the sound of his breathing began to consume his thoughts. Still… the feeling did not waver.

I'm being followed.

Finally, just as dusk began to fall over the region, Rapture's gates were towering over the adventurer's head. He wasted no time calling out to the guard, stating his intention, and keeping a watchful eye on his surroundings.

"I need to speak to The Council *immediately*," he yelled up to them, looking over his shoulder to see whether a Gang Member had followed him.

"State your name," called a voice from above.

The teen grew impatient. "Tommy McAvoy. I work with Xander in the farms. You know who I am."

For a moment, there was silence. Tommy considered whether he, too, had been exiled for warning Eva. Perhaps they found out, somehow. Did they send out a small group of scouts to watch him? No. He would have known. He would have seen or heard them during his journey.

Before he dwelled too much, the gates opened to a handful of bobbing kerosene lamps. It wasn't the Council, but Jake and a few guards that greeted him at the threshold. His elder brother was wearing his sleeping clothes, a loosely fit tunic and pants. When his gaze met Tommy's, his eyes widened.

"Why were you out here?" he grabbed him by the arm and snatched him inside. "I've been looking *everywhere* for you. You could have been *killed.*"

"Shit Jake," Tommy looked at his brother in disgust, snatching his wrist from his brother's grasp. "What is wrong with you? I'm not a child anymore. I don't need you telling me what to do. So shut up because we need to talk."

Jake completely ignored him. "Why were you gone so long? It's been *days*. Where were you? I was worried sick. Were you with *her*? Did she hurt you?"

Tommy couldn't take the tone any longer. His fist connected with Jake's jaw, knocking him off balance and into the mud. With a fistful of his brother's shirt, Tommy dragged him up, bringing their faces inches apart.

"Listen to me, for shit's sake! I'm so sick of you hiding behind everyone and letting them fight your battles. Our father sent his Tigers out to kill Eva. He knew that she'd be at the Rover Colony, somehow. They massacred everyone. But let me guess. You don't care, do you? Unless your life is threatened, you don't give a shit about anyone else. Well, guess what? Eva destroyed dad's warriors. All. Except. One. She challenged our father. He's coming. And if you don't face him with me, you deserve to die just as much as he does."

Jake was at a loss for words. He looked around at the guards for reassurance while rubbing his swollen cheek, but found neither pity nor concern. Tommy was well respected in Rapture, and for that reason alone, no one spoke.

Suddenly, Tommy burst into tears when the rage became too much. He shook Jake violently. "What the hell has gotten into you? You were starting to stand up for yourself out there. Then we get here. *People start dying*... And all you do is hide and lie to yourself."

The crowd watched as Jake stood up and shoved his brother into the road. “Fine. You want to know the truth? I’m *glad* Eva left. When we were out there, danger found us everywhere. I thought being here would change that. But it didn't. Not with her around. You don’t find that to be more than just a coincidence? Really, Tommy? People like her aren’t meant for places like this. Walls aren’t built to cage monsters like her.”

By the time Jake finished speaking, Tommy’s face burned white-hot, his jaw clenched so tightly it throbbed with pain. He shoved his brother aside and shot him a sharp look when he heard him mutter under his breath. His grip tightened around his weapon until his knuckles turned white.

If Eva was here…

One of the guards demanded that Tommy disarm himself before entering the city. “Where are you going? You know the laws.”

Tommy ignored him. Another guard along with Jake called to him again, but he continued down the cobblestone path towards the Council Chambers. Something in his gut said that they would be there, even though it was dark. A plan formulated in his mind as he reached the doors. He opened them and stormed into the Gathering.

“The Tigers massacred the Rovers,” he interjected. Virginia huffed and looked down her upturned nose. “They’re going to kill Eva and come straight here.”

The silver-haired woman cleared her throat. “They *will* kill or they *have* killed? Shame if our guards couldn’t get to her first… regardless… her tyranny will be dealt with. Justice will be served.”

Tommy’s eyes darted from one council member to the next. When he realized Virginia had directed a question at him, he answered.

He lied.

“Their Chief slaughtered her. But Gavin’s still out there… somewhere. McAvoy has already ordered his men toward Rapture. We need to send guards to the Rover Colony and stop them before they get here."

"How is it that *you* managed to escape?" Lee asked, leaning forward in his chair and interlacing his fingers. "Over the former Commander of the Guard? Gavin is well-trained… but you…"

Tommy brandished his weapon. "I was trained by The Wanderer and the Nomads. I stayed hidden."

"If what you say is true, we *must* fortify here," Bruce said. He shifted his weight in the chair and interlaced his fingers. "Without having anyone to spare… Rapture would be left unguarded. Citizens would be burned in the streets. And if you speak the truth about Eva, our men would stand no chance. We have survived this long here. Rapture *will* endure."

Even Tommy understood now that his fight would never truly end. Eva and Gavin would be alone when the Tiger Chief returned with his men. At least the Council believed the Wanderer was dead. Rapture would continue to hide behind its walls, just as it always had.

Cowards.

At that moment, Tommy realized he no longer wanted this life.

He vowed to stand beside Eva and never return to this place again. When the battle was over and his father was gone, he would return to the Nomads and spend the rest of his life among them, fighting for those who could not defend themselves.

Turning on his heels, he did not say another word until he reached the gate. His final exit. To his surprise, he found Jake waiting for him, dressed in the armor they had been gifted years ago. A dark bruise was forming around his eye where Tommy had struck him. He looked sternly at his younger brother, took a deep breath, and spoke slowly.

"This isn't about her…" he started. "You're my brother… and… I just have to see this for myself. Prove me wrong. Mara left and hasn't returned in days so I'm worried about her, too. I don't even know where she went. She left almost right after you did…"

"Fine," Tommy said shortly. "But I'm not coming back here."

***

After much convincing, Eva had reluctantly agreed to let Gavin remain in the Rover Colony as they waited for the Tigers. They settled near a cluster of shacks, dragging out old furniture to break down for firewood and pulling out a few chairs to rest on.

The Wanderer surveyed her surroundings after returning with a few rabbits for dinner and vegetables harvested from the Rover gardens. At the center of town stood the gnarled tree that had once displayed two Rovers as a message to her. Now it loomed over a square littered with bodies. Fresh Tiger corpses sprawled beneath its twisted branches, mingling with the charred, bloated remains of the Rovers. Only one word could describe the stench. *Death*.

Gavin's whisper barely reached Eva's ears. "It is only right to give them a proper burial. We can't leave them like this."

But The Wanderer's response was cold as she recalled the final conversation between her and the Rovers. "I will not waste my breath or strength on these people."

"But Eva," Gavin gently placed his hand on the small of her back. "There are children."

She sighed. Guilt surged through her as memories of her daughter, Anya, filled the emptiness in her chest. It felt like a lifetime had passed since her murder. *I can't even really remember what she looked like. My beautiful baby girl. My Anya.* Tears welled in her eyes and spilled down her cheeks. She buried her face in her hood and finally responded to Gavin by nodding gently.

"Just the children," she choked. Gavin could tell that she was crying, but said nothing. "Not those who brought this doom upon themselves."

Suddenly, Eva's attention shifted elsewhere. Her home. Something or someone was standing in the doorway. Just as Gavin started to carry the small children to a garden where they could be buried, The Wanderer slipped inside the metal shack. The door groaned and screeched as she closed it behind her. One of her blades was drawn and ready to strike. She swore she saw something dark slink behind the doorway, but there was nothing in her front room.

They must be in the back.

The Wanderer strained to hear any movement before she lunged into the back room.

Nothing.

Eva exhaled sharply and began overturning large pieces of furniture, searching for any proof that she was not alone. She rammed her weapon back into its sheath and tore through everything she could find, convincing herself someone had to be here.

There was no way she was wrong.

Beads of sweat ran down her face when suddenly, a shuffling sound reached her ears. The Wanderer's head snapped up in the direction of the sound. First, a laugh. Then, a familiar voice. A shiver made her hair stand on end. *How the shit is he here so quickly? Was he waiting for me the entire time? Shit. Shit. Shit. Shit.* Eva was not prepared. She had just made herself completely vulnerable. If he still carried her pistol from years ago, she would already be dead. With considerable effort, she pushed herself upright and slowly turned toward the source of the noise.

"Dan McAv-," she started to say, then gasped.

There he was, standing between her and the only exit in the home. But something was different about him. Confusion twisted through her mind. The figure looked and sounded like McAvoy, but something in her gut felt conflicted. If it was the Hooded Shadow that haunted her, it was stronger than ever.

"Well Wanderer?" his voice rose from a murmur. "What do you have to say for yourself? Do you truly believe that I am simply a figment of your imagination and nothing more? And if I am truly this *demon*, then what is my purpose?"

Eva felt the cold metal wall against her back as she pushed herself further into the corner of the room. She said nothing. She would not let her internal battles cloud her mind again, but it seemed like it already had.

"You. Are. Weak," it continued, stepping closer to her with each word. "You were known across the Region as the Serpent's Mistress, not the "hero" you pretend to be now. You were merciless. Calculated. *Powerful.* Time has softened you, and I admit… I almost pity you. *Almost.* Will our battle be as simple as I've calculated? Perhaps. Unless, of course, you choose to *fight.*"

I will fight harder than I ever have before. Until there is nothing left in me to give.

Eva drew in a deep breath, and a tingling sensation surged through her body. Every muscle tightened as she tore both blades from their sheaths. Digging her foot into the dust-covered ground, she sprinted toward Dan McAvoy, slashing with a fire she had not felt in years.

Her blade came down.

The effigy vanished.

She slid on her knees into the wall, her shortswords clattering to the floor. And then, there was nothing. Her face lifted toward the ceiling as she squeezed her eyes shut, fists clenched, the surge of power still coursing through her veins.

Change is coming and I'm letting it take me.

"Good, good," the familiar voice of McAvoy was now behind her. "The battle before was only a taste of revenge. Drink in it. Let the anger take hold. Let it pierce its claws deep within you. Only then can you truly be powerful. Only then can you truly become what you were meant to be."

McAvoy wouldn't say that, she thought. *He would never help me. Unless he's trying to weigh me down with thoughts.*

Eva slowly turned around and rose to her feet. During the tousle with her imagination, her pants had ripped at the knees. The hilts of her blades were dusty in her palms, but sweat slicked her skin and strengthened her grip.

One glaring question extinguished the blaze in her heart.

"What's the matter Eva?" it tormented. This time, it wasn't McAvoy standing face-to-face with her. It was another Eva.

She breathed. "*What the shit are you*?"

The creature raised an eyebrow. "Silly question." It paused and smiled maniacally. "Why... *I'm you.*"

"But why are you here?" Eva fought to keep panic from rising as she pieced together clues about the Demon. When was the first moment she could remember this thing? Not as Mistress. She could not recall seeing it then, nor had it been present when she became the Rover's protector. No. It began after the Vault. With Jake. With Tommy.

But why?

"I am here because you need me," her likeness straightened up. The only difference between Eva and this Shadow was the eyes—crimson red—same as McAvoy's effigy. "You have gone astray."

"Astray from what? I still don't understand."

"Therein lies the problem, doesn't it? I don't have all the answers. I was only sent to do so much."

"Sent?"

Eva just stood there, staring into her reflection. The armor that this demon wore was exactly what she had worn as the Serpent's Mistress. How could she forget? Leather, dark as the night sky and a crimson red cape that covered only one arm. And there sat, just over the tops of each shoulder, her blades. The pommels glinted against the light of the setting sun. Her hair was short and angled, almost as crimson as the cloak. This woman seemed so confident. So *powerful.*

Memories flooded in as Eva sheathed her blades and dropped to her knees before the shadow. She longed for the old days. Power. Prowess. Anything was attainable and nothing was impossible. The Serpents ruled with an iron fist… *her* iron fist. Was this 'being' speaking the truth? Had she really lost her way? Was her true path to conquer the weak rather than protect them?

As her eyes turned upward, her double vanished. She was alone in the room again, but it still felt like someone was watching her. A single whisper. A single sentence trickled through her ear in McAvoy's voice.

"I'm coming for you Eva," it whispered.

Gavin was standing in the doorway. Though he had witnessed everything that followed her scream, he would never admit it. He knew she was fighting the weight of everything that had happened over the past few years and trusted she would return to herself once the battle was over. For her sake, he backed out of the doorway and entered again, pretending as though he had just arrived.

"Gavin?" The Wanderer had almost forgotten that he had stayed behind when Tommy left.

"All of the Rover children have been buried," he said. His sorrowful blue eyes were fixed on the floor.

She nodded in thanks. "I'm sorry I didn't help… I was—"

"Are you hungry?" He changed the subject. "I'll go hunting and bring something back. It may be a while though. Not sure how many animals are on the forest edge. They seem to sense this place is cursed."

Eva nodded again.

You okay?"

"Fine. For now."

Gavin stood there for a moment, replaying what he had just witnessed. Stroking his short, red beard, he nodded, glanced at her again, and left. Eva followed him to the doorway and stopped, observing as he zigzagged between the corpses and out of view. The latch squealed as the door shut, locking Eva inside her home, just as she liked it. Her back pressed against the door as she sank to the floor, stretching her legs out in front of her. Clarity spread through her mind as she began to process what awaited her.

McAvoy's coming. I know he is. He believes he's trapped me, but he's made one dangerous mistake. The very same mistake that he made all those years ago. He forgot who he's angered. He will come with an army, but I will be ready. This is what I was born to do. This is how I remake my mark. Rebirth from fire.

"It's time," Eva said to herself. "I'm ready to face my mortality once again."

***

Hours later, Jake and Tommy found themselves peering through the cracks in Eva's shack. They could barely make out the dark silhouette sitting on the other side of the wall.

Jake's heart was racing. "Should we go in?" His instincts urged him to stay away from the door, yet he found his hand pressed against it. As he pushed against the frigid metal, the rust-weakened bolt lock shattered, spraying Eva with shards of reddened steel. She shot up and readied her weapons as the door swung open.

"Just like when we first met," Jake said with a nervous laugh, hands raised. His voice was shaking. "On the other side of your blade."

Eva did not smile. She only grasped the hilt a little tighter. "This time, I won't make the same mistake by allowing you to live."

Chapter 17

"*No*," the Demon hissed loudly behind Eva, whose blade was still pointed at Jake. "We need him alive."

She glanced over her shoulder and whispered, "What? Why?"

"Trust me," it replied. "He remains… necessary."

Jake stared at the space where Eva was looking but saw nothing. *Is she talking to her Demon? Has she gone completely insane?* The room groaned under a gust of wind that whistled through the cracks in its walls. Nightfall had already swallowed the town, and only scattered glints of moonlight touched the McAvoy brothers. Because Eva was further inside, the darkness concealed her face. They could only feel her gaze… deciding whether they deserved to live.

But something held her back.

Eventually, after a few moments of maddening silence, The Wanderer yielded. She released a long, labored breath as she slid her weapon into its sheath. "You'd better be right," she whispered to her back.

"Who are you talking to?" Jake asked.

She ignored him, walking over to the end table near her bed. Grabbing a box of matches, she struck one, studying the small flame for a moment before touching it to a lamp with just enough oil left to catch. A cloud of dust exploded from the bed as Eva sat down. Without making eye contact, she rested her forearms against her thighs and fixated on the floor.

Jake repeated his question. This time using *were* instead of *are*.

"Why are you here?" she snarled. "Come to destroy my life even more than you already have?"

Tommy and Jake furrowed their brows and spoke simultaneously. "What are you talking about? We didn't—"

"*Look around you.*" Eva shot up and stomped towards them. Her arms flew out to her sides and she was inches from Jake's face. "Before *you*. Before the Vault. Before a-all-all this bullshit. I was *fine*. The region. *Was fine*. People died because of *you two*. Every time I was forced to save your ass… chaos. But one, singular thing I cannot seem to grasp, is why… Why is everyone blaming *me* for this? All I did was protect *you two*… Your safety has cost enough lives. And your betrayal won't cost me mine."

Tommy took a step back. He glanced outside to see if anyone was coming. Unlike his brother, he kept his mouth shut. Eva may have spared their life for the moment, but that could all change in an instant.

"You're blaming all this on *me*?" Jake spat. "How is this my fault?"

Eva stopped for a moment and stiffened her shoulders. The three of them knew that when The Wanderer went silent, trouble followed. But lucky for Jake, a punch in the face was her only reaction.

He dropped to the floor in a heap, grasping his face in the same spot where Tommy had struck him. "Oops," Eva said without emotion. She may have broken his nose. Tommy rushed over to his brother but tried to cover his smile by biting his lip. He glanced up at Eva when Jake wasn't looking and mouthed, *he deserved it*.

She couldn't help but to crack a half-smile. No matter how hard Eva tried to understand, she could never figure out why she had such a soft spot for Tommy. But there was only one thing she was sure of. Somehow, in some way, he was like her.

“Why are you here?” Eva repeated, slumping back down on the bed, sending another plume of dust into the air around them. “I told you to stay in Rapture and stay away from me. But you just don’t listen, do you?”

Tommy lifted his brother to his feet. Jake muttered something to himself about Eva, while he wiped away the trail of blood from under his nose. No one paid him any attention.

“We came to help,” Tommy explained.

“Ha! Please tell me you’re joking.”

“No.”

“See?” Jake snipped, still holding his face. His voice sounded more nasally now. “I told you this would be pointless. You punch me in the face and make me come out here. Then we come all the way out here and I get punched in the face by her. And we haven’t seen Mara this entire time.”

“Oh, so *that’s* why you’re here. The truth finally comes out. Spare me the ‘help’ Jake, save the bitch who secured my imprisonment. What’s the matter? Did she leave you once she got what she wanted? Sounds familiar, doesn’t it?”

He kept his gaze glued on the floor. *I won’t let her words affect me. I did what was right leaving her.*

All of a sudden, Eva became overwhelmed by a familiar feeling. The Hooded Demon stood before her, its pooling darkness seeping across the floor and crawling up her legs. She rose to her feet and quickly shoved Jake and Tommy outside, saying nothing aside from, “Leave me.” Dread started to gnaw at her knees, making them weak. Just as the door closed behind her, the breath was sucked from her lungs. The room swayed beneath her as she dropped down on all fours. Beads of sweat formed on her brow and dripped down her nose, creating a small puddle in the dirt between her hands.

“Time is quickly approaching,” the Shadow warned. Its form had returned to the hooded and cloaked creature with skeletal hands. “McAvoy will be here soon. But you are not ready. You have gone astray.”

Eva couldn't hold herself back. She raised her voice over the Shadow's and pleaded. "Why do you keep saying that? What do I need to do? I don't understand. I've done *everything* you've said."

But the Shadow ignored her questions. It floated to the corner of the room and quadrupled in size, draping over her crumpled body. The Wanderer could feel its weight rapidly increasing. From her palms shaking under the pressure, she fell to her elbows, then prone on the floor.

"You have gone astray Wanderer," it repeated again and again. "Still… you hesitate. You must face him in battle. Only then will you discover your path."

The figure transformed to McAvoy again. He straightened his armor and hummed. "We are so alike, you and I. Trust me when I say that your life was never meant to be free. Your path has already been laid out before you. Fate cannot be changed for you and I. We were destined for greatness. Stray from that path and chaos ensues."

"What does that mean?" Eva could barely speak with the Shadow pressing against her back. *Is this all in my head? There's no way I'm imagining this.*

"Rise and face me. You have one day left to prepare. Then, our fates will be sealed."

This sounds like bullshit, Eva said. Her emotions shifted from panic to anger. *This whole thing is bullshit. Why does this keep happening to me? What is this thing? Why is it following me? Why does it keep trying to take over? I've been so scared of this thing for so long, even if I pretended not to be. But maybe…*

Finally, Eva answered loudly. "Fear is the only reason you still exist. I'm finished running from you. I will face you. I will *end* you."

All at once, the image, the pressure, and the voices vanished. Air rushed back into the Wanderer's lungs, and she pushed herself to her feet. She was shaking, sweating, and exhausted. Just as she stumbled to the doorway, Gavin rushed in, nearly knocking her backwards. He must have heard the struggle because he stormed in brandishing his weapon.

"What happened?" he said. Six rabbits were strung around his neck, three on each side. They were swinging violently as he rushed into the back room, brushing Eva aside.

She grabbed his shoulder. "No one is in here. Just… me and that thing in my head."

I sound so crazy, she thought, realizing what she said. *You've lost your damn mind. Gavin probably thinks you're crazy.*

Her Shadow whispered once more. "You have gone astray."

Gavin sighed in relief. "Okay… but are *you* alright?"

Eva nodded and glanced at the doorway, pressuring him to leave without saying a word. But it looked like he wanted to say something else. He shifted his weight uncomfortably, avoiding eye contact.

"What is it?" Eva snapped.

"Do you really think we can take McAvoy and his army?" he asked, bouncing uncomfortably in his stance. "Aren't you scared at all?"

"Of death?" she said. It was a question she'd been asked countless times before. "No. We've been… *close friends*… ever since I was a child. But I never felt like it was ready for me. But facing McAvoy again… I'm not so sure. I guess it's because I don't feel like myself right now. Something's wrong and I don't have much time."

Gavin grabbed her shoulders. "What do you need from me? How can I help? I will stand by you until my dying breath."

"Um," Eva paused. "Thank you. Nothing. Unless you want to cook that food for us. I'll rest until McAvoy arrives. Hopefully, that will be enough to clear my head."

Her Commander bowed and left the shack, strolling to the center of town. Jake and Tommy sat down beside him. Tommy grabbed a few large rocks and laid them in a circle while Jake carried over a few dry timbers and placed them in the center of the makeshift fire pit. Gavin started a fire and began dressing the rabbits he trapped. The Wanderer just watched from her home. After a while, she finally shuffled to her bed, laid down, and closed her eyes.

"Is she okay?" Tommy broke the agonizing silence after they stuck the last rabbit onto a skewer.

Gavin poked at the meat and grunted. "She's fine. Quit asking."

Rapture's former commander and Jake McAvoy glared at one another through the crackling flames. The thought of fighting alongside each other sickened and angered them both. Tommy could feel the tension pulling tight between them.

The shrill chorus of cicadas filled the desolate Rover Colony until the older McAvoy finally spoke. "What's wrong with you Gavin?" he started. "You were so kind to us when we arrived. Now you—"

Gavin kept his eyes glued to Jake. "Are you serious? You *can't* be serious."

"I am serious."

Jake stood up. Gavin followed suit. Tommy watched them both.

"You are an absolute imbecile, Jake. You know that? I've already told you. *She's* already told you. Eva has been threatened, undermined, attacked, and humiliated for the last year. All while you sit back, in your stupid little trinket shop, making stupid jewelry and shit, and let her take the fall for everything *you* dragged into her life. Pretty much everything's changed for her since the Vault."

Jake tensed up, and Gavin continued.

"Eva's been your human shield since the start and you've done *nothing* but hurt her. She's risked her life for you over and over again. And this is how you thank her? You show up thinking that standing beside her in one fight somehow makes up for all the times you didn't? Honestly, you probably aren't even out here to stand with us. We are way past cordials, Jake. In my eyes, there is *nothing* you can do to make me forgive you."

Jake raised his voice but took a step back. His body language turned submissive when faced with Gavin, fully aware of his capability in battle. "*We're out here now aren't we? Maybe it will make up for something.*"

"Did you not hear anything I just said? You aren't even out here for her. Are you? When your father shows up tomorrow, you'll just run back to Rapture with your tail between your legs."

Gavin was ready when Jake tried to lunge at him. He shoved him over the boulder that had served as his seat. Jake stumbled across uneven ground and crashed onto his back. Blood and dirt smeared his clothes as he scrambled back to his feet.

"Don't. Test. Me," Gavin warned. "I'm not doing this for anyone but *her*. I owe you nothing. If you get in my way or hers, I will not hesitate to strike you down."

Neither Jake nor Tommy had ever heard him so stern. His voice and the look on his face made their hearts leap into their throats. Jake awkwardly sank back into his seat without another word. Then, almost instinctively, all three of them glanced toward Eva's shack. She watched the exchange, but slipped back into the shadow of her home before anyone noticed.

Honestly, The Wanderer didn't care whether any of them stayed to face McAvoy or his army.

They'll just get in my way, she thought to herself. *At least Gavin is a warrior. Unlike the other two. He's been loyal through all of this. If we survive, I think I'll let him stay with me.*

She realized how deeply Gavin cared about her. While Jake would use her as a human shield against a hail of bullets, her former commander would face death with the same ferocity as the Wanderer, ready to offer his life without hesitation. Even after witnessing the Demon's hold over her, he still responded with kindness and compassion… things she had never learned how to accept.

Light from the campfire spilled golden waves across the walls beyond her doorway, casting ominous, dancing shadows behind her. She peeked through a slit between two metal sheets and admired Gavin from the solitude of her home. Before she realized it, he disappeared from his seat and was standing in the doorway, brow raised.

"Watching us, are you?" he joked. "Food is cooked. Would you like me to bring it to you?"

Eva smiled then glanced at the far corner of her home. The Shadow was standing there, watching in silence. "No… I'll come out."

Lingering in her room for a few moments, The Wanderer stepped out past the bodies and sat on an overturned log near the fire. Gavin handed her a stick with a rabbit skewered through the middle. She brought it up to her face and examined it closely. The outside was scorched but the inside appeared edible.

I've had worse.

No one said a word during the meal. Midnight clouds had cleared away and yielded to a glittering sky. As they looked around, taking in the space they shared with the dead, a cool fog crept in from the South. Starlight and moonlight shone like a beacon upon them, illuminating the graveyard.

Gangs. Rovers. Nomads. Rapture. Eva hadn't realized how small her world had been before she found the Vault. She had spent time as a Doxie in the Serpent's Nest, became its Mistress, and traveled throughout the southern region after escaping a mutiny. But she had never had reason to venture beyond the city. Discovering an entirely new civilization beyond the metropolis changed everything. Her experiences had become a double-edged sword. On one hand, she had met Gavin and, for a brief time, lived something resembling a normal life. On the other, Rapture became the catalyst for betrayal and loss.

Even now, as the Wanderer stared blankly into the fire, surrounded by echoes of her past, she still did not know who in Rapture had sold them out to the Tigers.

Maybe when McAvoy arrives, the snitch will reveal herself. Part of her still firmly believed that it was Virginia who had orchestrated the attacks. She feigned concern for Rapture's people but fought tooth and nail to keep her position of power. Only a veil of deception kept the citizens from realizing her true intent. Eva imagined the ecstasy she would feel burying a blade deep inside Virginia's chest cavity. Goosebumps rose on her arms.

A whisper from the Demon came and left with the wind. "Death will come to those who deserve it. Many more will fall by your hand. Soon."

The Wanderer tossed the remainder of her food in the fire, nodded at Gavin, and started back towards her shack. Jake watched until she was enveloped in darkness before returning to his meal.

After the door was shut and she stood in the darkness of her room, Eva unsheathed her blades and kicked the larger pieces of furniture aside. *I can't rest yet. I have to prepare.* When there was enough space, she held one blade straight out in front of her and started to practice her form. The Shadow and the voices disappeared as she twisted and turned with swiftness and accuracy. She drifted into a trance.

War was calling.

Over an hour passed before The Wanderer finally retired for the night. She took one more look out at the town. Red coals glowed just bright enough for her to see Jake and Tommy's prone figures lying around the fire. A lump formed in her throat. Where was Gavin?

"Hey Eva," he whispered through the crack in the door. "Can I come in? I don't want to be around Jake. I may *accidently* kill him in my sleep."

"Yeah," she yawned. "Better you than either of those two. Even though I told you to stay away from me until this battle is over."

"You know I never listen."

They smiled at each other and Gavin made his way over to the side of her bed and laid on the ground next to it. He squirmed around until he was on his back and comfortable. A comforting exhale, then a serene tranquility. Even the insects had quieted in the twilight hours.

"So, you think you can do it?" he whispered up to Eva. "Kill, McAvoy I mean."

Eva whispered softly. "Which one?"

"You know which one. How many of his men will he bring?"

"Depends. He will want enough of his men at the Gang to keep their fires going. The day-to-day never stops, even if the Chief goes to battle. But he will bring his best. Maybe a handful or a couple dozen. Why? Are you scared?"

Gavin smiled in the dark. "Never… Not with you by my side anyway. You're the best right? Or so they say."

"Well Gavin, you're about to find out."

Just then, they both shot upright and stared through the doorway into the adjoining room of the shack.

"Did you hear that?" Eva's voice was barely audible. "It sounded like someone speaking."

But Gavin did not hear anything. Rather, he felt something. "Something tripped over my foot and ran in the other room."

Before he could stand, Eva was already in the back of the shack with a blade in each hand. She walked in and out of the room three times before she was uneasily satisfied that there was no one there. Gavin could barely see her in the darkness.

"What the shit just happened?" she whispered. At first, she thought her mind was playing tricks on her again. Maybe it was her Shadow. But Gavin had felt something too.

His hands started to become clammy. "Well… This place is tainted with the blood of innocent people. Nomads say that if someone dies a horrific death, they remain here and can't move on. If that's true, I wouldn't be surprised if spirits of the Rovers are still here. Probably dozens or hundreds even."

The Wanderer's mind drifted to a memory from years earlier. The day she trained the McAvoy brothers to survive in the city, she experienced something she could never explain. Footsteps of a child. The sound of laughter. Yet the child was nowhere to be found. *Spirit*. Could these things truly exist? Was death truly not the end for the mortal creatures of this world? The whispers and questions curling around her did little to offer rest.

Gavin was only able to sleep for a few hours. Anticipation and fear left him tossing and turning until he finally sat up and walked out of the shack. *Eva will be alright*, he reasoned as he made his way past the ancient highway towards the forest's edge. *Besides, I'll only be gone for a few minutes. I'll be back before dawn. I just need to try and clear my head.*

But the demons Eva had fought for over a decade began rising to the surface once more.

Nightmares had always plagued The Wanderer. How was someone who witnessed and caused so much pain capable of coping in a healthy way? Only during her reign as a Gang's Mistress were her dark dreams ever silenced. Things had changed the second she ventured from those towering walls of steel. What began as fleeting grimaces, prickles of pain, and a nightmare here and there had grown into something far worse. A physical being manifestation. Trauma made flesh.

But this night was different. Perhaps the worst she had ever endured.

Because tonight, Eva thought she had escaped it when she awoke.

***

Echoes of the previous nightmare dwindled as The Wanderer opened her eyes. She found herself shivering despite the warm air. A shroud of malicious intent seemed to be draped over her entire shack. McAvoy's voice whispered nonsense in every corner of the room, echoing through the metal walls.

She slowly turned to the open door. A dark, tar-like liquid started oozing through the cracks in the walls. Panic spread through her body like spiderwebs. Each time she tried to stand, an overwhelming force shoved her deeper into the bed. She forced herself onto her stomach and dragged herself out of bed. Inch by inch, sweat pouring down her face, Eva dragged herself toward the door and reached for the opening. The door slammed shut, and she yanked her hand back just before it crushed her fingers.

This isn't real, she repeated. *This isn't real. Shit. What is happening? I'm awake. This is my old home. This isn't real, but I'm awake. This can't be happening right now. I have to be ready.*

"You have gone astray," a metallic voice screeched in her ear. "You will be tested. Destiny is waiting, but it is not patient. Fate is slipping through your fingers. Stand among the strong. Prove your worth. Rise."

Anger erupted inside The Wanderer. She clawed for control of her body, but it would not budge. *Am I still asleep? Wake up!*

The voice roared so loudly she was certain her eardrums would burst. Her face twisted in pain as the Demon continued to speak. "Oh Eva. But you are awake… you have gone astray… This is your punishment. Return to your path and everything will be revealed. Just. Let. Go."

Get out of my head!

With one desperate surge, Eva forced herself to her feet, her muscles screaming as though they might rip beneath the crushing weight. The sound that escaped her lips sent Jake and Tommy scrambling into consciousness. They froze.

"W-was that…?" Jake stopped.

Tommy simply nodded as they pressed their backs against a tree and stared into the darkness.

But the grasp of Eva's Shadow did not ease. It pierced deeper into her mind and circled like a gathering storm.

"Enough!" she screamed against her burning throat. "*I'm. Not. Weak.* Those who I called family have betrayed me. My child lies dead. My very existence is pain. From this moment, my life is by my blade. I will destroy Dan McAvoy with the skills that I have built *on my own.* When the sun sets on this day, The Tiger Chief will lie at my feet in a river of blood. *I. Am. In. Control. Obey me!*"

Gavin was strolling along the border between the Rover Colony and the forest when he heard the guttural scream. His heart hammered in his chest as he tore toward the village, sprinting as fast as his legs would carry him. He feared McAvoy had come early and attacked Eva in her sleep. But when he burst into the shack, Eva was alone, back pressed against the wall, her skin glistening with sweat.

Jake approached the shack and wasted no time patronizing her, just as Mara and Virginia had in Rapture. "See? Eva isn't well. We need to return to Rapture with her. Let the Council—"

Gavin snapped. He barreled into Jake and slammed him to the ground, pinning him beneath his legs. Tommy, who would have protected his brother a long time ago, stood aside. The young man turned away when his brother attempted to get his attention. Gavin jerked Jake's face back towards him.

"Why?" Rapture's exiled Commander spit in his face. "So they can hang her? *Huh?* Is that what you want? After all she's done for you! It isn't *her* that's the problem here. It's *you,* Jake. And I'm done with hearing your shit. *So, I'm going to end you. Right here. Right now.*"

But it was Eva who, once again, came to the rescue of Jake McAvoy. “Let him go.”

The murder in Gavin’s eyes dispersed when they met that of The Wanderer’s. She was following the orders of her Shadow, nothing more. Tommy felt the chill in those three words. He understood that she was merely sparing him, not saving him.

Jake crawled to her feet, sobbing in thanks. She took the toe of her boot and raised his chin. “Remember this day… For you were spared from both of us. Despite your poisonous words.”

“Thank you Eva-,” Tommy started.

“Go,” she interrupted. “Both of you. Out of my sight. Return to the safety of your town. This was your last mercy.”

Gavin crossed his arms and stared straight ahead. Tommy and Jake opened their mouths to speak, but something caught their attention behind The Wanderer. She noticed them looking over her shoulder in horror and turned to face the direction of the compounds. Just on the horizon was the sea of morning dew. Above it, silhouettes of over two dozen armored enemies approaching the town.

The Tigers were here.

And McAvoy was leading them.

Chapter 18

Jake and Tommy hid behind Eva. *Typical.* Gavin stepped to her side and nodded.

Fear rooted the men where they stood. There was nowhere to run. Weapons clenched in their grasp. Each breath, shallow and shaky. Heartbeats roared in their ears and pulsated through every muscle of their body. A whimper escaped their lips, but it was enveloped by the fog.

The Wanderer, however, remained calm. The cold hand of her Demon rested on her shoulder, but did not antagonize her. She glanced back at its skeletal face. It nodded and pointed to the center of the group, now more visible, as the first row broke through the mist. Unlike those fighting at her side, she had not unsheathed her blades yet. With her hood concealing her face, she lifted her head to greet the Tigers.

What she saw was simultaneously expected and shocking. Dan McAvoy was alive and well. The thought that she had missed her mark all those years ago twisted in her stomach, but she vowed she would not fail a second time. Still, what truly surprised her was not that he marched with his own high-ranking gang members, but that the Serpents stood beside them.

"I thought the memories would be nostalgic for you, Wanderer," he taunted.

The years had not changed him one bit. Salt-and-pepper colored hair, slicked back in deliberate perfection. A sly smile that held no warmth. His voice, melodic yet hollow.

And his icy blue eyes. They were just as dead and soulless as when they first met at her compound, fifteen years before.

"You still don't understand, so I've brought you a display. My subtleties clearly failed to penetrate that thick skull of yours, so I'll be more… obvious. People like us find happiness *only* in power."

But Eva did not flinch. Gavin and Jake watched as she stepped forward, her glare unwavering. Tommy inhaled sharply as his father shifted his cape, exposing The Wanderer's pistol.

"Look familiar?" he sneered.

Eva's brow furrowed for a split second.

"I've been saving it, you see. Cleaning and maintaining it every day for this very moment. One bullet left. One single target. Call it a sign of fate, if you will. Still… I find myself longing to feel my hands around your throat. To witness the life drain from your eyes would make every ounce of pain you caused me worthwhile."

A shiver of excitement ran through the Tiger Chief's body. He shook it off, smiling devilishly. Starting out as a muted snicker, his laughter was cut short by Eva's words.

"Again, McAvoy, you've made one slight miscalculation," she said.

"Hmm?"

"You are so certain you will walk from this battle victorious." A smirk flashed across her face. "Today is not the first time you've underestimated me. Have you learned nothing?"

She started to lift her hand to one hilt when her Shadow's grasp pinched her shoulder. "Not. Yet." it whispered. "Patience."

The moment she lowered her hand, more Gang Members appeared through the fog. Now, about fifty guards bearing all sorts of blunt weapons, blades, and guns stood before The Wanderer. Her smile immediately faded.

"What's wrong, Wanderer?" McAvoy lifted his arms to either side. "You managed to escape my compound unharmed. Then you cut down a dozen of my most elite warriors. And you think I underestimated you again? Audacious. But I never make the same mistake twice. Your luck has finally run out."

His voice rose above the marching and clanking of steel. "My wonderful brothers and sisters in arms. The day of reckoning for The Wanderer is upon us! This region will, once again, be whole. Leave her to me. I'm sure the others will be short work. Too bad though… to end my own sons' lives. My heart hurts for you Jacob and Thomas. You have disappointed me *and your mother*."

"Lies," Tommy called back. "Our mother would fight for what is right."

"How do you know, child?" McAvoy's lifeless gaze turned to his younger son. Suddenly, there was a flicker of something darker behind his eyes. "She was slain before you even stand."

Jake choked back tears. It had been so long since he had thought about his mother. *Tommy's right... but she isn't here to protect us now.* Temptation pulled at him, urging him toward his father to save himself. He took a step toward the gangs when a battle cry fractured the tension. Everyone but The Wanderer jumped and turned toward the sound. Fear shifted into elation. From the north, echoing down the cracked highway, came the steady rhythm of marching boots. At the front of the platoon was Councilman Bruce.

Chief McAvoy's lip quivered at the sight of armored guards filing in behind his adversary. Rapture had spent decades perfecting its armor and forging deadly weapons. But how would it fare in real battle? The figures behind Eva were not soldiers, but Scouts, quietly summoned from their posts. Most of them carried concealed caches of guns and ammunition, reserves that only Bruce appeared to have knowledge of. Clad in intricately decorated armor, he took his place at Eva's side.

"I'll admit," she whispered, "I'm glad to see you. But I didn't think the Council would let you fight *with* me. I thought you were sent to kill me."

Bruce chuckled. "I don't ask for permission to do what's right."

Eva couldn't help but smile. The fire inside her burned brighter than before.

"Ah yes... That reminds me," Chief McAvoy called to Eva over the crowd. The pleasantries and greetings stopped. "There is one more piece of our puzzle that must be addressed. Isn't that right, Wanderer? I am a man of my word, afterall. There is someone I want you to meet... though I suspect you've met before."

From just behind the front row, a willowy young woman stepped into view. She was clad in the same leather armor as the Tigers and plastered on her upper arm was the tattoo of the Gang. Her golden hair was braided and pulled back except for two wavy strands on either side of her face.

I was wrong, Eva thought. Her heart skipped a beat. *This whole time.*

Bruce's eyes widened in shock. "No. It-it can't be. All this time..."

Eva felt her fists tighten. The reason she had been imprisoned in the Stronghold. The reason she was forced to mourn her daughter's untimely death. The reason every citizen of Rapture had sought her execution. The notes. The warnings. The blame.

Now it all made sense.

I'm not crazy, she breathed, fighting back tears. *I was right all along. It wasn't all in my head.*

"*Mara!*" Jake shrieked. "What? Wait... you're with *him*? How? When? *Why*?"

The Councilwoman's daughter tried to play coy at first. "Ever since you arrived. But Jake, I had to… to protect you."

Jake's face went blood red and he started to cry. "*Protect* me? You killed your own people for shit sake. *You killed my daughter. My child*. For what? To protect me?"

"That abomination was never meant to spread her filth," she said, pointing at Eva. "I would never harm an innocent child. But the spawn of a demon… I carried out your father's will."

"You poisoned my daughter," Jake sobbed. "After all I've sacrificed for you. I never spoke up for Eva because *I believed you*."

Her lip trembled. "Jake. Please understand that I did all of this for you. For us. Everything I said was true. She is a *monster*. You needed to see it."

Mara dropped to her knees in front of Jake. Eva and the rest of the army watched the exchange. "I swear on my life I would never hurt you. I love you, Jake. Please. Believe me. Your father promised to spare you if I obeyed. Now we can have the life we talked about. The life you wanted. Don't you see? You were never meant to suffer like this. You were meant to stand with us. With me."

A slow, steady breath filled Jake's lungs as his burning gaze fixed on Mara. She reached for him, fingers trembling as she clasped his hand, her eyes wide and pleading.

"Mara—I…"

He sank to his knees, cupping her cheek and brushing his thumb across her skin. It was so soft. So warm.

"I love you, Jake," she whimpered. "More than you could ever know."

He brushed his lips against hers, gentle. Almost tender.

His free hand slipped toward his boot. No one noticed the faint glint of metal.

In the space of a heartbeat, he rose just enough to drive the dagger beneath her ribcage and into her heart.

"For Anya," he whispered.

Mara staggered upright, ripping the blade from her body, gasping and choking on blood. She tried to scream, but only a wet gurgle escaped her mouth. Blood soaked her fingers as she stared at Jake in disbelief. The dagger slipped from her hand and fell into a patch of grass. She toppled onto her side, drawing a few ragged breaths before her body went still.

Jake fell back onto the ground, breathing hard. He lifted his hands to his face. They were drenched in warm blood. When he tried to wipe it away, it thickened into a dark red clay across his palms.

So it wasn't Virginia... Eva studied the fresh kill, trying to process everything. *But she must've known her daughter was involved with this. Somehow, she had to have something to do with it.* Her eyes traced the spray of blood down to the weapon. She recognized it immediately. It was the dagger Jake had given her for their wedding ceremony. Guilt flickered through her for a single, searing second before the numbness swallowed it again.

"Shame," McAvoy shook his head. "She was so beautiful, Jake. The two of you would have given me stunning grandchildren… unlike that *creature* you've grown so fond of. Disappointment is something I've grown far too familiar with… especially from you. Mara convinced me that she could change you. Rule alongside me. You could have been so happy with her. Instead, you chose this cretin."

Jake wavered on his legs and locked eyes with his father. "I'm not choosing The Wanderer. I'm choosing Anya McAvoy. I'm choosing my little girl."

"Pity. Vengeance doesn't suit you. You lack the… stomach… for it."

Bruce tensed up and his army followed suit. Both sides were ready for battle and their two bloodthirsty leaders looked at one another in anticipation.

“Shall we do this?” The Tiger Chief held a hand out towards Eva as if he wanted to dance. When she did not respond, he stiffened up, adjusting his armor and fixed a single strand of hair that was out of place. Clearing his throat, “Well then. Everyone, I expect nothing less than a merciless battle. Do not disappoint. Leave The Wanderer for me. Those are your orders.”

Dawn crept into the battlefield as the two sides converged. Bruce and the Rapture Guards charged towards the Tigers and Serpents as gunshots rang through the village. Tommy weaved between friend and foe, knocking Gang Members over as he passed. He refused to kill, but aided those with weapons. Armies fueled by anger and revenge massacred one another. Bodies hit the ground, joining the corpses of the Rovers scattered around them.

But The Wanderer and her adversary had not moved.

“See what your presence has done?” The flat, emotionless voice of Dan McAvoy was just loud enough for Eva to hear through the commotion. “All of this is the direct result of *your* actions. Families have been torn apart in your wake. Since the day you rose to power with the Serpents, the bloodshed has not ceased. Your mere existence is a cancer on this region… and I will cleanse this land of you.”

“You speak as though you’re their savior,” Eva taunted. She still had not drawn her blades. Not yet. “You claim to do them favors while sacrificing their lives for your own ambition and twisted mind games.”

McAvoy bent back and cackled loudly. “If I’m not mistaken, I believe it was *you* who said this whole existence was a game. *A game you play better than everyone else*. So tell me, Wanderer, have you truly changed that much? Grown a heart and decided to embrace the weakness of mercy?”

Eva began to formulate a reply, but he continued.

“I know what ails you. Those years ago in the Tiger’s Den… when I mentioned that we are not so different. I meant every word. Whether either of us like it, we are very similar. For I, too, am haunted by a demon."

"He's lying," her Shadow hissed, elongating the words. It no longer bore the resemblance of McAvoy, only the skeletal figure that had appeared in her shack after The Vault. "Do not trust him."

I know that, she said angrily in her head. *But how does he know about mine?*

There was no reply.

"Contemplating how I know… aren't you?"

"Quit stalling," she provoked as a bullet went whizzing past her face. "Let's end this."

But McAvoy had to make the first move. She needed to see what type of condition he was in so she could adjust appropriately. Still, she was ready for an attack from any direction. Her hearing, smell, sight, touch, and even taste were all sharply attuned to the battle.

By now, the warriors on both sides were out of ammunition, resorting to their swords and blunt weapons.

"Will you accept death?" McAvoy inquired.

"Gladly," she smirked. "But I'm sure as shit taking you with me."

Eva was too impatient to wait any longer. She tore her blades from their sheaths and lunged at the Tiger Chief. He sidestepped with ease. *Just as I predicted.* A familiar exhilaration surged through her core, igniting the abilities that had given her such fame. She was in her element. Dragging one foot through the dirt, she skidded to a stop and spun around. He was already sprinting at her, tucking away Eva's handgun and drawing his own weapon. Eva dug two craters into the soft ground and darted back towards him, aiming low.

They collided.

The Wanderer drove the hilt of one blade toward McAvoy's knee, but he evaded again.

"I see you've healed up nicely."

"Better than ever my dear," he mocked and rushed at her again. Coming down with a hard blow from his massive hammer, McAvoy forced Eva to roll left. She barely had time to lift her blade before a Tiger swung down, aiming to sever her arm. She shoved her sword upward, driving it through the man's torso. Hot intestines spilled across her chest. Before she could regain her footing, McAvoy brought his hammer down again. Lucky for her, he missed the mark because one of his own Gang Members nearly knocked him over.

Not wasting a single breath, he tore a dagger from his boot and stabbed his guard right through the eye. "*I almost had her*," he screamed as the Tiger writhed in pain and slumped to the ground, dead.

"Savior for the people, huh?" Eva called from a short distance. "Does that include killing every one of your loyal followers? What's a leader with no one to lead?"

Dan McAvoy let out an animalistic growl and lunged at her again. His anger and desperation were starting to get the best of him. Eva took notice and prodded at every opening she could. But he was fast. Just fast enough to dodge the flail of attacks.

So was The Wanderer.

***

As chaos erupted, Jake had slipped out of the fight, dodging blows and slinking away from battle, hoping no one would notice. After killing Mara to avenge his daughter, he was too shaken to continue. *I'm not a monster*, he whispered to himself, hiding in a vacant shack and tucking his knees to his chest. *I'll wait until the fighting's over. Then I'll return. Rub some dirt and blood on me. No one will notice I was gone.*

But his disappearance did not escape attention. Tommy saw his brother slipping away, and when he tried to pursue him, a large Serpent cut him off.

"*Coward*," he screamed over the crowd, but his brother didn't hear him.

The Serpent assumed the insult was meant for him. He smiled, revealing teeth filed into sharp points. "Ima enjoy killen yew boy. Oooh, yew look tasty."

Carnage was strewn across the town. People tripped over bodies, old and new, as they fought one another. Bruce and Gavin had each killed a handful of Gang Members, and their soldiers were driving several others into retreat. "*No mercy*," Bruce bellowed above the chaos, and the deserters were cut down as they fled.

Gavin found himself on the other side of the battlefield, fighting four Gang Members at once. Hesitation lasted only a heartbeat. Then his blades found their mark. One by one, they fell. He scanned the chaos for Eva and spotted her locked in combat with the Tiger Chief. Whatever doubt remained vanished. He surged back into the fray.

Fatigue began to creep up through The Wanderer's legs, but she forced herself to ignore it. She could tell Dan McAvoy was starting to falter as well. Small mistakes slipped into his stance, and his breathing grew heavier with each strike. Unlike her blades, his weapon was bulky and demanded far more strength to swing.

"Getting. Tired?" he gasped.

Eva exhaled slowly. "Underestimating me again, Dan Avery?"

She lunged at him again, sending mud and grass shooting up into the air with each step. Calculating each maneuver as she attempted another slash or stab. Each time, he parried or dodged. Eva was not able to connect a single hit for what felt like hours. But then, her Demon gave her an idea. "Stop fighting metal against metal. *Think*."

In a short moment of silence, she studied her opponent. Beneath his weapon was a narrow stance, enough to knock him off balance if she allowed him to take a swing at her. She had to be quick, though. Very quick. *Please let this work.* She sheathed her blades and sprinted towards his left side, preparing to duck below his hammer as he swung it around. McAvoy believed she had conceded. A ruse. The moment he turned his body, his ankles caught one another. He tripped. Momentum from the weapon lurched him forward, sending him sliding across the bloodstained ground.

When he lifted his face out of the mud and glanced around, he found the entire battlefield still, eyes fixed on him, waiting for his rebuttal.

"Getting tired?" Eva mocked.

She reveled in the chaos. It was never the kill that thrilled her, but the fight. The struggle. The desperate climb toward dominance. That was indescribable. Victory was sweeter still, and facing the Tiger Chief was the pinnacle of it all.

McAvoy trembled with fury. His men had seen him fall. Filthy, sweating, humiliated. The embarrassment gnawed at him, growing rabid, as he drew Eva's handgun and aimed directly at her head.

"Laugh… One more time," he threatened, wiping his face with his coat sleeve. His hands shook slightly. "For everyone will bear witness to the last thing you ever do in my presence."

Bang. The final bullet burst from the barrel, swirling through the air toward The Wanderer. She stiffened up, knowing that dodging a bullet is impossible. Even for her.

She braced.

The impact came like a hammer.

Her body snapped backward and slammed into the dirt, breath ripped from her lungs.

The world went dark and terribly still.

Something changed. The battlefield felt it before they saw it. One by one, weapons lowered as the gunshot's echo lingered in the air. McAvoy, convinced the bullet had done its work, rose slowly, bracing on one knee, and called for the battlefield's attention. A grin of pure ecstasy crawled across his face.

"Today is a grand day," he smiled, his voice carrying over the clash of steel and the cries of the wounded. Blades stilled and silence fell upon the Rover Colony. "The Wanderer has fallen. The region is *mine*. Surrender now and I will spare you a slow death."

A few of the Gang Members cheered. Bruce watched Eva's body frantically, searching for any sign she was still breathing. He thought he saw some movement, but he was too far from her to be sure. Meanwhile, the Tiger Chief began parading through the crowd, arms outstretched.

He drew in a slow, dramatic breath. "Yes. The scales of this world are balanced once more. Until now, no one had ever managed to touch this creature without meeting the edge of her blades. Some believed she was an immortal monster. Others thought her nothing more than a fable to frighten children. Why? Because all who crossed her path were mercilessly slaughtered. Only a trail of blood and those silver blades remained in her wake. But now… she falls with them."

Tommy caught his father's eye and scowled at him with immense hate.

Dan McAvoy took the chance to further humiliate those who fought alongside Eva. He dramatically clasped his hands together and pretended to weep. "Poisoned my own son's mind. And it appears my eldest has run off like a coward, for I see no sign of him among the living or the dead."

The battle had suddenly calmed outside the shack Jake was hiding. He immediately recognized his father's voice rising above the moans of the wounded. Only muffled humming reached his ears. He didn't know Eva had been shot.

In the shack farthest from the fighting, Jake McAvoy remained where he was, paralyzed. Curled in the corner, he tightened his arms around his legs.

It's not over yet.

"Behold my brothers," The Tiger Chief continued preaching. "You are fortunate enough to bear witness to the end of a legend. In the days when I slaved under her tyranny, this monster spoke the truest observation ever to slip from those traitorous lips—*history is only written by the strong*. So I say, let us erase her from existence. Let us build a new world upon the body of a murderer… the first sacrifice to cleanse this region of weakness."

Gavin's anguish erupted as he shoved through the crowd. "*No! Eva!*" He managed to shove his way through most of the crowd to get to her, but was stopped by two brawny Serpents. They grabbed him by the arms, kicked him on the backs of his knees, and forced him to the ground.

In his disheveled state, Chief McAvoy waltzed over to Gavin and stood directly in front of him. He knelt down and lifted the Commander's chin with a dagger. A trickle of warm blood dripped down the blade as it pierced flesh.

"Well, well, well," his icy eyes studied Gavin. "I'll admit, I say I never forget a face… but I seem to have misplaced yours in my mind. I can't put a finger on it… Please, enlighten me to where I have seen you before."

Gavin let out a shaky exhale. "You killed my parents… When I was a child."

"Hmm," McAvoy bit his lip and dug the tip of the blade a little deeper into Gavin's neck. Although he stiffened up, he did not make a sound. "Shame… I should've killed you too… but no… I'll put you to work in a place that will make you *beg for death*."

Gavin said nothing. He kept his eyes glued on Eva, praying that she wasn't dead.

Please. Just get up. This can't be the end. We need you. I need you.

"Forgive me for being slightly confused," the Chief stopped. "But you said that I killed your parents. I was a footsoldier while working for The Wanderer. And yet, you idolize her. The very person who sent me to murder your own family."

"She's changed. *You* haven't."

"Ha! You fight beside the very woman who condemned your mother and father to death. And you probably call it *loyalty*, don't you? Smile, young man. Today you escape the cold embrace of death. I will find a use for you."

The entire battlefield held its breath. Everyone knew the Tiger Chief showed mercy only when it benefitted him. They watched him push to his feet, weigh his decision, and slowly turn back to Gavin.

"However…" he said, letting his voice sweep over the crowd. "Why would I spare someone who seemed so close to The Wanderer? Torture? Tempting. But you seem like the sort that would steal that from me… End yourself before I could break you. And that would rob me of the pleasure."

He took a step closer and sighed. "I suppose you're right. I have not changed. And I am no merciful hero."

It happened in a single, blinding instant. Eva shot to her feet, charged at McAvoy, and caught his arm before anyone realized she'd moved. Yanking backwards, he nearly fell on top of her. She was barely able to disarm him without being stabbed herself. Gavin glanced up at his savior. *Thank the Great Mother. She's alive.* Shoving against the dazed Serpents, he broke free just long enough to snatch a loose knife and plunge it into one man's thigh while deflecting blows from the other.

War resumed. Numbers were dwindling, yet no winner had been crowned. Eva desperately tried to break McAvoy's arm, pinning it between her thighs and wrenching it towards the ground, straining as hard as she could. She didn't have enough force. He broke free.

"*How*?" he snarled, brandishing his weapon at her.

She pointed to her shoulder. A thin line of blood trailed down her arm. "Grazed me," she breathed. "I guess I forgot to tell you. That old thing never shot straight. I've adapted over the years… Silly me for thinking you were more thorough than that."

McAvoy lunged, slamming into her with blind force, the impact ripping the breath from her lungs. Eva seized his clothing and braced her feet against his hips, flipping him over her body as they crashed onto a patch of softened earth. They scrambled to their feet, but the ground suddenly gave way beneath them, and they plunged into an Old Time tunnel below. Gavin, Tommy, and Bruce were still fighting off the last of the Serpents and Tigers.

No one noticed them disappear.

Chapter 19

It was well into the night before the last Gang Member lay dead, and a few more hours until the survivors were able to gather themselves. By morning, a thick fog had rolled in, mingling with the bloodshed and casting the field in a deep crimson hue. An eerie silence settled over the stench of battle as fires were lit among the carnage. Bruce, Gavin, Tommy, along with a handful of Rapture's guards and scouts were all that remained. Battered and exhausted, they trudged to the center of the battlefield to count the dead.

Gavin instantly noticed The Wanderer's absence and began to panic. "Where is Eva? Where is she? Did any of you see her? Is she–?"

He paused, face drained of color.

Bruce scoured the bodies nearby and gestured for his men. "Search the dead."

While the others worked to identify the fallen, Tommy charged toward the last place he'd seen his brother. He ripped through the shacks, throwing doors open, tears streaking down his face with every violent slam. For his entire life, Jake had been the only person he'd had to look up to. But after meeting Eva, everything changed. She was smart. She was strong. Most importantly, she never backed down from a fight if it meant protecting others. And the one time she needed the McAvoy brothers at her side, Jake abandoned her. Outrage had nearly drowned out any worry he had for his elder brother. A dark, shameful part of him even hoped Jake was dead, because he couldn't fathom the words to express how deeply he felt betrayed.

He wiped the dirt and blood from his face while tearing apart the inside of another Rover shack. "When I find him," he yelled. "If he isn't dead. I'm going to kill him myself."

As he reached the shack farthest from the town center, he threw the door open to find his brother crouched in the corner. Jake scrambled to his feet, staring at him as though he barely recognized the figure standing in the doorway. Tommy was drenched in blood, dirt, and sweat. The look on his face was an explosive mix of exhaustion and rage.

Jake knew every ounce of it was aimed at him, especially after Tommy raised a bloodstained dagger.

"Wait a second," he pleaded.

His brother took three steps towards him, saying nothing.

"Hey-hey-hey-hey. D-don't do me like that Tommy. I'm your brother."

"*Are you*?" Tommy's voice trembled with fury. Jake had never seen him like this. Even The Wanderer, at her angriest, had never frightened him so deeply. "Some shit brother you are. You don't even stand up for your family. The people who have stood beside you through all this shit. I'm out there risking my life, and you *hide*? You *always* hide, Jake. Eva was right about you. *Dad* was right about you. *You. Are. A. Coward*."

Jake's tone changed, but his voice squeaked. "So what, Tommy? What now? You're going to kill me? If you do, you will be just like him."

Though it was pathetic of Jake to compare Tommy to their father, the words still caught him off guard. "No. I-I'm not him. I wouldn't be…" he trailed off. Both of them stood there for a moment, watching the dust settle in the room. Tommy finally lowered his weapon along with his head.

Jake started towards his brother, stopping dead in his tracks when he spoke again.

"Go," he warned. "Get out of here."

"What? Wait… what happened out there? Where's Eva?"

Tommy lifted his head and stared at his brother, tears welling in his eyes again. "You *really* want to know? We're trying to find her body right now, Jake. We don't know where she is. Or Dad. But maybe, if you had been there, she would not be missing."

Jake opened his mouth to speak. Then, he closed it and nodded sheepishly.

"So, now you know… Get out of here. I don't want to see you ever again. You go back to your *perfect life* in Rapture. Oh wait. That's right. You have *nothing* now. Why? Because Mara was the one who killed Anya. Mara was the reason for this shit. *All of it. Not Eva.* You never listen. You threw your life away for a fraud."

Jake was silent for a moment. "Where will you go? Are you coming back?"

"No. I'm staying as far away from *you* as possible."

Tommy turned on his heels and slammed the door shut with a deafening clang. Jake waited until he could no longer hear footsteps before exiting the vacant home. He turned a sharp corner around the edge of the Rover Colony. Bruce was standing there, clearly waiting for him.

His face bore the look of disgust. "You are so predictable… so *pathetic*." He shoved Jake toward the search party. "Help us find Eva. *Then* you can return to Rapture to drown in your humiliation."

Maybe it was the look on the Councilman's face, or the sight of the carnage sprawled out before him. Whatever the reason, the severity of the moment finally settled into Jake's chest. As he shuffled toward the rest of the survivors, they stopped what they were doing. The eldest son of Dan McAvoy stood before those who had risked their lives for The Wanderer. Some knowing her only by name. He scanned the hardened faces staring back at him. When he caught Gavin's gaze, he straightened and stepped toward him. The others gradually returned to their search.

But Rapture's former Captain said nothing. He looked Jake up and down, circling him like a vulture. It was plain to see he had not taken up arms. Unlike those around him, he was not covered in blood, dirt, or even sweat.

"How can I help find Eva?" Jake finally broke the silence.

Gavin stopped, pointed to the pile of bodies, and said two words. "Start there."

Inside, though, he was overcome with worry. If The Wanderer wasn't among the dead, then where had she gone? Was she still alive? He and Bruce met each other's eyes, sorrow weighing heavily between them. They gripped one another's shoulders and pressed their foreheads together in shared agony.

"I swear that my men and I will do our best to track her down," Bruce squeezed his grip slightly. He understood how deeply Gavin cared for Eva. "If she's out there, we *will* find her, Captain."

For the first time that he could remember, Gavin was choking back tears. His lip trembled. He nodded to his friend and returned to a pile of remains.

All of a sudden, a gasp escaped Tommy's lips. He began whispering to himself, frantically searching the bodies he had just looked over. When he repeated the question a little louder, those around him heard it. Someone else was missing.

"Where's the Tiger Chief? Where is McAvoy?"

"His body isn't amongst the dead?" one of Rapture's Scouts asked.

Gavin started to overturn more corpses nearby. "No. I don't see him anywhere."

"Maybe they're still fighting?" Jake offered. Several heads turned toward him, but he ignored them. "Listen. Do you hear anything?"

Unfortunately, the dense fog swallowed nearly all sound. No wind. No wildlife. Even if Eva and McAvoy were still locked in conflict, no one would have heard them. Fatigued and bruised, the survivors continued their search for several more hours. Bruce and Gavin circled the perimeter of the Rover Colony, searching for any trace of where The Wanderer might have gone. They found nothing.

Tommy's intuition pointed him in the right direction again. Some unknown force seemed to pull him next to an unassuming shack near the center of town. *Wait a minute... The ground here...* His experience as a farmer told him something was wrong. He pushed his foot against the ground, shifting all of his weight on one foot. Soft, freshly disturbed earth was strange to find so far from any garden, especially in a town that had been desolate for weeks.

The teen knelt down and started to feel the grass, pressing against the ground. *Not spongy enough to be oversaturated.* He picked up a handful of dirt and sifted through it in his hand. *It looks like someone or something did this very recently*. Just ten feet ahead, he found a dip in the ground. Tommy's eyes widened as he approached the hole. His stomach dropped the moment he looked inside.

"Hey! Tunnel! Tunnel. There's a tunnel here. I think I know where Eva went."

Elation drifted back with Tommy's words. Gavin shoved through the gathering crowd and practically dove into the opening. When he reached the bottom, it was so dark, he couldn't see his own hand in front of his face.

His heart skipped a beat when the faint sound of clashing metal reached his ears.

Eva.

But the echoes obscured the exact location of the sound.

Bruce knelt down near the hole, careful not to let the ground fall from underneath him. "Do you see anything?"

"I can't see shit," he called back up to the group. "But I definitely hear something. She's still alive. Eva is still alive."

Tommy chimed in, proud that his years of farming had mattered in a moment like this. "Can we get to her?"

"Hang on," Gavin replied and carefully stepped deeper into the tunnel. "I'll be right back."

With each sliding foot, he felt around to make sure that there were no rocks or an uneven pathway. Running his hands along each side of the Old Time Sewer, he found himself in a large, circular room. Although he could not see them, he could hear the wind howling through a number of tunnels. He turned around and Bruce helped him to the surface.

Gavin was shaking his head long before he surfaced. "There are at least a dozen tunnel entrances fifty feet from this drop," he explained. "We would have to convince Rapture to send more guards to search each one. And by that time, they would be long gone… Well, whoever wins will be. McAvoy's down there, too. I'm sure of it."

All of a sudden, a scream echoed up from the tunnel. Everyone's heart skipped a few beats. The group froze, straining to listen. But nothing followed. Only silence.

Most of them believed it was Eva, but no one dared to voice their worst fears.

Except for Jake.

"So there's nothing we can do?" he begged. "We have to do something. *Anything*."

"Like you give a shit," Gavin spat. "You hid like a coward while she fought your father. And now you expect to be welcomed back with open arms?"

Bruce stepped in, turning his attention towards his former Captain. "Where will you go then? Your heart clearly isn't in Rapture anymore, so I assume you won't return."

Gavin shook his head. He was sure that Eva would emerge victorious, and he would be there when she did. "I will find her. No matter how long it takes."

"I'm coming with you," Tommy insisted, but was refused.

"No kid. If she doesn't make it… I can't imagine what your father would do… to her *or* you. I-I just don't want you to see that. Okay? Nothing personal."

Tommy sighed and reluctantly agreed. Truthfully, he feared searching for Eva only to find her dead. He trusted that if Gavin found her, their paths would cross again someday. That instinct was the small spark of hope he clung to.

The older McAvoy brother stood there in disbelief. "So we're just going to *leave*? Don't you all understand? They're going to *kill* each other. Neither will stop until the other is dead. We *have* to do something."

Vision narrowing, Gavin had enough. He seized Jake by the neck and slammed him into the wall of a nearby shack, tightening his grip as Jake fought for air. Their faces were inches apart.

"I should kill you, y'know?" he said through gritted teeth. "If she dies, at least it would avenge the fact that *you* deserted her."

Jake tried to speak but was starting to lose consciousness.

"Take a look around. No one is coming to save you. Shit, you've literally buried yourself in your own shame. And you know what? You're *lucky* that Rapture will take you back. Out here, you wouldn't last a day. Because your father was right. You are *weak*."

Cold, numb darkness had nearly overtaken Jake when Gavin finally released his grasp. He dropped to the ground in a heap, dragging air into his lungs, coughing and sputtering until he could stand.

The Scouts began to disperse towards Rapture. A few of them grabbed mementos of the fallen to take back to their families. Bruce beckoned for Tommy, but he politely declined. His eyes never left the fog-shrouded colony.

“I’m going to the Nomads,” he said softly, making sure his brother was out of earshot. “Don’t tell Jake. I want to be alone. I-I need to start over. It’s time I finally do something for myself.”

Bruce bid the young McAvoy brother farewell, then turned his attention to Jake, who was hunched over Mara’s body. He was sniveling, whimpering. The Councilman stepped closer, watching with a mix of curiosity and disgust as he realized what Jake was doing.

Jake was sawing through Mara’s neck. Tears streamed down his face, his hands slick with blood.

“I have to bring something back,” he sniffled. “To clear Eva’s name with Rapture.”

Bruce remained cold. “It won’t matter. She won’t come back to you. Even if she’s still alive.”

He ignored the Councilman. With a sharp twist, he snapped the willowy woman’s spine, then carved another incision from her neck across her shoulder to her upper arm. He wrapped the severed head in a tunic torn from another corpse and vomited onto the body of a nearby Serpent. Crying softly, Jake stood and tossed the sack over his shoulder. Bruce was already on the Old Time highway, leading the remainder of his men toward the city.

“We’ll make camp at the outskirts,” he instructed. “In a few days, we’ll all be home. I thank you for your sacrifice and your service. You fought well. I’m confident the Tigers won’t trouble us again.”

Jake rushed to join the ranks of Rapture’s guard, keeping his gaze fixed on his feet. He looked back only once. Gavin and Tommy sat beneath the tree where the Tigers had hanged two Rovers years ago. *Tim and Lyla.* He had never forgotten the names of the dead. In his heart, he knew it would be the last time he saw his brother. Separation hurt.

What have I done…?

***

"You loved her, didn't you?" Tommy asked Gavin as they built a fire for the evening. Together, they had dragged the bodies of the Gang Members to one side of the outskirts and Rapture's Scouts to the other. Only then were they able to take in the calm that had settled over the desolate colony. The curse on the land seemed to lift once the bloodshed ended.

Gavin sighed and dropped his forearms onto his thighs. "Yeah… Of course I did. How could you not? Eva has such passion for what she does." He smiled to himself. "She lives to fight, but she fights for justice. Most of her life, she spent standing up for those who were weak. Protecting them. You don't see that in the world we live in. Everyone is out for themselves. But not her."

Tommy felt like he could finally confess his closeness to The Wanderer to someone who would truly understand. "Growing up in the Vault, we would read about superheroes from the Old Times, but I never imagined meeting a real one. Something about her was different… that night she rescued us. I saw her as one of those superheroes. When I was kidnapped by the Tigers, she saved me. And when we infiltrated the Tigers to find our dad, she had to save our asses again. One person versus an entire Gang and we *still* managed to escape. Twice."

"She's definitely one-of-a-kind," Gavin tossed a few sticks into the fire. "Reckless. Lucky. Skilled. All of it. I don't think I ever told you this, but I admire your passion too. I mean, you are just a kid and you speak wisdom beyond your years. The Nomads were right to make you an owl. But what's more, you have the same spark as Eva does. Jake on the other hand…"

"Please. I don't want to talk about him or even think about him ever again. This whole time—I mean—the whole time in Rapture, I defended him. 'He's my brother.' I convinced myself that my Jake cared about me. But then, Mara…"

"Because you started to follow your gut. A sign of a great warrior."

"So, do you think my calling was a farmer? Or maybe something else?"

"Not for me to say. That's for you to find out."

Tommy considered returning to his fields for a moment. Harvest time was approaching. Plants are so predictable. You water them, they grow. You take care of them, they flourish. On the other hand, it was not nearly as exciting as being out here. The stars looked much brighter outside the city walls. Freedom without structure awaited him. Yidi and Masha would welcome the Owl Spirit with open arms. Travelling the city and learning the Nomad's secrets sounded like a life worth living.

It felt like Gavin had read his mind. "So, you're going to go back to the Nomads?"

Tommy nodded. "Mhmm. I just feel like I belong there. Always have. What about you? Do you want to come with me?"

"No," he replied. "I have to find her. Something tells me that she's out there. Ignore that sound we heard earlier. That could've been anything. Remember that gut instinct? Yeah. Mine is telling me that she'll win… and I need to find her when she does. As long as I'm alive, I won't let her feel alone again."

Even though Tommy had complete faith in The Wanderer's ability to kill his Father, he remembered what Jake had said. *They're going to kill each other. Neither will stop until the other is dead.* Dan McAvoy was a ruthless man that was just as calculated as The Wanderer. Not to mention, their skill was matched in battle. Tommy made the unsettling realization that it was equally likely for his own father to win. And if he was victorious, what would happen to the region? What would that mean for the free people who still roamed it? And what would that mean for the other Gangs in the West?

"Do you really think she's alive?"

He already knew Gavin's answer. He just needed to hear it.

"I really do, Tommy. Trust her. The good guy always wins, right?"

***

Right?

Eva had survived the fall into the sewers, but so did McAvoy. She barely had enough time to catch her breath before the Tiger was back on her. *Clang*. Metal on metal. She grabbed at his shirt and shoved him against the side of the sewer. He punched her in the face. Clambering to her feet, she rushed at him in the darkness. Whispers from her Demon had completely vanished, but she could feel it clawing at her, trying to get her attention.

A sudden, blinding pain sparked across the right side of her face. She yelped, throwing up her free hand to block another strike as her fingers slid over warm blood. McAvoy's blade had carved a line from her cheek to her brow bone, narrowly missing her eye. Reeling backward, she pressed her hand hard against her face.

"What's the matter?" The Tiger Chief's taunts echoed through the ancient sewers. "Did I cut you?"

She shoved him into a vast chamber where dozens of tunnels branched in every direction. They crashed together, blades still hacking and slashing as they fought for footing. Her eyes adjusted to the darkness, and the silhouette of her enemy came into focus. Steel rang through the hollow space, echoing down the intersecting passageways. As the battle between The Wanderer and the Tiger Chief raged on, so did the war within her, the Demon's whispers pressing harder with every strike.

"You have gone astray," it repeated again and again. *What the shit is going on?* She still did not know what it meant.

The Wanderer let the Shadow distract her three times, and three times she nearly died for it. That was enough. Rage surged through her, and she crushed the voices beneath it.

"Shut up!" she screamed. "Leave me alone."

Dan McAvoy believed she was addressing him. "So you're yielding to me?" he mocked. "Mercy is not in my repertoire, unfortunately. Especially not for you."

He raised his arms as they entered through an adjacent tunnel. For a moment, Eva thought she heard Gavin's voice echoing in the distance. *That's probably just in my head too*, she told herself. Something cold and dark crept up her leg as she pushed deeper into the sewer… and deeper into the abyss of her mind.

Questions seeped in, at first as faint ripples, then swelling into consuming thoughts. She couldn't hold them back any longer. In an instant, she was consumed by the clash with Dan McAvoy and in the war waged inside her skull.

My purpose is to protect others, isn't it? Then why does it feel like a curse? Every time I try to help someone, they turn on me. Jake. Mara. Rapture. The Rovers. All of them.

They tried to change who I am. Twist me into something I'm not. When I saved them, they called me a savior. But when I tried to save myself, they cast me aside and called me a monster.

They've taken everything from me. Everything except my name. My title.

The familiar metallic-like voice began to answer her concerns. *You were born into greatness. Abilities that many only dream of possessing. Use your gift. Order. Utopia. Peace. All of this is attainable. But there are two things standing in your way.*

Two things? Eva wrestled with the thought while blocking another of McAvoy's strikes. She'd slipped fully into defense now, her mind growing muddled and unsure.

One is before you, it explained. *The other is within you.*

McAvoy was the only thing standing in her way at the moment. Slowly, as they continued to dance on their mortality, she began to understand. *McAvoy was right. He and I aren't so different. Except... he allowed his anger to become him. What fuels his hate... is me. And, if he achieves his goal, what then?*

"This is not a battle between good and evil," McAvoy said. "Neither of us are innocent. But once you are gone, I will shape this world as it should be."

With a single, violent exchange, McAvoy and Eva collided, sword against sword, so hard that the recoil sent them both crashing to their backs. For a few moments they lay there gasping. Eva forced herself upright and tried to press the attack, but McAvoy had already slipped behind the corner of a tunnel. Nearly blind in the suffocating darkness, and with every sound echoing in a dozen directions, she couldn't tell where he was hiding.

"The world you want is a figment of your imagination," she replied. "Delusion fuels your ideals. Just as it did when you attempted a mutiny against me. People will not bow to your whim so easily."

"Then they are not fit for my new world," he spat. "No different from the way you ruled the Serpents."

The Wanderer pictured settlements and smaller gangs burning under Chief McAvoy's rule. Fire blazed across the landscape, spreading toward the city until nothing remained. Men, women, and children fell victim to his cruelty. Homes reduced to coals. Trees left brittle and black. Only the obedient were allowed to live. Those who begged were condemned to slavery, and the rest received the mercy of death. Scarred and hollow faces of Nomads, Western Rovers, and rival gangs lined the largest compound Eva could fathom. Utopia was reserved for those who blindly followed his reign.

"You owe these people nothing," her Demon whispered, sinking his claws into her brain. "Fight for yourself. *Give in.*"

The two of them raised their weapons. Steel met steel. Shadow swallowed them whole.

Some things are inevitable.

Darkness consumes.

And whatever it consumes...

It becomes.

www.ingramcontent.com/pod-product-compliance
Lightning Source LLC
LaVergne TN
LVHW041113080826
845145LV00007B/1791
* 9 7 8 1 9 7 0 3 2 3 0 9 2 *